WELCOME TO

The Abyss line of cutting-edge psychological horror is committed to publishing the best, most innovative works of dark fiction available. Abyss is horror unlike anything you've ever read before. It's not about haunted houses or evil children or ancient Indian burial grounds. We've all read those books, and we all know their plots by heart.

Abyss is for the seeker of truth, no matter how disturbing or twisted it may be. It's about people, and the darkness we all carry within us. Abyss is the new horror from the dark frontier. And in that place, where we come face-to-face with terror, what we find is ourselves.

"Thank you for introducing me to the remarkable line of novels currently being issued under Dell's Abyss imprint. I have given a great many blurbs over the last twelve years or so, but this one marks two firsts: first *unsolicited* blurb (*I* called *you*) and the first time I have blurbed a whole *line* of books. In terms of quality, production, and plain old storytelling reliability (that's the bottom line, isn't it?), Dell's new line is amazingly satisfying . . . a rare and wonderful bargain for readers. I hope to be looking into the Abyss for a long time to come."

—Stephen King

"The quality of the Abyss line really is remarkable. Right from the start, I was impressed with its distinction and ambition. It's wonderful to see this excellent line continuing."

—Peter Straub

Also by Poppy Z. Brite:

LOST SOULS

DRAWING BLOOD

POPPY Z. BRITE

Delacorte Press
Abyss

Published by
Delacorte Press
Bantam Doubleday Dell Publishing Group, Inc.
1540 Broadway
New York, New York 10036

Library of Congress Cataloging in Publication Data

Brite, Poppy Z.
　　Drawing blood / Poppy Z. Brite.
　　　　p.　cm.
　　ISBN 0-385-30895-7
　　I. Title.
　　PS3552.R4967D73　1993
　　813'.54—dc20　　　　　　　　　　　　　　　　　　93-26675
　　　　　　　　　　　　　　　　　　　　　　　　　　　CIP

Manufactured in the United States of America

Published simultaneously in Canada

November 1993

10　9　8　7　6　5　4　3　2　1
RRH

For
Christopher DeBarr
and
David Ferguson,
who knew when to be there
and when to go away

ACKNOWLEDGMENTS

A number of people have kindly assisted me with research on computer hacking. Greatest possible thanks to Bruce Sterling, Darren McKeeman, Forrest Cahoon, John Carter, and the digital underground at large. Any technical errors are my own.

Thanks also to Connie B. Brite, Harlan Ellison, Dan Simmons, Brian Hodge, Jodie & Steve, Mary Fleener, Leslie Sternbergh, Steve Bissette, Don Donahue, Paul Mavrides, John & Craig, Linda Marotta & Kaz, Ed Bryant, Dan Matthews, Andrew Cayce, Kevin & Valerye, Darrell, Virginia, John "Foetus" Corry, Matthew Grasse, Ellen Datlow, F. Christian Grimm, Heidi Kirsch, Tom Montelone, J. R. McHone, Ian & Anne, Tigger Ferguson and 5-8, Wilum Pugmire, Tom Piccirilli, Bob Brite, the Go Figures, Devlin Thompson, Bob and Ron, Steve and Ghost, Miss Sunbeam, Evan Boorstyn, Brian Emrich, Miran Kim (for the wonderful art!) and Steven E. Johnson, Wayne Allen Sallee, Brooks Caruthers, St. Janor Hypercleets, Will O'Dobbs, the Rev. Ivan Stang, and "Bob" Dobbs himself. All of you helped in some way, whether you know it or not, whether you like it or not.

To my editor, Jeanne Cavelos; my agents, Richard Curtis and Rich Henshaw; and to Monica Calheira Kendrick and Michael Spencer, as always.

Major sources of inspiration: R. Crumb, Chester Brown, Julie Doucet, Tom Waits, William S. Burroughs, Trent Reznor, and Charlie Parker.

"Art is not a mirror. Art is a hammer."
—phrase scrawled on a whiteboard in the Media Lab at
MIT (home of the first computer hackers),
attributed to Bertolt Brecht

Missing Mile, North Carolina, in the summer of 1972 was scarcely more than a wide spot in the road. The main street was shaded by a few great spreading pecans and oaks, flanked by a few even larger, more sprawling Southern homes too far off any beaten path to have fallen to the scourge of the Civil War. The ravages and triumphs of the past decade seemed to have touched the town not at all, not at first glance. You might think that here was a place adrift in a gentler time, a place where Peace reigned naturally, and did not have to be blazoned on banners or worn around the neck.

You might think that, if you were just driving through. Stay long enough, and you would begin to see signs. Literal ones like the posters in the window of the record store that would later become the Whirling Disc, but was now still known as the Spin'n'Spur. Despite the name and the plywood cowboy boot above the door, those who wanted songs about God, guns, and glory went to Ronnie's Record Barn down the highway in Corinth. The Spin'n'Spur had been taken over, and the posters in the window swarmed with psychedelic patterns and colors, shouted crazy, angry words.

And the graffiti: STOP WAR with a lurid red fist thrusting halfway up the side of a building, HE IS RISEN with a sketchy, sulkily sensual face beneath that might have been Jesus Christ or Jim Morrison. Literal signs.

Or figurative ones, like the shattered boy who now sat with

the old men outside the Farmers Hardware Store on clear days. In another life his name had been Johnny Wiegers, and he had been an open-faced, sweet-natured kid; most of the old-timers remembered buying him a candy bar or a soda at some point over the years, or later, cadging him a couple of beers. Now his mother wheeled him down Firehouse Street every day and propped him up so he could hear their talk and watch the endless rounds of checkers they played with a battered board and a set of purple and orange Nehi caps. So far none of them had had the heart to ask her not to do it anymore.

Johnny Wiegers sat quietly. He had to. He had stepped on a Vietcong land mine, and breathed fire, which took out his tongue and his vocal cords. His face was gone to unrecognizable meat, save for one eye glittering mindlessly in all that ruin, like the eye of a bird or a reptile. Both arms and his right leg were gone; the left leg ended just above the knee, and Miz Wiegers *would* insist on rolling his trouser cuff up over it to air out the fresh scar. The old-timers hunched over their checkers game, talking less than usual, glancing every now and then at the raw, pitiful stump or the gently heaving torso, never at the mangled face. All of them hoped Johnny Wiegers would die soon.

Literal signs of the times, and figurative ones. The decade of love was gone, its gods dead or disillusioned, its fury beginning to mutate into a kind of self-absorbed unease. The only constant was the war.

If Trevor McGee knew any of this, it was only in the fuzziest of ways, sensing it through osmosis rather than any conscious effort. He had just turned five. He had seen Vietnam broadcasts on the news, though his family did not now have a TV. He knew that his parents believed the war was wrong, but they spoke of it as something that could not be changed, like a rainy day when you wanted to play outside or an elbow already skinned.

Momma told stories of peace marches she'd gone to before the boys were born. She listened to records that reminded her of those days, made her happy. When Daddy listened to his records now, they seemed to make him sad. Trevor liked all the music, especially the jazz saxophonist Charlie Parker, who Daddy always called Bird. And the song Janis Joplin sang with his daddy's name in it. "Me and Bobby McGee."

Trev wished he could remember all the words, and sing the song himself. Then he could pretend it was just him and his daddy driving along this road, without Momma or Didi, just the two of them. Then he could ride up front with Daddy, not stuck in the back with Didi like a baby.

He made himself stop thinking that. Where would Momma and Didi be, if not here? Back in Texas, or the place they had left two days ago, New Orleans? If he wasn't careful he would make himself cry. He didn't want his mother or his little brother to be in New Orleans. That city had given him a bad feeling. The streets and the buildings were dark and old, the kind of place where ghosts could live. Daddy said there were real witches there, and maybe zombies.

And Daddy had gotten drunk. Momma had sent him out alone to do it, said it might be good for him. But Daddy had come back with blood on his T-shirt and a sick smell about him. And while Trev huddled in the hotel bed with his arms around his brother and his face buried in Didi's soft hair, Daddy had put his head in Momma's lap and cried.

Not just a few tears either, the way he'd done when their old dog Flakey died back in Austin. Big gulping, trembling sobs that turned his face bright red and made snot run out of his nose onto Momma's leg. That was the way Didi cried when he was hurt or scared really bad. But Didi was only three. Daddy was thirty-five.

No, Trev didn't want to go back to New Orleans, and he didn't want Momma or Didi to be there either. He wanted them all with him, going wherever they were going right now. When they passed the sign that said MISSING MILE TOWN LIMITS, Trevor read it out loud. He'd learned to read last year and was teaching Didi now.

"Great," said Daddy. "Fucking great. We did *better* than miss the highway by a mile—*we found the goddamn mile.*"

Trevor wanted to laugh, but Daddy didn't sound as if he were joking. Momma didn't say anything at all, though Trev knew she had lived around here when she was a little girl his age. He wondered if she was glad to be back. He thought North Carolina was pretty, all the giant trees and green hills and long, curvy roads like black ribbons unwinding beneath the wheels of their Rambler.

Momma had told him about a place she remembered, though, something called the Devil's Tramping Ground. Trevor hoped they wouldn't see it. It was a round track in a field where no grass or flowers grew, where animals wouldn't go. If you put trash or sticks in the circle at night, they would be gone in the morning, as if a cloven hoof had kicked them out of its way and they had landed all the way down in hell. Momma said it was supposed to be the place where the Devil walked round and round all night, plotting his evil for the next day.

("That's right, teach them the fucking Christian dichotomy, poison their brains," Daddy had said, and Momma had flipped him The Bird. For a long time Trevor had thought The Bird was something like the peace sign—it meant you liked Charlie Parker, maybe—and he had gone around happily flipping people off until Momma explained it to him.)

But Trevor couldn't blame even the Devil for wanting to live around here. He thought it was the prettiest place he had ever seen.

Now they were driving through the town. The buildings looked old, but not scary like the ones in New Orleans. Most of these were built of wood, which gave them a soft-edged, friendly look. He saw an old-fashioned gas pump and a fence made out of wagon wheels. On the other side of the street, Momma spied a group of teenagers in beads and ripped denim. One of them, a boy, flipped back long luxuriant hair. The kids paused on the sidewalk for a moment before entering the record store, and Momma pointed them out to Daddy. "There must be some kind of a scene here. This might be a good place to stop."

Daddy scowled. "This is Buttfuckville. I hate these little Southern towns—you move in, and three days later everybody knows where you came from and how you make a living and who you're sleeping with." He caressed the steering wheel; then his fingers tightened convulsively around it. "I think we can make it through to New York."

"Bobby, no!" Momma reached over, put a hand on his shoulder. Her silver rings caught the sunlight. "You know the car can't do it. Let's not get stranded on the highway somewhere. I don't want to hitch with the kids."

"No? You'd rather be stranded *here*?" Now Daddy looked away from the road to glare at Momma through the black sunglasses that hid his pale blue eyes, so like Trevor's eyes. Didi had eyes like Momma's, huge and nearly black. "What would we do here, Rosena? Huh? What would *I* do?"

"The same thing you do anywhere. You'd draw." Momma wasn't looking at Daddy; her hand still rested on his shoulder, but her head was turned toward the window, looking out at Missing Mile. "We'd find a place to rent and I'd get a job somewhere. And you'd stay at home with the kids, and there'd be nowhere to get drunk, and you'd start doing comics again."

At one time Trev would have chimed in his support for Momma, perhaps even tried to enlist Didi's help. He wanted to stay here. Just looking at the place made him feel relaxed inside, not cramped up and hurting the way New Orleans and sometimes Texas had made him feel. He could tell it made Momma happy too, at least as happy as she ever felt anymore.

But he knew better than to interrupt his parents while they were "discussing." Instead he stared out the window and hoped as hard as he could that they would stop. If only Momma needed cigarettes, or Didi had to go pee, or something. His brother was toying with the frayed cuff of his shorts, dreaming, not even seeing the town. Trev poked his arm. "Didi," he whispered out of the corner of his mouth, "you need to pee again?"

"Uh-uh," said Didi solemnly, too loudly. "I peed last time."

Daddy slammed his hands against the wheel. "Goddammit, Trevor, don't encourage his weak bladder! You know what it means if I have to stop the car every hour? It means I have to start it again too. And you know what starting the car does? It uses extra gas. And that gas costs money. So you take your pick, Trev—do you want to stop and take a piss, or do you want to eat tonight?"

"Eat tonight," Trevor said. He felt tears trying to start in his eyes. But he knew that if he cried, Daddy would keep picking on him. He hadn't always been like that, but he was now. If Trev stood up to Daddy and answered back—even if the answer was giving in—Daddy might be ashamed and leave him alone.

"Okay, then, leave Didi alone." Daddy made the car go faster. Trevor could tell Daddy hated the little town as much as he and Momma liked it. Didi, as usual, was lost in space.

Daddy wouldn't stop on purpose now, not for any reason. Trevor knew the car was going to break down soon; at least, Momma said so. If that was true, he wished it would go ahead and break down here. He thought a place like this might be good for Daddy if he would only give it a chance.

"God*DAMN!*" Daddy was wrestling with the shift stick, slamming it with the heel of his hand. Something in the guts of the car banged and shuddered horribly; then greasy black smoke came streaming around the edges of the hood. The car coasted to a stop on the grassy shoulder of the road.

Trevor felt like crying again. What if Daddy knew he had been wishing for the car to break down *right that very second?* What would Daddy do? Trevor looked down at his lap, noticed how tightly his fists were clenched against the knees of his jeans. Cautiously he opened one hand, then the other. His fingernails had made stinging red half-moons in the soft flesh of his palms.

Daddy kicked the Rambler's door open and flung himself out. They had already passed through downtown, and now the road was flanked by farmland, green and wet-smelling. Trevor saw a few patches of writhing vine dotted with tiny purple flowers that smelled like grape soda. They had been seeing this plant for miles. Momma called it kudzu, and said

it only flowered once every seven years. Daddy snorted and
said it was a goddamn crop-killing pest that wouldn't even
die if you burned it with gasoline.

Daddy walked away from the car toward a cluster of trees
not far from the road. He stopped and stood with his back to
the Rambler, his hands clenched at his sides. Even from a
distance Trevor could tell Daddy was shaking. Momma said
Daddy was a bundle of nerves, wouldn't even fix him coffee
anymore because it just made him nervous. But sometimes
Daddy was worse than nervous. When he got like this, Trevor
could feel a blind red rage pulsing from him, hotter than the
car's engine, a rage that did not know words like *wife* and
sons.

It was because Daddy couldn't draw anymore. But why
was that? How could a thing you'd had all your life, the thing
you loved to do most, suddenly just be *gone*?

Momma's door swung open. When Trevor glanced up, her
long blue-jeaned legs were already out of the car, and she was
looking at him over the back of the seat. "Please watch Didi
for a few minutes," she said. "Do some reading with him if
you're up to it." The door slammed and she was striding
across the green verge toward the taut trembling figure of
Daddy.

Trevor watched them come together, watched Momma's
arms go around Daddy from behind. He knew her gentle,
cool hands would be stroking Daddy's chest, she would be
whispering meaningless soothing words in her soft Southern
voice, the way she did for Trevor or Didi when they woke
from nightmares. His mind framed a still shot of his parents
standing together under the trees, a picture he would remember for a long time: his father, Robert Fredric McGee, a smal-
lish, sharp-featured man with black wraparound sunglasses
and a wispy shock of ginger hair that stood straight up on
top, the lines of his body tight as a violin string; his mother,
Rosena Parks McGee, a slender woman dressed as becom-
ingly as the fashions of the day would allow in faded, embroidered jeans and a loose green Indian shirt with tiny mirrors at
the collar and sleeves, her long wavy hair twisted into a braid

that hung halfway down her back, a thick cable shot through with wheat and corn silk and autumn gold.

Trevor's hair was the same color as his father's. Didi's was still the palest silk-spun blond, the color of the lightest hairs on Momma's head, but Momma said Trev's hair had been that color too and Didi's would likely darken to ginger by the time he was Trevor's age.

Trevor wondered if Momma was out there soothing Daddy, convincing him that it didn't matter if the car was broken, that this would be a good place to stay. He hoped so. Then he picked up the closest reading material at hand, a Robert Crumb comic, and slid across the seat to his brother. Didi didn't understand all the things that happened in these stories—neither did Trevor, for that matter—but both boys loved the drawings and thought the girls with giant butts were funny.

Back in Texas, Daddy used to joke that Momma had a classic Crumb butt, and Momma would smack him with a sofa pillow. There had been a big, comfortable green sofa in that house. Sometimes Trevor and Didi would join in the pillow fights too. If Momma and Daddy were really stoned, they'd wind up giggling so hard that they'd lose their breath, and Trevor and Didi could win.

Daddy didn't make jokes about Momma's butt anymore. Daddy didn't even read his Robert Crumb comics anymore; he'd given them all to Trevor. And Trev couldn't remember the last time they had all had a pillow fight.

He rolled the window down to let in the green-smelling air. Though it was still faintly rank with the odor of the frying engine, it was fresher than the inside of the car, which smelled of smoke and sour milk and Didi's last accident. Then he started reading the comic aloud, pointing to each word as he spoke it, making Didi follow along after him. His brother kept trying to see what Momma and Daddy were doing. Trevor saw out of the corner of his eye that Daddy had pulled away from Momma and was taking long strides down the highway, away from the car, away from the town. Momma was hurrying after him, not quite running. Trevor pulled Didi against him and forced himself not to look, to concentrate on the words and pictures and the stories they formed.

After a few panels it was easy: the comic was all about Mr. Natural, his favorite Crumb character. The sight of the clever old hippie-sage comforted him, made him forget Daddy's anger and Momma's pain, made him forget he was reading the words for Didi. The story took him away.

Besides, he knew they would come back. They always did. Your parents couldn't just walk away and leave you in the back seat, not when it would be dark soon, not when you were in a strange place and there was nothing to eat and nowhere to sleep and you were only five years old.

Could they?

Momma and Daddy were far down the road now, small gesturing shapes in the distance. But Trevor could see that they had stopped walking, that they were just standing there. Arguing, yes. Yelling, probably. Maybe crying. But not going away.

Trevor looked down at the page and fell back into the story.

It turned out they couldn't go anywhere. Daddy called a mechanic, an immensely tall, skinny young man who was still almost a teenager, with a face as long and pale and kindly as that of the Man in the Moon. Stitched in bright orange thread on the pocket of his greasy overalls was the improbable name *Kinsey.*

Kinsey said the Rambler had thrown a rod that had probably been ready to go since New Orleans, and unless they were prepared to drop several hundred bucks into that tired old engine, they might as well push the car off the road and be glad they'd broken down close to a town. After all, Kinsey pointed out, they might be staying awhile.

Daddy helped him roll the car forward a few feet so that it was completely off the blacktop. The body sagged on its tires, two-toned paint a faded turquoise above the dusty strip of chrome that ran along the side, dirty white below. Trevor thought the Rambler already looked dead. Daddy's face was very pale, almost bluish, sheened with oily-looking sweat. When he took off his sunglasses, Trevor saw smudgy purple shadows in the hollows of his eyes.

"How much do we owe you?" Daddy said. It was obvious from his voice that he dreaded the answer.

Kinsey looked at Momma, at Trevor and Didi in the crooks of her arms, at their clothes and other belongings heaped in the back seat, the duffel bags bulging up from under the roped-down lid of the trunk, the three mattresses strapped to the roof. His quick blue eyes, as bright as Trevor's and Daddy's were pale, seemed to take in the situation at a glance. "For coming out? Nothing. My time isn't that valuable, believe me."

He lowered his head a little to peer into Daddy's face. Trevor thought suddenly of an inquisitive giraffe. "But don't I know you? You wouldn't be . . . no . . . not Robert Mc-Gee? 'The cartoonist who blew the brainpan off the American underground' in the words of Saint Crumb himself? . . . No, no, of course not. Not in Missing Mile. Silly of me, sorry."

He was already turning away, and Daddy wasn't going to say anything. Trevor couldn't stand it. He wanted to run to the tall young man, to yell up into that kind, curious face, *Yes, it is* him, *it is* Robert McGee *and he's everything you said and he's* MY DADDY TOO! In that moment Trevor felt he would burst with pride for his father.

But Momma's arm tightened around him, holding him back. One long lacquered nail tapped a warning on his forearm. "*Sh,*" he heard her say softly.

And Daddy, Robert McGee, *Bobby* McGee, creator of the crazed, sick, beautiful comic *Birdland*, whose work had appeared beside Crumb's and Shelton's, in *Zap!* and the L.A. *Free Press* and the *East Village Other* and everywhere in between, all across the country . . . who had received and refused offers from the same Hollywood he had once drawn as a giant blood-swollen tick still clinging to the rotten corpse of a dog labeled *Art* . . . who had once had a steady hand and a pure, scathing vision . . .

Daddy only shook his head and looked away.

Just past downtown Missing Mile, a road splits off to the left from Firehouse Street and meanders away into scrubby countryside. The fields out here are nearly barren, the soil gone infertile—most believe from overfarming and lack of crop rotation. Only the oldest residents of town still say these fields are cursed, and were once sowed with salt. The good land is on the other side of town, the side toward Corinth, out where the abandoned railyard and the deep woods are. Firehouse Street runs into State Highway 42. The road that splits off to the left soon becomes gravel, then dirt. This is the poorest part of Missing Mile, the place called Violin Road.

Out here the best places to live are decrepit farmhouses, big rambling places with high ceilings and large cool rooms, most of which were abandoned or sold years ago as the crops went bad. A step below these are the aluminum trailers and tarpaper shacks, their dirt yards choked with broken toys, rusting hulks of autos, and other trash, their peripheries negligently guarded by slat-sided, soporific hounds.

Out here only the wild things are healthy, the old trees whose roots find sustenance far below the ill-used layer of topsoil, the occasional rosebush gone to green thicket and thorns, the unstoppable kudzu. It is as if they have decided to take back the land for their own.

Trevor loved it. It was where he discovered that *he* could draw even if Daddy couldn't.

Momma talked to a real estate agent in town and figured out that they could afford to rent one of the dilapidated farmhouses for a month. By that time, she said, she would find a job in Missing Mile and Daddy would be drawing. Sure enough, a few days after they moved their things into the house, a dress shop hired Momma as a salesgirl. The job was no fun—she couldn't wear jeans to work, which left her with a choice of one Indian-print skirt and blouse or one patch-

work dress—but she ate lunch at the diner in town and sometimes stopped for coffee after her shift. Soon she met some of
the kids they'd seen going into the record store, and others
like them.

If she could drive to Raleigh or Chapel Hill, they told
Momma, she could make good money modeling for univer-
sity art classes. Momma talked to Kinsey at the garage, who
let her set up a payment plan. A week later the Rambler had a
brand-new engine, and Momma quit the dress shop and
started driving to Raleigh several times a week.

Daddy had his things set up in a tiny fourth bedroom at the
back of the house, his untidy jumble of inks and brushes and
his drawing table, the one piece of furniture they had brought
from Austin. He went in there and shut the door every morning after Momma left, and he stayed in there most of the day.
Trevor had no idea whether he was drawing or not.

But Trevor was. He had found an old sketchbook of
Daddy's when Momma unpacked the car. Most of the pages
had been torn out, but there were still a few blank sheets left.
Trevor usually took Didi outside to play in the daytime—
Momma had assured him that the Devil's Tramping Ground
was more than forty miles away, so he didn't have to worry
about accidentally coming upon the pacing, muttering demon.

When Didi was napping—something he seemed to do
more and more often these days—Trevor wandered through
the house, looking at the bare floorboards and the water-
stained walls, wondering if anyone had ever loved this house.
One afternoon he found himself in the dim, shabby kitchen,
perched on one of the rickety chairs that had come with the
house, a felt-tip pen in his hand, the sketchbook on the table
before him. He had no idea what he was going to draw. He
had hardly ever thought about drawing before; that was what
Daddy did. Trevor could remember scribbling with crayons
on cheap newsprint when he was Didi's age, making great
round heads with stick arms and legs coming straight out of
them, as small children do. This circle with five dots in it is

Momma, this one is Daddy, that one's me. But he hadn't drawn for at least a year—not since Daddy stopped.

Daddy had told him once that the trick was *not* to think about it, not in your sketchbook anyway. You just had to find the path between your hand and your heart and your brain and see what came out. Trevor uncapped the pen and put its tip against the unblemished (though slightly yellowed) page of the sketchbook. The ink began to bleed into the paper, making a small spreading dot, a tiny black sun in a pale void. Then, slowly, Trevor's hand began to move.

He soon discovered he was drawing Skeletal Sammy, a character from Daddy's comic book, *Birdland*. Sammy was all straight lines and sharp points: easy to draw. The half-leering, half-desperate face, the long black coat that hung on Sammy's shoulders like a pair of broken wings, the spidery hands and the long thin legs and the exaggerated bulge of Sammy's kneecaps beneath his black stovepipe pants—all began to take shape.

Trevor sat back and looked at the drawing. It was nowhere near as good as Daddy's Sammy, of course; the lines weren't straight, the black inking was more like scribbling. But it was no circle with five dots, either. It was immediately recognizable as Skeletal Sammy.

Daddy recognized it as soon as he walked into the kitchen. He leaned over Trevor's shoulder for several moments looking at the drawing. One hand rested lightly on Trev's back; the other tapped the table nervously, fingers as long and thin as Sammy's, faint lavender veins visible beneath the pale skin, silver wedding ring too loose on the third finger. For a moment Trevor feared Daddy might snatch the drawing, the whole sketchbook; he felt as if he had been caught doing something wrong.

But Daddy only kissed the top of Trevor's head. "You draw a mean junkie, kiddo," he whispered into Trevor's ginger hair. And he was gone from the kitchen silently, like a ghost, without getting the beer or glass of water or whatever he had come for, leaving his elder son half elated and half dreadfully, mysteriously ashamed.

The carefully drawn fingers of Sammy's left hand were blurring. A drop of moisture on the page, making the ink bleed and furl. Trevor touched the wetness, then put his finger to his lips. Salty. A tear.

Daddy's, or his own?

The worst thing happened the following week. It turned out Daddy *had* been drawing in his cramped little studio. Had finally finished a story, only a page long, and sent it off to one of his papers. Trevor couldn't remember if it was the *Barb* or the *Freep* or maybe one of the others—he got them mixed up sometimes.

The paper rejected the story. Daddy read the letter aloud in a hollow, mocking voice. It had been a difficult decision, the editor said, considering his reputation and the selling power of his name. However, he simply didn't feel the story approached the quality of Daddy's previous work, and he thought publishing it would be bad both for the paper and for Daddy's career.

It was the kindest way the editor could find to say *This comic is a piece of shit.*

The next day, Daddy walked into town and called the publisher of *Birdland*. The stories for the fourth issue were already nearly a year overdue. Daddy told the publisher there would be no more stories, not now, not ever. Then he hung up the pay phone and walked a mile across town to the liquor store. By the time he got home, he had already cracked the seal on a gallon jug of bourbon.

Momma had begun staying later and later in the city after her modeling jobs—having drinks with some of the other models one night, going to someone's apartment to get stoned the next. Daddy didn't like that, had even refused to smoke the joint she brought him as a present from her friends. She said they wanted to meet him and the kids, but Daddy told her not to invite them out.

Trevor had gone into Raleigh with Momma one day. He brought his sketchbook and sat in a corner of the big airy studio that smelled of paint thinner and charcoal dust. Momma stood gracefully naked on a wooden podium at the front of the room, joking with the students when she took her breaks. Some of them laughed at him, bent over his sketch-book so quiet and serious. Their laughter faltered when they saw the likenesses he had produced of them during the class period: the stringy-haired girl whose granny glasses pinched her beaky nose like some torture device made of wire; the droopy-eyed boy whose patchy beard grew straight down into the collar of his black turtleneck because he had no chin.

But on this day Trevor had stayed home. Daddy sat in the living room all evening, sprawled in a threadbare recliner that had come with the house, his feet tapping out a meaningless tattoo on the warped floorboards. He had the turntable hooked up and kept playing record after record, anything that his hand fell upon, Sarah Vaughan, Country Joe and the Fish, frenetic band music from the twenties that sounded like something skeletons might jitterbug to—it all ran together in one long musical cry of pain. Most of all Trevor remembered Daddy searching obsessively for a set of Charlie Parker records: Bird with Miles, Bird on Fifty-second Street, Bird at Birdland. He found them, slammed one onto the turntable. The saxophone spiraled through the old house, found the cracks in the walls and spun out into the night, an exalted sound, terribly sad but somehow free. Free as a bird in Bird-land.

Daddy hefted the bottle and chugged bourbon straight from it. A moment later he let out a long, wet, rippling belch. Trevor got up from the corner where he'd been sitting, keeping an eye out for Momma's headlights, and started to leave the room. He didn't want to see Daddy get sick. He'd seen it before and it had nearly made him sick too, not even so much the sight of the thin, stringy whiskey-vomit as that of his father's helplessness and shame.

His foot struck a loose piece of wood and sent it skittering across the floor. Daddy had been doing repairs around the house a few days earlier, nailing down a board that had begun to curl away from the wall. Long silver nails and a hammer were still scattered around the hall doorway. Trevor began to gather up the nails, thinking Didi might step on one, then stopped. Didi was smart enough not to go around the house barefoot, with all the splinters in the floorboards. Maybe Daddy would need the nails. Maybe he would still finish the repairs.

At the sound of the nails chinking together, Daddy looked up from his bottle. His eyes focused on Trevor, pinned him to the spot where he stood. "Trev. What're you doin'?"

"Going to bed."

"Thass good. I'll fixyer juice." Momma usually gave the boys fruit juice to take to bed with them, when there was any in the house. Daddy got up and stumbled past Trevor into the kitchen, slapping one hand against the door frame to support himself. Trevor heard the refrigerator opening, bottles rattling. Daddy came back in and handed him a glass of grapefruit juice. A few drops sloshed over the side, trickled over Trevor's fingers. He put his hand to his mouth and licked them away. Grapefruit was his favorite, because of the interestingly sour, almost salty taste. But there was an extra bitterness to this juice, as if it had begun to spoil in the bottle.

He must have made a face, because Daddy kept staring at him. "Something wrong?"

Trevor shook his head.

"You gonna drink that or not?"

He raised the glass to his lips and drank half of it, took a deep breath, and finished it off. The bitter taste shivered over his tongue, lingered in the back of his throat.

"There you go." Daddy reached out, pulled Trevor into his embrace. Daddy smelled of stinging liquor and old sweat and dirty clothes. Trevor hugged back anyway. As the side of his head pressed against Daddy's, a panicky terror flooded through him, though he didn't know why. He clutched at Daddy's shoulders, tried to wrap his arms around Daddy's neck.

But after a moment, Daddy pried him off and gently pushed him away.

Trevor went down the hall, glancing into Didi's dark bedroom. Sometimes Didi got scared at night, but now he was fast asleep despite the punishing volume of the music, his face burrowed into his pillow, the faint light from the hallway casting a halo on his pale hair. Back in Austin the brothers had shared a room; this was the first time they had slept apart. Trevor missed waking up to the soft sound of Didi's breathing, to the scent of talcum powder and candy when Didi crawled in bed with him. For a moment he thought he might sleep with Didi tonight, might wrap his arms around his brother and not have to fall asleep alone.

But he didn't want to wake Didi. Daddy was being too scary. Instead Trevor walked down the hall to his own bedroom, trailing his hand along the wall. The old boards were damp, faintly sticky. He wiped his fingers on the front of his T-shirt.

His own room was nearly as bare as Didi's. They had been able to bring none of their furniture from Austin, and hardly any of their toys. Trevor's mattress lay flat on the floor, a rumpled blanket thrown over it. He had pinned up some of his drawings on the walls, though he hadn't put up Skeletal Sammy and he hadn't tried to draw any of Daddy's other characters. More drawings lay scattered on the floor, along with the comics he had scrounged from Daddy. He picked up a Fabulous Furry Freak Brothers book, thinking he might read it in bed. The antics of those friendly fools might make him forget Daddy sprawled in the chair, pouring straight whiskey on top of his pain.

But he was too tired; his eyes were already closing. Trevor turned off his bedside lamp and crawled under the blanket. The familiar contours of his mattress cradled him like a welcoming hand. From the living room he heard Charlie Parker run down a shimmering scale. *Birdland*, he thought again. That was the place where you could work magic, the place where no one else could touch you. It might be an actual spot in the world; it might be a place deep down inside you. Daddy could only reach his Birdland by drinking now. Trevor had begun to believe his own Birdland might be the pen moving over the paper, the weight of the sketchbook in his hands, the creation of worlds out of ink and sweat and love.

He slept, and the music wove uneasily in and out of his dreams. He heard Janis Joplin singing "Me and Bobby McGee," and remembered suddenly that she had died last year. From drugs, Momma had told him, taking care to explain that the drugs Janis had been using were much worse than the pot she and Daddy sometimes smoked. An image came to him of Daddy walking hand in hand with a girl shorter and more rounded than Momma, a girl who wore bright feathers in her hair. She turned to Daddy and Trevor saw that her face was a swollen purple mass of flesh, the holes of her eyes black and depthless behind the big round glasses, her ruined features split in the semblance of a smile as she leaned in to give his father a deep soul kiss.

And Daddy kissed back . . .

Sunlight woke him, streaming through the dirty panes of his window, trickling into the corners of his eyes. His head ached slightly, felt somehow too heavy on his neck. Trevor rolled over, stretched, and looked around the room, silently greeting his drawings. There was one of the house, one of Momma holding Didi, a whole series of ones that he was pretty sure were going to turn into a comic. He knew he could never draw the slick, tawdry world of *Birdland* the way Daddy had, but he could make his own world. He needed to practice writing smaller so he could do the letters.

His head slightly logy but full of ideas, Trevor rolled off the mattress, pushed open the door of his room, and walked down the hall toward the kitchen.

He saw the blood on the walls before he saw Momma.

It would come out in the autopsy report—which Trevor did not read until years later—that Daddy had attacked her near the front door, that they must have argued, that there had been a struggle and he had driven her back toward the hall before he killed her. That was where he would have picked up the hammer.

Momma was crumpled in the doorway that led from the living room into the hall. Her back rested against the frame. Her head lolled on the fragile stem of her neck. Her eyes were open, and as Trevor edged around her body, they seemed to fix on him. For a heartstopping second he thought she was alive. Then he saw that the eyes were cloudy, and filmed with blood.

Her arms were a mass of blood and bruise, silver rings sparkling amid the ruin of her hands. (Seven fingers broken, the autopsy report would say, along with most of the small bones in her palms, as she raised her hands to ward off the blows of the hammer.) There was a deep gouge in her left temple, another in the center of her forehead. Her hair was loose, fanned around her shoulders, stiff with blood. A clear fluid had seeped from her head wounds and dried on her face, making silvery tracks through the mask of red.

And on the wall above her, a confusion of bloody handprints trailing down, down . . .

Trevor spun and ran back down the hall, toward his brother's room. He did not know that his bladder had let go, did not feel the hot urine spilling down his legs. He did not hear the sound he was making, a long, high moan.

The door of Didi's room was closed. Trevor had not closed it when he looked in on Didi last night. High up on the door was a tiny smudge of blood, barely noticeable. It told Trevor everything he needed to know. He went in anyway.

The room was thick with the smell of blood and shit. The two odors together were cloying, almost sweet. Trevor went to the bed. Didi lay in the same position Trevor had left him in last night, his head burrowed into the pillow, one small hand curled into a fist near his mouth. The back of Didi's head was like a swamp, a dark mush of splintered bone and thick clotted gore. Sometime during the night—because of the heat, or in the spasms of death—Didi had kicked off his covers. Trevor saw the dark brown stain between his legs. That was where the smell came from.

Trevor lifted the blanket and pulled it over Didi, covering the stain, the ruined head, the unbearable curled hand. The blanket settled over the small still form. Where it covered the head, a blotch of red appeared.

He had to find Daddy. His mind clung to some tiny, glittering hope that maybe Daddy hadn't done this at all, that maybe some crazy person had broken into their house and killed Momma and Didi and left him alive for some reason, that Daddy might still be alive too.

He stumbled out of Didi's room, felt his way along the hall, sprawled headlong into the bathroom.

That was where Momma's friends found him hours later, when they drove out to see why Momma hadn't shown up to model that day; she was so reliable that they became worried immediately. The front door was unlocked. They saw Momma's body first, and had nearly worked themselves into hysterics when someone heard the high toneless keening.

They found Trevor squeezed into a tiny space between the toilet and the old porcelain sink, curled as compact as a fetus, his eyes fixed on the body of his father. Bobby McGee hung from the shower curtain rod. It was the old-fashioned kind bolted into the wall, and had held his weight all night and all day. He was naked. His penis hung limp and dry as a dead leaf; there had been no last orgasm in death for him. His body was thin nearly to the point of emaciation, luminously pale, his hands and feet gravid with blood, his face so swollen as to be featureless except for the eyes bulging halfway out of their sockets. The rough strand of hemp cut a deep slash in his neck. His hands and his torso were still stained with the blood of his family.

As someone lifted him and carried him out, still curled into the smallest possible ball, Trevor had his first coherent thought in hours, and the last he would have for many days.

He needn't have worried about accidentally coming upon the Devil's Tramping Ground, he realized.

The Devil's Tramping Ground had come to him.

From the Corinth *Weekly Eye,* June 16, 1972

By Denny Marsten, Staff Writer

MISSING MILE—Grisly tragedy has struck just down the road. Hardly anyone knew that the famous "underground" cartoonist Robert McGee was living in North Carolina until he bludgeoned two members of his family to death, then committed suicide in a rented house on the outskirts of Missing Mile.

McGee, formerly of Austin, Texas, was 35. His work has appeared in student and counter-culture newspapers across the country, and he created the controversial adult comic book *Birdland.* Also deceased are his wife, Rosena McGee, 29, and a son, Fredric McGee, 3. Surviving is another son, name and age unknown.

A state trooper commented at the scene, "We believe drugs were involved . . . With these kinds of people, they usually are." Another trooper remarked that this was the first multiple murder in Missing Mile since 1958, when a man shot his wife and his three brothers to death.

Kinsey Hummingbird of Missing Mile repaired the McGees' car a few weeks before the murders. "I didn't see anything wrong with any of them," Hummingbird said. "And if I had, it would be nobody's business. Only the McGees will ever know what went on in that house."

He added, "Robert McGee was a great artist. I hope somebody takes good care of the little boy."

No one would speculate on why McGee chose to let his eldest son live. The child has been taken into custody of the state and will be placed in an orphanage or foster home if no relatives are located.

TWENTY YEARS
LATER

ONE

As he walked to work each afternoon, Kinsey Hummingbird was apt to reflect upon a variety of things. These things might be philosophical (quantum physics, the function of Art in the universe) or prosaic (what sort of person would take the time to scrawl "Robin Fuks" in a freshly cemented sidewalk; had they really thought the legend was important enough to be preserved through the ages in concrete?) but never boring. Kinsey seldom found himself bored.

The walk from his house to downtown Missing Mile was an easy one. Kinsey hoofed it twice a day nearly every day of his life, only driving in when he had something too heavy to carry—a pot of homemade fifteen-bean soup, for instance, or a stray amplifier. The walk took him past a patchwork quilt of fields that changed with every season: plowed under dark and rich in winter; dusted with the palest green in spring; resplendent with tobacco, pumpkin vines, or other leafy crops through the hot Carolina summer and straight on till harvest. It took him past a fairytale landscape of kudzu, an entire hillside and stand of trees taken over by the exuberant weed, transformed into ghostly green spires, towers, hollows. It took him over a disused set of train tracks where wildflowers grew between the uneven ties, where he always managed to stub his toe or twist his ankle at least once a month. It took him down the wrong end of Firehouse Street and straight into town.

Missing Mile was not a large town, but it was big enough to have a run-down section. Kinsey walked through this section every day, appreciating the silence of it, the slight eeriness of the boarded-up storefronts and soap-blinded windows. Some of the empty stores still bore going-out-of-business signs. The best one, which never failed to amuse Kinsey, trumpeted BEAT XMAS RUSH! in red letters a foot high. The stores not boarded up or soaped were full of dust and cobwebs, with the occasional wire clothes rack or smooth mannequin torso standing a lonely vigil over nothing.

One rainy Saturday afternoon in June, Kinsey came walking into town as usual. He wore a straw hat with a tattered feather in its band and a long billowing raincoat draped around his skinny shoulders. Kinsey's general aspect was that of an amiable scarecrow; his slight stoop did nothing to hide the fact that he was well over six feet tall. He was of indeterminate age (some of the kids claimed Kinsey wasn't much older than them; some swore he was forty or more, practically ancient). His hair was long, stringy, and rather sparse. His clothes were timeworn, colorfully mismatched, and much mended, but they hung on his narrow frame neatly, almost elegantly. There was a great deal of the country in his beaky nose, his long jaw and clever mouth, his close-set bright blue eyes.

The warm rain hit the sidewalk and steamed back up, forming little eddies of mist around Kinsey's ankles. A puddle of oil and water made a swirling rainbow in the street. A couple more blocks down Firehouse Street, the good end of town began: some shabbily genteel antebellum homes with sagging pillars and wraparound verandas, several of which were fixed up as boardinghouses; a 7-Eleven; the old Farmers Hardware Store whose parking lot doubled as the Greyhound bus depot, and a few other businesses that were actually open. But down here the rent was cheaper. And the kids didn't mind coming to the bad end of town after dark.

Kinsey crossed the street and ducked into a shadowy doorway. The door was a special piece of work he had commissioned from a carver over in Corinth: a heavy, satin-textured slab of pine, varnished to the color of warm caramel and carved with irregular, twisted, black-stained letters that seemed to bleed from the depths of the wood. THE SACRED YEW.

Kinsey's real home. The one he had made for the children, because they had nowhere else to go.

Well . . . *mostly* for the children. But for himself too, because Kinsey had never had anywhere to go either. A Bible-belting mother who saw her son as the embodiment of her own black sin; her maiden name was McFate, and all the McFates were psychotic delusionaries of one stripe or another. A pale shadow of a father who was drunk or gone most of the time, then suddenly dead, as if he had never existed at all; most of the Hummingbirds were poetic souls tethered to alcoholic bodies, though Kinsey himself had always been able to take a drink or two without requiring three or four.

In 1970 he inherited the mechanic's job from the garage where his father had worked off and on. Kinsey was better at repairing engines than Ethan Hummingbird had ever been, though deep inside he suspected this was not what he wanted to do.

Growing older, his friends leaving for college and careers, and somehow the new friends he made were always younger: the forlorn, bewildered teenagers who had never asked to be born and now wished they were dead, the misfits, the rejects. They sought Kinsey out at the garage, they sat and talked to his skinny legs sticking out from under some broken-down Ford or Chevy. That was the way it always was, and for a while Kinsey thought it always would be.

Then in 1975 his mother died in the terrible fire that shut down the Central Carolina Cotton Mill for good. Two years later Kinsey received a large settlement, quit the garage, and opened the first-ever nightclub in Missing Mile. He tried to mourn his mother, but when he thought about how much better his life had gotten since her death, it was difficult.

Kinsey fumbled in his pocket for the key. A large, ornate pocketwatch fell out and dangled at the end of a long gold chain, the other end of which was safety-pinned to Kinsey's vest. He flipped the watch open and glanced at its pearly face. Nearly an hour ahead of schedule: he liked to be at the Yew by four to take deliveries, clean up the last of the previous night's mess, and let the bands in for an early sound check if they wanted. But it was barely three. The overcast day must have deceived him. Kinsey shrugged and let himself in anyway. There was always work to do.

The windowless club was dark and still. To his right as he entered was the small stage he had built. His carpentry was unglamorous but sturdy. To his left was the art wall, a mural of painted, crayoned, and Magic Markered graffiti that stretched all the way back to the partition separating the bar area from the rest of the club. The tangle of obscure band names and their arcane symbols, song lyrics, and catch-phrases was indistinct in the gloom. Kinsey could only make out one large piece of graffiti, spray-painted in gold, wavering halfway between wall and ceiling: WE ARE NOT AFRAID.

Those words might be the anthem of every kid who passed through that door, Kinsey thought. The hell of it was that they *were* afraid, every one of them, terribly so. Afraid they would never make it to adulthood and freedom, or that they would make it only at the price of their fragile souls; afraid that the world would prove too dull, too cold, that they would always be as alone as they felt right now. But not one of them would admit it. *We are not afraid,* they would chant along with the band, their faces bathed in golden light, *we are not afraid,* believing it at least until the music was over.

He crossed the dance floor. The sticky remnants of last night's spilled beer and soda sucked softly at the soles of his shoes with each step. Idly brooding, he passed the restrooms on his right and entered the room at the back that served as the bar.

He was brought up short by the stifled screech of the girl bent over the cash drawer.

The back door stood open, as if she had been ready to leave in a hurry. The girl stood frozen at the register, catlike face a mask of shock and fear, wide eyes fixed on Kinsey, a sheaf of twenties clutched in her hand. Her open handbag sat on the bar beside her. A perfect, damning tableau.

"Rima?" he said stupidly. "What . . . ?"

His voice seemed to unfreeze her. She spun and broke for

the door. Kinsey threw himself over the bar, shot out one long arm, and caught her by the wrist. The twenties fluttered to the floor. The girl began to sob.

Kinsey usually had a couple of local kids working at the Yew, mostly doing odd jobs like stocking the bar or collecting money at the door when a band played. Rima had worked her way up to tending bar. She was fast, funny, cute, and (Kinsey had thought) utterly trustworthy, so much so that he had let her have a key. When he had another bartender, he didn't have to stay until closing time every night; on slow nights someone else could lock up. It was almost like having a mini-vacation. But keys had a way of getting lost, or changing hands, and Kinsey didn't entrust them to many of his workers. He had believed he was a pretty good judge of character. The Sacred Yew had never been ripped off.

Until now.

Kinsey reached for the phone. Rima threw herself across him, grabbing for it with her free hand. They struggled briefly for the receiver; then Kinsey wrested it free and easily held it out of her reach. The phone cord caught her purse and swept it onto the floor. The contents spilled, skittered, shattered. Kinsey tucked the receiver into the hollow of his shoulder and began to dial.

"Kinsey, no, *please!*" Rima grabbed futilely for the phone again, then sagged back against the bar. "Don't call the cops . . ."

His finger paused over the last number. "Why shouldn't I?"

She saw her opening and went for it. "Because I didn't take any money. Yes, I was going to, but I didn't have time . . . and I'm in trouble, and I'm leaving town. Just let me go and you'll never see me again." Her face was wet with tears. In the half-light of the bar Kinsey could not see her eyes. Her wrist was so thin that his hand could have encircled it two or three times; the bones felt as fragile as dry twigs. He eased his grip a little.

"What kind of trouble?"

"I went to the Planned Parenthood clinic over in Corinth . . ."

Kinsey just looked at her.

"You want me to spell it out?" Her sharp little face went
mean. "I'm *pregnant*, Kinsey. I need an abortion. I need *five
hundred dollars!*"

Kinsey blinked. Whatever he had expected, that wasn't it.
Rima had arrived in Missing Mile just a few months ago.
Among local guys who had asked her out and been turned
down, the word was that she carried a torch for the guitarist
of a speed metal band back in her native California. So far as
Kinsey knew, she hadn't been back to California recently.
"Who . . . ?" he managed.

"You don't know him, okay?" She swiped a hand across
her eyes. "An asshole who wouldn't wear a rubber because
that's like taking a shower with a raincoat on. There's plenty
of 'em around. They shoot their wad and that's the last thing
they have to worry about!" Now her mean face had collapsed;
she was crying so hard she could barely choke out the words.
"Kinsey, I slept with the wrong guy and he's not going to
help me out, he won't even talk to me. And I don't want *any*
goddamn baby, let alone his."

"At least tell me who. I could talk to him. There are
things . . ."

She shook her head violently. "NO! I just want to go to
Raleigh and get rid of it. I won't come back to Missing Mile.
I'll go to my sister's place in West Virginia, or maybe back to
L.A. . . . Please, Kinsey. Just let me go. You won't see me
around here again."

He studied her. Rima was twenty-one, he knew, but her
body seemed years younger: barely five feet tall, breastless
and hipless, all flat planes and sharp angles. Her straight,
shiny brown hair was held back with plastic barrettes like a
little girl's. He tried to imagine that childish body swollen
with pregnancy, could not. The very idea was painful.

"I can't give you any money," he said.

"No, I wouldn't—"

"But you can take your last pay envelope. It's there on the bulletin board." Kinsey let go of her wrist and turned away.

"Oh, God, Kinsey, thank you. Thank you." She knelt and began scraping together the contents of her purse. When she had searched out everything in the dimness of the bar, she went to the bulletin board and took down her envelope. Kinsey was hardly surprised to see her glance into it as if making sure enough money was there. She turned and stared at him for a long moment, as if deciding whether to say anything else.

"Good luck," he told her.

Rima looked surprised, and a little guilty. Then, as if the milk of human kindness were too heady a potion for her parched soul, she spun on her heel and left without another word.

There goes my mini-vacation, Kinsey thought.

Thirty minutes later, with the lights turned up and the swampy area behind the bar half-mopped, he found the little white packet.

It was nestled in a crack in the wooden floor directly below the spot where Rima's purse had spilled. With the lights off, as they had been when Kinsey caught her, it was unlikely that she would have spotted it. Kinsey bent, picked it up, and looked at it for a long time. It didn't look like much: a tiny twist of plastic, the corner of a Baggie perhaps, with an even tinier pinch of white powder inside. No, it didn't look like much at all. But Kinsey knew it for what it was: a towering monument to his gullibility.

She could still be pregnant, he reasoned as he walked to the restroom. *She really could need money for an abortion. Somebody could be giving her coke. Maybe she was even selling the shit to get the money she needed.*

Yeah, right. The things she had said about the father of her embryo—if embryo there was—hardly suggested that he would be giving her free drugs. And Kinsey knew that the market for cocaine in Missing Mile was very poor indeed. You could hardly turn around without bumping into a pothead or a boozehound, and they treated psychedelics like candy, but coke was another thing. Most of the younger kids seemed to think it was boring: it didn't tell them stories or give them visions, didn't drown their pain, didn't do anything for them that a pot of strong coffee couldn't do for a fraction of the price. They would probably snort coke if it was handed to them, but they wouldn't spend their allowances on it. And most of the older townie crowd couldn't afford it even if they wanted it.

Rima, though, seemed to have had a constant low-grade cold for the last couple of months. She was always going to the restroom to blow her nose, but she always came back still sniffling. How clear was hindsight.

You could still call the cops, Kinsey told himself as his cupped palm hovered over the toilet bowl, ready to tip the little packet in. *Show them this stuff. She couldn't be far out of town yet.*

His hand tilted. There was a tiny splash, barely audible; the packet floated serenely on the still surface of the water.

She had every intention of ripping you off. Bust her.

His fingers found the flush lever, pushed it. There was a deafening liquid roar—Kinsey thought the plumbing in this building was of approximately the same vintage as the Confederate boardinghouses up the street—and the packet was gone.

Pregnant or not, she's in some kind of trouble. That's one thing she wasn't lying about. Why make it worse for her?

Later, mopping the floor near the stage, he glanced up at the art wall. The words WE ARE NOT AFRAID gleamed softly at him, and he knew that wherever Rima was now, whatever she was doing, those words did not hold true for her.

He could not resent letting her take her last pay, though. There was always a chance she would use the money to help herself, to get away from whatever (or whoever) had made her stash cocaine in her pocketbook and steal from people who wished her well. There was always a chance.

Yeah. And there was always a chance that John Lennon would rise from the dead and the Beatles would play a reunion show at the Sacred Yew. That seemed about as likely.

Kinsey shook his head dolefully and kept mopping.

T W O

Zachary Bosch awoke from fascinating dreams, pulled the pillow off his face, rubbed his eyes, and blinked up at the green lizard on the ceiling just above his head.

He slept in a small alcove at the side of the room, where the ceiling was lower and cozier than the rest of his lofty French Quarter apartment. The plaster here was soft and slightly damp, cracked with age, yellowed from two years of Zach smoking in bed. Against the dingy plaster the lizard was a vivid, iridescent green. Children in New Orleans called such creatures chameleons, though Zach believed they were actually anoles.

He reached for the ashtray next to the bed and the lizard was gone in a brilliant flicker of motion. Zach knew from experience that if you were fast enough to catch them by the tail, the thready appendage would come off, still twitching, in your hand. It was a game he often played with the little reptiles but seldom won.

He found the ashtray without looking, brought it up and nestled it in the hollow of the sheet between the small sharp mountains of his hipbones. In the ashtray was a tightly rolled joint that had been the size of a small cigar, a *panatela* or whatever the things were called. Zach hated the taste of tobacco and its harsh brown scorch in his lungs; he never touched the stuff. His friend Eddy put it simply if inelegantly: "If it's green, smoke it. If it's brown, flush it."

Zach had smoked half of this particular green the night before, while concocting a news story to plant in the *Times-Picayune* just to amuse himself, a tasteful little number about

some petrified fetus parts removed from a woman's womb
ten years after an illegal back-alley abortion. If it wasn't true,
it ought to be—or rather, the public ought to think it was. In
today's moral climate (cloudy, with a fascist storm front
threatening), illegal abortions needed all the bad publicity
they could get.

He had made sure to stress that the woman suffered great
pain, bloated grotesquely, and was of course rendered infertile. By the time he finished writing the article, Zach had
caught himself feeling tender, almost protective, toward his
hapless fiction. She was a true martyr, the finest kind of
scapegoat, a vessel for imaginary pain so that real pain might
be thwarted.

Zach felt for a book of matches on the floor, found some
from Commander's Palace, lit the joint and sucked smoke in
deep. The flavor filled his mouth, his throat, his lungs, a taste
as bright green as the lizard. He stared at the matchbook,
which was a darker green. The restaurant was one of the
oldest and most expensive in the city. A friend of a friend
who was deep in hock on his American Express card had
taken Zach to the bar there recently, and charged Zach's four
extra-spicy Bloody Marys to his Visa. They always did shit
like that. Stupid patterns, intricate webs they wove that
ended up trapping themselves most tightly of all.

Geeks, marks, and conspiracy dupes. In the end they all
amounted to the same thing: sources of income for Zachary
Bosch, who was none of the above.

His third-floor apartment was full of dust and sunlight and
tons upon tons of paper. His friends who knew his reading
habits, his smoking habits, and his squirreling habits swore
the place was one of the most hair-raising fire hazards in all
New Orleans. Zach figured it was damp enough to discour-
age any flames that escaped his notice. In deep summer, water stains spread across the ceiling and the fine old molding
began to sweat and seep.

The paint had long since begun to peel, but this never bothered Zach, since most of the walls were covered with scraps
of paper. There were pictures torn from obscure magazines

that had reminded him of something; newspaper clippings, headlines, or sometimes single words he had put up for their mnemonic effect. There was a large head of J. R. "Bob" Dobbs, High Epopt of the Church of the Subgenius and one of Zach's favorite personal saviors. "Bob" preached the doctrine of Slack, which (among other things) meant that the world really *did* owe you a living, if only you were smart enough to endorse the paycheck. There were phone numbers, computer access codes and passwords scribbled on yellow Post-it notes whose glue would not stick in the damp. These last were constantly fluttering down from the walls, creating canary drifts among the debris on the floor, and sticking to the soles of Zach's sneakers.

There were boxes of old correspondence, magazines, yellowing newspapers from all over the world and in several languages—if he couldn't read an item, he could find someone to translate it inside of an hour—distinguished dailies and raving tabloids. And books everywhere, crammed into shelves that covered one wall nearly to the high ceiling, spread open or with pages marked beside his bed, stacked into Seuss-like towers in the corners. There was every kind of fiction, telephone books, computer manuals, well-thumbed volumes with titles like *The Anarchist's Cookbook, High Weirdness by Mail, Principia Discordia, Steal This Book,* and other useful bibles. A cheap VCR and a homemade cable box were rigged up to a small TV; the whole setup was nearly hidden behind stacks of videocassettes.

Pushed up against the far wall was the heart of the chaos: a large metal desk. The desk was not visible as such, though Zach could find anything on, in, or around it in a matter of minutes. It was heaped with more papers, more books, shoeboxes full of floppy disks, and the unmistakable signature of the ganja connoisseur: an assortment of ashtrays overflowing with ashes and matches, but no butts. Marijuana smokers, unlike those who indulged in tobacco, did not leave spoor.

In the center of the desk, rising above the ashtrays and drifts of paper like some monolith of plastic and silicon, was a computer. An Amiga with an IBM card and Mac emulation that allowed it to read disks from several different kinds of computers, a sweet little machine. It was equipped with a large-capacity hard disk, a decent printer, and—most important for his purposes—a 2400-baud modem. This inexpensive scrap of technology, which allowed his computer to communicate with others via any number of telephone lines, was his meal ticket, his umbilical cord, his key to other worlds and to parts of this world he had never been meant to see.

The modem had paid for itself several hundred times over, and he had only had this one for six months. He had an OKI 900 cellular phone and a laptop computer as well, with a built-in modem to keep him mobile in case of emergencies.

Zach hunched himself up on his elbows, stuck the joint in his mouth, and raked a hand through his thick black hair. Some French Quarter deathrockers spent hours before the mirror trying to achieve the precise combination of unnatural-looking blue-ebony hair and bloomless translucence of skin that had been visited upon Zach by simple genetics.

It came from his mother's side of the family. They looked as though they'd grown up in basements, not that most of them had ever been anywhere near a basement, since they'd been in Louisiana for five generations or more. His mother's maiden name was Rigaud, and she hailed from a muddy little village down in the bayou country where the most exciting thing that ever happened was the annual Crawfish Festival. The hair and dark almond-shaped eyes, he guessed, came from her Cajun blood. The pallor was anyone's guess. Perhaps it came from all the time she had spent in various mental hospitals, in gloomy dayrooms and harsh fluorescent corridors, as if such a thing could be inherited.

She was probably in some lockup now, if she was still alive. His father, a renegade Bosch who claimed a lineage back to Hieronymus but whose visions had all been seen through the bottom of a whiskey bottle, had long since disappeared into some steamy orifice of the city's nightside. Zach had just turned nineteen, and though he had lived in New Orleans all his life, he had seen neither of his parents for nearly five years.

Which was fine. All he wanted of them was what he carried with him: his mother's weird coloring, his father's devious intelligence, a tolerance for hard liquor that exceeded either of theirs. Drinking never made him mean, never made him bitter, never made him want to punch someone young and small and defenseless, to bruise tender flesh, to steep his hands in blood. He supposed that was the main difference between him and his parents.

Zach had a habit of pulling his hair and snarling it around his fingers while he was reading or staring at the computer screen between keystrokes. As a result, it grew into a kind of mutant pompadour that cast the sharp planes and hollows of his face into shadow, exaggerated his pointed chin and thin peaky eyebrows and the gray smudges of computer strain around his eyes.

Last year a ten-year-old kid on Bourbon Street had run after him calling *Hey, Edward Scissorhands!* He hadn't known what it meant at the time, but when Eddy showed him an ad for the movie of that name, Zach was as close to shocked as he ever got. The resemblance was scary. He held the picture next to his face and stared in the mirror for a long time. At last he took comfort in the fact that he never wore black lipstick and Edward Scissorhands never wore big, round, geeky black-rimmed glasses like Zach's.

The movie bothered him, though, when Eddy took him to see it. He always enjoyed watching Tim Burton's films—they were eye candy, for one thing—but they left him feeling vaguely pissed off. They all seemed to have an agenda of relentless normalcy hiding behind a thin veil of weirdness. He'd loved *Beetlejuice* until the last scene, which sent him storming from the theater and left him kicking things all day. The sight of Winona Ryder's character, formerly strange and beautiful in her ratted hairdo and smudged eyeliner, now combed out and squeaky clean, clad in a preppy skirt and kneesocks and a big shit-eating sickeningly *normal* grin . . . it was entirely too much to bear.

But that, Zach supposed, was Hollywood.

He took one more drag on the joint and snuffed it out in the ashtray. It was excellent pot, bright green and sticky with resin that smelled like Christmas trees, quick to set the brain buzzing and humming. He hoped somebody at the Market would have more. Zach felt around on the floor again, found his glasses, and put them on. The world stayed blurry at the edges, but that was just the drugs.

Something nudged his hip beneath the sheet. The remote control for the TV and VCR. He aimed it at the screen and smiled as he thumbed the ON button.

He found himself watching an Italian splatter movie called *The Gates of Hell*. Good old Lucio Fulci; his plots were brain-numbing nonsense, every character dumber than a bag of rusty nails, but he gave great gore. And nothing normal *ever* happened in *his* movies.

A girl began to bleed from the eyeballs—Fulci loved eyeballs—then proceeded to vomit out her entire digestive tract over the course of maybe a minute. She'd been parking with her boyfriend; such were the wages of sin. Zach pressed the reverse button and watched the actress suck up her intestines like a plate of spaghetti in marinara sauce. Tasty.

A moment later he realized that the movie was making him hungry, which meant it was seriously time for some food. The remains of a *muffuletta* from the Central Grocery were wrapped up in his little dorm-style refrigerator. Zach kicked the sheet off, swung his legs over the edge of the mattress, rode the ensuing headrush for a minute, then stood and picked an expert path through the debris to the fridge.

The savory smells of ham and Italian spices, oiled bread and olive salad wafted up as he unwrapped the greasy pink butcher paper. The big round sandwiches were expensive but delectable, and they made two or three meals if you weren't a big eater, which Zach was not.

It wasn't as if he couldn't afford a *muffuletta* anytime he wanted one. Money was free, or nearly so; all he could need was at his fingertips every time he sat down at his desk and switched his computer on. But he had never quite gotten used to having enough to eat. His parents' kitchen cabinets never had much in them but booze.

The movie raged on. A priest had hung himself in the town of Dunwich—original name, that—which flung wide the gates of hell, or something. Zombies with bad skin conditions seemed to be able to beam themselves around like refugees from the Starship *Enterprise*. Zach thought of the only priest he had ever known, Father Russo, who said the masses his mother used to drag him to every few months when she was coming off a bad binge. Twelve-year-old Zach had gone to confession alone one day, ducked into the booth and leaned his aching head against the screen and whispered, *Bless me, Father, for I have been sinned against.* Hot tears squeezed out of his eyes as his lips formed the words.

That is not how the Confession begins, the priest replied, and some of Zach's hope ebbed. But he persisted: *My mother kicked me in the stomach and made me throw up. My father slammed my head against the wall. Can't you help me?*

Bad boy, telling lies about your parents. Don't you know you must obey them? If they punish you, it is because you have sinned. The Lord says honor thy father and thy mother.

WHAT ABOUT THEM *HONORING* ME? he shrieked, slamming his hand against the flimsy wall of the confessional, a hot spike of pain shooting up his already-sprained arm. Raking the curtain back, bursting into the priest's side of the booth, yanking his shirt up to display the technicolor bruises and belt stripes across his skinny ribs. *WHAT ABOUT THIS, MOTHERFUCKER, WHAT DOES GOD SAY TO* THIS? Staring into the priest's startled face, seeing the tracework of broken veins deepen from red to purple, the weak watery eyes flare with pious anger, and knowing sickly that there was no help here, that the priest was not really seeing him, that the priest was as drunk as his parents had been last night.

He had been hauled from the church and told not to come back, as if he ever would; he collapsed on the stone steps and sobbed there for an hour. Then he got up, hawked an enormous goober on the steps, and left with a silent pain that went deeper than his bruises and abrasions, all the way down to the wounded soul that the Catholic church would never touch again.

It would be nice to see Father Russo hanging and burning and bleeding from the eyeballs. Maybe the priest was dead now; maybe he had the starring role in some hellish Lucio Fulci film. Zach hoped so.

He chewed the last bite of *muffuletta*, licked the grease off his lips, and went diving for clothes. He came up with a pair of army pants cut off at the knees and a T-shirt that pictured JFK grinning toothily as his brains exploded in vivid silk-screen color. Faded red Converse hightops without socks completed the ensemble.

It was time to go snag his two daily stashes. Then he could come back here and get some work done.

June, as far as Zach was concerned, was the last tolerable month in New Orleans until mid-autumn. The days were already hot, but not as mired in sodden swelter as they would be through July, August, and most of September. During these obscene months he slept all morning and afternoon, his dreams punctuated by the rattle and drip of his laboring air conditioner. He spent his nights cramming his head with information, words and images and the subtle semiotics they triggered in his brain, or hacking paths through the infinite mazes of forbidden computer systems, or simply skating around the boards where he was not just welcome but absurdly revered.

Only long after sundown would he venture into the French Quarter to prowl the gaslit side streets, to walk among euphorically drunken tourists and roustabouts on neon-smeared Bourbon Street, to meet his friends passing a bottle of wine in front of Jackson Square, or lingering in the dark bars and smoky clubs of Rue Decatur, or occasionally throwing a small party in Saint Louis #1, the old cemetery on the edge of the Quarter.

But today he descended the stairs to the sidewalk, pushed the iron gate open, and drew in a noseful of the humid air as if it were perfume. And it was, of a sort; it felt like wet cotton in his lungs, but it carried the fragrance of the Quarter, a heady mélange of thousands of odors: seafood and spices, beer and horseshit, oil paints and incense and flowers and garbage and river mud, and underlying it all the clean crumbling smell of age, old iron, softly sifting brick, stone trodden by a million feet, recording the infinitesimal imprint of each.

Zach's third-floor apartment overlooked tiny Rue Madison, one of the two shortest streets in the Quarter, along with its twin Wilkinson on the other side of Jackson Square. His row of buildings was decorated with intricate black ironwork. Only a block long, quiet little Madison ran straight into the technicolor melee of the French Market.

Zach passed the vintage clothing store on the corner, knocked on the open door and waved to the hippie proprietor (who had recently given him a neighborly deal on a black frock coat lined with royal purple silk, though it would be too hot to wear the thing until Christmas), then cut through an area housing an informal bazaar where you could find useless crap or the very treasures of Lafitte, depending upon the day and your luck. Then he was in the French Market, surrounded on all sides by delicious smells and harmonious colors and all the symmetry and bounty of the edible vegetable kingdom, heaped together in great glowing piles under one old stone roof.

There were pyramids of tomatoes so achingly scarlet that they hurt the eyes, bushel baskets of eggplants like burnished purple patent leather, the verdant green of bell peppers and the delicate, creamy green of the tender little squash called mirliton. There were onions as large as babies' heads, red and gold and pearly white. There were nuts and ripe bananas and cool frosted grapes, fresh herbs by the bunch, great thick braids of garlic and dried red tabasco peppers hanging from the rafters. There were stalks of fresh sugar cane, sold by the foot so you could gnaw and suck out the sweet juice as you walked through the market smelling and marveling. There was homegrown rice, and barrels full of shining red beans to cook it with, and long links of smoky Cajun sausage to throw in for flavor. There was a fish market to the side where you could buy fresh crabs and crawdads and catfish, bright blue Gulf shrimp as long as your hand, even alligator if you liked.

And in front of every stand were the vendors hawking their wares, old men who had come in laden pickup trucks before dawn, their faces seamed leather, black or tan, Cajuns, Cubans, occasional Asians. The Market, Zach thought, was probably one of the most culturally and racially diverse spots in the city. Good karma for a place where, not two hundred years ago, slaves had done the morning shopping.

Every vendor had the finest, the freshest, the cheapest goods in all the Market; they all proclaimed so, each more loudly than the next, until the clamorous praise for fruits and vegetables rose to the roof and spiraled out between the stone columns. They would sell it to you by the piece, or the pound, or the whole damn lot if you fancied.

But Zach fancied other things. He walked through, looking but not stopping, until he reached the fringes of the flea market that took up the rear part of the building. Here the wares tended more toward the tacky or the weird, tables full of shell magnets and ceramic crawfish salt shakers alternating with stands that sold leather jewelry, boot knives, essential oils and bundles of incense and suspicious-looking cassette knockoffs of whatever CDs the vendor had recently bought.

Several of the people running the weirder stands nodded to him. There was Garrett, a nervous kid with bleached-blond hair and great tragic angel-eyes, who painted pictures way too scary for the Jackson Square portrait crowd; he had a table full of crucifix pendants and rhinestone cat's-eye sunglasses, and was doing a brisk business. There was Serena, purple-haired patchouli-daubed priestess as calm as her name, nodding happily before her altar of bootleg Cure and Nirvana; serene until some unsuspecting light-fingered customer happened along and mistook her for an easy mark. Then she whipped into ultraviolent motion, straight-arming the hapless thief with one hand, retrieving her merchandise with the other. There was spooky Larese with her black Cleopatra eyeliner and tattered velvet dress, who did Tarot readings on the square when she wasn't selling her homemade voodoo dolls in the Market. Her readings were not lucrative; she told her customers so many accurate bad things about themselves that they almost always demanded their money back, and she always gave it back—but with a date scrawled across it in indelible Magic Marker, a day and year sometimes far in the future, sometimes ominously near.

Zach scanned the stands and tables. The sign changed locations every day, but someone always had it. Finally he spotted it taped to a table of hats manned by a lean young man with skin the color of *café noir* and a mass of dreadlocks that seemed to burst like snakes out of the top of his skull, twisting halfway down his back, some of the strands interwoven with threads of purple, red, yellow, and green—the colors of Rasta and Mardi Gras. This gentleman went by the mellifluous name of Dougal St. Clair. The sign taped to the edge of his table, neatly printed and discreet, read HELP US IN THE FIGHT AGAINST DRUGS! ANY DONATION APPRECIATED.

"Zachary! I t'ink you need a hat, mon!" Dougal's face split into a grin sunny and stoned as his native Jamaica as he waved Zach over. His voice was deep and jovial, with an accent like dark, sweet syrup. He plucked a broad-brimmed black hat from the jumble on the table. An Amish hat, circled with a handsome band of black leather and silver cockleshells. To his credit, Dougal did not plop it rudely onto Zach's head, just held it out until Zach had to take it. Zach held the hat in his hands but did not try it on. Some of these guys could sell you anything.

"Actually," he said, "I wanted to make a small donation to the cause."

"Ya mon. No problem." Dougal didn't exactly stick out his hand, just eased it to the edge of the table where it would be available in case anyone wanted to slip anything into it. Zach scissored two twenties out of his pocket and palmed them over. Dougal's dark eyes flickered, clocking the amount even as he made the money disappear. He reached under his table and came out with a thick pamphlet, which he handed over to Zach: *The Dangers of Marijuana*, ever so imaginative a title, the propaganda zombies were really knocking themselves out with creativity these days. Zach tucked the pamphlet into his pocket.

Dougal unscrewed the top of a thermos and sloshed a generous amount of steaming black coffee into the plastic cup. The odor touched Zach's nostrils, rich with chicory. Dougal saw him squirming and offered the cup. "Finish it off, mon. Fresh this morning from Café du Monde."

Zach's hands itched to grasp the cup. He knew how warm and comforting it would feel between his palms, knew how the smooth slow-roasted flavor would roll over his tongue. Unfortunately, he also knew how the subsequent effects would feel, his heart slamming like a caged thing against the inner meatwall of his chest, his brain drying out like a sponge, his eyeballs seeming to jitter and buzz in their sockets. "I can't drink coffee anymore," he admitted. "I used to love it, but now it just gives me the shakes."

Dougal's heavy eyebrows drew together in genuine consternation. "But we got de second-best joe in de world right here! Jus' have a slug, it'll do you right."

"I can't even drink decaf," Zach said sadly. "My imagination's too good."

"You're twenty?"

"Nineteen."

"An' you quit drinkin' coffee—"

"When I was sixteen."

Dougal shook his head. The frayed and festooned ends of dreads swayed gently around his face. "I t'ink you need to relax. If I couldn't drink New Orleans coffee, I guess I'd be makin' even more donations to de cause than you do."

"So what's the *best* joe?"

"Jamaican Blue Mountain, mon. Fry up some salt fish'n'ackee every morning, have two-three cups of Blue Mountain, you lose dem dark circles unda your eyes."

Yeah, thought Zach, *and die of a heart attack before I hit twenty-five*.

They shot the shit for a few more minutes. ("Party tonight," Dougal informed him, "buncha folks gonna dial de trip phone at Louie's," which translated to "Anywhere from three to twenty people are going to drop acid in St. Louis Cemetery tonight.") As he made his farewells and turned to go, Dougal stopped him. "You want de hat? Half price—no problem."

Zach had forgotten he was still holding the black Amish hat. He started to toss it back on the table, then stopped. He didn't have a hat, and this one would keep the sun off nicely. He put it on, a perfect fit. Dougal nodded. "Very fine. Make you look like a preacher man gone bad." That sunny grin again, and Zach laughed too. These guys *could* sell you anything.

On his way back, Zach stopped at a produce stand and bought a few handfuls of thin, twisted, lethally hot red and green peppers. Once in a while the Market would get some of the orange and yellow scotch bonnets, or habaneros, that grew on bushes in Dougal's home country. They were said to be the hottest pepper in the world—fifty times the heat of the jalapeño—and they had a sweet, fruity flavor Zach loved. But the Louisiana peppers would do for now. He would snack on them later, while swigging milk and speeding down the highways of hackdom.

He supposed his strange body chemistry had its rewards. He missed coffee like a dear lost lover, but he knew no one else who could hack on acid, thrive for days on pot and Bloody Marys made of equal parts vodka, tomato juice, and Tabasco, or munch ounces of near-pure capsicum without even a scorched tongue or a burning belly to show for it.

He walked back down Madison, checked his mail—two catalogs, one from Loompanics Unlimited, which sold books about how to obtain fake IDs and disable tanks and other useful things, and one from Mo Hotta Mo Betta, which carried every fiery sauce, spread, spice, and seasoning known to humankind. These he filed on the bed for leisurely perusal later, along with his sharp new hat. His fingers were itchy, ready to pound some keys.

First he took out the antidrug pamphlet and removed the bag of pot taped between its pages. Tight green bud, packed nearly flat, laced with delicate little red hairs that spelled P-O-T-E-N-C-Y. Zach stuck his nose in the bag and breathed deep. The smell alone was intoxicating, herbal and piney. Anything that smelled that good just had to be illegal.

He crumbled some onto a stray sheet of paper, removed a couple of seeds and set them aside to throw in a field later, packed the weed into his black onyx pipe and lit up. The sweet smoke curled down into his lungs, sent green tendrils into his bloodstream, uncoiled the knots in his brain.

Aaaahhh.

Time to work.

He flipped the box on, stuck the phone in the modem's cradle, and dialed an obscure local pirate bulletin board system known as Mutanet. The BBS was an information exchange for all sorts of hackers, phone phreaks, and assorted computer weirdos. Zach had discovered its existence by writing a program that dialed every phone number in the area code and kept a list of the ones answered by modems. A little time spent discovering which ones led to bulletin boards—and what other ones might be useful—had led him to Mutanet, and a combination of brashness, twisted humor, and demonstration of his abilities had gotten him on.

He had all kinds of work waiting and projects going: credit card accounts to shave pennies from like wafer-thin slices of salami, bank balances to augment, lists of phone codes to obtain for sale later. He had recently written a program that cracked the encrypted password system of the state police headquarters, and he was toying with the idea of wiping clean the records of every drug offender he could find.

But right now he felt like fooling around on Mutanet for a while. He wasn't sure what made him do it—it wasn't how he usually began a work session—and he was never sure what gods to thank, afterward. For the pirate board might have been the only thing that saved him.

The system's logo appeared, along with a screenful of warnings, exhortations, and dire pronouncements, then a prompt. Zach tapped in his Mutanet handle (LUCIO) and his current password (NH3GH3), and he was in.

A computer BBS worked much like a real bulletin board: you could put up items for anyone to read and respond to, or you could put messages in envelopes, so to speak, for the eyes of one person only. It was better than a real bulletin board, though, because no one could deface your messages or peek into your envelopes except the systems operator, who wasn't usually inclined to bother.

He had mail waiting, a message from a talented phreak named Zombi who had given him some good uncanceled credit card numbers of the recently deceased. Grieving relatives didn't usually think to notify the card companies right away, and in the meantime the numbers were ripe for misuse or dissemination. Maybe this would be something equally nifty.

He brought up his mail and sat back in his chair.

And the message filled his screen, flashing like Bourbon Street strip-club neon, pulsing like a vein in a junkie's fevered temple.

    LUCIO. THEY ARE ON TO YOU. THEY KNOW WHO
    YOU ARE. THEY KNOW WHERE YOU ARE. RUN.

THREE

The Greyhound bus was slow and hot and nearly empty. It smelled mostly of smoke and sweat, a tired smell like the ends of journeys, but underlying that was a faintly exotic sweetness that twined into the nostrils like opium smoke. Probably the industrial strength disinfectant they used to slop out the rest room at the back of the bus, but to Trevor it was the smell of travel, of adventure. At any rate, it was an odor he knew as well as that of his own skin. He had spent a good part of the past seven years on Greyhound buses, or waiting for them in the quiet despair of a thousand cavernous terminals.

The Carolina countryside rolled past his window, summer-green, then dusk-blue, then a deepening, smoky violet. When he could no longer see by the dying sunlight that came through the window, he switched on the small bulb above his seat and kept drawing, his hand moving to the rhythm of the Charlie Parker tape on his Walkman. Now and then he raised his head and stared briefly out the window. All the cars had their headlights on, rushing toward him in an endless dazzling stream. Soon it was so dark that he could see only his own hollow-eyed reflection in the glass.

The fat redneck occupying the two seats in front of him heaved a great sigh when Trevor turned on the light. Trevor was dimly aware of the man shifting in his seat, making a show of tugging his John Deere cap down over his eyes, his body giving off a strong stale odor of cheap beer and human dirt. At last he turned completely around and stared at Trevor over the back of the seat. Neckless, his head looked like a jug resting on a wall; the skin of his face was seamed and damp and blotchy, nearly leprous. He might have been nineteen or forty. "Hey, you," he said. "Hey, hippie."

Trevor looked up but did not remove his earphones. He always listened to music at a very low volume, and he could hear fine with them on. "Me?"

"Yeah, you, who the fuck you think I mean, him?" The redneck gestured at an ancient black man asleep across the aisle, toothless cavern of his mouth gaping, gnarled hands twisting around the nearly empty bottle of Night Train in his lap.

Ever so slowly Trevor shook his head, never looking away from the redneck's bleary, glittering eyes.

"Well anyway, you mind turnin' that goddamn light off? I got a real bad headache, you know?"

Hangover, more like. Trevor shook his head again, even more slowly, even more firmly. "I can't. I have to work on this drawing."

"The fuck you do!" More of the redneck's head rose over the seat, though there was still no neck in evidence. A large scarred hand appeared as well. Trevor saw black half-moons of dirt under each thick nail. "What's a freak like you drawin' that's so goddamn important?"

Silently Trevor turned his sketchbook around so that the redneck could see it. The light showed every detail of the drawing: a slender woman half-seated, half-sprawled in a doorway, head thrown back, yawning mouth full of blood and broken teeth. Her left temple and forehead were smashed in, her hair and face and the front of her blouse black with blood. The draftsmanship was stark and flawless, the frozen agony eloquent in every line of her body, in every stroke of her ruined face.

"My mother," Trevor said.

The redneck's fat face quivered. His lips twitched; his eyes went shocked, momentarily defenseless, then flat. "Fuckin' freak," he muttered loudly. But he didn't say anything else about the light, not for the rest of the trip.

The bus turned off the interstate at Pittsboro and got on the narrow two-lane state highway. It stopped for minutes at a tiny dark station in Corinth; then there were no more stops, and it was irrevocable, it was true, he was really going back to Missing Mile.

Trevor looked back down at his drawing. A line appeared between his eyebrows as he frowned at it. How weird. In the lower right-hand corner, without being aware of it, he had labeled the drawing. And he had labeled it wrong. In big, dark block letters he had printed the name ROSENA BLACK.

But his mother's name had been Rosena *McGee*. She had been born Rosena Parks, but she had died a McGee. Black was the name Trevor had chosen for himself years ago, the name he drew under.

He didn't erase the mislabel; it was too heavily penciled, would fuck up the paper. He wasn't much for erasing anyway. Sometimes your mistakes showed you the really interesting connections between your brain, your hand, and your heart, the ones you might otherwise never know were there. They were important even if you had no idea what they meant.

Like now, for instance. Coming back here might be the biggest mistake he'd ever made. But it might also be the most important thing he had ever done.

He couldn't remember his last sight of Missing Mile. His mother's friends had carried him out of the house that morning, and that was all he had known for a while. Only one of them, a man with large, gentle hands, had been brave enough to edge past Bobby's dangling body and pry Trevor from his niche between the toilet and the sink. The next thing he remembered was waking up in a blank white room, smelling medicine and vomit, then screaming at the sight of a tube that snaked out of a bag hanging by the bed and ran straight into the crook of his arm. The flesh where it went in was puffy, red, sore.

Trevor had thought the thing was alive, burrowing into him as he slept. He would never really trust sleep again. You closed your eyes and went somewhere else for a few hours, and while you were gone, anything could happen—anything at all. The whole world could be ripped out from under you.

The nurse said Trevor had not been able to hear people trying to talk to him, and could not eat or drink. The tube had pumped ground-up food into his arm to keep him from starving to death, or so he understood it. He was embarrassed to find himself wearing a diaper. Even Didi was too old for diapers. Then he remembered that Didi wasn't anything anymore but a memory of a smashed shape on a stained mattress. His family had been dead five days, had been buried while Trevor floated in that hazy twilight world.

The doctors at the hospital in Raleigh called it *catatonia*. Trevor knew it was Birdland. Not just the place where no one else could touch you, but the place you went when the real world scared you away.

After it became apparent that no relative or friend of the family was going to claim him, and a series of cognitive tests proved he was functional (if withdrawn), the court declared Trevor McGee a ward of the state. He was placed in the North Carolina Boys' Home on the outskirts of Charlotte, an orphanage and school whose operating budget had been shaved to the bone the previous year. There was no foster family program, no special training for the gifted, no therapy for the disturbed. There was only an enormous drafty pillared school building and four outlying dorms all built of smooth gray stone that held a chill even in the heart of summer. There were only three hundred boys aged five to eighteen, all kept crew-cut and conservatively dressed, each with his own personal hell and none of them much inclined to help ease the weight of anyone else's.

The place seemed to have no color, no texture. Trevor's thirteen years there were a collage of blurred edges, featureless gray expanses, empty city streets sectioned into little diamonds by the chain-link fence that surrounded the Home and its grounds. His room was a cold square box, but safe because he could draw there without anyone looking over his shoulder.

Most of the other boys used sports as their escape, built their dreams around athletic scholarships to State or UNC. Trevor was painfully clumsy; except for his right hand, his body felt wrong to him, like something he wasn't entitled to and shouldn't have. He dreaded the afternoons he was forced out to the playing fields with his gym class, hot dusty tedium broken only by occasional panic when someone screamed at him to run or swing or catch a hurtling ball that looked like a bomb falling at a thousand miles per hour out of a dizzying clear blue sky.

His life at the Boys' Home had been neither good nor terrible. He never tried to make friends, and mostly he was ignored. On the rare occasions that a group of predators chose him as their next target, Trevor returned their taunts until he goaded them into attacking him. They always attacked him eventually. Then he would hurt as many of them as badly as he could. He learned to land a hard punch with his left fist, to kick and claw and bite, anything that did not risk his drawing hand. He usually got the worst of it, but that particular group would leave him alone afterward, and Trevor would mind his own business until the next group came along. From things he read, he suspected it was a lot like prison.

The state had cut him loose at eighteen with an option to attend vocational school. Instead, Trevor headed for the Greyhound station and bought a ticket for as far as the hundred dollars in his pocket would take him.

He had traveled haphazardly in those years, zigzagging between cities and coasts, picking up work here and there, occasionally selling a sketch or a comic strip for the price of a bus ticket, often more. Sometimes he met people that under other circumstances he thought he might have called friends. At any rate, people in the real world were more interesting than any he had met in the Home. But as soon as he left a place, these acquaintances were gone as if erased from the world.

He never let anyone touch him. Mostly he preferred to be alone. If he was ever unable to draw, Trevor thought he would probably die. It was a possibility he always kept tucked away in a corner of his mind, the comfort of the razor or the rope, the security of poison on the shelf waiting to be swallowed. But he wouldn't take anyone with him when he went.

He had not cut his hair for seven years. He had never had a permanent address. He seldom visited a town or a city more than once. There were only a few places he avoided. Austin. New Orleans. And North Carolina, until now.

His twenty-fifth birthday had recently come and gone, celebrated only by the crossing of state lines, a thing that always exhilarated him a little no matter how often he did it. Trevor often came close to forgetting his own birthday. All it had meant in the Boys' Home was an ugly new shirt and a cupcake with a single candle on it, reminders of everything he didn't have.

And besides, his birthday was overshadowed by the more important anniversary just after it. The anniversary that fell tomorrow.

Twenty years since it happened, and every year strung heavy as a millstone round his heart. Four-fifths of his life spent wondering why he wasn't dead. It was too long.

Recently he had started having a dream of the house on Violin Road. All through his childhood Trevor had dreamed of that last morning, that bloody morning that seemed to drip through his memory like molasses, dark and slow. That was a familiar nightmare, infrequent now. But this new dream was different, and had been coming several times a week.

He would find himself sitting in the little back bedroom Bobby had used as a studio, staring at a blank sheet of paper on the drawing board. Trevor usually drew comics in his sketchbook, but Bobby had used looseleaf paper for *Birdland*. Only there was no Birdland on this sheet of paper. There was nothing on it, and he could think of nothing to put on it. It stared him in the eye and laughed at him, and Trevor could almost hear its dry sardonic whisper: *The abyss stares back into you? Ha! Nothing to see but a liver pickled in whiskey and the ashes of a million burnt-out dreams.*

Awake, Trevor couldn't imagine not being able to draw. He could always make his hand move. An empty page had always been a challenge, a space for him to fill. Awake, it still was. But in this dream, the blank sheet of paper was a mockery.

And he didn't drink whiskey, or any other kind of alcohol. He had never taken a drink in his life.

Trevor found that this dream bothered him more than the ones in which he saw his family dead. Drawing had been the only thing he cared about for such a long time. Now he was beginning to understand how the loss of it could drive someone insane.

He started to worry: what if the hollow, paralyzed feeling of the dream infiltrated his waking life? What if someday he opened his sketchbook and his hand went stiff, his mind numb?

The night he woke up with a broken pencil in his hands, the edges of the wood as raw as a fractured bone, the sound of the snap still echoing like a leftover shred of nightmare through his lonely boardinghouse room, Trevor knew he had to go back to the house. He was sick of wearing his past like a millstone. He would not let his art become one too.

The bus passed a wreck just outside Missing Mile, a small car crumpled in a ditch, sparkling shards of glass picking up the whirling red and blue lights, making the scene seem to revolve psychedelically. Trevor cupped his hands to the window, pressed his forehead to the glass. Paramedics were loading someone into the ambulance, strapped to a stretcher, already punctured with needles and tubes. Trevor looked straight down into the person's face and saw that it was a girl, maybe close to his age, face drenched with blood, chest crushed in, eyelids still fluttering.

Then—he saw it—the life left her. Her lids stopped moving and he saw her eyes freeze on a point beyond him, beyond anything he would ever see in this world. The medics kept moving, shoved her into the ambulance and slammed the doors, and she was gone. Yes, she was gone.

Great, he thought. *An omen. Just what I needed.*

A few minutes later the bus pulled into the parking lot of the Farmers Hardware Store, the flatiron-shaped building that stood lone and proud among lesser downtown structures like the prow of some landlocked ship. A small ticket office at the back and a bench in the parking lot served as Missing Mile's bus station. The Greyhound groaned to a stop alongside the deserted bench.

Trevor hoisted his backpack and made his way down the aisle, then down the steps. His feet touched North Carolina ground for the first time in two decades, and a shiver ran through him like a tiny electric chill. No one else got off.

The bus had seemed hot, but the humid swelter of the night outside made him realize it had been air-conditioned. The air pressed like a soft damp palm against his face, delicious with the scents of honeysuckle, wet grass, hot charcoal and the rich oils of roasting pork. Someone nearby was cooking out tonight.

The smell of barbecue made his stomach roll over, then growl: he was either sick or starved. Years of institutional food had blurred the two sensations. The Boys' Home was not quite Dickensian, but second helpings were neither kindly looked upon by the cafeteria ladies nor much desired by the boys.

Maybe by now Missing Mile had somewhere to eat besides that greasy diner. But if not, the diner would do. Trevor decided to take a walk through downtown. He couldn't go out to the house yet. Not at night. He was ready for anything, but he was still scared.

He would be there tomorrow, for the twenty-year reunion. Trevor only hoped he was invited this time.

Kinsey knew tonight was going to suck. Rima was scheduled to work, and Rima was gone, finding someone else to rip off, having raw meat scraped out of her womb, coking up her little brain until it spun like a whirligig, or maybe all of the above.

So Kinsey would be working by himself. Terry Buckett's new band Gumbo was playing. Owner and manager of the Whirling Disc record store, Terry also played drums and sang whenever he could get a gig. Gumbo was one of the Yew's biggest draws now that Lost Souls? were on the road, and it would be a busy night.

To distract himself, Kinsey decided to have a dinner special. It would make him even busier, but he loved feeding his kids. He ran through his limited repertoire. Curry? . . . no, it would take too long . . . lentil soup? no, he'd had that one twice last week . . . gumbo, for the band . . . but his skills weren't up to it, and there was nowhere to get fresh seafood, and he never had been convinced you could make good gumbo anywhere but New Orleans. The Mississippi River water gave it that special flavor, maybe. At last Kinsey decided tonight would be Japanese Night.

He hiked home and put together a quick broth from some elderly vegetables and a few pork bones in his freezer, loaded it into his car, and drove slowly back into town so as not to slosh it. The railroad tracks were tricky, but he managed them with aplomb. In town, he stopped at the little grocery next to Farmers Hardware and bought twenty packages of Oodles of Noodles and several bunches of green onions. The rain had stopped, which meant it would be even busier.

Back at the Yew, Kinsey took down the chalkboard over the bar, selected a piece of purple chalk, and with a flourish wrote JAPANESE NOODLE SOUP! $1.00!

If anyone ordered the special, Kinsey would ladle up a bowl of his homemade broth, pop in the noodles, throw away the sodium-laden "flavor packet," and zap the whole thing in the microwave he kept behind the bar. The green onions were for a garnish, and he set to chopping them into small, fragrant rounds. It was getting near eight. The band wouldn't start until ten, but the kids often started drifting in this early to drink and eat and talk. Sometimes he opened the club at five for happy hour, but he hadn't been happy enough today.

An hour later the Sacred Yew was nearly full. Admission was free until ten. After that he would have to find someone to work the door. That was never hard: all the door people had to do was collect money, shoot the shit, and watch the band for free. If they were of age they got a free beer too. The club served no alcohol but beer—bottled, canned, and draft.

Still, the vagaries of North Carolina law made the Yew a bar and forbade the presence of those under twenty-one.

For the place to be an all-ages club—as Kinsey had intended all along—it must qualify as a restaurant as well. Hence the noodle soup, the sandwiches, the odds and ends of snacks he served. At first making the food had been a bother. Then he grew to like it; now his cookbook collection was rapidly expanding. Regular customers gave them to him all the time, and Kinsey chose to take these as a compliment.

Some of the kids he knew, the ones from Missing Mile and surrounding areas, most of whom attended a nearby Quaker school called Windy Hill. There was a public high school too, but the kids there were mostly metalheads and shitkickers; Kinsey knew some of them, had even helped them work on their cars, but they didn't like the music at the Yew.

The kids who came here were of a more artistic bent, clothed in bright ragtag colors or ripped T-shirts and combat boots or chic, sleek black, according to their various philosophies and passions. Some dyed their hair and cropped it, some let their hair grow long and tied it with colored ribbons, some simply shoved it behind their ears and didn't give a shit, or pretended not to. There were poets and painters, firebrands and fuckups, innocents and wantons. There were Missing Mile townies and college kids from Raleigh and Chapel Hill, the ones with legal IDs and money for beer, the ones who paid his bills. There were younger kids furtively fumbling with flasks, adding liquor gotten from God knows where to their Cokes from the bar. Unless this was done in a particularly obvious or obnoxious manner, Kinsey usually turned a blind eye.

He had just hooked up a new keg of Budweiser when Terry Buckett sat down at the bar. The band had done their sound check earlier, and it was obvious they'd been practicing: they were tighter than ever, Terry's voice clear and strong, R.J.'s bass line thunderous. "What do you call that style of music?" Kinsey had asked after listening to a couple of numbers.

"Swamp rock," Terry had said with a grin.

Now he grinned up at Kinsey again, stoned and amiable,

muscular drummer's forearms propped on the bar, tie-dyed bandanna wrapped around his dark curly hair. "Noodle soup, huh? Where'd you come up with that?"

"A cookbook called *The Asian Menu*," said Kinsey. "With certain variations."

"I'll bet. Well, let's give it a try. Gimme a Natty Boho too." National Bohemian was the Yew's bar brand. At a dollar-fifty a bottle it was a hot seller. Kinsey opened a frosty bottle and set it on the bar in front of Terry, then started preparing the soup.

"Talked to Steve and Ghost today," Terry said.

"Yeah? They call the store?" Steve and Ghost were the two members of the band Lost Souls?; the spray-painted lyric WE ARE NOT AFRAID was from "World," the song they always used to close their set. Steve played a dark, fierce guitar; Ghost had a voice like golden gravel running along the bottom of a clear mountain stream. A couple of weeks ago they had returned from a gig in New York and promptly left town again for a cross-country road trip in Steve's old T-bird. San Francisco was their ultimate destination, but they would plan their route as they traveled, and they might be gone for as much as a year.

"Yeah. The new guy answered, and Steve goes 'This is John Thomas from the IRS calling for Mr. Buckett.' I about pissed myself when he handed me the phone. That little bastard . . ." Terry laughed and shook his head.

"Are they doing okay?"

"Sure. They're in Texas now. Steve said they played at a coffeehouse in Austin and the folkies loved 'em. Sold some tapes too. Maybe I ought to check out Austin. You ever been?"

"No. One of my favorite underground cartoonists came from there, though. Bobby McGee."

Terry frowned. "McGee? Wasn't he the guy who . . ."

"Yup."

"That house is still standing out on Violin Road," Terry mused. "I was only eight when the murders happened, but I remember. They say it's haunted."

"Of course they do. It might even be true. But his comic *Birdland* was brilliant, right up there with Crumb and—"

"Didn't he leave one of his kids alive?"

Kinsey served Terry a steaming bowl of noodle soup. "Yes, he left a kid. A five-year-old son, I believe. And no, I *don't* know what ever happened to him."

"I bet he was fucked up real good," said Terry, slurping thoughtfully.

"Excuse me. Could I get a bowl of that soup?" said a quiet voice from the end of the bar.

Kinsey turned. Neither he nor Terry had noticed the boy before; the bar was crowded and the kid fit right in, tall and slender, plain black T-shirt tucked into black jeans, wavy ginger-blond hair grown long and pulled back in a ponytail from a bony, almost delicate face. A battered gray backpack was slung over his shoulder. He looked about twenty and carried himself like someone maybe even younger, unsure of his welcome and not particularly wanting to be noticed.

But his eyes were arresting: a transparent, icy blue, large and round, irises rimmed with a thin line of black. They seemed enormous in the thin face. *Waif-eyes,* thought Kinsey; *hunger-eyes.*

"You new in town?" Terry asked through a mouthful of noodles.

The boy nodded. "I came in on the bus about an hour ago."

"That's new, all right." Terry offered his hand. The boy looked confused for a moment, then reached out and shook. "I'm Terry Buckett. I run the record store here, in case you need any sounds. Everything from Nine Inch Nails to Hank Williams."

"Hank Williams, *Senior,*" Kinsey interjected.

"Senior, absolutely. For Bocephus you have to drive to Corinth—he's a little too all-American for us. Who're you?"

"Trevor Black. I usually listen to jazz."

"Got some of that too." Terry grinned at the boy. After a moment's hesitation, the boy smiled tentatively back. Terry's friendliness was hard to resist; he would keep talking until a person starting answering, even if it was just to shut him up.

Kinsey set a bowl of soup in front of Trevor Black—the name seemed vaguely familiar, but he couldn't think why—and collected the boy's dollar. "I usually buy new customers a beer. If you're under twenty-one, I'll buy you a Coke."

Trevor tucked a neat bundle of noodles into his mouth. "I'm twenty-five. But I don't drink. I'll take a Coke." He chewed the noodles, then frowned. "This tastes just like Oodles of Noodles."

Terry snorted. "Kinsey practices what you call 'found cuisine.' "

"The broth is homemade," Kinsey said coolly. "Would you like your dollar back? Either of you?"

Terry just waved an impatient hand. Trevor seemed to consider it for a moment, then shook his head. "No. This is fine."

"So glad it meets with your approval," Kinsey muttered, turning away to get the kid's Coke. Behind him he heard Terry snort again. Kinsey closed his eyes and took several deep breaths. It was going to be a long night.

An hour later Gumbo was churning away onstage, Trevor Black was still perched on his stool nursing his third Coke, and the bar was a scene of utter chaos.

Kinsey had gotten a local kid called Robo to collect money at the door. Robo, at eighteen, was well on his way to becoming Missing Mile's resident stewbum—he got his nickname from the bottles of Robitussin he shoplifted from the drugstore—but Kinsey figured he was just capable of counting dollars, stamping hands, and managing not to pocket any of the band's proceeds as long as Kinsey slipped him a couple of beers during the show.

The club was packed. Terry and R.J. Miller, Gumbo's bass player, had sat in with Lost Souls? a number of times and were already known as solid players. The guitarist was a glam-rock dynamo, a kid named Calvin who in fact bore a strong resemblance to the Calvin of comic strip fame, but punked out and tarted up considerably. Gumbo served up a foot-stomping set, hot as Tabasco, intoxicating as Dixie beer.

Since the band started, Kinsey had been drawing constant cups of draft, popping endless bottletops. Just before eleven the keg of Bud ran dry. Kinsey ducked into the back room and walked a new one onto the dolly. The kegs were heavy and awkward, and when he was in a hurry he usually managed to roll them off the dolly and right onto his toes.

"*Shit!*" he said loudly as this very thing happened. As he jerked his foot away, the keg teetered and threatened to tip. Kinsey grabbed at it. If it went over, the beer inside would foam unmercifully. Customers were lined up three deep at the bar, waiting to be served, and last call was just an hour away. Silently he cursed the treacherous Rima, wishing he had busted her after all, if only for the cheap satisfaction it would give him right now.

Then suddenly someone was beside him, wrestling with the icy keg, pushing Kinsey toward the taps, the cooler, the impatient mass of drinkers. "Go wait on them—I'll hook it up. I know how." Skinny arms wrapped around the keg, heaving it into place; deft long-fingered hands were already tapping the valve. Trevor Black. Kinsey wondered if the kid really was twenty-five. He still looked more like nineteen, and the Yew could get busted if an underage person was caught serving beer. Kinsey shrugged and put it out of his mind. Taking the risk was better than losing business.

Fifteen minutes or so into the rush, Kinsey could tell Trevor had done this kind of work before. He was quick to figure out where everything was; he was able to duck and dodge around Kinsey without getting in his way. Since he didn't know the prices, he just served drinks as fast as he could and left the register to Kinsey. Dollar bills flew into Kinsey's hands. The tip jar jangled with change. At last the flood of customers flowed to a trickle, then stopped altogether: everyone was drunk and dancing, getting into Gumbo.

Kinsey went up front with a round of Natty Bohos for the band. Terry flashed him a big smile and did a little flourish on the drums. The club was hot and steamy, smelling of sweat and beer and clove smoke; the faces of the dancing kids were slick with light, lost in musical rapture.

When Kinsey made his way back through the crowd, Trevor was leaning against the cooler drinking another Coke. His smile was tentative, barely a flicker. "Was that okay? To just jump in like that?"

"Absolutely not. You're fired." They stared at each other for a moment; then Kinsey's mouth twitched, and all at once both were laughing. "Seriously, do you want a job? You can keep all tonight's tips, and I'll start you at four-fifty an hour."

Trevor shrugged. "I have stuff to do in Missing Mile—I don't need a job right away. And I'm not really a bartender. I've just filled in for one a couple of times."

Kinsey raised an eyebrow. "You could've fooled me. Well, you can fill in some here if you want. Pick up a shift every week or so."

Trevor stared at the floor. "Maybe. It depends."

Kinsey decided not to ask what it depended on. He seemed to have wrecked the moment of camaraderie already. Trevor was an odd bird, his conversation seeded with chill winds and ice pockets. Kinsey searched for a neutral topic to dissipate the tension. "So, if you're not a bartender by profession, what is it you do?"

Trevor kept looking at the floor, scuffed the toe of a ratty black sneaker over the worn boards. "I draw comics."

Kinsey had thought the name was familiar. "Trevor Black . . . Didn't you have a page in *Drawn and Quarterly?*" This was an underground comics magazine featuring some of the newest, most bizarre talent around.

Trevor looked surprised, then a little disconcerted, but he nodded. "Yes. That was me."

"It was a good strip. You know, it made me think of—"

A second wave of beer drinkers descended upon the bar clamoring for Natty Bohos. Trevor turned away to serve them so quickly that Kinsey wondered whether he was glad to get off the subject. As Kinsey rang up their purchases, his mind lingered on the comic. It had been an odd, brief tale, an epiphany of sorts, something about a flock of birds rising from a man's charred corpse like a feathered, jewel-eyed soul. Kinsey had been about to say how much the comic's style had reminded him of the late Robert McGee, the sharp inking and clean, graceful lines. He was sure Trevor had read *Birdland*. Possibly he knew McGee had died here. Kinsey might even tell him about the time he'd fixed the McGees' car, just before the tragedy.

But the band was winding down. The rush went on until last call, and then it was closing time, money to count, spills to wipe up, hundreds of cups, cans, bottles to find and empty and sort for tomorrow's recycling pickup. By the time they finished it was after three.

Kinsey popped a beer, then picked out a tape and stuck it in the little cassette player behind the bar. Miles Davis, something from the fifties. The sound of the trumpet filled the room, easy and slow, smooth as eggnog spiked with whiskey. Trevor put his head down on the bar. Kinsey leaned against the register and closed his eyes.

The music ended and an announcer's voice came on, part of the tape, which had been recorded live on Fifty-second Street in the golden bebop days. The voice was deep, white, and juicy, and somehow seemed a distilled essence of its time; you could easily picture the guy in his sharp suit with its deep-cut lapels, hair slicked back, cool ofay cat. *"Well! Yeah! Miiiiles Davis. Remember, you still have plenty of time to get to Birdland—"*

Kinsey heard a strangled sob. He opened his eyes and stared at Trevor, who was rolling his head back and forth on the bar, his hands clawing at the scarred wood. His lips were pulled back over his teeth, and tears poured from his eyes. Kinsey could actually see them forming salty little pools on the bar's varnished surface. He moved toward the boy. "Hey, Trevor? What—"

"I *don't* have plenty of time to get to Birdland!" Trevor cried. His voice sounded as if it were being pulled out of him, dragged over hot coals and rusty nails, tortured out of his throat. "I don't have any time at all—and I'm *scared*—"

"*Birdland?*" Kinsey said softly.

Trevor caught the puzzled inflection. He looked up at Kinsey, the pale flesh of his eyelids swollen, his clear eyes naked and wet and terrified. And suddenly Kinsey knew that face: a five-year-old boy, in bad need of a haircut by some standards, too thin and hollow-eyed by any, standing on the side of a country road staring first at his mother, then at his father.

"Trevor McGee," said Kinsey.

"Oh, goddamn . . ." Miserably, Trevor nodded. Then he was sobbing again. Kinsey went around the bar, put a cautious hand on the boy's trembling shoulder, felt the muscles bunch up and flinch away from his palm.

"Don't touch me!"

"Sorry. I didn't mean—"

"No, I just can't—"

They stared helplessly at each other. Trevor's face was flushed, slick with tears. Everything in the way he held himself—arms crossed over his chest, shoulders hunched—screamed *Don't touch me* as loudly as Trevor's mouth had done. But his eyes were five years old again, and begged *Hold me. Hold me. Help me.*

Trevor might hate him, might even think Kinsey was hitting on him, but that was just too bad. Kinsey could not ignore such pain. "I remember you," he said. "I was the mechanic who fixed your parents' car. I wanted to help you then, and I want to help you now." Before Trevor could flinch again, Kinsey wrapped his long arms around the boy and held on tight.

He felt Trevor's body go absolutely rigid, felt him try to pull away. If he had kept trying, Kinsey would have let him go. But after a few seconds of struggle Trevor sagged against Kinsey's chest.

"I remember you too," he said. "You recognized my dad . . . but he was ashamed of himself . . . ashamed of us . . ."

"You poor child," Kinsey whispered, "you poor, poor child." The thin body was all sharp angles, all elbows and shoulder blades; it felt as fragile against him as that of a wounded bird. Kinsey imagined Trevor's fear unfolding like treacherous wings to carry him back to that house, back to the strange and painful year 1972, to the death he no doubt thought he had deserved.

At last the crying faded to an occasional long tremor that jerked through the boy like an electric current. He had been leaning hard against Kinsey, his sharp chin digging into Kinsey's shoulder. Now he pulled away and slumped on the bar stool, swiping at his face. Kinsey decided not to give him time to be embarrassed. "Let's go."

Trevor gave him a half-wary, half-questioning look.

"You shouldn't be by yourself tonight," Kinsey told him. "You're coming home with me."

He expected argument, maybe refusal, and he was prepared to push the issue. But if anything, Trevor looked relieved. Kinsey wondered whether the boy had been planning to hike out to Violin Road, to sleep in that bad memory of a house. The house of Trevor McGee's thwarted doom and, perhaps, of Trevor Black's impending destiny.

Trevor slung his backpack over his shoulder, turned off the bar lights, and followed Kinsey out of the club, down the bad end of Firehouse Street, into the silent silver-lit night.

FOUR

Four rings. Zach counted them with his teeth gritted, his free hand viciously shredding a fundamentalist tract he'd picked up somewhere, *Tomb of the Unborn*.

Then the gentle click of a lifted receiver, muted Dixieland jazz playing in the background. "Hi, this is Eddy Sung."

"EDDY FOR CHRISSAKE YOU GOT TO HELP ME I GOT TO GET OUT OF—"

The Dixieland changed abruptly to grinding industrial hardcore. "I'm sorry I'm not here, but if you leave your number I'll call you back as soon—"

"AWWWW SHIT, GODDAMMIT, EDDY, PLEASE BE THERE!!! PLEASE PICK UP!!!"

A squealing snatch of violins; then Eddy's answering machine beeped in his ear. Zach took a deep sobbing breath, resisted the urge to slam his own phone into the cradle hard enough to crack its casing, and tried to speak calmly. "Ed— I'm in trouble. You always said you coveted my apartment, well, call me soon enough and you might get the goddamn thing."

He hung up, spun aimlessly in the middle of the room for several moments. The computer screen caught his eye, still pulsing like some obscene digital orifice. Yes, you could fall headlong into that screen, that alternate reality like a cradling mouth or womb, never coming up for air, never realizing that so slowly, so smoothly you took no notice, it was chewing and digesting you . . .

No. Blaming the computer for his troubles, that was like a terminal lung cancer victim blaming a pack of cigarettes or, worse, his faithful old Zippo. It was a tool and he had chosen to use it. His troubles were with They whose clammy suck- ered tentacle grasped the other end of that tool. William Bur- roughs had advised him to know what was on the end of his fork, but had he listened? Of course not—and now the dirty tines were on the verge of impaling his tongue.

But in that direction madness lay.

He leaned against the doorjamb that led into the bathroom —with its polished sea-green tiles and its skylight in the ceil- ing high above the tub, taking a shower here was like stand- ing beneath a sunlit waterfall, and where would he ever find such a place again? A green waterfall of a bathroom—an apartment with all his things in it, a block from the wondrous bazaar that sold everything he needed, two blocks from the bank of the Mississippi that coursed through the city like a throbbing brown artery?

Before moving in here two years ago, Zach had spent most of his time on the streets and at various friends' houses. This was the first place that had ever felt like home. He wasn't sure he knew how to live anywhere else, wasn't sure any- where else would have him.

But that didn't matter. He had been cutting things too close, taking too many dumb chances. When he started hack- ing three years ago, it had been just another lark, another way of amusing himself, a curiosity like getting drunk on sloe gin or watching the Psychic Friends Network on late-night cable TV. During his brief high school career he had taken an ele- mentary programming class and ended up getting himself kicked out of the school computer room, which robbed him of his only good reason to show up at the brain-numbing, tomb- like institution at an inhuman hour each weekday morning.

At sixteen, two years after leaving home, Zach dropped out and started casting about for something better. He had known immediately that hacking was it. He'd only had a cheap PC-clone with a slow modem at first, but fucking around on the underground bulletin boards he found with his automatic dialing program led him to wonder about other networks, secret systems and databanks that were supposed to be hidden but were actually *right there,* tantalizingly there, vibrating behind a thin membrane of commands and pass-words.

Free information and money, if only you could get at it. Zach soon discovered that he could. And it was *so damn easy* . . .

But if they caught you at things like stealing from credit card companies and breaking the systems of Southern Bell, affectionately known as the Gestapo among phreaks and hackers, it could be worth ten years in a federal prison. Sure, you might get out in half as many, or even less. But the thought of even one day in the pen was too much for most hackers, conjuring up vivid images of great tattooed baby-rapers and serial killers cornholing their lily-white butts, then snapping their skinny necks.

Zach let his knees buckle and slid down the door frame to the floor. He'd kicked off his sneakers at some point, and the green tiles were blessedly cool against the soles of his feet. He saw the round mirror above the sink reflecting his empty room, saw the dripping faucet that over the years had left a stain on the porcelain like the imprint of rusty teardrops, saw the blue ceramic mug that held two toothbrushes, one purple and one black. He kept an extra because Eddy had been known to sleep over on occasions when they watched one bad film too many or talked too far into the night or simply drank themselves into a stupor on the cheap bourbon Eddy loved.

There was nothing untoward to it, though, nothing sexual, not even a furtive drunken groping here or there. Zach liked Eddy too much for that.

But never mind who he liked. He was going to be on the road, playing it lonely for a while. Hackers were scared of prison, yes, and many of them would turn informer once they were nabbed. But most would also do anything they could to help a fellow outlaw, as long as they didn't endanger them-selves. He had been communicating with other Mutanet users for more than a year; it was like frequenting some weird little coffeehouse, getting to know the regulars. He trusted Zombi as much as any of his less remote friends, knew Zombi wouldn't send him such a message unless his lead was reliable.

And it surely was. Any number of scary companies and agencies could be after him: if they caught you stealing they would try to fuck you up. And he had stolen a *lot*.

And didn't he have to admit, begrudgingly, that in some extra-perverse corner of his brain the idea of having to get out of town before sundown appealed to him? New Orleans had been the only constant thing in his life. But didn't he get an itchy foot sometimes, didn't he sometimes think about just throwing all his stuff in his car and *going*?

Of course he did. Everybody did, even normal people, the ones with triple mortgages and orthodontists' bills and responsibilities to everything except what they really wanted. Everyone dreamed of the open highway unspooling like a black satin ribbon beneath his wheels. It was in the American blood, some kind of racial memory. But most people never really did it; they became tied to a place by friends, possessions, habits. If you stayed in one place long enough, you started to send down taproots.

And yet it was always a possibility, just getting up one day and taking off. It was the kind of thing you thought about, but seldom did.

Until you had to.

Zach felt a million possibilities starting to unfold within him like a garden of dark flowers. The perfume was heady: the scent of strangers, of unknown cities and towns; the subtle bouquet of adventure and its twin, danger.

He was only nineteen and he wanted to know everything there was to know in the world, to do all things, to grasp every experience in his hands and drink it down like whiskey. This couldn't break his spirit, couldn't keep him down. So They were after him, the shadowy, faceless, infinitely sinister They that seemed a peculiarly American archetype of terror: dark trench coat, glowing eyes beneath a black slouch hat, badge in hand emblazoned with the dread legend FBI, or NSA, or worse, extended like a red-hot iron ready to sear its brand into your forehead. Every hacker, every phone phreak, every intelligent criminal Zach knew had his or her own visions and nightmares of Them.

But just because They were after him didn't mean They could get him.

He realized that his hands were clenched into fists and his heart was pounding painfully. Excitement did that to him; he supposed it would kill him someday, but he was addicted to it. He willed his pulse to slow down, made himself unfold his hands. *Tomb of the Unborn* was still crumpled in one palm. Should have been a horror movie, he thought; too bad someone had wasted such a great title on a piece of anti-choice propaganda, for that was what it was, complete with color shots of shredded fetuses in puddles of their own gore.

He balled up the tract and threw it across the room, pushed himself to his feet, shook off the headrush, tested his balance. Cool. He'd had a few bad moments there, but now he was ready for the next reel of the Grand Adventures of Zachary Bosch.

Zach didn't know if thinking of your life as a movie serial was healthy, but it certainly helped keep him sane.

Bourbon Street runs through the Vieux Carré for fourteen blocks, beginning on the more-or-less north side, at the wide avenue called Esplanade. On that side of the Quarter, Bourbon is funky and fashionable, paved with cobblestones, lined with dark little neighborhood bars and dearly priced studio apartments, haunted on hot nights by boys sweating in brazenly tight leather.

The middle blocks of Bourbon are part tawdry carnival and part efficient tourist mill, the tinsel and glitter of Mardi Gras for sale year-round, plastic cups of beer and frozen daiquiris and Hurricanes sold right on the sidewalk, racks of T-shirts, postcards, plastic alligators and mammy dolls, and "N'Awlins Voodoo Kits" side by side with window displays of glitter condoms, penis neckties, lurid latex vibrators. Here are the big strip clubs with their hucksters and roustabouts outside, bars flashing neon and touting endless drink specials, a few famous restaurants and a slew of pretenders. Every souvenir shop has poppers of amyl nitrite for sale in the back. In combination with the abuse of other substances, indulging in these makes the head seem to lift off the shoulders and fill the skull with a dazzling, infinitely expanding light.

But at the other end of Bourbon, the end that runs into Canal and the downtown skyscraper sprawl of the Central Business District, a different miasma hangs over the street. An air of dinginess that is somehow timeless, a seedy, mysterious air. The city looms above the old buildings of the Quarter, making them look gray and small and slightly faded. The bars feature no specials or cutely named cocktails, but the drinks are cheap and strong.

On this end of Bourbon Street, sandwiched between a pawnshop and a po-boy stand was the Pink Diamond Lounge. It was identifiable as a strip club only by the design stenciled on the door, a nude female silhouette inside a figure that might have been a diamond but looked a great deal more like a vulva. A lone bouncer nodded in the recesses of the doorway, letting loose a halfhearted line of patter when any likely customers passed by, knowing they had already heard it all farther up the street.

The interior of the Pink Diamond was dark except for the tiny, garishly lit stage. Smoke lurked in the corners and in a swirling blue layer near the ceiling. A few dancers wriggled gamely in front of beer-stained tables—not on top of them, as was popularly believed of table dances. No table in the Pink Diamond could bear the weight of a healthy girl, and most could have been reduced to matchsticks by a ninety-pound junkie.

One dancer stood in the dust-choked area behind the stage waiting for her cue. A muffled cough and snort sounded over the P.A. She would bet her day's tips that Tommy, the DJ, was doing a line right there in the booth. Usually he went to the men's room, but the manager wasn't here today, and no one else cared.

"And now—in her last set of the day—The Sweetest Charm of the Orient—MISS LEE!"

The first notes of her music pounded out of the speakers, a Cure song cranked up so loud that the words were distorted, but it didn't matter because no one else in this club had ever heard of the Cure except maybe a couple of the other dancers, and no one cared what music she danced to anyway as long as she showed her tits. Miss Lee threw back the dusty velvet curtain and kicked one leg out, long and silky-pale, shod in a spike-heeled, silver-chained, black leather ankle boot, and the crowd went wild.

If you could call five or six unshaven, seedy-looking men a crowd.

And if a few listless hoots and whistles, the lewd waggling of a tongue in the general direction of her crotch, or the simple act of lifting beer to mouth could be considered wild.

Miss Lee undulated onto the tiny stage. A ring of globe-shaped bulbs lit her from below, playing over her black vinyl T-strap and bra as she moved, showing off what curves she had. Five or six of the bulbs were dead, spaced at uneven intervals like rotten teeth in a jaw. She stalked to the pole placed strategically at center stage, wrapped her arms around it, and straddled it. She arched her back and worked the pole with her hips, letting her mouth fall open and her eyes slip half-shut into the dazed, drugged-looking expression that was supposed to pass for ecstasy. Then she pushed away from the pole, paused in front of the first stage rat, and began a slow insistent grind in front of his face.

After a couple of minutes he pinched two crumpled dollar bills out of his shirt pocket and slid them into her garter, making sure to run his nicotine-withered fingers as far up her thigh as he thought he could get away with. His sour scowl never wavered. Miss Lee gave him a geisha smile and moved on to the next customer, who was marginally young and good-looking, and therefore less likely to tip.

She wondered what they would think if they knew where her stage name came from. She had been born in New Orleans of Korean parents, and Loup, the Pink Diamond's manager, had advised her to pick "some kinda fake Chinese name" to capitalize on her ethnic looks. ("Lotta guys go in for that kinda thing," he'd added as if letting her in on a big guy-secret.) She had chosen the name Lee after a character from her favorite book, *Naked Lunch*. When a customer was nasty or business was bad or she was just in no mood to shake her ass for a bunch of human dildoes, she would think of junk-filled needles jabbing into putrescent veins, of swollen cocks leaking foul greenish slime, of beautiful boys fistfucking by the light of a rotten-cheese moon. It didn't make her happy, but it helped.

Her second song began. The Pixies' "No. 13 Baby." She glanced over at the DJ booth and saw Tommy grimace at the whining voice and churning psychedelic guitar: his tastes ran more to bands like Triumph and Foreigner, fake corporate metal, maybe a little Guns N' Roses if he was feeling really radical.

Miss Lee reached back to unhook her bra and felt a bill being tucked into the back of her garter, a dry hand whispering over her left buttcheek and gone before she could turn her head. She caught sight of the customer in one of the mirrors that ringed the stage. A tall black guy, head down, already disappearing into the darkness of the bar. For some reason the black men who liked her seemed embarrassed by their attraction. Maybe because she was so pale.

Surreptitiously she reached around and palmed the bill, slid it to the side of her leg. It was a ten. *Jackpot*. That pushed her over the hundred-dollar mark, good money for the day shift: she could actually afford to go home.

She stared at her reflection receding into infinity as she peeled the vinyl top away from her small firm breasts. A thin silver chain connected them, attached to delicate rings through both of her *café-au-lait*-colored nipples. The rest of her skin was a pale matte almond, ribs showing through like slats in a shutter, body too scrawny except for her rounded shelf of a butt and her tiny potbelly, legs muscled from six-hour shifts on spike heels and long walks through the French Quarter.

Her face was rather flat, her wide lips unrouged—she hated the way she looked in lipstick, especially the greasy pink-orange stuff most of the other dancers smeared on their mouths—and her dark narrow eyes smudged with purple shadow and black mascara, half hidden by her messy platinum wig. "Yew got the most beautiful hair Ah ever seen," a rube tourist had once told her reverently, and how she had longed to whip it off and drop it in his lap.

Instead she had smiled sweetly and taken his money.

Third song. Prince's "Darling Nikki," a small concession to the crowd, give 'em something they've heard before. And it was a dirty song, the famous dirty song that had kicked off the PMRC's entire Crusade Against Dirty Music, or whatever it was, by using the word *masturbating* in its lyrics. Bless it. Miss Lee hooked her thumbs into the elastic of her G-string, pulled the tiny scrap of vinyl tight over her crotch, so that the folds of her labia were all but outlined in shiny black. To get away with this trick she had to shave her pubic hair to the approximate size and shape of a Band-Aid, and it still wasn't enough; they always wanted to see more.

"Pull it to the side," some old fart would croak, waving a dollar in her face as if it were worth her job.

"Lemme see some hair."

"Hey, are you a *natural* blonde?" That line was always good for a snigger.

The men who came here could never see enough of her body; it was as if they wanted to take her apart. If she could remove her G-string, they'd want her to bend over and spread her cheeks so they could look up her twat. If she could do that, she supposed, they'd want her to unzip her skin and peel it off.

But it was a job (though precious few of the men who paid her salary seemed to realize that; it was amazing how many thought the dancers did this to meet guys or get erotic thrills). It allowed her to set her own schedule and paid better than waiting tables, which she had also done; dancing was much less demeaning. People saw restaurant workers as automatons, extensions of the tables and chairs, fair game for anything from tip-stiffing to verbal abuse.

But dancers, especially ones with any kind of good looks, were often treated like the epitome of unattainable goddesshood. Even in a joint like the Pink Diamond, the men were crude and gross and often infuriating, but hardly ever flat-out mean. And if they were, the dancers could have them kicked out. Some girls tried to get customers thrown out just for making raunchy remarks. Miss Lee thought this was stupid. Men who made such remarks were usually drunk, and drunk men usually tipped better. And she couldn't help pondering the morality of girls who shook their tits in the face of any guy with a dollar to his name, but blanched when they heard the word *pussy*.

It was an okay job, but she wouldn't mind winning the sweepstakes tomorrow.

She sank to the stage in a modified split that set them peering at her crotch in the eternal Quest to See Hair, collected a few more dollars, and disappeared behind the curtain as the last strains of "Darling Nikki" died. She and the next dancer, a tall muscular girl with bleached-blond hair and smooth ebony skin who called herself Baby Doll, groped their way past each other in the cramped coffinlike area. "How are they?" Baby Doll whispered.

Miss Lee shrugged. "Not great."

"Honey, they're *never* great." Miss Lee laughed. Baby Doll dabbed at her liberally applied pinky-orange lipstick, hoisted her heavy breasts so that they rode high and round in the D-cups of her red sequined halter top, and ducked onstage as Tommy botched the lead-in to her first song.

Miss Lee walked down a short shabby corridor to the dressing room. The heels of her boots dug into the bare concrete floor and sent bolts of agony up her calves. Boots were more comfortable than the pumps most girls wore, since they gave her ankles some support, but at the end of a shift she could still feel every step she had taken on those four-inch spikes.

She tugged them off as soon as she hit the dressing room,

collected the sweaty dollars stuffed into her garter and her G-string, peeled off both, and dove into her bag for street clothes. An oversize black Ministry shirt, a pair of cutoffs, and her Converse All-Stars, one black, one purple, safety-pinned and scribbled upon; she had another pair just like it at home. After six hours on high heels, there was nothing more comforting than shoving your sore toes into a pair of soft, sloppy sneakers.

She stopped by the DJ booth to tip out—don't spend it all in one place, Tommy, sniffle snort—and cut through the club. A blubbery redneck she'd table-danced for earlier tried to wave her over, but she stared right through him and kept heading for the door. Once she was done, she was *done*.

Just outside the door she stopped, whipped off the platinum wig, and stuffed it into her bag. Her hair underneath was black, buzzed nearly to the scalp except for wispy bangs that fell over her face and a few long skinny braids sprouting here and there. One of her small ears was pierced with thirteen silver hoops beginning at the lobe and curling gracefully up around the delicate rim. From the other dangled a single cross with a tiny ruby-eyed skull at its juncture.

She ran her hand through her buzz cut and breathed in the twilight air of the French Quarter and let Miss Lee go for another night. She was Eddy Sung now, and her evenings were her own.

The gas lamps were just beginning to come on, their soft yellow glow flickering on every corner. She thought of stopping off for a beer and a dozen oysters on the halfshell somewhere. The salty, briny flavor of them always drove the taste of a day's false smiles out of her mouth. But no, she decided, she would go home and check her mail and her messages, and then maybe she would call Zachary and see if he wanted to go eat oysters. They were supposed to be an aphrodisiac; maybe they'd work on him.

Ha. She should be so lucky.

Eddy allowed herself a rueful little laugh and set off through the Quarter for home.

FIVE

*Z*ach was already throwing the last of his movable belongings into his car when Eddy arrived. She had run all the way from her apartment on St. Philip after hearing his message on her answering machine, and her face was flushed and sweaty, her breath coming in harsh shallow gasps.

But Zach looked worse. His green eyes had a feverish sheen. Beneath a ridiculous black bad-cowboy hat she hadn't seen before, his peaked pale face was nearly luminescent in the gaslit gloom of little Rue Madison. He crammed a box of papers into the back seat of his Mustang, turned to grab another box, and saw Eddy. His face froze. For an instant he looked terrified. Then he stumbled toward her and threw his arms around her. Her heart broke a little, but Eddy was used to this; it happened every time she saw Zach.

"They got you?"

He nodded. The words *I told you so* hung in the air, but she would not dream of speaking them.

"How bad?"

"The warning said *They know who you are, They know where you are.* I don't think They really know where I am yet or They'd be here. But They could be finding out right now. They could show up anytime."

Eddy glanced nervously back toward Chartres Street. Except for an occasional ripple of street jazz or burst of drunken laughter, all was quiet.

"I'm taking the incriminating stuff with me. The computers, my disks, my notebooks. The place will be clean if you want to move in. If They show up and want to search, let 'em search. They won't find a damn thing." He looked proud, defiant, exhausted. Eddy reached up to touch her fingertips to his perspiring face. Her heart was not just breaking but imploding. He was all but gone.

"Come sleep at my place tonight," she said. "No one can find you there. Leave in the morning, with some rest."

He didn't even hesitate. "I want to get as good a start as possible. If I go now I'll have the cover of the night."

The cover of the night. To Zach this was some big adventure. He was scared, yes—but more than that, he was excited. She could hear it in the tremor of his voice, see it in the blaze of his eyes. He was like a racehorse getting ready to run, elegant nostrils flaring, velvet flanks bunching and tensing.

She had thought perhaps one last night together . . . But she knew what it would have been like. They would have stayed up drinking and smoking pot and talking until dawn, maybe whipped up a batch of cayenne popcorn and watched a weird movie or two. And that would have been it. Zach didn't mind if she leaned against his shoulder, didn't mind a casual touch of the hand or ruffling of his unruly hair. But anything more obvious on her part—like the couple of times she'd leaned over and kissed him full on the lips—would be met with "I can't, Ed, I just *can't.*" And if she asked why, she would get the infuriating answer, "Because I *like* you."

It wasn't as if Zach were celibate or gay, either. She had seen him pick up scores of people at the clubs and bars they both frequented, and the ratio was only slightly in favor of cute young males. He always seemed to go for the good-looking and the empty-headed, preferably drunk, ideally with some absent girlfriend or boyfriend to absorb the aftershock. He had only one inflexible rule: they had to have a place to fuck. He would not take them back to his sanctuary of an apartment, would not share his nest with his bimbos. Maybe he was embarrassed for his computer to see them.

The next day—or night—he would brush them off, not in an especially cruel way, but in a manner that left no doubt that they had been nothing but caprices. It was, Eddy thought, as if Zach considered sex a biological need on the

order of going to the bathroom: you didn't form an emotional
bond with every toilet you took a crap in, and when you were
done, you flushed and walked away—feeling better, to be
sure, but not really *thinking* about what you'd just done.

It raised Eddy's blood pressure, and frustrated her, and
made her crazy. Any other friend or potential lover with such
an attitude would have been long since trashed. But Zachary
was so sweet, so smart, so cool otherwise that this seemed an
aberration, a flaw or handicap he could not be blamed for,
like a strawberry birthmark or a missing finger. She supposed
part of it was the hell he had watched his parents put each
other through, and the hell he had endured at their hands.
And she kept hoping part of it could be blamed on his age;
almost any character defect was forgivable at nineteen. (Eddy
was twenty-two, and far more worldwise.)

"Won't they know your car?" she asked.

"I've already switched the plates."

She glanced at the back end of the Mustang. Zach's license
plate read FET-213, which looked awfully familiar. "Isn't that
the same one you always had?"

"I didn't switch plates on the *car*," he explained patiently.
"I switched them in the DMV *computer*. My plate is completely wiped out of existence, and I gave myself the plate of
some Cajun's 1965 Ford pickup down in Houma."

"Oh."

"It can't be traced to me."

"Uh-huh."

"Trust me, Ed! I'm making a clean getaway. I just need to
get going."

They stood awkwardly in the deepening gloom staring at
each other. "You already have a key," Zach said. "You want
the extra?"

"No. You'll need it if you come back and I'm not home."

"I'm not coming back, Eddy," he said gently. "Not for a
long time, anyway. I'll kill myself before I'll let them lock me
up."

"I know." She would not lose her composure, would not

slobber and bawl, would not beg him to take her along. If he wanted her along, he would have said so.

"So—well—I can't call here, but I'll try to get in touch somehow."

"You do that." She crossed her arms over her chest, shook a few tiny braids out of her face, fixed him with a steely eye. "Eddy . . ."

"Don't you fucking Eddy me! You could have been more careful! You didn't have to show off and take so many dumb chances—it wasn't like you needed the money. You could have . . . *stayed!*" Now she was crying. She bared her teeth at him, narrowed her eyes nearly to slits to hide the tears.

"I know," he said. "I know." He took two steps forward and enfolded her in his arms again. She laid her wet cheek against the soft cotton of his T-shirt, breathed his smoky, slightly sweaty boy-smell, held his skinny body tight against her. This was how it should have been all along.

Too bad he hadn't agreed.

"Be safe," she told him at last.

"I'll be careful."

"Where will you go?"

He shrugged. "North."

They stared at each other again, at a loss for words but not yet ready to say good-bye. Then Zach leaned down and— ever so carefully, as if touching together two live wires— placed his lips against Eddy's. She felt the electric thrill of contact, the very tip of his tongue touching hers, and an exquisite heat exploded from the center of her womb. For an instant she thought her innards would simply melt out of her pussy and run down her thighs, so intense was the rush. But then Zach pulled back and stepped away.

"Gotta go."

Eddy nodded, did not trust herself to speak. She watched him walk around the front of the car, slide into the driver's seat, turn the key in the ignition. The powerful engine leapt to life, ready to carry Zachary Bosch far away from New Orleans, far away from Eddy Sung. The horn beeped twice and then he was pulling away from the curb, red taillights pausing at the corner, then merging into the nighttime traffic of Decatur Street.

Gone.

Eddy stood for several minutes in the shifting shadows cast by the wrought-iron balconies overhead. She glanced at the door that led up to Zach's place, touched the key ring in her pocket, then shook her head. The Madison Street apartment was much nicer than her own roach-infested closet, and she knew the rent was paid for the rest of the year. Zach hated thinking about mundane matters like rent, so he paid it off at the beginning of each year when he renewed his lease. She would start moving her things in tomorrow. But she could not go up there now, while his presence still lingered painfully strong, like a voice just beyond the range of hearing, like an atom-thin membrane between reality and memory.

She turned and walked back up Madison, turned left on Chartres, and headed for Jackson Square. The spires of St. Louis Cathedral loomed ahead, moon-pale and mysterious, stabbing like bony fingers into the purple night sky. A brick commons lay between the cathedral and the square, and kids in thrift-shop black and painted leather and torn denim were already beginning to congregate there, smoking cigarettes, passing bottles of cheap wine.

Eddy stopped at the bank machine on the corner of Chartres and St. Ann. She still had her day's pay in her pocket, a fat wad that rubbed against her leg and made her nervous. She would deposit it, saving out thirty dollars—enough to get good and drunk. Then she might go and join the kids on the square, or she might find a dark little bar and drown her sorrows alone.

She filled out a deposit slip, stuffed her money in the envelope, popped her card into the slot and punched in her personal number, then the necessary information. She heard little wheels grinding deep inside the machine. The screen asked her if she needed travelers' checks for that summer vacation. Finally her eighty-dollar deposit was processed and the machine spit back her card, then a printed receipt.

Eddy turned away, glanced idly at the receipt, and stopped

dead in her tracks. A couple of fratboy tourists crossing the commons nearly walked into her, swore at her, and stumbled on. She ignored them, kept staring dumbly at the slip of paper. She tried squinting and blinking, but the numbers stayed the same.

She'd paid her rent a couple of days earlier, and that put the balance of her checking account at a precarious $380.82. It now stood at $10,380.82.

She'd never let Zach give her money. It was too dangerous for him, and she liked taking care of herself.

But it appeared he had left her a farewell present.

He got on Highway 90—other than superinterstates 59 and 10, which were as dull as direct-dialing a long distance call and paying for it with your own credit card, the two-lane blacktop was pretty much the only way out of New Orleans —and left the city under cover of the night. The Rolling Stones song of that name pumped monotonously in his head (*curled up baby, curled up tight*), an unwelcome echo from the bruised ache and white-hot hatred of his eleventh year. It reminded him that he had hardly any tapes in the car. He'd left his music, books, and movies for Eddy, since he could always get more. But he should have brought a few for the road. He'd stop and get some later, when his thoughts quieted down enough to make listening worthwhile.

He was already sick of wearing his new hat, so he chucked it into the back and raked a hand through his hair. It was tangled, dirty, and felt like it was standing up at fifteen different angles. So much the better for that popular Edward Scissorhands look.

A few miles out of New Orleans, 90 wound past an enclave of Vietnamese restaurants and stores, an exotic little Asian village set down in rural Louisiana, nurtured by the bounty of the rivers, lakes, and bayous. Though Eddy was Korean, the sight made him think of her, gave him an empty feeling somehow. He'd eaten dinner at her parents' house in Kenner once, had been served oyster pancakes and a wonderful concoction of rice, fresh greens, seaweed, raw fish, and hot sauce heaped in a giant glass bowl and called *fea-dup-bop*. Zach kept hearing it as *fetus of Bob*, but that hadn't lessened his appetite. Once Eddy's mom saw he loved the turbo-hot sauce, she kept plying him with increasingly fiery tidbits and condiments until he was munching whole the deadly little red peppers she minced into her *kimchee*.

It was then, he guessed, that the Sungs had decided their daughter just might be able to marry an American. Not that they had much to say about any of Eddy's actions—though they believed she was a cocktail waitress at the Pink Diamond, or pretended they did—and not that Eddy expected Zach to marry her.

He felt a twinge of unease that was as close to guilt as he ever got. He knew perfectly well how different Eddy had wanted their friendship to be. But it was impossible for him. Loving someone was okay, and fucking someone wasn't bad either. But if you did both with the same person, it gave them too much power over you; it let them plunge their shaping hands into your personality, gave them a share of your soul.

He had grown up watching his father change his mother from a sickly-scared but harmless creature into a sadistic bitch with twisted knives for fingers and a spitting, shrieking mouth. A mouth full of broken teeth, to be sure—but all the pain she had taken from her husband she gave back to her son, a gift wrapped in cruel words, signed in blood.

And his parents *had* loved each other, in whatever mutually parasitic way they were capable of. He had watched their heart-ripping fights and sodden reconciliations, heard their anguished lovemaking through the thin walls of many cheap apartments too often not to believe that somehow they were passionately in love, or had been once.

There had never been room for him. Zach sometimes thought that if he had not been born, the two of them might have managed a kind of happiness together, Joe with his broken-backed dreams and his fierce intelligence tamped down by liquor, Evangeline with her bruises and black eyes and always-hungry loins. If only his mother had managed to scrape up, pun most certainly intended, the cash for the abortion she often wished aloud that she had had. If only his father's rubber hadn't broken—and how many times had Joe taunted him about that damn rubber? The thing was practically a Bosch family heirloom.

In the too-silent darkness Zach punched at the buttons of the radio, twisted the tuning knob. Frizzly static greeted him, then a spurt of jazz. A ripple of piano and tympani, a trembling, exalting alto saxophone. He disliked the Dixieland jazz he had heard all his life, as he did Cajun music and indeed anything with accordions or brass in it, anything that sounded like growing up in New Orleans. Such music twisted barbs into his memory, ran too deeply into his blood.

But this wasn't New Orleans stuff. Kansas City, maybe; it sounded less frenetically cheerful, exotic somehow, musing and dreaming. He left it on.

After the Vietnamese enclave, the highway passed through an interminable stretch of beach cabins with cute names (Jimmy's Juke Joint, Li'l Bit O'Heaven, Moon Mansion replete with a big plywood ass shining in his headlights) and private driveways that went straight down to the dark water on either side. This was the beginning of bayou country, and there was very little solid land. Zach pondered the name of his own imaginary cabin—Hacker Hideaway? Outlaw Asylum? No: Bosch's Blues. Check all Uzis and Secret Service badges at the door.

Gradually the cabins grew sparser and shabbier; some were bereft even of their names, or bore signs with the words and crude bright illustrations worn away. Then they were gone, and the road was empty, straight, flanked by dark expanses of water and woods and shadow. He crossed a bridge that arced high above the water, saw moonlight shimmering on the surface like pale jewels.

The radio station never faded out, though Zach thought he drove fifty miles or more, past bland green vistas and ugly stretches of consumerland, K marts and QuikStops and fast-food charnelhouses shut down against the night. In one of these towns a fried human ear had been found in a box of takeout chicken, like some cannibalistic remake of *Blue Velvet* by way of Colonel Sanders. Zach remembered reading the story in some tabloid out of Baton Rouge and wishing he'd thought it up himself, wondering if it were true or whether there was another prankster out there somewhere, creating urban mythology in giant digital strokes. The same song seemed to keep playing over and over, as if the DJ had set the CD on infinite replay and gone to sleep. The sax wailed and sobbed. The piano dreamed behind it.

At last he reached the Gulf Coast and began his meandering trek along it. The little coastal towns shut down after ten; there was only the long deserted stretch of white beach broken by marinas and piers, and beyond it the black expanse of the Gulf of Mexico.

His parents had brought him here once, when he was ten or so. Zach remembered smelling the salt air as they drove down, imagining the blissful caresses of the sand and water. In reality the sand had had an unpleasantly powdery feel, like ordinary playground dirt; there had been a scum of pollution at the water's edge, a pale brown froth that ebbed and flowed with the waves. It smelled faintly of dead fish, engine sludge, chemicals gone bad.

But out past the beach the water was the color of new denim, and felt so good on his parched, abused skin. He had ducked his head beneath the surface, seal-like, and hadn't stopped swimming out to sea until his father's harsh hands grabbed him by the hair and wedged the back of his swim trunks up the crack of his scrawny ass.

The car swerved slightly to the right. Zach caught it at once, but the memories were starting to hypnotize him, to pull him toward the water.

A town marker flashed by. PASS CHRISTIAN, pronounced not like "Christian," Zach knew, but like a girl's name: CHRISTIE-ANN. He was already in Mississippi, and hadn't even noticed. Fine old Southern mansions loomed sepulchrally along the left side of the road, shrouded in ghostly curtains of Spanish moss and the giant knurled oaks that had hung on through a hundred hurricane seasons or more. The beach on the right was pure white, shining.

Zach hooked a left off the highway and headed for Pass Christian's downtown, such as it was. A man was pissing against a wall outside the Sea Witch Tavern. A dim, tempting blue light burned somewhere deep in the bar, like a siren luring travelers to a watery grave. The other buildings were dark and still.

After driving several blocks, Zach came upon a lone convenience store called Bread Basket, its neon flickering fitfully, flooding its little patch of town with erratic dead white light. There were no cars in the parking lot, but Zach saw a clerk nodding at the register, blond head drooping over the Slim Jims and Confederate lighter displays.

As he parked the car, the jazz tune finally ended. He heard a guttural voice as of a DJ roused from long and peaceful slumber. "Uh. Yeah. That was, uh . . . 'Laura' by Charlie Parker . . . a whole buncha times . . ."

The inside of the store assaulted his corneas like an acid vision after the calm silver and charcoal of the night. Zach observed that the clerk had been not napping, but studying with rapt attention a magazine spread out on the countertop. It was open to a black-and-white photograph of a lanky, bare-chested, feral-faced boy who looked a lot like the clerk himself.

"C'n I help you?" A plastic nametag was pinned to the lapel of the boy's blue polyester store jacket. LEAF. Hippie parents would do the damndest things.

"Yeah. Can I smell your coffee?"

"Huh?"

"Your coffee." Zach waved at the coffee machine and its trappings against the opposite wall. "Can I just smell it?"

"Sure . . . I guess." Leaf glanced down at the photo again, then unhurriedly closed the magazine. It was an old issue of *GQ*. "If you're lookin' for Hawaiian Kona, though, you're out of luck. It's just evil ole homebrew."

"That's okay. I don't actually want to *drink* any." Zach crossed to the coffee maker, pulled the pot out of the metal apparatus that kept it at sub-boiling point, and passed it slowly back and forth beneath his nose. Hot bitter steam wafted into his face, moistened his tired eyes. He felt microscopic particles of caffeine traveling up his nostrils, into his lungs, out through the interfaces of his bloodstream and straight into the hard drive of his weary brain.

His heart gave a jump and began beating faster. The rush made his mouth dry. As he grabbed a bottle of mineral water out of the cooler, he found himself wondering why a cute kid who read *GQ* and knew about Hawaiian Kona coffee was working at a Bread Basket in Pass Christian, Mississippi.

At the register, Zach set his drink on the counter, added a lighter (patterned in gaudy pink and black zigzags, but no rebel flag), and pulled out his wallet. He hadn't tried to access any of his various bank accounts before he left town, knowing that all of them could be watched. And he could get more. He'd only brought the stash of ready cash he kept for an emergency such as this; he had always known that he might have to bail out someday, and that he would have to do it fast. Now he found that the smallest bill in his wallet was a hundred.

"Can't change it," Leaf said apologetically. "They only let me keep fifty dollars in the register after ten, and I haven't had shit for business."

"I'm really thirsty."

"Well—"

Zach caught the other boy's eyes with his own and held them. Leaf's eyes were long and slightly tilted, gimlet eyes, the same warm honey-gold as his hair. "Just give me the stuff," he suggested. "I'll get you stoned."

This was a simplified version of a hacker technique known as social engineering. It could be used to reassure an operator that she was talking to a bona-fide telco technician; it was good for all manner of scamming, impersonation, and general fraud. This cute clerk was no challenge at all. The seeds of rebellion were already planted. Zach could see the kid mulling it over, talking himself into it.

He leaned an elbow on the counter and offered his most charming smile. "What do you say?"

"Well . . . oh, fuck it. Take whatever you want. I don't care. I'm quitting soon anyway."

"Thanks. That's real neighborly of you." Zach whisked the lighter into his pocket, cracked the mineral water open, and took a long gulp. It tasted flat and dead, but then he was used to the carcinogenic soup that passed for tapwater in New Orleans. Plenty of flavor in that.

Leaf snorted. "Neighborly. Like you live in Mississippi. I'll bet you're from New York or something."

Zach hadn't heard that one before. People sometimes thought he was part Oriental—a fact that amused Eddy no end—but no one had ever accused him of being from New York.

He decided the idea appealed to him. "Well, yeah," he admitted. "How'd you know?"

"The way you talk. And you don't look like you're from around here. The only other place you could've come from is New Orleans."

"Never been there." In a burst of inspiration, Zach added, "Yet. It's where I'm headed."

Their eyes met again and locked. For an instant Zach imagined that Leaf was able to look straight into his brain, to see the lie and the convoluted reason behind it, the miles he had already run and all the miles still ahead. But Zach knew that was not true.

And even if it were, he could see in those warm honey-colored eyes that this kid wouldn't care.

Leaf accepted Zach's offer and locked up the store, and they went into the back room to smoke one of the joints Zach had rolled for the trip. Leaf lounged on a crate of toilet paper, long legs sprawled before him. There was a small defiant hole in one knee of the faded jeans he wore with his uniform shirt. The skin beneath was downed with fine gold hairs.

Zach leaned against the opposite wall watching Leaf's nervous gestures, tasting Leaf's lips on the joint. The stockroom of a convenience store in Mississippi seemed a stupid place to get waylaid this early in the trip. But the damn kid was making his mouth water.

"I'm quitting tomorrow," Leaf said after his third toke. "I hate this fuckin' place."

"What are you doing here, anyway?"

"I'm an art student in Jackson. Photography. I was supposed to spend the summer here taking pictures, preserving the goddamn history or something. But it sucks. None of the rednecks know anything and none of the rich old farts will even talk to me. I don't know which stuff is supposed to be important. I guess I'll fail my project."

"Can't you do some research?"

"What do you mean?"

"Go to the library, find out where people lived, what houses are haunted, that kind of thing. Most of the old newspapers are probably on microfilm."

Leaf looked up at Zach. The whites of his eyes were shot with a faint scarlet tracery of veins, but the irises and pupils were heartbreakingly clear. "I'm a totally visual person," he said. "I hate reading."

Zach bit his tongue hard, dug his fingernails into the soft meat of his palms. That was the kind of casual statement that could send his blood pressure rocketing if he let it. But now it produced only a faint twinge in his heart, like a filament stretched to the breaking point. So the kid was vapid; so much the better. It made things easy, and Zach would never have to see him again after tonight. "You hate all kinds of stuff," he said.

Leaf shrugged. "I guess."

"Tell me something you like."

This was evidently a tough one. Zach could see the kid sifting through possibilities, rejecting them one by one. "I like the beach," he said finally. "I never go in the water, but I like to sit on the sand and stare out to sea. It makes me feel like I'm looking into infinity. You know?"

A screen full of scrolling numbers flashed through Zach's head. He nodded.

"I like sleeping."

Another nod, this one coupled with the barest suggestion of a shrug. *Tell me something I couldn't have guessed.*

"I like you okay."

They had both known they weren't just locking themselves back here to smoke a joint, but the rest of their agenda had to be obliquely tested, so that no one would lose face. Zach knew the game and approved. He smiled and raised an eyebrow, waited for more.

"Oh, just come over here and let's fuck."

Now that was Zach's idea of an excellent pickup line. He slid across to the case of toilet paper and suddenly Leaf was upon him, face pressed up against his, one hand slipping under his T-shirt, the other squeezing his leg beneath his loose cutoffs. Leaf's mouth found his and closed over it, hot little tongue probing and searching, piney flavor of the weed still on his lips. His spidery hands flew over Zach's skin as if trying to memorize its warmth and texture. His touch was starving, frantic. The poor kid probably hadn't been laid all summer.

Zach pushed him gently back against the wall, unbuttoned the tacky polyester uniform, stroked the boy's smooth chest and the hollow of his ribcage, managed to calm him down a little. He kissed the side of Leaf's throat; the pulse that beat there was as agitated as his own. The skin smelled of soap and salt, tasted of clean sweat.

Leaf slid to the concrete floor and sprawled between Zach's knees, pressed his face into Zach's stomach and mumbled something unintelligible. Zach cupped the boy's chin, tilted the sharp feral face up to his own. "What did you say?"

"I want to make you come."

"How?"

Those exotic honey-colored eyes tried to meet his, then wavered. Leaf wasn't used to talking dirty. "How?" he asked again.

"I want to suck your dick."

The words increased his desire, made him ache and burn. "Go on," Zach said through clenched teeth. "Just do it."

The boy's hands fumbled with the button fly of Zach's pants, friction driving his hard-on nearly to the point of pain. Then all at once Leaf's hot mouth slid onto him, then pulled all the way back to a teasing, flickering tongue-tip, then swallowed him deeper yet. Zach felt the pot and pleasure swirling in his skull, deliciously mingling. God love the kid, it turned out he knew what he was doing after all.

Zach always appreciated it when people surprised him.

Twenty minutes later, stocked up with a handful of lighters, a sixpack of mineral water, and two bags of jalapeño potato chips, Zach renewed his acquaintance with Highway 90. It would take him through Biloxi, through the tag-end of Alabama, and all the way to Pensacola in another hour or two. After that, he thought, he would get off 90 but keep heading east, all the way to the coast of the Atlantic Ocean. Somewhere, he knew, there was a beach that was clean.

Leaf hadn't asked him to stay overnight, hadn't seemed put out in the slightest by the encounter. After getting each other off they had rested together for a few minutes, embracing loosely, catching their breaths. Zach had spent the moments appreciating the spare, elegant lines of the boy's face and body, admiring the sheen of his silky hair in the half-light of the storeroom. Then by some silent mutual consent they rose and pulled their clothes together and went blinking back out into the unmerciful brightness of the store.

At the door they clasped hands briefly. "By the way," Leaf told him, "I like your shirt."

Zach glanced down at himself. He was still wearing the exploding Kennedy head. He wondered idly if some buried sixth sense had made him put it on this morning as a twisted metaphor for what was to follow.

"Thanks," he said, and gave Leaf's talented fingers one final squeeze. In its way it was quite a tender farewell.

The day had followed a steep curve down to hell, but now

it seemed to be inching back up. The interlude with Leaf had relaxed him, left him feeling sharp and awake, as if Leaf had imbued him with some vital essence . . . as indeed he had. Surely there was some energy in come, some electrifying charge.

And Zach had given as good as he got. He always deserted in the end, like the bastard Eddy thought he was, but he always tried to make his lovers feel good in the brief spans of time he spent with them. He had even left Leaf with another tightly rolled, sticky joint to stave off tomorrow night's ennui.

All in all, Zach mused as he reconnected with the silent ribbon of highway, it had pretty much been the perfect relationship.

SIX

Trevor awoke from a dream of blank paper laughing up at him, his mind a monochrome wash of panic, his heart clenching around a core of emptiness. If he couldn't draw . . . if he couldn't draw . . .

The sheets Kinsey had given him were twined around his legs, sodden with nightmare sweat. Trevor kicked them away and shoved himself upright. His bag lay on the floor next to the sofa. He pulled out his sketchbook, opened it to a clean page, and sketched furiously for several minutes. He had no idea what he was drawing; he was only reassuring himself that he *could*.

When his heart stopped pounding and his panic began to fade, Trevor found himself staring at a rough sketch of his brother lying on a stained mattress, small hands curled in death, head crushed into the pillow. He remembered that today was the day his family had died.

Trevor felt like throwing the book across the room. Instead he closed it and slid it back into his bag, found his toothbrush in the zipper pocket, then stood up and stretched. He heard his shoulders crack, his spine make a noise like a muffled burst of gunfire.

Despite the flattened cushions and the occasional sharp end of a spring, Kinsey's sofa had been a welcome place to sleep. Trevor was surprised to find it comforting to be invited into someone's home, to have a known human presence in the next room. He had grown used to cheap hotels and run-down boardinghouses. On the other side of the wall might be drunken sobs or curses, the moist tempo of sex, the silence of an empty room—but never anything familiar, never anyone who cared that Trevor Black was there.

Kinsey's living room was sparsely furnished with more thrift-shop relics: an easy chair, a reading lamp, a wooden bookcase listing under the weight of too many volumes. Paperbacks, mostly. Trevor read some titles as he passed. *One Hundred Years of Solitude, The Stand, Short Stories of Franz Kafka,* whole shelves of Hesse and Kerouac, even *Lo!* by Charles Fort. Eclectic tastes, that Kinsey.

There were some crates of comics too, but Trevor did not look through them. He had his own copies of *Birdland.* Coming upon other copies in a comic shop or someone's collection was always unnerving, like seeing someone he had thought dead.

There was no TV, Trevor noted approvingly. He hated TV. It brought back memories of a crowded dayroom at the Home, the sweaty smell of boys, voices raised in fury over what channel to watch. The stupidest ones had always screamed for a cartoon show out of Raleigh called *Barney's Army.* Barney was a cartoon character himself, squat and ugly, announcing kids' birthdays and cracking lame jokes between Looney Toons shorts. He was so badly animated that no part of him moved but his pitifully stubby, flipperlike arms, his prognathous jaw, and his big googly eyes. Trevor figured he had probably hated Barney as much as any real person he had ever known.

The bathroom tiles were spotless, deliciously cold against his bare feet. He used the Tom's of Maine cinnamon-flavored toothpaste on the edge of the sink, then splashed cold water on his face. For a long moment he stood staring into the mirror. His father's eyes looked back at him, ice rimmed in black, faintly challenging. *Do you dare?*

You bet I do.

The door of Kinsey's bedroom was ajar. Trevor peeked into the shady room. Kinsey's tall form lay sprawled across the bed, skinny legs half-covered by a vivid patchwork quilt. He was the only person Trevor had ever seen who actually wore pajamas—bright blue ones, the same color as his eyes, patterned with little gold moons and stars. Trevor hadn't even known they made pajamas in Kinsey's size.

For a few minutes he watched the gentle rise and fall of Kinsey's chest, the draft from the open window that stirred Kinsey's scraggly hair, and he wondered if he had ever slept so peacefully. Even when Trevor wasn't having bad dreams his sleep was uneasy, sporadic, full of flickering pictures and half-remembered faces.

But the luminous face of the clock on Kinsey's nightstand (no cheap digital job, but a molded-plastic relic done in early sixties aqua, its corners rounded and streamlined) told him it was nearly noon. He had to go. Not to the house yet, no; but he had to take the first step toward the house.

Trevor slung his backpack over his shoulder, stepped out into the tranquil Sunday morning, and locked Kinsey's door behind him.

The road that led out to Missing Mile's small graveyard was hot and flat and muddy. Trevor was accustomed to walking city streets, where the languid haze of summer was shot through with blasts of air-conditioning from doors constantly opening onto the sidewalk, where you could always duck under an awning or the overhang of a building, into a little pocket of shade.

But this road, Burnt Church Road according to the crooked signpost where it ran into Firehouse Street, offered no shade except the occasional leafy canopy of a tree. The houses out here were few and far apart. Most had been built on farmland, and the road was bordered by fields of leathery tobacco and bristling corn. This was a nicer area than Violin Road; the dirt here had not yet been farmed to death. The houses were not new or fancy, but their yards were large grassy expanses unmarred by scrap heaps or the rusting hulks of autos.

The sun beat mercilessly on the road and on the coarse gravel that paved it, broken granite like the crushed leavings of a cemetery, mired in wet red clay, catching the light and shattering it into a million razored fragments. Trevor was glad when clouds began to blow in, a slow-brewing summer thunderstorm on the way. His brain felt baked in his skull, and his skin already tingled with fresh sunburn. His backpack was waterproof, to keep his sketchbook dry. If the storm held long enough, he would start a new drawing at the graveyard. If not, he would sit on the ground and let the rain soak him.

Trevor could feel the nearly silent presence of death up ahead, not precisely watchful, not even really aware, but somehow detectable. It was like a frequency on a radio, or rather the empty space on the band between frequencies: there were no signals to pick up, but still you heard a faint electric hum, not quite silence, not quite sound. It was like being in a room someone had just left, a room that still bore the faint scent of breath and skin, the subtle displacement of air. An epileptic kid had died on his hall at the Boys' Home once, pitched a grand mal fit in the hours before dawn, when no one was awake to help him. Trevor had woken in the cool, still morning and known that death was close by, though he hadn't known who it had come to, or how.

But the graveyard gave off only a quiet buzz like crickets in the sun, like the cogs of a watch beginning to wind down. Set back at the shady dead end of Burnt Church Road, surrounded by woods on three sides, it was a place that felt like surcease from pain. Trevor had never seen the burial place of his family. As soon as it came into view, he knew that this was a fitting prelude to going home.

Of course they hadn't let him attend the funeral. As far as Trevor knew, there had been no proper funeral. Bobby McGee had burned most of his bridges when they left Austin, and they had no family but each other. The town, he supposed, had paid for the interment of three cheap pine coffins.

Later, a group of comics artists and publishers had taken up money for a stone. Someone had sent Trevor a Polaroid snapshot of it years ago. He remembered turning the picture over and over in his hands until the oil from his fingers marred the slick paper, wondering who had cared enough to visit and photograph the grave of his family but not enough to rescue him from the hell that was the Boys' Home.

He also remembered a drawing he had done soon afterward, a cutaway view of the grave. He made the headstone look shiny and slick, as if some thick dark substance coated the granite. The earth below was loamy, seeded here and there with worms, nuggets of rock, stray bones come loose from their moorings. There were three coffins, two large ones with long shrouded forms within, their folds suggesting ruined faces. The shape in the littlest coffin was strange—it might have been one form grossly misshapen, or two small forms mingled.

Mr. Webb, the junior high art teacher who hid Listerine bottles full of rotgut whiskey in his desk, had called the drawing morbid and crumpled it. When Trevor flew at him, skinny arms outstretched, hands hooked into claws going unthinkingly for Webb's eyes, the teacher backhanded him before he knew what he was doing. Both were disciplined, Webb with a week's suspension, Trevor with expulsion from art class and confiscation of his sketchbook. He covered the walls of his room with furious art: swarming thousand-legged bugs, soaring skeletal birds, beautifully lettered curse words, screaming faces with black holes for eyes.

They never let him take an art class again.

Now here was the place of his drawing and his dreams, the place he had imagined so often that it already seemed familiar. The graveyard was much as he had pictured it, small and shady and overgrown, many of the stones listing, the roots of large trees twining through the graves and down into the rich soil, mining the fertile deposits of the bodies buried there. Trevor wondered whether he might find Didi's face in a knothole, the many colors of Momma's hair in a shock of sunbleached grass, the shape of his father's long-fingered hands in a gracefully gnarled branch.

Maybe. First, though, he had to find their grave.

Trevor rummaged in his backpack, found a can of Jolt Cola, popped the top, and tipped the warm soda into his mouth. The sickly-sweet taste foamed over his tongue, trickled into

the cracks between his teeth. It tasted horrible, like stale car-
bonated saliva. But the caffeine sent immediate electric tendrils into his brain, soothed the pounding at his temples,
cleared the red cobwebs from his vision.

It was the only drug he had much use for. Once he'd
started to develop a taste for speed, but quit the first time he
detected a tremor in his hand. Pot reminded him too much of
his parents in the good days, back when Bobby was drawing.
Alcohol terrified him; it was nothing more than death, distilled and bottled. And junk held such a morbid fascination
for him that he dared not try it, though he had been in plenty
of low haunts and back alleys where he could have had some
if he'd wanted to. He knew it was supposed to be clear, yet he
imagined it black as ink, swirling out of the needle and
through his veins, lulling him into some dreadfully familiar
nightmare world.

He drank the last vile swig of Jolt, stuck the empty can back
in his backpack, and set out on a meandering path through
the graveyard. The ground was uneven, the weeds in some
places tall enough to brush the tips of his fingers. He caught
at them, let them slip through his hands.

This was not Missing Mile's only burying ground. Trevor
had glimpsed a few small church cemeteries on his way into
town, and he remembered that the surrounding woods were
seeded with old Civil War graves and family plots, sometimes
just two or three rough-hewn stones in a lonely little cluster.

But this was the oldest one still in use. There were recent
stones, letters and dates chiseled so sharply that they seemed
to float just above the slick surface of the granite. Flecks of
quartz and mica caught the receding light. There were old
markers, stone crosses and arched tablets of slate, their edges
crumbling, their inscriptions beginning to blur. There were
the small white stones of children, some topped with lambs
like smooth cakes of soap partly melted in the shower. Some
graves were splashed with gaudy color, flowers arranged in
bright sprays or tortured into wreaths. Some had gone un-
decorated for a very long time.

And some had never been decorated.

Pain shot through his hands. Trevor found himself standing before a long, plain slab of granite. He realized he had been standing there for several minutes, working his hands against each other, twisting his fingers together until the joints screamed. He made himself flex them, one by one.

Then he raised his head and looked at the gravestone of everyone he had ever loved.

McGEE

ROBERT FREDRIC	FREDRIC DYLAN	ROSENA PARKS
B. APRIL 20,	B. SEPT. 6,	B. OCT. 20,
1937	1969	1942

DIED JUNE 14, 1972

Trevor had forgotten that his brother's middle name was Dylan. Momma had always told people it was for Dylan Thomas, the poet. Bobby pointed out that the kid was born in '69; no matter what anyone said, everybody would assume he was named after Bob Dylan. It would haunt him all his life.

But Bobby had taken care of that.

During his walk out here Trevor had wondered if they might all start yammering at him, their voices worming up through six feet of hard-packed earth, through twenty years of decay and dissolution, over the chirrup and buzz of insects in the tall grass and the slow rumble of the storm coming in. But, though he still sensed the soft hum of the collective dead, his own dead were silent. Now that he was here he felt curiously flat, almost disappointed; no one had spoken to him, no skeletal hand had thrust up to grab his ankle and drag him down with them. Left out again.

Trevor knelt and laid his palms briefly against the cool stone, then put his backpack down and stretched out on the ground. In the center of the grave, over Didi, he supposed. It was hard to believe that Didi's body, the body he had last seen stiff and cold in bed with its head smeared like overripe fruit across the pillow, lay directly beneath him. He wondered if any reconstruction of the heads and faces had been done, or if Didi's fragile skull had been left to fall to pieces like a broken Easter egg. The ground was warm under his back, the sky overhead pregnant with clouds, nearly black. If he was going to do any drawing here, he'd better get started.

He unzipped his bag and took out his sketchbook. A pencil was wedged into the coiled wire binding. Trevor fingered it but did not pull it out just yet. Instead he turned to the drawing he had finished on the bus. *Rosena Black:* the dead version of Rosena McGee, with none of her wit or warmth, with nothing but a cold ruined shell of a body. Seven fingers broken as she tried to fight Bobby off in the doorway to the hall, beyond which lay her sleeping sons. Had she been trying to grab the hammer, and if she got it, would she have killed her husband with it? Trevor thought so.

That would have changed every part of the equation but one: Bobby would still be dead, and Trevor would still be alive. Only if it had gone down that way, at least Trevor would know *why* he was alive.

He reached into his backpack again, felt way down deep in the bottom, found a battered manila envelope and took out three folded sheets of paper. The folds had worn through many times over, had been taped back together and refolded until some of the photocopied words on the paper were nearly illegible. It didn't matter; Trevor knew them by heart.

They all followed the same format. *Robert F. McGee, Rural Box 17, Violin Road, male Caucasian, 35 yrs, 5-9, 130 pounds, blond hair, blue eyes. Occupation: Artist. Cause of death: Strangulation by hanging. Manner of death: Suicide. Other marks: Scratches on face, arms, chest area . . .*

He knew Momma had made those scratches. But they hadn't been enough, not nearly enough. Fingernails weren't much use once the fingers were broken.

He folded the autopsy reports and slid them back into the envelope. He had stolen them from his file at the Home and carried them with him since then. The paper was worn soft and thin, read a thousand times. The ink was smudged with the whorls of his fingerprints.

The storm was very close now. The hum of insects in the grass, the trill and call of birds in the surrounding woods seemed very loud. The afternoon light had taken on a lurid greenish cast. The air was full of electricity. Trevor felt the fine hairs on his arms standing up, the nape of his neck prickling.

He flipped to a clean page in his book, freed his pencil, and began sketching rapidly. In a few minutes he had roughed out the first half of his idea for a strip.

It stemmed from an incident in a biography of Charlie Parker he had read at the Home. In his thirteen years there, Trevor had read just about everything in the meager library. Most of the other kids wondered why he wanted to read anything at all, let alone a book about some dead musician who had played a kind of music that nobody listened to anymore.

The incident had happened when Bird was touring the South with the Jay McShann Orchestra. Jackson, Mississippi, was a bad place for black people in 1941. (Trevor doubted it was any great shakes for them now.) There was a curfew requiring them to be off the street by eleven P.M., so unless they wanted to risk arrest or worse, the band had to be finished and packed up by ten-thirty. There was no hotel in Jackson that would admit them, so the musicians were farmed out to various shabby boardinghouses and private homes.

Bird and the singer, honky-tonk bluesman Walter Brown, drew cots on the screened porch of someone's house. They were out of the converted barn where they had played and back at the house by eleven, but since their usual lifestyle kept them up until the small hours, the musicians were far from sleepy. They lay on their cots under the meager yellow glow of the porch light, passing a flask and sweating the liquor from their pores as fast as they swallowed it in the sodden Mississippi heat, slapping at the mosquitoes that slipped through holes in the screen, shooting the shit, talking of music or beautiful women or perhaps just how far they were from Kansas City.

At midnight the police showed up, four beefy good old boys with guns and nightsticks and necks as red as the blood they were itching to spill. The burning porch light was a violation of the "nigger curfew," they said, and Bird and Brown could come along to the station with them, and if they didn't care to come peacefully like good boys, why then, they were welcome to a few lumps on the head and a pair of steel bracelets.

Charlie Parker and Walter Brown spent three days in Jackson jail for sitting up talking with the porch light on. Charlie had the sharpest tongue, and so came out of it the worst; when McShann was finally able to bail them out, Bird's close-cropped hair was still stiff with dried blood where the nightsticks had split the skin over his skull. He had not been allowed enough water to wash the crust of blood away. Brown claimed to have kept his mouth shut, but sported some lumps and bruises of his own.

Bird had composed a tune to commemorate the incident, first called "What Price Love?" but later retitled "Yardbird Suite." His fury and wounded pride wound through the song like a crimson thread, a sobbing, wailing undertone.

How to get all that into a single strip, a few pages of black-and-white drawings? How to best show the tawdry tenement where they had been sequestered, the weathered wood and torn tarpaper houses, the narrow, muddy streets, the stupid malice on the faces of the cops? It was the sort of thing Bobby had done effortlessly in the three issues of *Birdland*. His stories had taken place mostly in the slums and beat sections of New York or New Orleans or Kansas City, not Jackson, Mississippi, and his human characters had been fictional junkies and street freaks and jazz musicians, not real ones.

But the mood of *Birdland*, the stark, slick, slightly hallucinatory drawings, the distorted reflections in puddles and the dark windows of bars, the constant low-key threat of violence, the feeling that everything in the strip was a little larger than life, and a little louder, and a little weirder—that was what Trevor wanted to capture here.

For now, though, he was just sketching in the panels and their contents, space for captions and word balloons, rough figures and backgrounds, the barest hints of gestures and expressions. The faces and hands were his favorite part; he would linger over them later. He had already drawn Bird hundreds of times. The handsome fleshy features appeared on the margins of his pages and woven into his backgrounds nearly as often as the face of his father.

He reached the part on the porch, just before the police arrived, and the first time Walter Brown's face appeared in closeup. His pencil slowed, then stopped, and he tapped the eraser against the page thoughtfully. He realized he had never seen a picture of Brown, had no idea what the singer looked like.

No problem: he could wing it, improvise the man's face like a jazz solo. He already had a hazy picture in his head, and even as he thought about it, the features grew clearer. His fantasy Walter Brown was a very young man, about twenty—but then they had all been young, mostly younger than Trevor was now—and boyishly thin to Bird's fleshiness, with high cheekbones and slightly slanting dark-almond eyes. Handsome.

This was how he usually worked: pondering an idea for months, turning it over and over in his head until he had nearly every panel and line worked out. Only then did he put pencil or pen or brush to paper, and the thing spilled full-blown onto the page. Bobby had been the same way, working in feverish bursts and starts. And when the inspiration was gone, it was gone forever.

At least if that happens to me, Trevor reminded himself, *I won't have anyone to kill.* There was no person he had cared that much about. Incidents like the one with the art teacher were a different thing altogether. You could cheerfully rip such people's heads off and drink the fountaining blood from the neck-stumps in those first few minutes of blind rage, if the fragile constraints of civilization and lack of physical power did not bind you.

But later, when you had time to think on it, you realized that nothing could be gained by hurting such people, that perhaps they were not even alive enough to feel pain. You could make better use of your anger by keeping it to yourself, letting it grow until you needed it.

Still . . . if you loved someone, really loved them, wouldn't you want to take them with you when you died? Trevor tried to imagine actually holding someone down and killing them, just breaking them apart, watching as the love in their face turned to agony or rage or confusion, feeling their bones crack and their blood flow over your hands, under the nails, greasing into the palms.

There was no one with whom he would want such intimacy. Kinsey had hugged him last night in the club, had held him as naturally as one might hold a suffering child. It had been the first time Trevor had cried in another person's presence in twenty years. For that matter, it was as physically close to another person as he had been since the man with gentle hands carried him out of the house, since his last glimpse of his father's swollen face. These two brief meetings of clothed skin were all he'd had.

No, he remembered. Not quite all.

Once, when he was twelve, a slightly older boy at the Home had caught him alone in the shower and pushed him into a corner. The boy's hands had scrabbled over his slick soapy skin, and Trevor had felt something in his head *snap*. Next thing he knew three counselors were pulling him off the kid, who was curled in the fetal position on the stall floor, and the knuckles of his left hand were throbbing, bruised, and blood was streaking the white tiles, swirling down the silver drain . . .

The older boy had a concussion, and Trevor was confined to his hall for a month. His homework and meals were brought to him. The solitude was wonderful. He filled eighteen notebooks, and one of the things he drew over and over was the shower stall with the boy in it: head smacking the cold tiles at the precise moment of impact; skinny body curled in a half inch of water threaded with his own blood. His blood that Trevor had spilled before he even knew what he was doing.

And the weird thing was, the boy's hands had actually felt *good* sliding over his skin. He had *liked* the feeling . . . and then suddenly the boy had been on the floor with blood coming out of his head.

He had plenty of time to think about what he had done, and what had made him do it, the violence inherent in his genes, in his soul. That was the first time he could remember considering the comforts of suicide.

Trevor stuck his pencil behind his ear, laid his sketchbook on the ground in front of him. He let the fingers of his right hand slide down the soft inner skin of his left forearm. The skin there was mottled with old scars, years of slashes and cross-hatchings done with a single-edged Exacto razor blade, the same kind he used for layouts. Perhaps a hundred thin raised lines of skin, paler than the rest of his arm, exquisitely sensitive; some still reddened and hurt once in a while, as if the tissue deep inside his arm had never quite healed. But if you went deep enough into the tissue, no scar ever healed completely.

And this map of pain he had carved out of his skin, this had been no half-assed attempt at suicide, anyway. Trevor knew that to kill yourself you had to cut along the length of your arm, had to lay it open from wrist to elbow like some fruit with a rich red pulp and a hard white core. Had to cut all the way to bone, had to sever every major artery and vein. He had never tried it.

These cuts he had made over the years were more in the nature of experimentation: to test his domain over his own malleable flesh, to know the strange human jelly below the surface, part layer upon cell-delicate layer of skin, part quickening blood, part pale subcutaneous fat that parted like butter at the touch of a new blade. Sometimes he would hold his arm over a page of his sketchbook, let the blood fall on clean white paper or mingle with fresh black ink; sometimes he would trace it into patterns with his finger or the nib of a pen.

But he hadn't done it for years and years. He thought the last time had been on his twentieth birthday, two years out of state's custody, the ill winds of adulthood and poverty blowing down his neck. It was as if America had begun the decade of the eighties by shattering some great cosmic mirror, except that the seven years of bad luck hadn't ended yet. The wizened, evil-faced dybbuk in the White House had been as alien a being as Trevor could imagine, a shriveled yet hideously animated puppet thrust into power by the same shadowy forces that had controlled the world since Trevor was five, forces he could not control, could barely see or begin to understand.

He had spent the night of his twentieth birthday wandering around New York City, riding the subways alone, slamming down coffee and cappuccino and espresso in every dive he passed, finally achieving an exaggerated state of awareness that went beyond perception into hallucination. He ended up huddled in a grove in Washington Square Park, furtively slicing at his wrist with a dull and rusty blade he dug out of his pocket, trying to let some of this electric energy out with the blood before it rattled him to pieces. Toward dawn he fell into restless sleep and dreamed of angels telling him to do violence—to himself? to someone else? he could not remember when he woke.

He didn't know why he had stopped cutting himself after that. It had just stopped working: the pain couldn't come out that way anymore.

Trevor sat up straight, shook himself. He'd nearly started to doze here in the gathering storm on his family's grave. He saw an image of his flayed wrist above a white sheet of paper, dark sluggish blood making Rorschach blots on the page.

The first drops of rain were hitting the spongy carpet of grass and pine needles, dark streaking and blotching on the headstones. Lightning sketched across the sky, searing jagged blue, then thunder rolling in like a slow tide. Trevor closed his sketchbook and slid it into his backpack. He could work on the Bird strip later, at the house.

The rain began to come down in great gusting sheets as he left the graveyard. By the time he reached the road, the ground was already wet enough to sink and squelch under his feet, muddy water oozing into his socks and sneakers. The trees bowed low over the road, then lashed the wind-torn sky.

A ways down the road, Trevor realized that he had barely glanced at the headstone as he left, had not touched it at all past the first initial contact. It was numb, dead, like the fragments of memory and bone that lay beneath it. Maybe they had been there once, but as their flesh decayed and crumbled in the sodden Southern ground, their essences had leached away too. Maybe he could find his family in Missing Mile, or something of them. But not where their bodies lay.

He had plodded most of the way back to town when he heard a car coming slowly up the road behind him, grinding over the coarse wet gravel. He thought briefly of trying to thumb, just as quickly decided against it. He was already soaked through; nobody would want his soggy ass on their upholstery.

Now the car was close enough that he could hear its wipers sluicing back and forth across the windshield. The sound triggered a memory so distant it was barely there: lying in the back seat of his father's car one rainy afternoon in Texas, listening to the *shush-skree* of the wipers and watching the rain course down the windows. One of the great San Francisco contingent of cartoonists—Trevor couldn't remember which one—had been passing through town, and Bobby was showing him the sights of 1970 Austin, whatever they may have been. The other cartoonist was busily rolling joint after joint, but that didn't stop him from running his mouth as much as Bobby. For Trevor in the back seat everything blurred together like different hues of watercolor paint: the comfortable sound of the adults' voices, the sweet herbal tang of the pot smoke, the afternoon city light filtering through a veil of rain.

Momma must have been at home with the baby. Didi had

been sick with one thing or another for a good part of his first year. Momma worried over him, fixed him special nasty-tasting organic mush, kept watch over him as he slept. Just as if she thought it mattered, just as if they all lived in a universe where Didi was going to grow up.

Trevor kept walking, did not register that the car had pulled up behind him until a horn blipped. He turned and found himself staring at the headlights and grillwork of his father's old car, the one whose back seat he had dozed on that rainy day in Austin, the one they had driven to Missing Mile. The two-toned Rambler, or its twin, complete with a crimp that had graced its front bumper since 1970.

His father's car, the windshield opaque with reflected light, the windows obscured by beads and drips of rain. Bobby's car coming down Burnt Church Road, from the direction of the graveyard. And the window on the driver's side was slowly cranking down.

Trevor thought there might be tears on his face. Or maybe it was only the rain, dripping out of his sodden hair.

He stepped forward to meet the car and whatever was inside it.

SEVEN

Just after dawn, Zach left his car in the parking lot of a prefab pink motel and walked out onto the dirtiest beach he had ever seen.

He'd kept on a steady northeastern course all night. Shooting past Pensacola at two, he had intended to go straight on east to Jacksonville but had been diverted by a highway sign pointing out the turnoff to a town called Two Egg. Zach might never set foot in Florida again; he had to see Two Egg before he left.

But the town was eerie even for rural Florida in the small hours of the morning. The buildings on the downtown strip all seemed to have been built in the early fifties, that time of false prosperity and fake space-age optimism. There was that look of the Plexiglas pillar and chromium arch, the kidney shape and the fashionable sign of the atom. But now these fabulous structures were abandoned, left behind by the chill silicon void of the millinneum's end. Their aqua paint was faded and peeling, their once-wondrous swoops and starbursts and streamlined angles rusting, falling away.

The buildings seemed to sway and nod over the street as if trying to pull Zach into their sterile dream. The street was full of trash, crumpled fast-food bags and torn newspapers drifting like aimless ghosts. The swamp was reclaiming the town on all sides; stagnant tongues of water lapped at the sidewalks, cattails grew in every vacant lot. Altogether, the town made Zach think of the opening helicopter landing scene of Romero's *Day of the Dead* as filmed on the ruined set of *The Jetsons:* desolation in which rotting corpses might rise, set against a backdrop as garish and sad as a forgotten cartoon.

He got out of Two Egg in a hurry. Thirty minutes later he crossed the state line into Georgia.

Now he was on Tybee Island, according to the signs he'd been nearly too bleary-eyed to read by the time he finally hit the coast. Just east of Savannah, Tybee was a cheap resort area frequented by redneck and middle-class family groups all summer. The island was honeycombed with seaside motels, fried seafood shacks, shell stands, and those weird, ubiquitous little Indian boutiques with their unvarying inventory of gauzy cotton clothes, incense, out-of-date rock posters, cheap jewelry, and drug paraphernalia.

This early, nearly everything was closed. Zach paid cash for a room at the Sea Castle Motor Inn, parked his car behind the Pepto-Bismol-colored building, and walked down to the beach.

The Atlantic Ocean looked dark and murky, not quite slate, not quite green. The foam that laced the breakers was like whipped cream squeezed out of a can, thin and unappetizing, unnatural-looking. And the sand—a hundred times worse than the chalky whitish stuff on the Gulf—gray and wet and heavy, like silt, like sludge. Zach nudged a heap of it with the toe of his sneaker and uncovered a broken plastic shovel, the wrapper from a Payday bar, the gritty, sticky wad of a used condom. He kicked sand back over the whole mess and watched it fall in a dirty spray, only half hiding the trash.

He had thought the ocean would soothe his jangling nerves. Instead the sight of it endlessly heaving and churning made him feel tight inside, lost somehow, as if this was not the place he had meant to come to at all. He had also thought there would be other teenagers on the beach, that he would be able to blend in and look like part of some holiday crowd. But at this early hour the beach was nearly empty, and the few people he saw were middle-aged couples or terribly young parents with herds of tiny children. Even when he took his shirt off and let the fledgling sun beat on his pale back and shoulders, Zach felt about as inconspicuous as Sid Vicious at a Baptist covered-dish supper.

He was beginning to realize just how little he knew about

life outside of New Orleans. But that was all right: with intelligence and intuition, he could hack it.

Hacking was defined as the manipulation of any complex system, as in "I can't *hack* getting dressed tonight, so I'm going to the club in my bathrobe." The complex system could be numbers on a screen or the relays and interchanges of the phone system; those were mechanical, and all you had to do was learn them. The crucial fact many computer hackers never seemed to realize—and the reason some of them were perceived as such geeks—was that the world and all its sentient beings and their billions of stories comprised the most intricate, fascinating system of all.

He pushed himself up off the gray sand and walked to the edge of the water. The glare caught the round lenses of his glasses, made his eyes sting and tear. Fine; he felt like crying anyway. A breeze tainted with the odors of wet salt and crude oil caught his hair and pushed it back from his face, dried the faint sheen of sweat on his forehead and upper lip. The tears and the wind felt good together.

Zach looked up and down the beach, followed the juncture of sand and water until it merged into infinity. South of here were the Georgia Sea Islands, where the rich language and culture of the Gullah people had dried up over the past century like so many fronds of marsh grass never woven into baskets, like so many magical roots never fashioned into protective "hands." North was the rest of the Atlantic Seaboard, more than a thousand miles of that churning, strange-colored ocean stretching all the way up to the unimaginably toxic sands of New York and New Jersey.

Soon the beach began to get crowded, and Zach saw that he would never be able to blend in here. The redneck dudes in their drawstring jams and scraggly little mustaches, the dudettes with their bleached-permed-frosted hair and cottage cheese asses and scary, leathery tans, the kids that were hideous little replicas of their parents in Teenage Mutant Ninja drag—all stared at Zach as if he might be something nasty that had washed up overnight and hadn't floated back out yet. It was time to crash, time to sleep now so he could blow this boring joint by nightfall.

Back in his room at the Sea Castle, Zach stripped out of his sweaty cutoffs, laid his glasses on the nightstand, and crawled into the double bed. The sheets were worn but clean and cool. He nestled into the pillows, closed his eyes, felt delicious exhaustion wash over him, thought of the kid Leaf and suddenly had a raging boner that was never going to let him sleep in a million years, noway, nohow.

Zach leaned over the edge of the bed and rummaged in one of his bags, found a string of little blue plastic packets, and tore one off. He never used rubbers for sex unless the other person insisted—and many of his lovers in New Orleans had insisted; he was known for more than his pallid good looks and mysterious wealth (which combination had convinced a certain set of French Quarter kids that Zach was a vampire and another set entirely that he was dying of AIDS and whooping it up while he still could). But he always used them for beating off. Not a one had broken yet, and he figured he was getting into the thousands.

He fitted the slippery little sheath over the head of his dick and unrolled it, sliding his hand down with it, pretending it was Leaf's mouth. The weight of the sheet was Leaf's hands, the extra pillow was Leaf's skinny body pressed smooth against his own. But when he came, Leaf disappeared and Zach saw an achingly blue wave crashing and foaming on pure white sand.

The rubber, as always, remained intact. Maybe they had made the things flimsier back in '72.

For a few minutes he lay with his mind wandering and his hand still moving idly. Not until warm tendrils of come started trickling back down into his pubic hair did he pull the thing off, knot the end of it, and toss it in the general direction of the toilet. He heard a small wet plop that meant bull's-eye, though the room was so small it would've been hard to miss. If every sperm was sacred, Zach figured he had made more offerings to the altar of the porcelain goddess than any other.

When he woke up later and saw the condom floating like a

pale chrysalis in the blue-tinged water of the bowl, he would pee on it and then flush it. Zach thought his body was a nifty machine and had a healthy appreciation of its many functions.

He turned over, stretched his lanky arms and legs across the unfamiliar expanse of mattress, pushed his head into the mound of pillows. One of them lay snug against his side like a warm body sinking into sleep. For an instant he wondered how it would be to fall asleep and wake up with someone next to him every morning, bodies fitting together in easy familiarity, skin smelling of each other and the safe shared bed.

But only for an instant did he think he might like it. These were thoughts that usually only came to him on leaden winter mornings, when the needling rain of a New Orleans cold spell streaked his windowpanes.

The pillow was his only constant bedmate, in all its malleable, comforting forms. He held it close and pressed his face into it, smelled cotton and detergent and the lingering ghost of his come, damp and salty as the ocean, but cleaner. In a while the image of his own bed faded from behind his eyes, and Zach began to dream of a long expanse of silky, sugary white sand, of water the color of the sky, of sky the color of the sun.

When he woke the room was full of sunset's first light, deep pinks and lavenders that lay in overlapping petallike layers across the bedclothes and made him think he was still dreaming. As consciousness seeped back in, Zach contemplated going out to the beach to watch the sun set and get something to eat. A steady edge of hunger was gnawing at his stomach. But all the happy couples were probably strolling hand in hand in the grimy surf. Zach decided to stay in and order a pizza.

He paged through the phone book, ripped out the Domino's ad and tore it into tiny pieces—they supported Operation Rescue and other heinous fascist causes—then dialed a

local parlor and ordered a twelve-inch pie with triple jalape-
ños.

Thirty minutes later, his hair dripping from a fast shower,
Zach munched pizza and drank grape soda from the motel's
machine while he studied his new atlas. He'd stopped to fill
the Mustang's tank somewhere near Valdosta, and while it
had not been nearly as fine an adventure as his stop in Pass
Christian, he had scored three tapes, a hot Slim Jim, and the
book of maps. He saw that I-95 north from Savannah would
take him all the way into North Carolina. Zach didn't like
interstates, but he was well away from New Orleans now and
ready to cover some more distance in a hurry.

And after North Carolina, where? Leaf had thought him a
New Yorker. Zach had always been intrigued by the idea of
such a tiny island-bound city crammed full of people of every
possible race, gender, and persuasion, entire cultures and culture wars, systems of magic and religion, infinite microcosms.
Maybe now he could get lost there.

He finished his pizza, dropped off his room key at the office, slapped on his new Hank Williams tape, and headed
north.

Just before midnight Zach sat drinking a Bloody Maria at
the Sombrero Lounge, a colorful confection of a building
molded primarily of pink stucco, orange neon, and thousands
of twinkling white fairy lights. The South of the Border theme
park on I-95 had drawn him in like a bug to a gaudy flame.

SOB's increasingly surreal billboards loomed along the
highway for thirty miles before the park, all 3-D papier-
mâché sculpture and moving parts, giant hot dogs and spinning sheep and the smirking mustachioed mug of pedro, the
SOB mascot. It was like a little city set down in the middle of
nowhere, halfway between New Jersey and Disney World (as
one of the signs bragged), and after three hours of dark interstate flanked by monotonous stretches of farmland and
stands of pine, its tacky bars and souvenir shops with their

Easter egg paint jobs of purple and pink and chartreuse had looked to Zach like the lights of Bourbon Street at Mardi Gras.

As he finished his drink, an eye-watering blend of tequila and Tabasco with a splash of tomato juice, an idea came to him. He left the bar and drove across the complex to pedro's motel, paid cash for one of the "heir conditioned" rooms, dug his battery-powered laptop computer out of the back seat and took it inside, along with the OKI 900 cellular phone he carried everywhere. Zach had tumbled the phone, or reprogrammed it to generate a new ID number each time he used it. It could not receive calls, but neither could his calls be traced.

The furniture and walls of the room were painted pink, the bed heart-shaped, with a mirror on the ceiling and a slick spread of lurid red satin. No doubt you could put a quarter in and summon the Magic Fingers. Instead, Zach turned on the laptop, entered a stolen MCI credit card number, and dialed into the composing department of the New Orleans *Times-Picayune.*

Over a year ago he had discovered that the newspaper had a program that let reporters type in their stories from home. He'd created an account for himself, changing his password every time he planted an item in the paper. Currently it was ZYGOTE, thanks to his last story about the petrified abortion. He logged on and changed it to *pedro.* Then he typed:

```
   GODDESS SEEN IN BOWL OF GUMBO
  by Joseph Boudreaux, Staff Writer
   The Goddess Kali is known in Hin-
 duism as the Mother and Destroyer
 of Creation. But can she make a
 roux?
   In  a  twist  on  the  well-known
 Jesus-in-the-plate-of-spaghetti
 theme,  Parvata  Sanjay  of  India
 spied the Hindu goddess in his bowl
 during  a  recent  visit  to  New  Or-
 leans, while sampling the seafood
```

gumbo at a popular French Quarter
restaurant. ''Her four terrible
arms were outstretched,'' said
Sanjay, ''and her bloody, lolling
tongue was clearly visible. It was
only a pattern in the soup, formed
by the oil on the surface, but I believe all patterns have significance.''

Might Mr. Sanjay have sampled a
few Dixie beers as well?

The Calcutta native plans to continue his American travels in North
Carolina, where he says he wants to
try the barbecue.

Zach added the sequence of characters that meant an editor
had approved his copy. Then with a few more keystrokes he
sent it on its merry way to the printing department, where it
joined the other stories ready to be printed in next Sunday's
edition. It was easier to bury items in the Sunday paper—they
were hungry for filler and didn't look twice at the shit that
came in.

He knew Eddy would be watching the paper for hidden
news of him. The mention of Kali would catch her eye, and
she might also notice that he had reversed the Indian sur-
name and first name. Calling the guy Mr. Parvata Sanjay was
something like calling an American Mr. Rogers Fred.

Other friends and outlaws might see it and recognize his
hand too. Maybe some of Them would see it too, for that
matter, but Zach didn't think They would connect it with a
hacker on the run.

He logged out and broke the phone connection, turned off
the computer, and carried it back out to his car. A quick pee
in the pink-tiled bathroom, room key left in the door, and
Zach was gone. After sleeping all day he was ready to drive
all night, and anyway he couldn't stand the thought of lying

there in that slick red heart-shaped bed, staring at his own lonely, horny body in the mirror overhead.

South of the Border disappeared behind him. Soon it was only a faint fuchsia glow on the horizon. As the night deepened and the traffic thinned to nothing, it seemed to Zach that the whole country lay over the next rise, around the next bend of the highway all lit up and wide awake, violent and strange and joyous, just waiting for him to come find it.

EIGHT

Trevor didn't know what he expected to see inside the Rambler as the driver's window wound down: a grinning skeleton dirt-crusted and worm-festooned, dry bone finger beckoning him in? His father's flesh restored, black shades balanced on his blade of a nose, intense eyes blazing through smoky lenses? Or Bobby as he had looked the last time Trevor saw him, dead eyes bulging, tongue jutting like a rotten melon, chin and bare scrawny chest slicked with drool, streaked with gore?

Whatever he expected, it wasn't the smiling face of Terry Buckett, the affable second-generation hippie who had introduced himself at the bar last night. The owner of the record store, Trevor remembered. Procurer of jazz sides, retailer of the magic that had made Bird so little money during his own lifetime.

"Hey, Trevor Black. It's pouring down rain, or didn't you notice? Catch a ride, man."

Terry cocked a thumb toward the passenger door. Trevor made himself walk around the front of the car, heard wet gravel crunching under his feet though he could not feel it, heard the roar and thrum of the idling engine. Perched high on its wheels, the Rambler looked like a child's sketch of an automobile, a small rectangle atop a larger one precariously balanced on two circles. It was a boxy, plain, yet somehow rakish machine. It was not the sort of car in which you expected to see a ghost; it was not the sort of car you expected to *be* a ghost.

Trevor raised his left hand and wrapped his fingers around the door handle. It was cold to the touch, beaded with rain.

He pulled the heavy door open and slid in, across the dirty-white vinyl seat his butt had polished in cloth diapers and Osh-Kosh overalls, the seat that had stuck to the backs of his legs when it was hot, the seat that Didi had peed on a couple of times, though most of his accidents had been confined to the back.

Terry lounged comfortably on the other side of the seat, curly hair pulled back in a faded blue bandanna, dark amused eyes looking Trevor up and down. Terry's features were blunt, not quite handsome; his bushy eyebrows nearly met over the bridge of his nose, and he needed a shave. But his face had a friendly, squared look, a face that wouldn't take any bullshit but wouldn't give you any either. Make him a little seedier-looking and he could have been a character drawn by Crumb.

Terry put the car in gear, eased off the clutch, and started rolling down Burnt Church Road again. He seemed to be in no great hurry to get anywhere.

"Where did you get this car?" Trevor asked.

"Aw, I've had it forever. Kinsey used to help me fix it whenever it broke down, but I've learned to do most of the work myself. I love these old engines. No damn electronics to get fucked up, just a bunch of metal and grease. You know these wipers still run on *vacuum tubes*?" Terry indicated the slushing windshield wipers as though pointing out an artifact of some forgotten civilization. "Something else Kinsey told me about this car. It used to belong to a famous cartoonist who killed himself here in Missing Mile. Pretty weird, huh?"

Trevor sagged back in the seat and let out a long unsteady breath. Terry glanced over. "You okay, man?"

"Yeah." He sat up, swiped water out of his eyes. His shirt was sticking to his skin, outlining his ribs. His jeans were sodden, unpleasantly heavy. "Just wet. And cold."

"Well, look, I was going into town to do some errands, but my house is just back down the road. You want to stop by there and towel off? I'll even give you a dry T-shirt, I've got a million of 'em."

"No, I'm fine—"

But Terry was already turning the car around. "I forgot to get stoned before I left anyway. Consider it done."

A couple of minutes later the Rambler turned into a long gravel driveway and stopped in front of a small wooden house whose paint was not so much peeling as fraying at the edges. A couple of rocking chairs were stationed on the porch among various whirligigs, wagon wheels, pirated street signs, and crates of empty beer bottles. Country kitsch gone weird.

Terry led the way up the porch steps, through the towers of junk, and unlocked the front door. "Watch out for the hex sign. It's supposed to be bad luck to step on it or something."

Trevor looked down as he crossed the threshold. Someone had painted two interlocking triangles, one red and one blue, with a silver ankh at their juncture. "What's it for?"

"Don't ask me. This house belongs to my friend Ghost, who's even spookier than you might guess from his name. His grandmother was some kind of witch."

"He isn't here, is he?" Trevor hoped he wasn't about to meet yet another of Missing Mile's friendly freaks. He had only wanted a ride, not an impromptu afternoon party.

"No, his band is on tour. *Extended* tour. I'm minding the farm, which means free rent and a lifetime supply of good karma."

"How come?"

"Oh, I don't know." Terry shrugged. "Miz Deliverance was a *good* witch. What color shirt do you want?"

"Black."

"But of course."

Terry tossed him a cotton T-shirt printed with the Whirling Disc logo—a little long-haired man who looked like a hippie version of the man on the Monopoly game, twirling a record on the end of his candy-striped cane—and pointed him down the hall to the bathroom. Trevor placed his wet feet carefully on the mellow hardwood floors. He was intrigued by the idea of a house with good karma, a house that held memories of love and music.

He pulled the heavy wooden door of the bathroom shut behind him, tugged his wet shirt over his head and dropped it on the floor. It was just a plain black tee like almost every other shirt Trevor owned; he had one with a pocket, but that was getting fancy. The little Whirling Disc man was a radical departure for him.

Trevor unbound his ponytail, leaned over the old clawfoot bathtub and wrung a stream of water from his hair. Then he rumpled it with a towel and let it hang loose to dry. It rippled halfway down his back, ginger like Bobby's, shot through with a few strands of pale gold like Momma's.

The mirror in the bathroom made him nervous; he had a strong sense of someone looking back at him from its depths. He put his lips close against the wavy silver surface, whispered "Who is it?" But nothing answered. There was only his own high pale forehead melding with its own reflection, his own eyes merging into one misshapen transparent orb that stared mercilessly back at him, his own long somber face dissolving to mist at the edges. He stood back from the mirror and watched his nipples shiver erect, his skin prickle into goosebumps.

Trevor pulled the Whirling Disc shirt over his head and hurried back down the hall to the living room, where Terry was just firing up a fat, pungent joint.

"I don't suppose you do this?" Terry asked after a long toke. Blue smoke leaked out of his nostrils and the corners of his mouth; narrowing his eyes against it, he looked sybaritic and handsomer than before. Trevor hesitated. Terry held out the joint, waggled it enticingly.

What the hell, Trevor decided, and reached out to take it with his left hand. He'd smoked pot before, but not for a long time, and never much. It had been one of Bobby's drugs. But pot had never made Bobby puke and sob like a baby, had never made him pick up the hammer or whispered in his ear how he might use it. And Bobby had smoked it when he was drawing. Trevor thought it might be good to try some right before he went in the house.

So he wrapped his lips around the wrinkled end of the joint, slightly damp with Terry's spit but not unpleasantly so, and took a deep drag.

Big mistake.

He hadn't eaten anything since Kinsey's dubious noodle soup last night at the club, hadn't drunk anything but a few Cokes and a warm, noxious Jolt. Suddenly his stomach felt like a small pouch of cracked and shriveled leather, his tissues and the meat of his brain felt scorched by the fire that burned inside him.

The joint slipped from his fingers and skittered down his arm, leaving a long singed trail along the old tracework of scars. He heard Terry say something, felt his knees begin to buckle.

Big round bursts of light appeared in front of his eyes, blue and red and sparkly silver, spinning like crazy constellations. Then blackness waltzed in and wiped them all away.

Terry couldn't believe it when the kid collapsed on his living-room floor. He had seen stoners toked to the point of zombification, staring at a TV screen as if it might bring nirvana. He had seen drinkers gone to drooling stupor in every sort of compromising position and location, including on the toilet. He had even seen a nodding junkie or two. But never in his twenty-eight years had Terry Buckett watched anyone pass out from one toke on a joint.

He retrieved the burning spliff from the folds of Trevor's shirt, patted down the kid's scrawny chest to make sure no stray embers were setting him aflame, checked out the glowing end of the joint but saw nothing amiss, smelled nothing weird. The pot couldn't be laced with anything: Terry had already rolled three or four joints out of this particular bag, which came from a trusted source. His own buzz was just starting to tickle the edges of his brain, leafy and benign. It was nothing but good Carolina homegrown. This pale trembling youth must be in pretty sorry shape.

He checked to see if Trevor was breathing, gently pulled up one of his eyelids to make sure he hadn't had a brain embolism or something. The silvery-pale eye glared at Terry, making him think Trevor was in there somewhere, not too far away. As he wedged a cushion from the sofa under Trevor's lolling head, the kid started muttering, ". . . m'okay . . . fine . . ."

"Yeah, you look great," said Terry. He went to the kitchen, found a dishrag that was mostly clean, ran it under cold water, went back and draped it over Trevor's face. Trevor raised a limp hand to swipe at it, got halfway, then let the hand fall like a dead white bird by his side.

"Hang loose," Terry told him. "Don't go away." He paused beside the stereo and scanned the portion of his vast record collection he had already managed to cart over here, wondering what music Trevor might like to surface from oblivion with. Jazz was one of the few categories Terry's collection lacked; he liked it okay but had never accumulated any of his own, had always vaguely figured it was the sort of music you had to be an expert on to really appreciate.

Finally he selected an old Tom Waits album, dropped the needle on it, and returned to the kitchen to be a gracious host.

Trevor woke with a damp sour-smelling membrane over his face and a strange guttural voice groaning in his ears. He clawed frantically at the membrane and it came away in his hands, cold and dank and foul. How long had he been gone? It felt like minutes but could have been an hour, no more; the light hadn't changed.

The walls seemed to tower toward an infinitely high point overhead. They were decorated with vintage acid rock posters whose lurid colors swirled and gyred, the bands' names taunting him: Jimi Hendrix Experience, Captain Beefheart, Strawberry Alarm Clock. All had been in his parents' record collection.

The room was furnished much like his childhood home in Austin: bookshelves of cinder blocks and particleboard, comfortable sofa with sagging cushions and the nap on the arms worn thin, table that looked like a refugee from someone else's trash pile. Early Starving Artist, or Poverty Deco. Trevor saw parts of Terry's drum set strewn about the room, a cymbal in the corner, a snare propped between a bookcase and the doorway that led to the hall. There was only one difference between this stranger's house and the one he remembered living in with his family: this one felt somehow safe. His parents' home had felt safe once too, but that was so long ago Trevor could barely remember.

He tried to sit up and felt his brain starting to spiral off into the ether again. A snippet of dialogue from *Krazy Kat* drifted through his mind: *Just imegine having your "ectospasm" running around william & nilliam among the unlimitless etha'—golla, it's imbillivibil—*

Imbillivibil it was. Yet it would seem he'd swooned in Terry's living room, or whoever's living room this was. How fucking embarrassing. Terry didn't seem to be around, and Trevor thought that when he felt able to stand he might just slink out of this safe place, walk the rest of the way into town, then out to Violin Road.

Yes, that was what he thought he would do—until he smelled the aroma wafting from the kitchen. It rooted him to the floor, made his nostrils flare and his head throb with longing. Oily-dark, bitter-rich, utterly compelling.

Coffee.

Terry finished making two generous sandwiches, poured two mugs of joe, picked up the plate in one hand and both steaming coffees in the other. Precariously he edged back through the kitchen, into the living room, and held out the mugs to Trevor. "Do you want sugar or—"

He was surprised again when the kid seized a mug and drank down the hot black coffee in what looked like a single swallow. Terry winced, imagining the bitter brew blazing down his own smoke-seared throat, but Trevor just sighed and licked his lips and held up the empty mug. "Can I have another?"

"Should I just bring the whole pot?"

"Yes." He seemed serious, so Terry went back to the kitchen and got it, along with the bag of sugar and a couple of spoons. Trevor poured himself another cup, stirred in a meager spoonful of sugar almost as an afterthought, and drank half of it at once. Terry took his first sip. "I thought you might could use a bite to eat too."

"What is it?" Trevor hadn't noticed the plate of sandwiches until now.

"Olive loaf and mustard on whole grain."

"Olive loaf?"

"Yeah, it's kind of a classic around here. A while back, Kinsey wanted to have New Orleans Night at the Yew and serve *muffuletta* sandwiches, right? But he didn't know how to make the Italian olive salad. So he made these fucked-up things on sub rolls with boiled ham, sliced pepperoni, and olive loaf. They were awful but we all choked 'em down. Since then I've kind of gotten to like it."

Trevor took a sandwich and bit cautiously at the very edge of it, stayed poker-faced, managed not to shudder. Then he seemed to inhale and the whole thing was gone. He picked up the other half of the sandwich and repeated the process, then poured himself another cup of coffee.

"You, uh, want me to fix another pot of java?"

"I don't know." Trevor looked up, and an odd shadow passed over his face. It was as if he had managed to relax for a few minutes, to let down a little of his guard, and then he had suddenly remembered some awful thing he had to do. "Maybe I better just go."

"It's okay, man. I'm in no hurry. That's the whole point of owning a business, you know—you set your own hours and pay people good money, nobody yells at you if you're a little late." *Or a little stoned.*

Spooning coffee out of its foil bag, Terry mused over the enigma in his living room. There was something very strange about this new kid: he seemed nervous and aloof, but at the same time terribly lonely. It was as if he had no social skills, as if he were some kind of space alien who had read extensively about people and their habits and customs, maybe *wanted* to know more, but was only now making first contact.

And he put away java the way Terry's car chugged motor oil. Terry wondered what Trevor was trying to stay awake for.

One thing was certain: Missing Mile had itself another live one.

Trevor stayed long enough to drink most of the second pot of coffee. Terry finished the joint and ran his mouth in what seemed like a friendly way, talking about music, the town, even comics once he found out Trevor drew them. Trevor didn't usually talk about it, but Terry asked so many questions that he couldn't help answering some.

At least Terry didn't mention Bobby McGee, but then *Birdland* probably wasn't his sort of thing. He liked the Freak Brothers, predictably, but most of his other favorites featured guys in capes and long underwear beating up guys in black. (There was an awkward silence here; then Trevor, unable to help himself, mumbled "I hate that shit." Terry just shrugged.)

Terry seemed kind enough; still Trevor could not shake the idea that he was being surreptitiously examined like some three-headed sideshow attraction. In few other places had people seemed as curious about him, as *interested* in him, as here. It was as if they sensed that he was a hometown boy, or nearly so.

Finally Terry stood up and stretched. Trevor saw a flash of bare belly beneath his T-shirt: the skin lightly tanned, with the barest beginnings of a roll of fat and a thin line of pale brown hair disappearing into the waistband of his jeans. "Guess we better get moving. You want a ride somewhere?"

"Violin Road."

"Pretty dead out there, man. You sure?"

"That's where I'm staying now."

Terry glanced at Trevor, seemed to wrestle with something he wanted to say, evidently decided it was none of his business. "Okay. Violin Road it is."

The rain had stopped but the day was still overcast. The air felt heavy and moist against Trevor's skin, like an unwanted kiss. The Rambler gunned through town and bumped over the railroad tracks. It was Sunday afternoon, and nearly everything seemed to be shut down, doors locked tight, windows dark and shaded. Freak subculture or not, Missing Mile was still in the heart of the Bible Belt. The thought of his lambs being able to buy a tube of toothpaste or get a cup of coffee on Sunday was surely a terrible affront to the Lord.

Then they were turning off Firehouse Street onto another gravel road, one that changed to rutted dirt after half a mile or so. Violin Road. Trevor felt a loosening in his chest, a hot ribbon of excitement uncoiling in his stomach. The scrap heaps and rusted hulks of automobiles, the unpainted trailers, the castlelike spires of kudzu slipped past, less substantial than blurry images in old photographs. His eyes swept the roadside.

Then, suddenly, there was the house: his hell, his Birdland.

It was set farther back from the road than he remembered. The porch and the peak of the roof were barely visible through the rioting growth that had taken over the yard. A weeping willow at the side of the house had not been much taller than Momma's head; now its pale green fronds caressed the roof. A verdant tangle of goldenrod and forsythia, Queen Anne's lace and pokeweed and brown-eyed Susans ran right up to the porch steps, which were partly crumbled. Kudzu was draped over everything like a green blanket, tendrils twining between the porch railings, through the broken windows.

"You can let me out here."

Terry slowed the Rambler to a crawl, looked around. This far out, Violin Road was sparsely populated; there was no other house in sight. "Where?"

"Right here."

"The murder house?"

Trevor didn't say anything, waited for the car to slow enough so that he could jump out. Terry seemed to have forgotten that his foot was on the gas; the Rambler inched along at ten miles per hour. "Oh shit," he said. "I think I know who you are."

"Yeah, I'm starting to feel like a local celebrity or something. Thanks for the ride. I'll see you at the Yew."

Trevor grabbed his bag and pushed the passenger door open, prompting Terry to apply his brakes at last. Trevor's sneakers hit the scrubby grass at the side of the road; then, before he could think about it, he was sprinting toward the house.

"Be careful, man!" Terry yelled. Trevor pretended not to hear. Then the Rambler was speeding up, disappearing down the road, throwing mud in its wake. It rounded a bend and was gone.

Trevor stood alone in the yard, panting, staring at the house. A few patches of weathered wood and broken glass were visible through the growth; other than that the face of the house was mostly hidden.

The grass just brushed his knees. As he pushed through it, sparkling drops of water scattered to earth, grasshoppers whirred away from his invading feet. He ducked under a dripping bower of vine and was there. No more obstacles lay between him and the house. The steps were mostly intact, and he thought the porch would hold him. The front door was barely ajar. Beyond that was dusty darkness.

Trevor closed his eyes for a long moment, heard the sigh and hush of leaves, the high shrill drone of insects, the distant conversation of birds . . . and beneath that, a subliminal voice whispering to him, making itself heard over years of absence and decay?

He was afraid so. He hoped so.

He opened his eyes, took a deep breath of sunlight and the verdant smell the rain had left, and put his foot on the first step.

NINE

The air in Birdland was golden as slow syrup, green as the light that filtered through the kudzu, weighted with dampness and rot. The cool decaying scent of a house abandoned for decades, made up of many things: the black earth under the floor, the dry droppings of animals, the drifts of dead insects sifting to shards of iridescent chitin beneath shimmering tapestries of cobweb. In the random shafts of sunlight that fell through the lattice of roof and vegetation, dust motes slowly shifted, turned. Each one might represent a memory Trevor had of this house, a particle of the universe charged with the terrible energy of years.

He moved deeper in. Here was the living room, the husks of the ugly chair and old brown sofa that had come with the house moldering in a corner, reduced to skins of brittle colorless cloth stretched over skeletons of wood and wire. The rain had come in through the holes in the roof, and the room smelled of slow damp decay, of fungal secrets. Here were the remains of the stacked milk crates where the records had been stored. Most of the records were gone, probably stolen by kids who had made it this far in, though by the end of that summer the magical vinyl wheels would have been as warped as if they had spent two months in a slow oven.

A few fleeting images of album covers came to him: Janis Joplin's *Cheap Thrills* with art by R. Crumb, the psychedelic hologram of the Rolling Stones' *Satanic Majesties Request* that could induce dizziness if he stared into it too long, a photograph of Sidney Bechet that had scared him a little to look at, because the muscles of the jazz saxophonist's cheeks and neck

were so developed that his head appeared swollen, elephan-
tine.

Here was the doorway leading into the hall, where Momma
had died. Her blood had long since faded to a barely discern-
ible pattern of streaks and spatters on the wall, not much
darker than the shadow and grime around it. But here and
there the wooden frame had been splintered by hammer
blows that missed. And in two spots, one on either side of the
door, Momma's fingers had dug into the wall hard enough to
leave gouges in the plaster. That must have happened when
Bobby didn't miss.

In the autopsy report was a list of substances found under
her fingernails: wood, plaster, her husband's blood and her
own. And little divots of Bobby's skin, strands of Bobby's
hair. She had fought him off hard. She had died in intimate
contact with him.

*Cause of death: blunt trauma. Victim had fifteen separate wounds
made by a claw hammer, five to the head, three to the chest area,
seven to the arms and hands. Three of the head wounds and two of
the chest wounds could in and of themselves have been fatal.*

Had Momma died quietly? This was something Trevor had
wondered about for a long time. She might have wrestled
with Bobby in a desperate silence at first, not wanting to
wake the boys and scare them with another fight. But once
she realized that Bobby meant them harm, Trevor thought,
she would have started screaming. She would have tried to
hold Bobby off long enough to let them get out of the house.

And the injuries she had taken before her death: seven broken fingers, a splintered collarbone and a shattered tibia,
three cracked ribs, a blow sunk so deeply into her chest that it
penetrated the breastbone. Could she have remained silent
through those?

Trevor didn't think so. He probably could have slept
through anything that night. He remembered the bitter-tast-
ing grapefruit juice Bobby had given him before bed, the dull
loginess of his head the next morning when he woke. And a
notation in his file at the Home said there had been Seconal in
his blood when he was brought in.

Bobby had drugged him, which meant he had planned the murders. But had he planned to leave Trevor alive, and drugged him so he would sleep through it all? Or had he drugged both boys, planning to kill both, and changed his mind about Trevor for some reason?

And what about Didi? Trevor wondered if his brother had seen his death coming. He had found Didi curled on his belly, ruined head burrowed deep into the pillow, as if Bobby had killed him in his sleep. But unless Bobby had given him Seconal too, Trevor didn't think Didi could have slept through the sounds of his mother dying. Bobby could have killed him sitting up in bed—or cowering—and then arranged him back into the peaceful sleeping position as if trying to absolve himself.

Fredric D. McGee, Box 17, Violin Road, male Caucasian, 3 yrs, 2-6, 25 pounds, blond hair, brown eyes. Occupation: None. Cause of death: blunt trauma. Victim had approximately twenty-two separate wounds, all in head/neck area. Cranium and brain were completely destroyed . . .

Trevor imagined Didi's eyes as the hammer descended. He squeezed his own eyes shut and slammed the heel of his hand against the door frame. A rain of dust sifted down. The pain in his hand—his *left* hand, of course; he didn't hit things with his drawing hand—made the image of Didi fade. And, in a far corner of the living room, a crumpled sheet of newspaper suddenly rustled, then tore. The sound was nearly heartstopping in the silent room.

Trevor turned away from the doorway, walked over to the corner and nudged the paper with his toe. He could see no mouse or insect, nothing that could have made it move, let alone tear. He picked it up and smoothed it, and the headline screamed off the page at him. "I HAD TO DO IT," SAYS KILLER. The word *killer* was ripped neatly in half.

Trevor examined the paper more closely and saw that it was a Raleigh *News and Observer* dated October 1986, years after he had left Missing Mile. The headline story was about a man in Corinth who had given his pregnant wife an abortion with a 30.06, firing sixteen shells into her belly. Even in the womb children were not safe from their fathers. Trevor imagined the sizzle of hot lead tunneling into unformed fetal flesh, the raw, bloody reek edged with the firework smell of cordite. But Bobby hadn't been giving any interviews after murdering his family, not in this world anyway.

Trevor pictured the front page of hell's daily, printed on asbestos but still singed at the edges, Bobby's huge-eyed, shellshocked face in grainy black and white on the front page. And the headline would say—what?—ANOTHER FUCKED-UP GUY KILLS FAMILY, THEN SELF. ONE KID LEFT ALIVE; "WE'LL GET HIM LATER" SAYS DEVIL. Minor demons yawning over steaming mugs of bitter black coffee and brimstone, blearily scanning the news but not thinking much about it; this was business as usual in hell.

He felt the house drawing him in, filling his mind with images and icons till he overflowed like a pitcher of dark liquid. Caffeine sang in his veins. He dropped the newspaper, walked through the doorway stained with his mother's blood, past the kitchen on his left, and slowly down the hall, cocking his head and listening as he passed each room, trying to see through the half-closed doors.

On the right side of the hall was his parents' bedroom, then Bobby's studio. On the left was Didi's room, then Trevor's, then the tiny bathroom where Bobby had died. He remembered standing here before, looking at the afternoon light filtering in through the rooms, falling in golden slants across the hall floor, and wondering if he would ever be able to draw well enough to capture it.

He could do it now. But the light was subtly different, murkier, with a greener tinge to it. After a moment Trevor realized it must be because of the kudzu growing over the windows of the rooms, catching the sunlight and staining it.

He continued to the end of the hall, trailing his hand along the water-stained wall. On his right was the studio, on his left the bathroom. Bobby's hell and purgatory. Or was it the other way around? Trevor guessed that was one of the things he had come to find out.

He looked to his left and saw the faint gleam of light on

dirty porcelain, the buckled shower curtain rod above the black chasm of the tub. How many hours was it now until the exact moment when Bobby had fastened the rope and stepped off the edge of the tub? How many hours until the twentieth anniversary of his neck snapping?

Trevor's eyes moved over the peeling walls, over the dark rectangle of the mirror, found the space between sink and toilet where he had curled his five-year-old body into the tightest possible ball. He wondered if he could fit there now. He wondered what he would see if he did.

Instead he turned and went into the studio. The two large windows were intact, and the room was dusty but otherwise clean. Trevor brushed off the tilted surface of Bobby's drawing table. He preferred to draw on a flat surface, having gotten used to his desk at the Home, but the folding table was one of the few things Bobby hadn't sold or thrown out when they left Austin. It had his stains and gouges, his razor slits and scars, his sweat grimed into its grain, maybe his tears too. Maybe his secrets. And maybe his nightmares.

Trevor sat on the sawed-off bar stool that Bobby had used as his drawing chair. It wobbled as it always had, but held. The light in here was good, even with the vines and tall grass covering the window, but some drawings tacked up on the wall were in shadow. He didn't want to see them now anyway; he had enough of Bobby here to suit him for a while.

Trevor got his own pencils and sketchbook out of his bag, arranged them on the table, and flipped to the story he had been working on at the graveyard. The story of how Bird and Walter Brown went to jail in Jackson, Mississippi, for talking on a screened porch one fine summer night.

Left arm curled around his sketchbook, head bent down far over the page, hair hanging like a pale curtain around his thin, determined face, Trevor drew for three hours. When he looked up, the room was veiled in blue shadows and he realized he had barely been able to see the page for ten minutes or more. He saw Bobby's old gooseneck lamp still clamped to the edge of the table, and without thinking he reached out and pushed the button that turned it on.

Stark electric light flooded the room, threw the spidery shadow of his fingers clutching the pencil onto the pitted tabletop.

Trevor's drawing trance broke. He shoved himself back from the table, nearly tipped the stool over. Only his fear made him keep his balance. He did not want to be on his back on the floor of this room just now. His gaze swept the corners, the ceiling, the darkening windows, came to rest on the brown cord snaking from the base of the lamp to the wall socket below. The thing was plugged in. But how could the wiring, the bulb, last twenty years? And as long as he was asking stupid questions, *how could the fucking electricity be on?*

He wondered if it might never have been turned off, if their delinquent bill might have been passed over by an idling computer or some such. He distrusted all engines and mechanical systems but especially computers, whose insides he pictured as like some silver, sinister, impossibly intricate painting by Giger.

But Trevor didn't think the power could have stayed on for two decades without someone at the switches noticing or the house catching fire. When you subtract the impossible, what's left? The improbable, the strange but true. The supernatural, or if you liked, the *supra*natural: outside the boundaries of most experience, but possible in a place where no boundaries are drawn.

Trevor settled back on the stool and glanced up at the wall, at the drawings tacked there, done on sketchbook paper now yellowed and curling at the edges. Most had sifted away to faint scratchings of ink or graphite, impossible to make out. But the one his eyes came to rest on was still clear enough.

It was Bobby's last drawing of Rosena, of whom he had done so many: facial studies framed in cascading hair, with tender mouth and large lustrous eyes; sinuous nude fantasies made flesh; long graceful hands like rapid sketches of birds in flight. But in this one Rosena sprawled in the hall doorway, head thrown back, face battered in. Except for slight differences in style—Bobby had a heavier hand with the shading, and a way of capturing the fall of light on hair that made it look nearly wet—it was identical to the drawing Trevor had done in his sketchbook on the Greyhound, on his way to Missing Mile.

Trevor stared at the faded picture, nodding ever so slightly, not even surprised anymore. Either Bobby had known how she would look in death before he killed her, as if he'd had some vision, or he had gotten out his sketchbook and drawn her broken body before he had gone into the bathroom to hang himself. Maybe somewhere around here was a sketch of Didi dead too. Trevor had done one this morning, barely awake, coming out of his dream of not-drawing.

But now he was here, on the very spot where he sat in the dream, and he could still draw.

His jaw was set, his eyes wary, a shade darker than before. Though he did not know it, he looked like a man who has taken blows but is now ready to deal some of his own.

He glanced down at his own sketchbook and for the first time really saw what he had just drawn, and all the hardness drained out of his face. His mouth fell open; his throat slammed shut; tears started in his eyes. Caffeine and adrenaline sizzled through his veins, made his heart carom against the walls of his chest. He could barely remember drawing this. It wasn't even how the story was supposed to *go*.

The cops were meant to show up with their nightsticks drawn, bash Bird and Brown around some, then haul them off to jail with bruises and bleeding scalps. That was what had really happened.

But in this version, the cops never stopped bashing.

There were closeups of hard wood connecting with skulls, skin splitting and curling back from the edges of wounds, a freshet of blood coursing from a nostril, an eye gone to pulp and swollen tissue, a spray of broken teeth on the ground like splinters of ivory scattered on dark velvet. Bird and Brown lay crumpled at the bottom of the final page like animals hunted down and killed for their pelts, adrift in a spreading pool of gore.

The gore was darkly shaded and looked slick, nearly wet. Trevor could not remember drawing it.

The house and whatever lived here had cast some nightmarish pall across his vision, hypnotized his hand, ruined his story.

Or had it?

The true story as Trevor had intended to tell it would have been strong and affecting in an understated way. Maybe this could be something splashier, stranger, and ultimately more memorable. He envisioned an ending for this version. The cops realize they've killed the musicians and sneak off, figuring they can blame the murders on niggers killing other niggers. But, as white men have failed to realize for too long, people aren't stupid just because they're poor. The black people of Jackson can read the death of their heroes like a bitter book whose pages are bound in dusky skin, writ large with blood spilled in hatred.

Jackson is not so far from New Orleans, cradle of dark religion and herbal wisdom from Africa, from Haiti, from the heart of the Louisiana swamp. And hoodoo knowledge has a way of traveling . . .

Trevor imagined the bodies of Bird and Brown rising back up, seeing dimly through smashed eyes, thinking dimly with smashed brains. They would be only shells, drained of music, of life. But like all good zombies they would be able to hone in on their killers. And they would have help . . .

In his mind he saw a full-page final frame. The cops crucified and burning on their own front lawns, nailed to crosses of blazing agony, their blackening, yawning forms silhouetted against the rich texture of the flames. It would have a crudely moralistic, E.C. Comics feel to it. But he wouldn't ink it or color it; he would do it entirely in pencil, meticulously shaded and hatched and stippled, and it would be beautiful.

And he would sell this fucker, sell it to a market that could afford to print it right. *Raw* maybe, or *Taboo*. He loved *Taboo*, an irregularly published anthology of beautifully rendered, lovingly produced, weird and twisted comics printed mostly in stark blacks and whites, shot through here and there with a few pages of color alternately subtle, vivid, and disturbing. Everything from Joe Coleman's mutilation paintings to the numerous intricate collaborations of Alan Moore had appeared in its pages, all printed on fine heavy paper.

Trevor's jaw was set again as he bent back over his sketchbook. But now the emotion in his face looked more like strength than hardness. If he did this right, it would be the best thing he had ever drawn.

He drew for four more hours in the harsh electric light, until his eyelids grew heavy and sandy, until his fingers could barely uncurl from the pencil. Then he folded his arms on the tabletop and cradled his head and went effortlessly to sleep.

Sometime later the gooseneck lamp clicked off, leaving him in darkness broken only by the trembling, shifting moonlight that came in the windows, filtered through kudzu and twenty years of dust.

Trevor did not dream that night.

TEN

Kinsey Hummingbird woke on Monday morning hoping Trevor might have come back in the night, though he had not seen him all day Sunday. Kinsey couldn't imagine anyone sleeping in that house. But apparently Trevor had; at any rate, he wasn't here.

There were so many things Kinsey wanted to say to the boy —but he had to stop thinking of him as a boy. Trevor was twenty-five after all; even if he had had reason to lie, the chronology was right. Kinsey remembered the date of the McGee deaths well enough.

It was just that Trevor looked so young. That scared five-year-old was still a big part of him, Kinsey thought as he got up and went to the kitchen, though some flintier core must have kept Trevor alive and sane. There was an undeniable strength there; many people in Trevor's situation would have retreated into the numb fog of catatonia or blown their brains out as soon as they were able to lay hands on a gun.

But even for a soul of enormous strength, what would a night in that house have been like?

After the investigation of the McGee deaths was over—and of course there had been little investigating to do; the bodies told their own mute tale—the cops had locked the door behind them and the family's things had sat in the house, gathering dust in the silent, bloodstained rooms. A FOR SALE sign went up in the scrubby yard, but no one saw it as anything other than a ghoulish joke on the realtor's part. That house would never be rented again, let alone sold.

Browsing the aisles of Potter's Store one day deep in the summer of 1972, the FOR SALE sign outside the murder house already niggling at his mind, Kinsey found himself wondering what had happened to the McGees' things. Potter's was a cavernous thrift establishment downtown, huge and dim and cool, its rickety rows of metal shelves crammed with chipped plates and battered silverware and obsolete (though usually functional) kitchen appliances, its cracked glass display case filled with strange knickknacks and costume jewelry, its bins heaped high with musty clothing. Kinsey, with his love of junk, often spent long afternoons browsing here.

But he didn't think the McGees' belongings had ended up at Potter's Store. He wasn't sure what he thought he should have seen: bloodstained mattresses, maybe, or splattered shirts and dresses woven through the pile marked MISC WOMENS CLOTHS 25 CENTS. But there hadn't been any jazz records or underground comics either, and there sure as hell hadn't been a drawing table. He supposed everything was still out there, moldering in the silent rooms.

The house on Violin Road never sold. The FOR SALE sign was stolen, replaced by the realtor, whose optimism apparently knew no bounds. The paint on the new sign faded throughout the long dry summer. Tall weeds grew up around it, and it began to list. At last it fell face forward and was soon hidden in the long grass.

By that time kudzu had begun to climb the walls of the house. Where the children of Violin Road had thrown rocks through the windows, the insidious vine snaked in. Kinsey imagined it twining through the rooms, sucking nourishment from blood long dry. He did not doubt that this was possible. As a child, he had seen a kudzu root unearthed from the Civil War graveyard where his own great-great-great-uncle Miles was buried. The root, fully six feet long, had eaten its way through a grave and taken on the shape of the man buried there. Its offshoots formed four twisted limbs, the root-tips bursting from them at the ends like a multitude of fingers and toes. At the top had been a skull-sized tangle of delicate fibers in which the planes and hollows of a face could almost be made out.

Twenty years later the house was nearly hidden under its

twining green blanket. Driving past it, you could barely tell that there was a house on the overgrown lot at all. Only the wooden porch and the peak of the roof showed forlornly through the vines. A stand of oaks shaded the house, their heavy canopy of foliage turning the yard into a deep green cave of light and shadow. The fronds of a willow brushed the roof, fingering the jagged edges of glass in the rotting window frames, strumming the kudzu like the strings of a lyre.

Kinsey wondered again how much of the family's stuff was still in there. He knew kids had broken in over the years, daring each other, showing off. Terry, Steve, and R.J. had been in years ago, though Ghost would not even go as far as the porch.

So most of the things in the front room would be long spirited away. But not many kids would have gotten past the gouged and bloodied doorway to the hall, and Kinsey doubted that any would have made it farther than the first bedroom, where the little boy had died. The back rooms would be dusty but intact. He wondered what Trevor would find in them.

Kinsey measured coffee, poured cold tapwater into the machine, and, as the old percolator began to bubble and steam, fell to gazing out his kitchen window at his own backyard. He had a little vegetable garden, but otherwise the grasses and trees grew wild. Kinsey liked it that way, home to any flying, slithering, or crawling thing that cared to take up residence. But it was not as snarled and shadow-stained, not as forbidding a landscape as the house on Violin Road.

The house where Trevor must be now, even as Kinsey sipped his first milky cup of morning coffee.

Kinsey's mother had cured him of Christian prayer long ago. He tried to think of a Zen koan that might be of use to Trevor, but the only one he could remember was "Why has Bodhidharma no beard?" which didn't seem to apply. But then koans weren't supposed to apply.

His head full of ghosts, little smirking Buddhas, and secondhand treasures, Kinsey stood woolgathering for the better part of an hour in his own clean comforting kitchen.

* * *

Hank Williams's nasal twang poured out of the car speakers as raw and potent as moonshine spiked with honey. Zach pondered it as he drove. It should not have been a remarkable voice; it was nothing but a po'bucker whine straight from the backwoods of Alabama. But there was something golden and tragic in it, some lost soul that fell to its knees and sobbed every time Hank opened his mouth.

He'd been meandering north on I-40 and surrounding roads when he saw the turnoff for Highway 42. Zach loved the *Hitchhiker's Guide to the Galaxy* series, and the sign reminded him that the number forty-two was the answer to life, the universe, and everything. It pulled him as inexorably as the lights of South of the Border had done. Soon he was driving down a two-lane blacktop shrouded in rags and tatters of predawn mist, and several times he caught himself singing lustily along with Hank.

The little town only caught his attention because of its curious name and weird architecture; to his road-weary eyes it seemed that the entire downtown was decorated with wagon wheels and spinning barbers' poles. He almost drove on through, but caught himself drifting across the center line and decided to stop for a quick nap.

Zach pulled into an alley and came upon a small lot where several other cars were already parked. The friendly local deputy-dawg wouldn't bother him here; at any rate he was only going to stretch his tired bones across the seat, close his eyes for a few minutes, then get moving again . . .

He slept for six hours in the parking lot behind the Whirling Disc record store. The lot was also used for storage by an adjacent auto parts store, and the Mustang was not noticed among the other junkers for some time. When he finally woke, the sun had risen high and hot, his body was bathed in sweat, and Terry Buckett was peering into the car, tapping worriedly on the window.

* * *

"Man! I thought you were dead for sure!" Terry took a hit off Zach's pipe and passed it back, shaking his head, letting the fragrant smoke leak out the corners of his mouth. "You looked like somebody had shot you and left you lyin' there across the seat. All that was missing was the brains on the window."

Zach suppressed a shudder. He didn't think the FBI would shoot a hacker on sight, but he wasn't sure about the Secret Service. (The NSA probably kept hackers alive for torture and interrogation later, but their jurisdiction was largely military, and military secrets had never much appealed to him.)

They were sitting on crates in the dim, cool back room of the record store, and though Zach felt an undeniable echo of Leaf and Pass Christian, Terry was obviously as straight as the day was hot. There was no definable characteristic that told him this; the pheromones just weren't there. It was a good thing too, Zach thought; after stewing in his own juices all morning he was sure he stank abominably.

As if to confirm this, a girl with long brown hair stuck her head through the curtain, blinked big Cleopatra eyes against the gloom, and wrinkled her nose. "Terry?"

"Back here, Vic." The girl picked her way through the boxes and rolled-up posters, long gauzy skirt swishing around her ankles. When she got closer, Zach saw that she was wearing a skintight tank top, as if to accentuate the fact that she had absolutely no breasts. Eddy had had a phrase for strippers built like that: *Nipples on a rib.*

The girl leaned down to Terry. Zach thought they were going to kiss, but instead Terry blew into her mouth a long stream of smoke, which she sucked in expertly. Tendrils of it seeped from her narrow nostrils and curled around her head. Terry cupped the back of her thigh through the full skirt. "This is my gal Victoria. Vic, meet Zach. He just rolled into town this morning."

"Looks like we gain two for every one we lose." At Terry's questioning look, she added, "You told me about that guy who came in Saturday. Now him."

"Yeah, so who'd we lose?"

"Omigod, you don't know!" Victoria clapped her hands over her mouth. Zach wasn't sure, but it looked as if she might be hiding a sudden, guilty smirk. "That girl Rima? The one Kinsey fired for stealing from the Yew? She had a wreck out on the highway. Totaled her car and broke her back. They found cocaine all over the place."

"Gee, Vic, you sound pretty upset about it."

"Yeah, right." From the sudden chill in the air Zach guessed that Rima had come on to Terry at some point, though if she was such a loser he doubted Terry had slept with her. Terry seemed like that rarest of all creatures, a genuinely guileless Decent Guy. Besides, you probably couldn't get away with much in a little town like this.

"Well . . ." A shadow passed over Terry's face. He obviously felt bad about the girl, but didn't want to hurt Victoria's feelings. "She didn't kill anyone else?"

Victoria shook her head, and Terry brightened a little. Zach believed this was known as Looking on the Bright Side, also as Pulling the Wool Over Your Own Eyes. He didn't say anything, though; the last thing he needed now was to annoy anyone.

So he loaded another bowl and sat around the back of the store with them for a while longer, listening to gossip about people he didn't know, occasionally asking a question or offering a comment, hacking the scene, making the connections, weaving himself into the net. It was possible anywhere, though it could be a damn sight tougher than breaking into a computer.

When Terry's morning crew (one sleepy-looking teenager with a tattoo so fresh it was still bleeding) showed up, Terry and Victoria took Zach down the street for greasy grilled cheese sandwiches at the local diner. The waitress refilled Zach's water glass with tea, and when he took a sip of it without noticing, his nerves began to crackle and fizz like a string of firecrackers. For all of that, he felt good. He liked this town.

After lunch Victoria had to go to work—she sorted and mended old clothes at some downtown thrift shop—and

Terry offered to show Zach the local dive before he went back to the record store. By the time they were halfway down the street, Zach was eagerly picturing the inside of a bar. It would be calm and dark and air-conditioned, like a little pocket of nighttime in the middle of the hot afternoon. It would be comforting with the sharp scents of liquor and the grainy smell of beer on tap, lit by the soft watery glow of a Budweiser clock or a neon Dixie sign. He might have been picturing any of a hundred bars in the French Quarter, but the Sacred Yew was like none of them, and Zach had yet to learn how difficult it was to find Dixie beer anywhere but New Orleans.

Trevor woke at the drawing table with cramped muscles, an aching head, and a painfully full bladder. The green-tinted sunlight streaming through the studio windows made him wince and rub his eyes as he had seen Bobby do in the grip of countless bourbon hangovers. But he hadn't had the dream of not-drawing last night.

He stood up without looking at the pages he had drawn, stumbled out of the room, back through the hall and living room, out onto the vine-shrouded porch where he stood urinating into the kudzu, squinting out at the empty road.

The day glistened in emerald splendor, grass stems and spiderwebs still bejeweled with yesterday's rain, inviting Trevor to come out and enjoy the sun awhile. Instead he stood for a few minutes in the shelter of the porch, breathing deeply of air that did not smell like mildew or dry rot. From the quality of the light he thought it was early afternoon.

This time twenty years ago, Momma's friends from the art class had been coming up these steps, knocking worriedly on the door, then letting themselves into the house and finding him among the bodies. The man with the gentle hands had been picking him up, carrying him out of the carnage. For an instant Trevor almost remembered what he had been thinking at that moment: something about the Devil. But it eluded him.

Soon he turned and went back into the soft gloom of the house. Without giving himself time to think about it he crossed the living room, walked a few paces down the hall, and let himself into Didi's room.

It looked smaller than he remembered, but that might have been due to the kudzu vines that had burst through the window and taken over more than half the room. They twined up the walls, around the light fixture on the ceiling. They trailed into the closet on Trevor's left, where he could still see a few of Didi's toys mired in the leaves, as if the kudzu had actually twined around them and lifted them off the floor. A smiling plush octopus, a windup grandfather clock, a once-red rubber ball. All were covered in dust, faded with time and neglect. Twenty years never touched by a little boy's hands, a little boy's love.

The kudzu filled the left half of the room with rustling heart-shaped leaves and shifting green shadows. The mattress sat in a clear spot to the right. Instead of a tiny body it bore only a huge, irregular bloodstain, dark crimson and wet-looking in the center, fading to the most delicate pale brown around the edges. Trevor noticed splotches and runners of blood on the wall above the mattress too, five or six feet up. How many blood vessels were in the brain? And how far could they spray when the head was crushed like a juicy grape, made to spill out the red secrets of its wine, the electric potion of its cerebral fluid, the very chemistry of its thoughts and dreams?

It's a glorious summer day, some remotely, annoyingly sane voice in his head nagged him, *and here you are buried in this tomb of a house staring at the twenty-year-old deathstain of a brother you barely had time to know.*

And another part of him answered, *We get to the places where we need to be.*

He pulled the Whirling Disc T-shirt over his head, let it fall to the floor, and stretched out on Didi's mattress. Stale dust puffed up from the ticking as he centered his head on the bloodstain. It was stiff and dry against his cheek, and smelled only of age, with perhaps a faint sour undertone like the memory of spoiled meat. He nuzzled his face into the stain, spread his arms wide as if to embrace it.

From somewhere in the room came a faint *popping* sound, then the noise of something heavy hitting the floor. Trevor jerked reflexively but did not look around. He wasn't sure he wanted to see what new surprise the house had dealt him. Not yet. *Can't you even give me a minute with Didi?* he thought. *Can't I even have that before I have to start thinking about you again?*

But by now he knew he wasn't calling the shots, not many of them anyway. He had come here to learn, and whatever was here would teach him . . . something. He pushed himself up on his elbows and turned to look into the corner of the room from which the sound had come, over by the closet. A small dark object lay near the edge of the kudzu, as if it had tumbled out of the vines. The object was perhaps a foot long, half-shrouded in shadow. Trevor tried to tell himself it could be anything. A stick. A stray piece of wood.

A hammer.

He got up and crossed the room, stared at it for a long moment, then leaned down and picked it up. The stout wooden handle was scuffed and streaked with dark stains. It felt slightly warm in his hand. The head and claw were rusted, caked with a delicate, crumbling dry brown matter like powdery fungus, like desiccated petals. He touched his finger to it, rubbed it against his thumb. The scrim of matter between them felt dusty, gritty. Pale brown, like the edges of the bloodstain. He remembered reading somewhere that any human tissue would turn to some shade of brown eventually, given time. It was the color of all skin, the color of waste, the color of rot.

Cause of death: blunt trauma . . .

Trevor had no idea what had happened to the hammer that had killed his family, but he knew it could not have stayed in the house. It would have been taken as evidence, photographed, probably even fitted into the holes in their skulls to prove it was indeed the murder weapon. That was how they did things. Yet he knew too, just as surely, that this was the same hammer.

He stood for a long time turning it over and over in his hands. He felt a few slow tears leaking from his eyes, running into his mouth or dripping off his chin. But he had done most of his crying last night, with Kinsey. Now he was beginning to feel as if he were being taunted. *Here's a hammer; what can you do with it?*

He didn't know yet.

But when a noise came from the living room—no scrape or creak of the house, he was already starting to get used to those, but a distinct footfall—he whirled and raised the hammer before he knew what he was doing.

And when he heard a stranger's voice, Trevor moved swiftly and silently toward the door.

"Shit! I better get back to the store before it pours. Tell Zach I'll see him later if he decides to hang out."

Terry tipped a quick salute at Kinsey, who was on his knees ripping several weeks' worth of silver duct tape off the stage, and took his leave of the Sacred Yew. A few minutes later Zach came out of the rest room, his face and hands freshly scrubbed, his dark eyelashes still beaded with water, settling his glasses on the narrow bridge of his nose. "It's raining," he told Kinsey.

"I heard. How could you tell?"

"The ceiling's leaking. I put the trash can under it."

Kinsey sighed, pushed his feathered hat back over his stringy hair, and kept tugging at the duct tape.

"Did Terry leave? I was going to ask him if he knew a place I could crash."

"He'll let you have his spare bedroom if R.J. isn't camped there. You can sleep on my couch, too, if you'll do me a favor. I was going to do it myself, but I need to stay here and make sure the place doesn't flood. The landlord won't fix our pipes and sometimes a heavy rain just comes right in."

Zach had an open Natty Boho in his hand—he'd grabbed it

out of the cooler and slapped two dollars on the counter before Kinsey could card him—and looked in no great hurry to
go anywhere, but he agreed readily enough. "Sure, I'll do you
a favor."

"There's a young man living in an abandoned house out on
the other side of town." Kinsey explained briefly about
Trevor, giving none of the details of why he was in the house.
"He has no electricity or running water. I brought in a few
things for him—blankets, bottled water, some food. Think
you could take it out to him?"

Zach looked dubious. "Okay."

"He doesn't bite."

"Oh, well then forget it." Zach saw Kinsey's blank look.
"Sorry. What's he doing in this abandoned house?"

"I'll let him tell you himself, if he wants to. You'll like
Trevor. He's lived in New York—the two of you can compare
notes on that pestilent hellhole."

Zach followed Kinsey behind the bar to get the box of supplies. Kinsey noticed that Zach's hands were restless, nervous, their slender spatulate fingers always manipulating
something: skating over the keypad of the adding machine,
toying with the phone. Once he reached for the keys of the
cash register, but drew back as if realizing that would be im-
polite. The boy seemed to have a fascination for switches and
buttons. He refrained from actually pushing them, but
stroked and tapped them gently as if wishing he could.

Kinsey gave him directions to the house and let him out the
back door. Zach could hardly miss the place; there were several run-down houses on Violin Road, but only one that was
barely even there. Kinsey went back into the club. Now a thin
trickle of water was seeping from under the door of the men's
room. If the rain kept up, he could spend the whole afternoon
mopping and wringing, mopping and wringing. Damn the
landlord.

He wasn't sure he had done right by sending Zach out to
Violin Road, but it felt right somehow. He hated the thought
of Trevor staying out there another night without food or

water. Someone should at least make sure he hadn't fallen through a rotten floor and broken his neck.

Zach was an all right sort, if a little shifty. Kinsey didn't think he was really from New York, or anywhere near it. There was a type of New York accent that sounded something like his voice, true. But Kinsey had heard a distinctive one from New Orleans—a weird blend of Italian, Cajun, and deep-South—that sounded a lot closer. And Zach had perked up visibly when Terry mentioned that the name of his band was Gumbo.

But if he wanted to be from New York, then he was from New York as far as anyone around here was concerned. Kinsey only asked questions when he could tell a kid wanted him to. Right now Zach, no last name offered, looked like he wanted to stay as far away from questions as possible.

Zach swerved to avoid the swollen carcass of a possum in the road, slowed, and turned into a likely-looking driveway. It was barely more than a rutted track losing a battle to tall grasses and wildflowers; the house itself was so overgrown that it was invisible from the road unless you were looking for it. Zach thought it looked like a wonderful place to live.

He finished his beer, got out of the car, and pulled the box of supplies out after him. Kinsey had put a six-pack of Coke in with the bottled water, blankets, and various packaged food. There was even a pillow in a flowered case at the bottom of the box. Whoever this Trevor Black was, Kinsey had done him up right.

The rain had slacked off some, but it was still drizzling drearily, beading on his glasses, making his hair straggle into his face. The day had taken on a cool, slightly eerie cast. Zach hoisted the box and lugged it up the steps to the vine-draped porch.

The front door hung askew on its hinges, half open. Zach knocked, waited, knocked again. No response. He squinted into the damp gloom of the house, then shrugged and let himself in.

For a moment he stood in the center of the living room letting his eyes adjust to the absence of light. Gradually details resolved themselves and he saw the holes in the ceiling, the vines twisting in the windows, the rotting hulks of furniture. A tendril of unease touched him. He cleared his throat. "Hello?"

Nothing. The doorway to the hall was a black rectangle, the wall around it smeared with indistinct dark stains. Zach stared at it, feeling worse. What had that old hippie sent him into?

He would just put the box down here on the floor and turn around and go. Nothing to it. He lowered it halfway, his eyes never leaving the hall door.

When a tall pale form appeared in the doorway, Zach stifled a scream and dropped the box. It hit the floor and tipped over on its side. A can of Chef Boyardee ravioli rolled across the floor, disappeared under the couch. Absurdly, Zach wondered if Kinsey had remembered a can opener.

The pale form came out of the darkness toward him. A shirtless, skinny, ridiculously beautiful boy, long blond hair spilling over his shoulders and dirt-smudged chest, eyes wide and blazing and utterly mad, a rusty claw hammer clutched in his upraised hand. He looked like some malevolent avenging angel, like a pissed-off Christ come down off the cross ready to pound in some nails of his own.

Zach stood paralyzed as the hammer-wielding angel, presumably Trevor, descended on him. He could not seem to make himself speak. He did not want to die like a character in a splatter movie, did not want to die quick and stupid or slow and mean, with a chunk of metal buried in his frontal lobes and syrupy blood gradually obscuring the dumb, startled expression frozen on his face for all eternity. But even less did he love the idea of turning to run and feeling the claw end of the hammer take a divot out of his skull.

His heart caromed crazily off the walls of his chest. A wire-thin pain shot down his left arm. Maybe he would just have a heart attack and avoid the whole thing.

Trevor's other hand snaked out, wrapped long fingers

round Zach's wrist. His touch was galvanizing, akin to an electric shock or a whole pot of coffee. Zach thought his nerves might just rip out of his skin and go twining up Trevor's arm like the stinging tentacles of jellyfish.

But his synapses refused to save him. *Think,* his mind yammered, *flex your brain and THINK because if you don't it's going to end up splattered all over this dirty floor, and is that any fate for this rare and superior organ that has served you so well for nineteen years? Wanna go for twenty? Then HACK THIS SYSTEM, DØØD! What's the first thing you need? THE PASSWORD!*

"TREVOR!" he hollered. "NO!!!"

He had made his voice as loud and sharp as he could. He saw Trevor hesitate, but his grip on Zach's wrist didn't loosen, and the hammer stayed upraised, ready to fall.

But passwords always required more than one try. *"Trevor!"* he shouted again, letting an extra edge of fear and deference creep into his voice. *"Kinsey sent me! Please don't kill me! Please!"*

Zach felt a tiny bright pain deep in his head, wondered if that was the spot where the hammer would go in or if he had just managed to have an aneurism instead of a heart attack. It seemed the body always had some time bomb lurking in its depths.

But some of the madness appeared to melt off Trevor. His eyes met Zach's, really *saw* Zach, and a glassy film cleared from them. The black-rimmed irises were the palest, most delicate ice-blue; moments ago they had been muddy with killing rage. Now Trevor looked horrified, and years younger. He let go of Zach's wrist. His shoulders sagged. He tried to swallow but could not seem to work up the spit; the curve of his throat worked convulsively. The skin there was creased with sweat and grime, as if he had not shaved or bathed in days.

Okay. You found a crack in the system; that doesn't necessarily mean you're in. Verify yourself. Reassure the system that you belong here.

"Trevor? I . . . didn't mean to scare you. My name's Zach

and I'm new in town too and . . . uh, Kinsey from the club sent me out to bring you this stuff."

The quicksilver eyes flickered; then Trevor's lips moved. His voice was deeper than Zach had expected, and very quiet. "You must think I'm crazy."

"Well—" said Zach, and stopped. Trevor tilted his head. "Well, it would help if you put the hammer down."

Trevor stared at the grisly tool in his hand as if he had no idea how it had gotten there. Then, very slowly, he bent and placed the hammer on the floor. "I'm sorry," he muttered. "I'm really, really sorry."

Bingo! In with full user privileges! Bells and whistles should have been going off in Zach's head. But he didn't feel as triumphant as he usually did when he cracked a system. He was starting to remember that Trevor was more than a system; he was a person, and people were volatile things, and that hammer was still within easy reach.

And on top of all that, the stricken look on Trevor's face and the jagged catch in his voice were so genuine that Zach actually felt a little sorry for him. He was a beautiful boy with fierce intelligence behind the craziness flickering in his eyes. Zach wondered what had brought him to this place, to this extremity.

"You're the only person who ever tried to kill me that apologized for it afterward," he said. "So I guess I accept."

A trace of a smile might have crossed Trevor's face. It was gone before Zach could be sure. "How many other people have tried to kill you?"

"Two."

"Who were they?"

"My parents."

Trevor's eyes went very wide, paler still. Then suddenly they shimmered with tears. A couple spilled over the rims of his eyelids before he could stop them, great fat crystal drops of pain.

Once in a while you happen purely at random upon the right

*password in a million, the unguessable code sequence, the needle in
a program's haystack. Once in a while, you just get lucky.*
"I can explain everything," said Trevor.

The thought of what he had nearly done made Trevor feel
light-headed. The house spun around him; the floor threatened to tilt, to yawn wide open beneath his feet.

He couldn't remember what he had been thinking as he
grabbed Zach's wrist. He wasn't sure he *had* been thinking;
his mind had felt as empty as the rooms of the house, and
that scared him worse than anything.

"I can explain everything," he said, though he doubted he
really could, and doubted even more that Zach would want
to hear it.

But Zach just shrugged. "Sure, if you want to talk about it.
I'm not hurt. It's no big deal."

Trevor looked at him. Zach was trying to smile, but his face
was terribly pale in the gloom, and his eyes still showed too
much white. Even his hands were shaking. Trevor wondered
what kind of threat Zach *would* consider a big deal.

"I want to talk about it," he said. "Let's go outside."

They walked around to the side yard and sat beneath the
glistening canopy of the willow. The leaves back here were so
thick that the ground was almost dry, though a shimmer of
droplets fell on them from time to time. Trevor was still shirtless, and the water beaded on his shoulders, made trickling
paths through the dirt on his chest and back.

Zach seemed to be watching him closely, waiting to hear
what he had to say. In the daylight Trevor saw that his eyes
were a startling shade of green, large and slightly tilted. His
face was fine-boned, sharp-featured, interestingly shadowed
by his wild spiky hair and the round black frames of his
glasses. Trevor realized who Zach resembled: his drawing of
Walter Brown, the singer who'd been arrested with Bird in
Jackson, Mississippi. The singer whose face Trevor had had to
imagine because he'd never seen the man's picture. The like-
ness wasn't exact, but it was strong enough to put him more

at ease with Zach. This was a face he knew, a face that pleased his eye.

Trevor began to talk. The words came slowly at first, but soon he could not stop. Never in his life had he talked for so long at one time. He told Zach everything: the deaths, the orphanage, the dreams, the things that had happened since he'd been back in the house. He even talked about the time he had cracked that kid's skull open in the shower, though he didn't mention how much he had liked it.

He was surprised at how good talking felt. Not since he stopped letting blood from his arm with a razor blade had he felt such a welcome sense of release, of poison draining from his system.

He wasn't sure why those two words Zach had spoken— *my parents*—had opened him like this. Certainly there had been other kids at the Home who had taken plenty of abuse from their parents, and probably would have told Trevor about it if he had asked. But those kids had not appeared in the house of his childhood like embodiments of someone he had drawn. Those kids had not stood their ground and talked him out of . . . whatever he had been about to do. He had never gripped those kids' thin wrists hard enough to leave red impressions of his fingers in the flesh.

And if he had, he doubted they would have stayed around to hear his reasons why.

Trevor's face was hidden behind curtains of long hair, and his voice was so low that Zach had to lean in close to hear it. Trevor kept sneaking looks at Zach as if to gauge his reaction, but would not look him full in the face.

Slowly the tale unfolded, beginning with the bloody history that had been branded upon the house before Zach was even born. He would have heard much of this in town soon enough, Trevor said rather bitterly; word was no doubt getting around Missing Mile that the last survivor of the murder family had come home. He said it just like that, *the murder family*, as if he knew that was what they would be called in the local legends that must have unfolded around them. But Trevor's own story got weirder and weirder until hammers were appearing from thin air and drawings were undergoing sinister mutation betwixt hand and page.

Zach kept nodding his encouragement. He was far too fascinated to let Trevor quit. Back in his familiar French Quarter, back in his comforting little corner of cyberspace, Zach thought he had seen strange things, maybe even done some. But he had never met anyone who had lived through experiences like this, anyone who had taken such damage and remained among the walking wounded.

Eventually Trevor's flood of words ran down and he sat staring out through the drifting, glistening fronds of the willow. Through the undergrowth one weathered corner of the house was just visible, paler gray than the threatening afternoon sky. Zach watched a single raindrop making its way down the knobby ridge of Trevor's spine. At last Trevor said, "I don't know why I told you all that. You still must think I'm crazy."

"Maybe," Zach told him, "but I don't hold it against you."

It was obvious no one had ever said such a thing to Trevor before. He didn't know what to make of it. He looked wary, then surprised, and finally tried a tentative smile.

Zach thought Trevor might indeed be quite insane, but was developing a healthy respect for him in spite of it. Terry, Victoria, and Kinsey were fun to hang out with, but if he was going to stay in Missing Mile for any length of time, he wanted Trevor for his first friend.

He'd have to sublimate the attraction, though. He'd done it before, once he realized that he actually liked someone. He didn't think it would be a problem: whereas Terry gave off the wrong kind of pheromones, Trevor didn't seem to give off any. It was as if he had no sexual awareness at all. Zach caught himself wondering how hard it would be to teach him.

He watched the raindrop finish its navigation of Trevor's spine and disappear beneath the waistband of his jeans. There was a dusting of the palest golden hair there, slightly damp, right in the hollow of the back . . .

He bit his lip painfully and realized that Trevor was asking him something. "Huh?"

"I asked what you do."

"Oh." After the raw honesty Trevor had shown him, Zach could not entirely bring himself to lie. "Well, I work with computers." With great relief he watched Trevor's eyes glaze over. It was the look of the willful computer illiterate, complete with the hasty little nod that said *that's enough, that's all I need to know, please don't start talking about bits and bytes and drives and megarams and all that incomprehensible mojo.* Zach had seen that look hundreds of times, welcomed it. It meant he wouldn't have to answer any uncomfortable questions.

He dug into his pocket and found his last prerolled joint, flattened and mauled but more or less intact. "Do you mind?" he asked. Trevor shook his head. Zach produced one of the lighters Leaf had given him and set it afire.

Trevor's nostrils flared as the smoke drifted past his face. "I better not," he said when Zach offered him the joint, though Zach saw his fingers twitch as if wanting to reach for it. "I smoked some pot yesterday and almost passed out. I'm not used to it."

Zach gathered all his considerable nerve. "Want a shotgun?"

"What's that?"

Oh god. How to explain a shotgun without making it sound like the obvious scam it is? I'm not going to take this any further, I'm really not, I LIKE him, dammit, but there's no harm in a little innocent frustration. "It's, uh, where one person breathes in the smoke and then blows it into the other person's mouth. See, my lungs filter the smoke before you get it, so it won't be as strong." *Yeah, right. Heavy science goin' down.*

Trevor hesitated. Zach tried not to slip into social-engineering mode, but he thought he could feel the power radiating in great joyous waves through his brain now. He felt as if he could convince absolutely anybody of absolutely anything.

"C'mon," he said. "Pot's good for you. It relaxes you, clears out your brain."

Trevor eyed the smoldering joint, then shook his head. "No, I better not."

"What?" Zach couldn't hide his surprise. He had known Trevor would say yes as surely as he'd known Leaf would give him those damn lighters. *"Why?"*

Trevor studied Zach's face as intently as anyone ever had, more intently than most of his one-night lovers had done. Zach felt almost uncomfortable under the scrutiny of those striking, serious eyes. "You really want me to do it, don't you?"

Zach shrugged, but he felt Trevor had looked straight through his skull to the whorls of his devious, treacherous brain. "It's more fun getting stoned with somebody, that's all."

Another long searching look. "Okay then. I'll take one." Zach thought Trevor might as well have added, *But don't fuck with me too much, hear?* He realized that his heart was beating more rapidly than ever, that his blood was surging and his head felt like a helium balloon ascending fast into an achingly blue, cloudless sky. No one ever got to him this way; this was the way he liked to make *other* people feel.

He took a deep hit off the joint, held it in for a second, then leaned over and exhaled a long steady stream of smoke into Trevor's open mouth. Their lips barely grazed. Trevor's felt as soft as velvet, as rain. Ribbons of smoke twined from the corners of their mouths, swathed their heads in an amorphous blue-gray veil. Zach kept his eyes open and saw that Trevor had closed his, as if being kissed. His eyelashes were a dark ginger color, the pale parchment of his eyelids shot through with the most delicate lavender tracery of veins. Zach thought of putting his mouth against those eyelids, of feeling the lashes silky against his lips, the secret caged movement of the eyeball beneath his tongue . . .

. . . and he was doing a damn fine job of sublimating his attraction, wasn't he?

He pulled back, shaken. Once he decided he wasn't going

to be turned on by someone, he just *wasn't* anymore. At least
that was how it had always been. He let himself have anyone
he wanted unless he had good reason not to want them, and
his libido had always paid back by giving him complete control.

Until now.

Trevor lay back on the damp grass and put a hand to his
forehead. Zach saw pine needles snarled in his long hair,
fresh dirt under his fingernails, tiny beads of water trapped in
the fine hairs around his nipples.

"So," said Trevor, blowing out his shotgun, "how did your
parents try to kill you?"

"My dad beat the shit out of me for fourteen years. My
mom mostly just used her mouth."

"Why did you stay?"

Zach shrugged. "Nowhere else to go." From the corner of
his eye he saw Trevor nod. "Sure, I could have run away
when I was nine or ten, but there would've been a lifetime of
stiff dicks in Town Cars waiting for me. I waited until I knew
I could take care of myself some way besides giving blowjobs.
Then I ran. Just disappeared into another part of the city.
They never tried to find me."

"What city?"

Zach hesitated. He still didn't want to lie to Trevor, but he
couldn't start giving different stories to different people.

"You don't have to tell me if you don't want to."

"New Orleans," Zach said, not even sure why. "But don't
tell anybody."

"Are you on the run or something?"

Zach's silence spoke volumes.

"It's okay," said Trevor. "I've been running from this place
for seven years. But you know, you get sick of it after a
while."

"Yeah, so you come back and it tries to make you bash
people's brains out."

Trevor shrugged. "I wasn't expecting company."

Zach started laughing. He couldn't help it. This guy was *so
fucked up* . . . but smart, and despite his weird asexuality,

entirely too beautiful. Trevor stared at him for a moment, then tentatively joined in.

They grinned at each other in ganja-swirled camaraderie. Suddenly Zach found himself wondering again if it mightn't be possible after all to love someone and make love with them too. Something about such a spontaneous sweet smile on a face that didn't smile too often made him wonder why he had always denied himself the physical pleasure of a person he truly cared for. Wouldn't it be fun to see someone—all right then, someone like Trevor—smile that way just because Zach knew how to make him feel good? Maybe even more fun than getting sucked off by a cute, all-but-anonymous stranger in the back room of a convenience store in a state he might never see again?

Probably not. Probably it would end in cutting words and tears, pain and blame and regret, maybe even blood. Those were the risks of such a relationship, almost guaranteed.

But where along the line had he decided that he could not take those particular risks, while cheerfully taking—indeed, *seeking out*—so many others?

Trevor was watching him closely. He looked as if he wanted to say *What are you thinking?* but didn't. Zach was glad. He'd always hated that question; it seemed people only asked it of you when you were thinking about something you didn't want to share.

Instead, very hesitantly, Trevor asked, "Have we met before? Do I know you?" He frowned as if that weren't precisely the question he wanted to ask, but he could not find the words for the right one.

Zach shook his head. "I don't think so. But . . ."

"It feels like we have," Trevor finished for him.

Zach snuffed the half-burnt joint and put it back in his pocket. They sat in silence for a few minutes. Neither wanted to be the first to say too much, to take this strange new notion too far. Zach mused on how irretrievable words were in the real world. In many ways he preferred the simplicity of the computer universe, where you could revise and delete things at will, where you acted and the system could only react in certain ways.

But there you ran up against an eventual wall of predictability. Here the slightest shift in semantics could make a situation run wild, and that appealed to him too.

The rain had nearly stopped. Now it began to come down harder again, though they were still protected beneath the canopy of branches and vines. The sky rumbled with nascent thunder, then erupted. All at once it was pouring.

Zach saw a chance to defuse the awkwardness. He caught Trevor's arm and pulled him up, noticing how Trevor's flesh seemed to simultaneously cleave to and cringe from his touch. "Come on!" he urged.

"Where?"

"Don't you want a shower? This is our chance!"

"Out here?"

"Sure, why not? Nobody can see us from the road." Zach ducked out from under the curtain of willow fronds and ran to a clear patch in the yard. He kicked his sneakers off, pulled his shirt over his head, stuck his glasses in his pocket, and started unbuttoning his pants. Trevor followed, looking doubtful. "Are you going to get naked?"

Zach undid the last button and let his cutoffs fall. He wasn't wearing any underwear. Trevor raised his eyebrows, then shrugged, unbuckled his jeans, and pushed them down over his skinny hips. If he'd grown up in an orphanage, male nudity was probably no big deal to him.

The rain sluiced over their bodies, washing away the grime of the road and the old crumbling house. Trevor was only a wet blur several feet away; Zach could barely see him flinging his arms about as if dancing or performing some wild invocation.

Zach raised his face to the downpour and let it fill the tired hollows of his eyes, wash the taste of smoke from his lips. He was not aware that he was grinning like a fool until he felt rain trickling between his teeth, over his tongue, and down his throat in a little silver river.

ELEVEN

Kinsey was mopping up the last of the water as the early evening barflies began to drift in. Terry was closing up shop at the Whirling Disc and wishing Steve Finn were in town. The new guy had fucked up an invoice and ordered twenty copies of *Louie's Limbo Lounge,* an obscure album of exquisitely bad strip-club music, instead of the two Terry had meant to special-order. Now they could hear such classics as "Torture Rock," "Beaver Shot," and the amazing "Hooty Sapperticker" by Barbara & the Boys whenever they so desired.

Terry started to call Poindexter's in Durham to see if they wanted any, but decided *fuck it* and went instead to buy his girl a beer. A gaudy sunset bathed the downtown in red and purple light, and the slowly darkening streets glistened with the rain that had fallen all afternoon.

One by one the streetlights flickered on. Terry remembered a summer two or three years ago when there had been a plague of Luna moths. The huge insects beat against windows and swarmed around streetlights, their broad fragile wings catching the light and making it shift strangely, their color like nothing else in nature—the palest silver-green, the color of ectoplasm or the glow of radiation. You could find drifts of them tattered and dead in the gutter, their fat furred bodies shriveled to husks.

Soon a flock of bats descended upon the town, roosting in the treetops and church bell towers by day, swooping out at night to catch the Luna moths in their tiny razored jaws. If the show at the Sacred Yew was boring, the kids would congregate on the street and watch the shadowplay of leathery and iridescent wings, strain to hear the high needling squeal of the bats over the churn of guitars and percussion from the club. One night Ghost had mused aloud that to the bats, the moths' blood must taste like crème de Menthe.

Terry wondered what had become of the new kids. He thought Zach might have just hit the other side of town and kept driving; that boy looked like he might have someplace to be in a hurry. And he guessed Trevor was still out at the murder house. Hell of a thing, Bobby McGee's son coming back after all these years.

Well, Kinsey would know the lowdown. Terry hastened his step toward the Yew, toward friends and music and the taste of a cold beer in his favorite bar on a summer's evening.

By ten o'clock Terry had had five cold beers and had forgotten all about Zach. But Zach had not hit the other side of town, had not even returned to his car except to check the locks and pull it around to the side of the house. He had found a place he liked, and he had every intention of setting up camp here for a few days unless Trevor objected. But he didn't think Trevor would.

When they came in from the rainstorm, Trevor excused himself to put on dry clothes and disappeared down the hall. Zach followed a few minutes later and found him sprawled on a bare mattress in one of the back bedrooms. Naked and almost painfully thin, long hair spread out around his head like a corona, he was already deeply asleep.

Zach watched him for several moments but could not disturb him. Trevor had spent the last three nights sleeping on a Greyhound bus, a couch, and a drawing table; he deserved some bed rest. Zach got one of Kinsey's blankets and covered him. As he did so he saw gooseflesh shivering across Trevor's chest, water droplets still caught in the cup of his navel and the damp tangle of his pubic hair. He imagined the salty taste those droplets would have if he were to bend down and lick them away.

Now you want to molest him in his sleep. It was Eddy's voice, out of nowhere. *Christ, Zach, why don't you just buy a blow-up love doll on Bourbon Street and be done with it?*

Fuck you, Eddy.

As he turned away from the bed he noticed drawings tacked to the walls. Monsters and fanciful houses, unfamiliar landscapes. And faces, all kinds of faces. A child's drawings —but a child with obvious talent, with an eye for line and proportion, with an untrammeled imagination. This was Trevor's own room.

Zach left Trevor to sleep and started exploring the house. At the end of the hall was the bathroom where Bobby had died. There was no window in this room, and Zach did not think to try the switch. He stood on the threshold staring into the unlit chamber, saw porcelain gleaming dully beneath layers of dirt and cobweb. The shower curtain rod was bent, almost buckled. Zach wondered if Trevor had seen that yet.

Something about the bathroom's geometry seemed wrong, as if the angle at which walls met ceiling were slightly skewed. It made Zach feel dizzy, almost nauseated. He turned away and went into the room across the hall, which was the studio. He saw Trevor's sketchbook lying open on the drawing table and slowly flipped through the pages. The drawings were very good. Zach had read one issue of *Birdland*, and he thought Trevor's style was already technically better than Bobby's. The lines were surer, the faces finer and more subtle, with layer upon layer of nuance lurking in the expressions he captured.

But Bobby's work had always had a certain fractured warmth to it. No matter how sordid and vile his characters were—the junkies and glib beatniks and talking saxophones who got laid more often than their human counterparts—you always felt they were pawns in an indifferent universe, butts of an existential joke with no punch line. Trevor's work was harsher, icier. His universe was not indifferent but cruel. He knew his punch line: the crumpled, bleeding woman in the doorway, the broken bodies of the musicians, the burning cops.

And others, as Zach paged back through the book. So many others. So many beautifully drawn dead bodies.

He checked out the master bedroom and its walk-in closet, saw little of interest—the parents hadn't brought much of their own stuff, probably; after fitting Bobby's art supplies and the kids' things in the car there wouldn't have been much space left.

He crossed the hall to Didi's room, stopped dead on the threshold and stared at the huge dark mass boiling through the window, then realized it was kudzu. Zach wondered how long it would be before the vines filled the room from floor to ceiling. He took in the bloodstain on the mattress, the spatters high on the wall. Trevor said the hammer had appeared in the opposite corner, next to the small closet. Zach looked at the area, even prodded the kudzu with the toe of his sneaker, but found nothing unusual.

He had heard of objects instantaneously being transported from one place to another; they were called "apports" and were supposed to be warm to the touch, as Trevor said the hammer had been. Zach wasn't sure he believed in apports, but he couldn't think of another way it might have gotten there. If it was the same hammer.

But if it wasn't, where had the dried blood and tissue come from? Zach didn't even want to wonder. It had to be the same one; that made more sense than thinking Trevor had bought another one and smeared it with sheep brains or something. Zach was not an implicit believer in the supernatural, but he didn't believe in scaring up improbable natural explanations just to rule it out, either. Nature was a complex system; there had to be more to it than anyone could understand from looking at the surface.

The kitchen was large and old-fashioned, with a freestanding sink and a gas range. A real farmhouse kitchen, or so Zach imagined. He opened the refrigerator and was surprised to see the light come on. He hadn't tested the electricity, he realized; he had forgotten about it until now.

In the fridge was a juice bottle with a half inch of black

sludge at the bottom, some kind of vegetable matter mummi-fied beyond recognition, and a Tupperware container whose contents he dared not contemplate: he'd heard Tupperware coffins could preserve human remains for twenty years or more, so who knew what they could do to leftovers? Zach retrieved the Cokes and bottled water from the living room and arranged them on the shelf next to the juice.

He checked Trevor again, found him still sleeping. Zach began to get bored. He picked his way across the living room, went out to his car, and got the bag that held his laptop computer and cellular phone. He thought he might be staying here for a few days, and he wanted to give Eddy a more specific message than the one he had left last night. If he dialed in now, he thought he could just make the deadline.

Zach accessed the *Times-Picayune*'s computer, typed rapidly for several minutes, then pressed the keys to send his article. After he had done that, he was still restless. He found a square of yellow Post-it notes in his bag, scribbled down a few phone codes, and stuck them on the edge of the table. They were numbers he might need in a hurry, and he didn't think Trevor would mind.

Then, just for the hell of it, he dialed into Mutanet. He didn't log in with his own password, of course, since They might be monitoring the board. But Zach had long since ac-quired full systems-operator privileges on Mutanet, though he had discreetly neglected to mention this fact to the sysop. The sysop fancied himself a Discordian, or worshiper of the chaotic goddess Eris, and his password was POEE5.

First Zach read the messages on the main board, scanning them for his handle.

```
MESSAGE: 65
FROM: KØDEz KID
TO: ALL MUTANTS
''Lucio''    got    busted    today!!
Hahahahahahaa!!!!!
```

```
MESSAGE: 73
FROM: ZOMBI
TO: KØDEz KID
If you had a googolth of Lucio's hack-
ing skill you would not take such sick
joy in his misfortune. You're wrong,
Kidd□-somebody warned him Sat. nite
and he's long gone.


MESSAGE: 76
FROM: AKKER
TO: MUTOIDS
Zombi's right! I, Akker the H-akker,
founder of the Data Acquisition and
Retrieval Team (DART), cracked the Se-
cret Service's system and found the
warrant to search Lucio's house. It
was I who warned him in time!! Power to
DART!!! :-)


MESSAGE: 80
FROM: ST. GULIK, YR. HUMBLE SYSOP
TO: ANYONE READING THIS
Lucio can't get on this board anymore.
I disabled his account. If he tries to
contact you, don't talk to him. For all
we know he could have gotten busted and
turned informant. Anyone known to
still have contact with him will be
kicked off Mutanet! A paranoid hacker
is a free hacker!
```

That caught Zach's interest, so he checked the sysop's personal mail. There was only one message.

```
FROM: ZOMBI
TO: ST. BOGUS
FUCK YOUR FASCIST BOARD, DØØD! YOU'D
BE THE FIRST TO TURN RAT IF A KKKOMPUTER
KKKOP NAILED YOUR WHITE ASS!!! YOUR
ADDRESS IS 622 FRAZIER ST. IN METAIRIE
AND IF YOU KEEP TELLING kidZ WHO NOT TO
TALK TO, I WILL FIRST POST IT ON BOARDS
ALL OVER THE COUNTRY, THEN COME OVER
THERE AND PERSONALLY INTRODUCE YOUR
TEETH TO SOME OF THAT CHAOS YOU'RE SUP-
POSED TO WORSHIP (BUT DON'T SEEM TO)!
AND BY THE WAY, AKKER DIDN'T WARN LUCIO
. . . I DID!!!
```

Zach nearly fell off his chair laughing. He'd known he could count on Zombi. He left two messages, the first on the main board where everyone could read it, the second personal.

```
FROM: LUCIO
TO: ST. PARANOID
Pleez don't kick me off the board,
Br'er   Sysop!    Pleez!    Pleez!!
Pleeeeeez!!!
```

```
FROM: LUCIO
TO: ZOMBI
A googol times, thanks.
```

Then Zach logged off Mutanet, maybe for the last time.

After turning the computer off, he felt disoriented. He was used to spending hours each day in front of the screen. Those few minutes had only whetted his appetite, had made his fingers tingle but hadn't given them the supersensitized buzz he got from a marathon session of pounding the keys. But he didn't need money yet, and he wanted to lie low for a few days.

He noticed Trevor's backpack sitting on the kitchen counter. The zipper was half open, and Zach could see the corner of a comic book poking out. He glanced toward the door, then went over to the bag, cautiously tugged the zipper all the way down, and began to nose through the contents.

To Zach this was no different from examining Trevor's credit rating or police record, either of which he would have done guiltlessly and without hesitation if he had reason to. But he didn't care about those things. He wanted to know what Trevor carried around with him, what he kept close to him.

Here were all three issues of *Birdland*, battered copies in plastic bags. No surprises there. A Walkman and some tapes . . . Charlie Parker, Charlie Parker, and, just for good measure, Charlie Parker . . . a black T-shirt, a pair of underwear, a toothbrush and other assorted toiletries. Pretty boring. Zach dug deeper, and his fingers touched worn paper. An envelope.

He pulled it out, unfolded the contents carefully. The three sheets of paper were taped and retaped at every crease, wrinkled to the texture of fine silk. Much of the text was indecipherable, but from what Zach could make out, he suspected Trevor had it memorized.

Multiple defensive wounds . . . A blow to the chest penetrated the breastbone and ruptured the heart, and could in and of itself have been fatal . . .

Due to gross trauma, victim's brain could not be removed in one piece . . .

Robert F. McGee . . . Occupation: Artist . . .

Each report was signed by the county coroner and dated June 16, 1972. Yesterday had been the twentieth anniversary of the McGees' deaths; tomorrow would be the twentieth anniversary of their autopsies.

Zach imagined the three naked bodies lined up on steel tables whose blood gutters were black with clotted gore. He could picture them much more clearly than he wanted to, their skin shockingly livid, their wounds black and purple, their torsos crisscrossed with Y-shaped autopsy scars that bisected each pectoral muscle and went all the way down to the pubic bone. The woman's breasts hanging slack and darkly veined like fruit gone rotten on the tree, her long hair stiff with blood. The little boy's head tilted at an awkward angle because the back of his skull was gone, his soft pink lips sealed with a crust of dried blood, his fingers permanently curled like a doll's. The man with his eyes squeezed halfway out of their sockets by the pressure of the rope, giving him a goggle-eyed stare that would last until the eyeballs fell into the cranial cavity.

Zach folded the autopsy reports and jammed them back into the envelope. It was as if Trevor had imagined the scene so many times that it was imprinted on these sheets of paper like some sort of psychic snapshot. Zach glanced over his shoulder again, but the doorway was still empty. He wasn't sure if he had been afraid of seeing Trevor, or something worse.

Enough snooping for now. It was making him jumpy. He put the envelope back and found a fat paperback book in the very bottom of the bag. *Thou Shalt Not Kill* was the true tale of a man named John List who had calmly and systematically murdered five members of his family—wife, mother, two sons, and a daughter—and then disappeared for eighteen years. The back cover said they had caught him through the TV show *America's Most Wanted*.

The book fell open in Zach's hands to page 281, where the spine was cracked. List was killing his older son, fifteen-year-old Johnny. He'd struggled with the boy in the kitchen, shot him in the back as he ran down the hall, caught up with him and shot him nine more times as he tried to crawl away from his father toward some imagined safety.

Zach checked out Johnny's school picture in the section of photographs at the center of the book. A skinny, grinning kid with badly cut dark hair and birth-control glasses and ears that stuck out goofily. Looked like a hundred computer geeks Zach had known, not so different from how he had looked at fifteen. This shit could happen to *anybody*.

He sat down at the table and began to read about the Lists.

He didn't usually read this kind of thing, but it was a pretty interesting story. They didn't find List's family until a month later, lined up on sleeping bags in the giant ballroom, their bodies black and swollen.

When it grew too dark to see the page, Zach got up and switched the overhead light on without thinking about it. He read for two hours, until he heard stirring and yawning from the bedroom.

Trevor appeared in the kitchen doorway, his hair rumpled and tangled, knuckling sleep from his eyes. He had put on a pair of baggy black sweatpants but remained shirtless. "Was I out long?"

"Couple hours. I thought you could use it."

"Why are you reading that?"

Zach put the book down. "Why are *you*? I mean, it's none of my business, but it seems a little depressing for someone in your situation."

Trevor pulled out the other chair and sat down at the table. "I always read books like that. I keep hoping one of them will make me understand why the guy did it."

"Any luck?"

"No." Suddenly Trevor looked up, speared him with those eyes. "Anyway, I meant why are you reading that book that was in my bag? I didn't say you could go in my bag."

Zach held up his hands. "Sorry. I just wanted something to read, and you were asleep. I didn't touch anything else."

Great. They'd make a perfect pair: a professional snoop and a privacy freak. Zach guessed now was probably not the best time to tell Trevor how much he had liked the drawings in his sketchbook, and he didn't think he'd better mention the autopsy reports at all.

Trevor still didn't look happy about the matter, but let it drop. He noticed Zach's Post-it notes, peeled one off the table and read it. "What's this?"

"A phone card number."

"What's it for?"

"Making phone calls."

Trevor gave Zach a look, but decided to let this pass too. "Are you hungry?"

"Starved."

They retrieved Kinsey's can of ravioli from under the couch and ate it cold with forks scrounged out of a kitchen drawer. It was awful, but Zach felt better after he had choked it down. He watched Trevor drink two Cokes the way some guys drank beer, putting the stuff away with more regard for quick chemical effect than thirst or taste. He was starting to think he could watch Trevor all night.

"Do you want something else?" he asked, thinking they might go out to the diner.

Trevor looked at him rather sheepishly. "Could I . . ."

Anything, Zach wanted to say, but settled for "What?"

"Could I have some more of that pot?"

Zach laughed and fished the half-burnt joint out of his pocket. It was a bit damp, but fired up fine. "I thought you weren't used to it," he said.

"I'm not. I never really liked it before. But my dad used to smoke a lot back when he was drawing, and I just thought . . ."

"What?" Zach asked gently. "That you could figure out why he stopped?"

Trevor shrugged. "If I really wanted to figure *that* out, I'd start drinking whiskey. Bobby used to say pot made him more creative, and after he went dry, he wouldn't smoke even when Momma tried to make him. It was like he didn't even want to *try* anymore."

"Maybe he just knew it was gone no matter what he did."

"Maybe."

They sat at the table talking and smoking. As Trevor passed him the joint, Zach noticed the tracery of slightly raised white scars on his left forearm. *He had to put some on the outside,* Zach thought, *to match the ones on the inside.* But he didn't yet know Trevor well enough to say that. Instead he talked of New Orleans, the daytime bustle of the French Market, the way the cobblestone streets looked at night under the gas lamps all black and gold, the neon smear of Bourbon Street, the river like a dirty brown vein pulsing through the city.

At last they both began to yawn. Trevor stood up, stretched hugely. Zach watched the loose sweatpants ride low on the ridges of his hipbones, then wondered why he was staring; he'd already seen it all this afternoon. "Do you want to crash here?"

Finally. "That'd be great."

"You can have the big bedroom. There's a mattress and, uh . . ." Trevor stared at the floor. "Nobody died in there or anything."

Zach hadn't expected an invitation to bed down with Trevor, was still trying to convince himself he didn't *want* one. But he couldn't help feeling disappointed as he said good night and left the kitchen.

He untied his sneakers, took off his glasses, and was about to lie down on the sagging double mattress when he realized that his head and back were throbbing in tandem. He'd been running on pure adrenaline for more than twenty-four hours; now the pot and the long drive had finally kicked in to give him the great-granddaddy of all body aches, and he hadn't brought any kind of medicine.

He padded down the hall to Trevor's room, saw that the light was still on, and tapped at the door. "Do you have any aspirin?"

Trevor was sprawled in bed reading the John List book. "Yeah, I think so." He sat up and rummaged in his bag, came up with a single white pill. "Here you go. I think this is my last one."

"Thanks. G'night again." Zach went to the kitchen and drank from the faucet, put the pill in his mouth, and washed it down. A chill ran along his spine as he passed the hall doorway and returned to his room. It was dank and dim, empty except for the mattress and some moldering cardboard boxes in the shadowed recesses of the closet, the window an inky rectangle beaded with rain.

For the first time in hours Zach found himself unnerved by the house. Sitting in the bright kitchen talking with Trevor was one thing. Sleeping by himself in the bedroom of a suicide and a murder victim whose blood still stained the place . . . that was another.

But he wasn't afraid of ghosts, he reminded himself. He lay down on the dusty mattress, pulled one of Kinsey's blankets over him, and closed his eyes.

A few minutes later his heart gave a nauseating lurch and began to race so hard he thought it might just punch right through his breastbone like an angry fist made of muscle and blood. Then his whole chest seized up and he was sure the tortured organ had simply ceased to beat, that in seconds he would realize he was dead.

He felt the house gather itself around him, its rotting boards alive and watchful, its darkness ready to enfold him in velvety arms and claim him for its own.

Trevor turned out the light and lay back on his mattress, listening to the slow creak and drip of the house. He thought that somewhere deep within the hundreds of tiny noises there might be a murmuring voice. He wondered what having Zach here would do to the house's subtle chemistry. He wondered why he had let Zach stay.

It was only for one night, he told himself. Zach was an outsider too, and he would surely want to move on tomorrow.

But that didn't explain the weird sensation they'd had of almost recognizing each other this afternoon. And it didn't explain the tightness Trevor felt behind his eyes when he looked at Zach, or the uneasy warmth deep in his stomach when he thought about Zach now. He was so *smart* . . . and so *strange* . . . and he had the smoothest skin, like matte paper . . .

Probably it was just the pot. Trevor had smoked too much. Stupid to think it could teach him anything of his father; it was only a drug, its effects as subjective as those of sleep or sorrow. Even alcohol was nothing but a drug. In his heart he knew it hadn't made Bobby kill his family any more than the hammer had.

The idea of being drunk still made Trevor feel sick, though. All he could remember was the stinging scent of whiskey that had surrounded Bobby like a cloud as he watched his five-year-old son drink Seconal, then hugged him goodnight for the last time.

Trevor heard a floorboard creak in the hall, then a closer sound. The door of his room, which he had pushed to, slowly swinging open. His body stiffened and his ears strained; he felt his pupils dilating hugely, painfully against the blackness.

"Trevor? You still awake?"

It was Zach.

He thought of not answering, of pretending to be asleep. He couldn't imagine what Zach wanted now. But Zach had listened to him this afternoon.

"I'm awake," he said, and sat up.

"What was that medicine you gave me?"

"Aspirin, like you asked for."

"Are you sure it was aspirin?"

"Well, Excedrin. That's what I always take."

"Oh, god." Zach laughed weakly. "That shit has sixty-five milligrams of caffeine in every tablet. I can't deal with caffeine."

"What happens?"

"It hits me like speed. *Bad* speed."

"What do you want me to do?"

"Nothing." He felt Zach's weight settle onto the edge of the mattress. "I'm not gonna be able to sleep for a while, though. I thought maybe we could talk some more."

"Why?"

"Why what?"

"Why do you want to talk to me?"

"Why shouldn't I?"

"I don't understand why you like me. The first time I ever laid eyes on you, I tried to knock your brains out. Now I've poisoned you. How come you're still here?"

He heard Zach try to laugh. It came out more like a moan. "Just persistent, I guess."

"No. Really."

"Well . . ." A shudder ran through Zach's body, into the mattress. "Do you mind if I stretch out here?"

"I guess not."

Trevor moved to one side of the bed. He felt Zach arranging himself on the other side, thought he could feel electricity crackling off Zach's skin. When Zach's elbow brushed his, it gave Trevor a sensation like the shock one gets from walking across a carpet and then touching metal.

"First of all," said Zach, "you *didn't* try to knock my brains out. You stopped. Second, you didn't know caffeine would hurt me."

"Even so—"

"Even so, seems like I would have figured out by now that you aren't exactly good for my health?"

"Something like that, yeah."

"Maybe I'm not in this for my health."

"In what?"

"Life."

"Then what are you in it for?"

"Um . . ." He felt Zach shiver. "To keep myself amused, I guess. No, not amused. *Interested.* I want to do everything."

"You do? Really?"

"Sure. Don't you?"

Trevor thought about it. "I think I just want to *see* everything," he said at last. "And sometimes I'm not even sure I *want* to. I just feel like I *have* to."

"That's because you're an artist. Artists remind me of stills."

"Of what?"

"Of stills. What they use to make moonshine. You take in information and distill it into art." Zach was silent for a moment. "I guess that's not such a good analogy from your point of view."

"It's okay. A still doesn't have much choice about making moonshine. The choice is up to the person who drinks it."

"Then I'll drink your moonshine anytime you want to give me some," said Zach. "I admire you. That's why I didn't leave this afternoon. You may be crazy, but I think you're also very brave."

Suddenly Trevor felt like crying again. Here was this young kid on the run from some sinister unknown, this curious, generous, resilient soul who could stand up to a stranger with a hammer and make friends afterward, and he thought Trevor was brave. It didn't make sense, but it sure made him feel better. He couldn't remember the last time anyone had told him he was doing something right.

"Thanks," he said when he could trust his voice. "I don't feel very brave, though. I feel scared all the time."

"Yeah. Me too."

Something brushed the side of Trevor's hand, then crept warmly into the palm. Zach's finger, still trembling a little. Trevor nearly jerked his hand away, actually felt his muscles tensing and pulling. But at the last second, his own fingers curled around Zach's and trapped it.

If he went, he wouldn't take anyone with him. That was the one thing Trevor had promised himself.

But if he had someone to hang on to, maybe he wouldn't have to go. At least, not all the way down.

Zach's touch sent little currents through his hand, into his bloodstream. The old scars on his arm throbbed in time with his heartbeat. In the darkness he could just make out Zach's shining eyes. "What do you want?" he whispered.

"Could you . . ." Zach squeezed his hand, then let go. "Could you just hold me? This damn Excedrin . . ."

"Yes," said Trevor. "I think I can. I'll try."

Gingerly he reached out and found Zach's bare shoulder, slid his arm around Zach's chest, moved closer so that their bodies were nestled like two spoons in a drawer. Zach's heart was hammering madly, his muscles so taut it was like hugging an electrical coil about to blow. His body felt smaller and frailer than Trevor would have expected. It reminded him of sleeping with Didi; they had often nestled together in just the same way.

"The damndest thing," Zach said into the pillow, "is my head still hurts."

Trevor laughed. He could hardly believe any of this was happening. He would wake up and find that he'd slept another night at the drawing table, had invented this boy, this impossible situation. He wasn't supposed to be feeling like this. He had never felt like this. He was supposed to be finding out why he was alive.

But he was very aware of Zach's skin against his own, as smooth as he had imagined it, and he didn't want to pull away. If anything, he wanted to get closer.

He wondered if this might have something to *do* with why he was alive.

Trevor pressed his face into the soft hair at the back of Zach's neck. "Are you supposed to be here?" he asked very softly, half hoping Zach would not hear him. "Is this part of what's supposed to happen?"

"Fuck *supposed to*," said Zach. "You make it up as you go along."

Holding each other like a pair of twins in the womb, they were able to sleep.

Sometime just before dawn, a slow shimmering began in the air near the ceiling just above the bed. It deepened into a vaguely circular whirlpool pattern something like the waves of heat that swim above asphalt in the heart of a Southern summer. Then tiny white fragments of paper began to fall, appearing in the air and seesawing slowly down. Soon a funnel-shaped cloud of them was swirling like a freak snowstorm in the hot, still room.

Trevor and Zach slept on, not knowing, not caring. The bits of paper collected on the floor, the bed, the boys' sweaty sleeping bodies.

Dawn found them still locked tightly together, Trevor's face buried in the hollow of Zach's shoulder and his arms clamped across Zach's chest, Zach's hands clutching Trevor's so tightly that Trevor would later find the indentations of Zach's nails in his palms.

Awake, they had been afraid to touch each other at all.

Asleep, they looked as if they would be terrified to ever let go.

TWELVE

As luck would have it, Eddy had a hacker in her apartment when the Secret Service kicked the door down.

His name was Stefan, better known on Zach's beloved pirate boards as "Phoetus," and he was one of the few local computer outlaws who knew Zach's real name and where he lived. Even if Zach hadn't wanted him to have this information, Phoetus could easily have chivied it out of the vast grid of data kept under electronic lock and key by the phone company. Zach said he was very good.

He ran with a local gang of hackers who called themselves "The Ørder Øf DagØn." (Hackers, Zach had explained to her, often employed a unique spelling system in which *f*'s were replaced with *ph*'s, plural *s*'s with *z*'s, and ordinary *o*'s with zeroes.) It amused Eddy to picture Lovecraft's blasphemous fish-frogs of nameless design flopping, hopping, croaking, bleating, and surging inhumanly through the spectral moonlight all the way from Innsmouth to New Orleans and the surrounding swamps, where they had presumably set themselves up with the latest technology and started tapping phone lines and cracking databanks.

He came knocking at her door early Tuesday morning, sometime around eleven. Eddy had spent all day Sunday and most of Monday trundling her stuff from her old apartment over to Madison Street in a little red wagon she usually used for shopping and laundry. It didn't dawn on her until she was making the second-to-last trip that she could have hired a moving van. Having thousands of dollars in the bank was difficult to get used to. She kept expecting someone to stop her on the street and tell her there had been a mistake.

Which of course there had been—but with luck, They wouldn't find out about it.

By Monday night she was sore and exhausted. She had collapsed on Zach's bed, thinking she would just rest for a few minutes, then get up and go to the corner liquor store for a flask of rotgut. She could drink if she wanted to; she didn't have to get up and drag herself to the Pink Diamond tomorrow afternoon; she could call that hairy failed rock star Loup and tell him to blow.

Of course, she would do no such thing. She would inform him politely that she was taking some time off, and she hoped it wasn't too inconvenient, and he could call her if he needed a dancer to fill in sometime. Then, if he called, she would have to search madly for excuses not to.

Sometimes the leftover shreds of her upbringing could be a real bitch. In Korean etiquette there was no such thing as a flat *no*. You left all possibilities open, no matter how ambiguous. You never caused the other person to lose face. Not even if he was a sexist, coke-snorting asshole.

She took one last look at the twenty-five wagonloads of her stuff strewn around the room along with everything Zach had left. It was a mess. Eddy decided to rest her eyes for a few minutes.

When she opened them again sunlight was streaming through the open window, a green lizard was poised on the ceiling spearing her with its jeweled gaze, and someone was knocking lightly but rapidly at the door.

She opened it and Phoetus slipped through the crack. He was perhaps seventeen, very thin, tall, and loose-jointed. Something about his posture and gait reminded Eddy of those posters of Evolving Man. Phoetus was somewhere around the midpoint, where the head and muscle structure were more human than ape, but the arms still dangled a bit too low. His curly brown hair looked as if it might lighten two or three shades if he washed it, and his eyes were nearly hidden behind lenses as thick and swirly as the bottoms of Coke bottles.

He looked blankly at her. "You're not Zach."

"No, Stefan. I'm Eddy, remember? We met at the Café du Monde once." She had been having coffee and beignets while Zach nibbled the Thai bird peppers he'd just bought in the Market and chased them with a cold glass of milk. They had a table by the railing, and Zach hailed the nervous, pasty-skinned boy as he skulked by, dodging street performers, avoiding the eyes of tourists.

When introduced, the guy stared at Eddy as if petrified by the sight of her, leaned over the railing to mumble something to Zach—it sounded like "the eunuchs' holes are wide open" —and sidled quickly away toward the river.

"Who was that?" Eddy inquired.

"That was one of the most brilliant phone-systems guys on the planet. He's also the sysop of a pirate board called 'The Lurking Fear' and a member of the Ørder Øf DagØn. He's way underground. Sociable type, isn't he?"

As usual when Zach talked about his hacker buddies, Eddy understood about half of it, but she always looked at her telephone a bit more warily afterward. Who knew what un-speakable presences waited within those wires like swollen silver spiders clinging to a fiber-optic web?

Stefan stood by the door wringing his hands and staring at her in sweaty panic. Eddy realized with something like awe that he might never have been alone in a room with a girl before. The thought was oddly touching. She would have to remember not to make any sudden moves, otherwise she might frighten him clean away.

"Zach's not here," she told him. "He doesn't actually live in New Orleans anymore."

"I heard he might have gotten busted."

"Who said so?"

"I hear things."

That much she didn't doubt. "He wasn't busted. He got away. But he's okay—I got a message from him."

The hacker looked aghast. "He didn't call you *here*?"

"No. He put a message in the paper, in secret code." She showed him the folded page of yesterday's *Times-Picayune*. Goddess in a bowl of gumbo, indeed. "See, I think this means he's in North Carolina, maybe heading for New York next."

He scowled at the paper. "Secret code? This is kid stuff!"

"I suppose shutting down the 911 system is *mature*," Eddy said coolly. Zach had told her how Phoetus bragged on the boards that he could overload every emergency telephone circuit in the city if he wanted to.

Not seeming to register the insult—or perhaps not considering it an insult—Stefan edged past her into the room. "Where's the phone?"

She pointed to Zach's desk, which was still piled high with books and papers but looked rather forlorn without the computer and boxes of floppy disks. Zach had left his printer behind, though; Eddy guessed she would drag it out and hock it sometime soon.

Stefan took the receiver from the hook and pried off the plastic earpiece before Eddy could protest. He removed a small black box from his pocket and clipped some wires running from it to something inside the phone, then peered owlishly at the box. "Well, nobody else has a tap on this line, but the government might. They can tap straight from the phone company if they've got a warrant. Assume it's bugged."

"What did you do to it?"

He held up the black box. "This is called a multitester. It reads your standard off-hook voltage. If it's too low, there's probably another device sucking volts off your line."

"Oh."

Stefan had become briefly animated. Now he seemed to sink back into his sniffling, nervous fugue. "Look, I've got people after me too. Why, if They knew I was here—"

Eddy had closed the door as Stefan entered but had not yet bothered to lock it. There was an iron security gate at the street entrance that led up to the apartment, and while French Quarter residents were generally careful about locking all their doors, the gate offered some semblance of privacy, some illusion of safety.

This illusion was shattered as the door flew open and banged against the wall, making a dent in the soft plaster. All the policemen in the world seemed to come pouring into her tiny apartment. Eddy had no idea how many there actually were. All she saw was the guns, great oily insectile things unholstered and dripping death, pointed straight at her.

Eddy crouched and wrapped her arms around her head and screamed "NO! NO!" She couldn't help it. She had always had an instinctive terror of guns; perhaps in another life she had been a revolutionary sentenced to the firing squad or a gangster cut down in a street battle.

Behind her, she heard one of the most brilliant phone-systems guys on the planet burst into tears.

The raid team totaled fifteen men: Secret Service agents, BellSouth phone-security experts, and curious New Orleans cops along for the ride. Most of them faltered at the sight of the two cowering kids. Several guns went back into their holsters.

The German machine pistol carried by Agent Absalom Cover wasn't one of them. He kept it trained on the suspects and watched them writhe. Either of these two could be Zachary Bosch, or the person hiding behind that name.

Agent Cover had wanted Bosch for a long time. Other hackers goaded him unmercifully, threatened his credit and disrupted his phone service, left taunting messages in his E-mail, had done all but beard him in his New Orleans field office. But Bosch was smarter than ten such crooks, and far more dangerous. He didn't brag much. He didn't leave cute little clues in his wake. He just breezed through systems nobody should be able to get into, stealing information and wreaking havoc, and he covered his tracks like an Indian.

Finally a fifteen-year-old software pirate under interrogation had given them the keys they needed to trace him. Scratch a hacker and find a rat; ask him the right questions, marvel a little at his amazing technical feats, and turn him into an *eager* rat. Some of these kids were terrifyingly smart, but they were still kids. And Agent Cover believed all kids were basically amoral.

He got his warrant and moved in fast. Bosch couldn't have had time to slip between his fingers.

Still, once the first flush of adrenaline began to wear off, he found himself looking doubtfully at the two bawling kids. He hadn't expected Bosch to fold so easily. Most of these teenage whiz kids turned to jelly when they saw a few guns and badges, but then most of them had only broken into a system or two and browsed through sensitive files, maybe used a stolen phone code here and there or downloaded some software they shouldn't have. Most of them weren't brazen enough or criminally inclined enough to rip shit off on the scale that Zachary Bosch had.

Cover took one last loving look at his Heckler & Koch and tucked it back into the holster inside his jacket. He hadn't needed a gun on a hacker raid yet. These kids loved to brag on the boards about how they would go down shooting, but the deadliest weapon Agent Cover had found in a hacker's possession was a dental probe the kid used for jimmying phone jacks.

As he approached the suspects, the punked-out Asian girl lifted her head and stared at him in teary defiance, like a gut-shot deer watching a hunter loom over her in the bloody snow. She had enough crap dangling from her earlobes to set off a metal detector, and her hair looked like she'd cut it with a weedeater in the dark. Cover always wondered what had been done to these kids in early childhood to make them want to look the way they did. He'd busted one hacker who had a blue mohawk and scorpions tattooed on the shaved sides of his skull. Scorpions!

The tall, sickly-looking boy bolted for the bathroom. Two of the cops were right behind him. Cover heard the toilet lid bang up, the thick liquid sound of vomiting.

"Hey!" One of the cops stuck his head back in, an expression of dismay plastered across his broad shiny face. "He just chunked his wallet an' keys in the crapper!"

"Fish 'em out."

"But they're floatin' in a puddle of puke—"

"Fish 'em out," Cover repeated. The girl was watching him with a mixture of terror and loathing. The rush of forced intrusion left him and he felt suddenly weary. From the bathroom he heard "Awright, you little crook, fish 'em out," followed by another round of puking.

The U.S. Secret Service was charged with all manner of important duties and missions, any of which Ab Cover might have been assigned to upon his graduation from the Federal Law Enforcement Training Center at Glynco, Georgia. He could have protected the President from freaks and commies and assassins. He could have guarded the precious metals in Treasury vaults, or fought the clear-cut war on counterfeiting and forgery of U.S. currency.

Instead, he was part of an ongoing crackdown on computer crime that had begun with Operation Sundevil in 1990. Based in Arizona, Sundevil had targeted hacker abuse of credit card numbers and phone codes. More than forty computers and twenty-three thousand floppy disks had been seized from private citizens across the country. Since then, the Secret Service had acquired a taste for the slippery little anarchists who loved to hide behind their keyboards in their dark dens of iniquity, but could be so rewarding once they were dragged out into the sun.

So instead of guarding the President, Cover busted funny-looking misfit geniuses who weren't usually old enough to go to prison for crimes that nine tenths of the American public didn't understand.

In Washington they told him it was an honor. At any rate, it was a living. But sometimes he wondered if it was a good one.

Eddy clutched her copy of the search warrant and watched the cops swarm over the apartment. Now that the guns had been put away—though she was very conscious of the filthy things bulging under jackets and dangling from carelessly snapped holsters, looking as if they might crash to the floor and go off at any moment—she was able to take a look at the men behind them.

The Secret Service drones were sleek and broad-shouldered and well dressed, with razor-cut hair combed severely back from feral faces, with clean square jawlines and hard glittering eyes. They all seemed to be wearing expensive leather tassel loafers, and Eddy was hardly surprised to see that several even sported mirrorshades. She assumed that the guys in the cheaper jackets and plain loafers were lower-echelon agents, though in fact they were from the telephone company.

And of course she recognized the New Orleans cops. She had a long and bitter acquaintance with them, from her bust for a joint's worth of marijuana at sixteen (which Zach had since wiped from her record) to the clumsy attempts at entrapment she had been subjected to at the Pink Diamond ("How much wouldja charge to show a little *more*?" they'd leer, tugging at the crotches of their tacky plainclothes slacks).

After the agent in charge had examined her driver's license and realized that there was no computer equipment left in the place except the printer, he seemed to view Eddy as a minor threat at best. She still saw his mean, handsome face glowering in her direction from time to time as he snapped out orders, but she had mostly been forgotten. The printer quickly disappeared out the door in the arms of another sharp-dressed, eerily efficient Secret Service man.

"Zach moved out months ago," she said. "I think he left the country." No one paid any attention. A suit with a camera clicked off shot after shot of the desk, the bookshelves, the towering stacks of paper. Two others busily sorted and packed computer printouts, smudgily printed zines, cassettes and CDs. With a sinking heart she saw the folded page from the *Times-Picayune* going into one of their goodie boxes, along with a copy of the science fiction novel *Neuromancer*. That had been one of Zach's favorite books. The main character plugged his computer directly into a jack in his brain and entered the matrix, where he stole information from huge, faceless corporations. To Zach, William Gibson's seamy world must have read like the paradise of his wildest dreams. To these guys it was just more proof of sedition.

They unplugged the phone and the answering machine and took those too. They took poor Stefan; Eddy saw him being hustled out the door between two broad blue backs, a thin string of puke still dripping from his chin. She wondered what they'd gotten him for. Tampering with evidence, probably, for throwing his ID in the toilet. Eddy thought it had been a pretty good trick; too bad he hadn't managed to flush and send them fishing in the sewers.

New Orleans' finest, busting pitiful teenage geeks while old ladies visiting their husbands' graves stood a good chance of getting robbed or raped in the cemetery. Real heroes. And robbed and raped was how she felt right about now, watching these cookie-cutter robots swarm over her home and sift through her belongings and not being able to do a damn thing about it.

As soon as this nightmare was over, Eddy decided, she would go to the bank and withdraw part of the ten thousand dollars. Not all of it, that might look suspicious, but enough to have around in case . . . what? In case she needed to leave in a hurry?

Goddammit, she thought, *I haven't even broken the law yet and I'm already as paranoid as Zach was. Is this any way to live? Is it worth the gnawing in your stomach, the constant urge to look over your shoulder?* For Zach she supposed it had been; he was addicted to the thrill, the risk. But for her, this state of affairs would not do for long.

She didn't know if she should go anywhere near that money, and wished she had been able to ask Stefan if it was safe. But Eddy thought she would feel more secure with wads of cold cash sewn into her mattress than with illegitimate funds lurking in any electronically accessible part of her life. She wished she had never seen a computer.

Right now, if she was to be perfectly honest, she wished she had never met Zach. He was the best friend she had ever had, he was generous and brilliant, he had introduced her to all manner of exotic things she might never have found on her own. But he was also confusion and trouble and heartache.

And, on top of all that, she missed him so badly she thought it might kill her.

THIRTEEN

Trevor was in a small square room with a high ceiling lost in the shadows of dawn, a room whose walls were painted shabby gray to match the city beyond. He heard rain hitting the loose panes of the window. Soon would come the sound of doors opening, boys' footsteps in the hall, boys' voices in the early morning stillness, and it would be time to get up, time for breakfast and school, the sameness of another day.

He often dreamed that he was back at the Boys' Home, that he had been handed all those years like penance to do over and over again until he got them right . . . whatever right would be.

Trevor opened his eyes and found himself staring at the back of a neck in extreme closeup. The dark hair at the nape had been recently shaved and stood up in baby-fine bristles. The skin was translucent white, almost poreless. The neck curved down to a bony shoulder; Trevor saw his own hand resting on that shoulder, encircling the sharp knob of the bone. The rest of the body was nestled cozily into the curve of his own.

He was amazed that the sensation of another person in bed with him—the slow rise and fall of breathing, the vibration of the curious heart—hadn't kept him awake all night. He was used to sleeping in unfamiliar beds, but always alone. What happened when you woke up in bed with someone? What were you supposed to do?

The shoulder moved beneath his hand, and Trevor felt muscles shifting liquidly, bones rotating in their sockets, the smooth texture of skin under his palm. He felt the spine arch and ripple against his chest. He realized he had never thought about how much anatomy you could learn by touching someone.

Then Zach rolled over and looked at him with those almond-shaped dark green eyes, those eyes that were the exact shade of a colored pencil Trevor had once worn down to a nub. It was a pencil he used for coloring deep waters and strange shadows, and it had been labeled simply JADE.

Zach looked at him and smiled without saying anything. Even yesterday, even before the rain it had seemed that Zach was seeing too much of him, was perhaps half-hearing his thoughts. *I don't mind being in bed with you,* Trevor thought, not really wanting Zach to hear it but perversely hoping he would. *I don't mind being this close to you. I don't seem to mind it at all.*

Like a dark pulsar from the depths of his subconscious, on the heels of that thought came: *Yes, you could learn anatomy by touching someone. But Bobby took that method to its worst extreme, didn't he?*

And that was when he noticed the tiny bits of paper scattered across the blanket, over the pillow, through the tangle of Zach's dark hair.

He reached out and took one. Zach turned his head to look, and his cheek barely grazed the back of Trevor's hand. Trevor held the scrap of paper close to his eyes, trying to see it in the poor light. It was less than half an inch square, but its heavy texture felt terribly familiar. He sifted through a few more scraps. Pencil marks, mostly unidentifiable lines and shading. But here and there a detail had survived. A hastily lettered word. A pair of lips sealed around the mouthpiece of an alto saxophone. A dark eye filling with blood.

Zach propped himself on one elbow, shook the stuff out of his hair. "What is it?"

But Trevor was already up off the mattress, out of the room, running down the hall and slamming into the studio. He had left his sketchbook neatly centered on the drawing table. Now it lay wide open at a crazy angle on the floor, its spiral spine pulled askew by whatever force had ripped out the five pages of his story. The sight gave him a sick sensation in his stomach.

He picked up the sketchbook. It felt dirty, as if the pages were lightly coated with slime. Trevor supposed they might be. He made himself hold it between the thumb and forefinger of his left hand, made himself walk slowly back down the hall instead of caroming off the walls, beating his head against the door frames, or simply throwing himself to the floor and sobbing.

Zach's hands were full of the scraps of paper. He was trying to examine them in the watery light from the window. Trevor held up the sketchbook. As Zach made out what it was, a stricken expression dawned on his face. "Not the Bird story?"

So he had read it, the little snoop. Trevor couldn't bring himself to care much now. "Yeah, that's it you're holding."

Zach spread his hands and let the fragments flutter to the floor. He rubbed his palms together to dislodge the ones that had stuck, then started brushing them off the pillow and blanket. "Did you . . . were you . . ."

He read the question in Zach's face. Zach was wondering if Trevor could have torn up the story himself. The realization didn't even make Trevor angry; he supposed it was a reasonable enough doubt. "I was in bed with you all night," he said. "You know I was. I could just as well ask you the same thing."

"But I didn't—"

"I know you didn't."

"What are you gonna do?"

"Draw it again, I guess."

Zach started to speak, stopped, then could not seem to help himself. "But . . . but . . . Trevor . . ."

"What?"

"Aren't you *pissed*?"

"What? That you read my story?"

"No," Zach said impatiently. "I'm sorry but . . . no. I mean, aren't you mad that it's *gone*?"

Trevor sat down on the edge of the mattress. He looked at

Zach, who was leaning forward, his hands clenched into fists against his bare chest, his muscles tensed, his eyes very wide and blazing. "Well, *you* obviously are."

"Why aren't *you*? It destroyed your work and threw it in your face! How can you *not* be pissed?"

Trevor took a deep breath. "There's something in this house. I think it might be my family."

"Yeah, I think maybe so too. And you know what I'd do if I were you? I'd say *so fucking what* and get the hell out of here. If it'll tear up your work, it'll hurt you."

"I don't care."

Zach opened his mouth to reply, could not find anything to say and closed it again.

"If I hadn't been here, I wouldn't have drawn that story in the first place. Birdland gave it to me. What can I say if Birdland wants it back?"

"Try *bullshit*."

Zach slid across the mattress and laid his hands on either side of Trevor's head, his fingertips pressing gently against the temples. "*This* is your Birdland. And *these*." He dropped his hands to Trevor's, took away the mutilated sketchbook, wrapped Trevor's hands in his own and squeezed. "If you came back here to find something, at least admit what it is. Don't get to thinking you need this place for your art, because you don't. That would be suicide."

"Maybe I want to commit suicide."

"Why?"

Trevor pulled his hands away. "Why don't you just drop it?"

"Because your father did? Is that why you think it's so fucking romantic? 'Cause if you do—"

"Why don't you shut the fuck up and get your stuff—"

"—maybe you ought to think about this: HE JUST LOST HIS GODDAMN SENSE OF HUMOR!"

Zach reached for Trevor's shoulder, maybe only wanting to grab it and shake it to belabor his point. Trevor didn't want to be grabbed. He brought his right arm up to shield himself, and Zach made the mistake of trying to pull it down. Trevor saw his left hand curl into a fist, watched it draw back and piston forward into Zach's still-talking mouth. He felt the skin split warmly against his knuckles, felt spit and blood smear across his hand. It hurt where it had connected with the hardness of teeth and gums. But it wasn't his drawing hand.

Zach's head hit the wall hard and he slid to the mattress, dazed. Above his bloody mouth, his eyes were a more vivid green than ever, wide, stunned, scared. Those eyes begged mercy. It was a wonderful emotion to see in someone's eyes. You could grant it if you wanted. But you also had the power to refuse it.

Trevor pulled his fist back to do it again. His other hand curled around Zach's wrist, felt the small bones grind deliciously beneath his fingers. He watched Zach's eyes. This was what they had looked like before they died. This was how it had been on the other side of the hammer.

He's right, you know.

Trevor stopped.

If Bobby couldn't stand to live without his art, okay. Suicide is always an option. But he didn't have to kill them. You didn't have to spend the rest of your life alone. Momma would have taken care of you and Didi. Is saying he lost his sense of humor so far wrong?

He'd had such thoughts before, usually late at night in a cheap bed in an unfamiliar city. Now they came again unbidden and made him realize what he had been about to do. He had been ready not just to hit Zach, but to hit him again and again, as many times as it took . . . to shut him up? To kill him? Trevor didn't know.

He shoved himself away from Zach, rolled off the mattress and lay on the floor in the dust and the ruins of his story. Half of him hoped Zach would come over here and beat the shit out of him now. Trevor would lie still and let him do it.

But half of him hoped Zach would stay away. Because the softness of Zach's lips spreading and splitting open against his hand had felt *so damn good* . . .

*   *   *

Zach pressed the heels of his hands into his eye sockets and willed himself to disappear into the mattress. He was sure Trevor's fist was going to smash into his face at any moment, and he only hoped that blow would knock him out before the next one came. He knew he should defend himself. He couldn't land a punch, but he could kick.

But fighting back was the one thing he could not do. He had a stoic dread of physical pain born of hard experience: you took what you couldn't avoid, but you didn't ask for more. Zach had learned long ago that if you fought back, they only hurt you worse.

When the blow didn't come, he risked a look, though he had a particular horror of being punched in the eye so hard that it just squirted out of its socket. But Trevor didn't hit him again. Trevor was halfway across the room, lying on the floor with his arms wrapped around his head.

Zach swallowed a mouthful of blood, felt hot helpless tears spilling over the rims of his eyelids, stinging his wounded lips. Blood dripped off his chin, made deep red blossoms on the bare mattress, ran down his chest and traced the pale arc of his ribs in vivid scarlet. Zach felt it pooling in his navel, trickling into his crotch. He put his fingertips to his mouth and they came away slicked nearly purple. He looked again at Trevor, still curled miserably on the floor.

Why bother? I was right all along: the second you make yourself vulnerable to someone, they start drawing blood.

Yeah, but if a real *vampire came along, you'd bare your neck in a second.*

Zach almost laughed through his tears. It was true; he was always ready to take the flashy risks, always ready for the rush of impending doom as long as he could thwart it at the last second. But the slower-acting and ultimately more dangerous risk of involving his life with someone's, of laying his soul open to someone, that was just too much.

He felt a surge of self-loathing. His whole life had been lived by the Siamese-twin philosophies of *Do what thou wilt* and *Fuck you, Jack, I've got mine.* Beyond all his digital daring he was a coward, unable to fight or love. No wonder he made such a good punching bag.

Trevor might be crazy, probably *was* crazy, but at least he was looking for the source of his craziness instead of running from it.

Trevor raised his head. His face was wet with tears too. He saw Zach looking at him, saw the blood, and his expression of uneasy calm crumbled into fresh woe. "You can leave if you want. I won't . . . hurt you."

"I don't want to leave."

Trevor tried to speak, could not make his throat work, lowered his face into his hands again.

"Trevor?"

"Wh . . ." He forced back a sob. "What."

"Why don't you get back in bed with me?"

Amazed, not trusting his ears, Trevor looked up. He saw Zach's face, scared but not angry. Even with blood dripping fresh off his chin, Zach wanted him over there. Trevor couldn't imagine why. He only knew that he did not want to stay here alone on the dirty floor of his childhood room, with his faded drawings staring down from the walls.

He crawled across the rough floorboards, through the drifts of torn paper and dust, toward the mattress. When he was halfway there Zach held out his hand, and Trevor crawled toward that.

Zach clasped the outstretched hand and pulled Trevor onto the mattress, into his arms. He pulled Trevor's head into the hollow of his shoulder, buried his face in Trevor's hair. Zach's body felt to Trevor like a reflection of his own; Zach's bones seemed to interlock with his like atoms in the structure of a molecule. Trevor thought he could feel their very souls, their molten cores of pain, flowing together like white-hot metals.

How can you know that? Is this falling in love? And if it is, how the hell does anyone SURVIVE it?

He realized that he was sobbing and Zach was too, that their faces and throats and collarbones were wet with each other's tears, that their skin was spattered and streaked with Zach's blood. Zach's arms were wrapped tightly around

Trevor's chest, and his sharp chin dug into Trevor's shoulder. Trevor turned his head slightly and his mouth found Zach's jawline, still bloody.

Without thinking, Trevor rubbed his lips across the blood, then licked some of it away. Then Zach's mouth moved to meet his, and Trevor supposed this was kissing, this warm, strange, melting thing. He tasted salt and copper and the sharp smoky flavor of Zach's mouth. Zach's torn lips were very soft against his, surely sore. As they kissed more deeply Trevor felt the wounds come open again, felt Zach's blood flowing over his tongue. He sucked at it and swallowed it. He had spilled it; now he could take it into himself. And it tasted so sweet, so full of the twin energies of life and death.

Zach's hands traced light patterns across his chest, making the skin shiver into goosebumps. Trevor moved his mouth to Zach's ear, smelled yesterday's rainwater in Zach's hair. "What are you doing?" he whispered.

Zach placed his lips against the hollow of Trevor's throat and left them there for a moment before he answered. "Do you mind?"

"No, I don't think so. I just don't *know* . . ."

"Don't know what?"

"Anything."

Zach glanced up, met Trevor's eyes. "You mean you've never . . ."

Trevor was silent. Zach's eyes widened and he started to speak, but was apparently struck dumb with awe. Finally he said, "What did you *do*?"

"Nothing."

"Jerk off?"

"Not much."

Zach shook his head slowly, marveling. "I'd be dead in a week if I didn't do *something*. I'd be splattered all over the walls."

Trevor shrugged.

"Well—" Zach lowered his head so that the longer strands of his hair fell forward and tickled Trevor's chest. Most of his face was hidden, but Trevor saw a fierce spot of color blazing in one pale cheek. "I would show you. If you wanted me to."

"Zach?"

He looked up. His eyes were full of doubt and desire, enormous-pupiled, insanely green.

"I don't even know how to say yes."

Their hands found each other and intertwined. Zach squeezed Trevor's fingers, brought them to his lips and kissed them. His tongue slid over the ball of Trevor's thumb, soft as velvet. Trevor felt something uncoil deep inside him, some unfamiliar warmth seeping like liquor through his innards. Only it didn't dull his senses, it heightened them; he was aware of every inch of his skin, every hair on his body, every pore and cell. All of them were straining toward Zach, thirsting for him.

Then they were kissing again, carefully at first, learning the shape and texture of each other's lips, testing the sharpness of the teeth behind them. Trevor felt Zach's hands sliding down his back and straying beneath the waistband of his sweatpants, cupping his buttocks and squeezing, moving down to the sensitive juncture of his thighs and lightly stroking the downy hairs there. He had an erection for the first time in as long as he could remember, had almost forgotten what one felt like. It felt a hell of a lot better snuggled into the warm hollow of someone's hipbone, that was for sure.

It's too fast! said a panicky voice in his mind. *And too dangerous! He'll drink your juices, taste your brain, crack your soul open like an egg!*

Hell, I think I want him to do all that.

The thought released Trevor, gave him abandon. He sucked at Zach's tongue and pulled it deep into his mouth. You became so used to the texture and mass of your own tongue that you seldom noticed it nestling in the cradle of your lower jawbone, pressing against your teeth. Having another tongue there felt alien at first, like trying to swallow some small slippery animal, a baby eel or perhaps an energetic oyster.

Their hands roamed the planes and hollows of one another's bodies. Now Zach's clever fingers were teasing

Trevor's nipples, plugging into unfamiliar nerve endings, webs of sensation that seemed to radiate from his chest up his spinal cord and into his brain, down through the pit of his stomach to his aching penis. Never mind when he had last had a boner; he couldn't remember *ever* having had one that felt like this.

Then Zach's hand slid down to cup it through the soft cloth, and Zach's lips kissed a slow trail down his chin, along the curve of his throat and the hollow of his collarbone, and wrapped hot and wet around his left nipple. Trevor felt his heart lurch, his mind begin to dissolve in pleasure. He choked back a throatful of saliva. "Don't!"

Zach's mouth paused but did not go away. His hand moved to the ridge of Trevor's hipbone and squeezed gently. "Why not?"

Trevor caught his breath, searched for a reply. "It hurts," he said at last, though that was not precisely what he meant.

"You mean it feels too good?"

Silver motes swarmed in the air above his face; his vision was drowning in red filigree. Trevor closed his eyes and nodded.

"Sometimes you just have to ride it. But we can slow down." Zach shrugged. "I'll kiss you all day if that's what you want." He lowered his face to Trevor's, brushed his lips ever so lightly across Trevor's. Trevor felt tears starting again behind his eyelids for the kindness of this boy.

Do you want to do this? he thought. *You were finally able to come back to this house, to come home. You haven't had that damn dream in two nights. You're on the verge of finding whatever is left here for you to find. Do you want to add this to the equation?*

But he was sick of listening to the voices in his head and the slow settling of empty rooms. There were other things to hear. Zach's breathing and heartbeat, the whisper of Zach's hands against the slight stubble on Trevor's face, the liquid sound their mouths made together. Zach lay half on top of him, holding him loosely, kissing him languorously. It became impossible to think of anything but tastes and textures.

They kissed dreamily, then searchingly, then with increasing urgency. Then Zach was nuzzling his neck and chest again, but this time Trevor wasn't scared. He arched his back, twined his fingers into Zach's thick soft hair. Zach's fingers strayed again to the band of Trevor's sweatpants, found the drawstring and deftly untied the bow. His lips moved across the concavity of Trevor's stomach, paused just above the cloth. Trevor thought his penis might simply explode soon. He imagined shimmering globules of semen dripping from the ceiling, nestling in Zach's hair like diamonds on blue-black velvet.

Zach looked up at Trevor and suddenly his serious, almost-scared face split into a wide dazzling grin.

"This feels *so good*," he said, "you won't even *believe* it."

He tugged the cloth away and kissed the tip of Trevor's penis, then took the whole throbbing burning thing into his mouth. He was right. All at once there was no more house, no childhood room, no dirty mattress under Trevor's back. There was only this moment and this boy, only the smooth glide of saliva and fingertips and tongue, only the deep silken tunnel of Zach's throat surrounding him. It was like nothing else ever.

He felt a stream of pure white energy blazing along his spine, sending twin bolts into his balls and his brain, filling every cell with light. His scalp and the palms of his hands tingled madly. He felt his pores open and bead with sweat, heard himself moaning and Zach moaning muffled encouragement back at him. *Does he really want me to come in his mouth?* Trevor wondered. *Can I do that?—can I—OMIGOD—*

Thought deserted him again. He felt like a man made of television static, of a million roaring, hissing silver dots. Then the stream of energy filled him completely and husked him out clean. A year's pain seemed to leave his body as he came, ebbing from his balls, leaking out of his eyes, expelling from his lungs in short harsh gasps.

For several minutes Zach stayed where he was, his mouth and hands still working gently. Then he crawled up and rested his head next to Trevor's on the pillow. His lips were swollen, smudged with fresh blood and milky traces of semen. The light sheen of sweat on his face turned his pale skin nearly opalescent.

Zach took handfuls of Trevor's hair and pulled it over their faces. The effect was like being inside a sheer tent or a tawny ginger cocoon. Their foreheads and the tips of their noses touched. Trevor could taste his own come in Zach's mouth when they kissed, a fresh, faintly bitter organic flavor. Was that how Zach's would taste too? He realized he wanted to find out.

He pulled Zach close to him and rolled on top. The feeling of Zach's body beneath him was exhilarating, this complex, delicious bundle of blood and bones and thoughts and nerves and muscles captive in his arms, willingly so, gladly so. He laid his head on Zach's chest. The skin stretched tight over Zach's breastbone and ribs like a drum, milk-white, without hair or blemish. Tentatively, Trevor let the barest edges of his teeth graze one pale pink nipple.

"AAH—" Zach stretched like a cat. "MMMM. Do that some more."

"Can I bite?"

"Hell, yes."

Trevor's teeth closed on the defenseless bud of flesh. He sucked at it, nipped harder and made Zach groan. He worried at it, gnawed on it. Surely Zach would yell at him to stop. But Zach only writhed beneath him and gasped appreciation laced with pain. If he wanted his nipples sore, Trevor didn't mind obliging him. They were pliant and tender between his teeth, flavored with the salt of Zach's sweat and the faintly spicy taste of Zach's skin.

"ARRR . . . ah . . ." Zach groped for Trevor's fingers. "Put your hand on my dick. Please."

His dick? The term jarred Trevor for an instant, reminded him of the Boys' Home, snickers and whispers in health class, scrawled graffiti on toilet walls. It sounded like a word R. Crumb would use, Trevor thought irrelevantly—though Crumb drew penises rather more often than he mentioned them, with plenty of unsightly hairs, popping veins, and oozing come-drops. He realized he was terrified again, but now it was like being on a carnival ride that had started looping out of control: you couldn't stop, so you just had to hang on tight and lean with the curves.

Zach had grabbed his hand and was pushing it down, making a weird, urgent growling sound in his throat. He wore only a pair of skimpy black briefs made of some soft silken material. Trevor's fingertips skated over the cloth, and his hand closed on the warm pulsing shape beneath. He rubbed his face over Zach's ribs and the hollow of his stomach, pressed his lips against the silky cloth. He heard Zach's breath sobbing in and out.

Trevor hooked his thumbs into the elastic of the briefs and tugged, and Zach managed to squirm out of them without untangling his hands from their grip in Trevor's hair. Zach's penis—Trevor could not quite bring himself to think of it as his dick—bobbed up and brushed softly against Trevor's lips. Trevor cupped his hands around it, felt Zach's heartbeat throbbing between his palms. The skin of the shaft was textured, slightly rippled beneath the surface. The head was as smooth as satin, as rose petals. Trevor rubbed his thumb across it, squeezed gently, heard Zach suck air in through his teeth and moan as he let it out. He could see blood suffusing the tissue just beneath the translucent skin, a deep dusky rose delicately purpled at the edges, crowned with a single dewy pearl of come. It was as intimate, as raw as holding someone's heart in his hands.

Zach's body shifted beneath him. Zach's legs wrapped loosely around him. Out of the corner of his eye he saw Zach arching his back off the mattress, rubbing thick handfuls of Trevor's hair up across his belly and chest.

All at once it hit him: this was power too, just as surely as smashing your fist into someone's face, just as surely as putting a hammer through someone's skull. The power to make another person crazy with pleasure instead of fear and pain, to have every cell in another person's body at your thrall.

And this way, the person was still alive when it was over.

"Please suck my dick," Zach said faintly.

"I—" Trevor searched for the right thing to say. "I'd love

to," he whispered at last, and slid his hands under Zach's butt, and very carefully took Zach's penis deep into his mouth. It seemed to nestle against his tongue and the walls of his throat as if it had been made to fit there. He slid one hand up between Zach's legs, cupped his balls and felt them draw tight, felt the skin shivering, seething. Zach was tossing his head and moaning, trying not to thrust too hard. Trevor grabbed his bucking hips and swallowed him deeper, willing his throat muscles to open, to liquefy. He almost gagged, but forced the reflex down. He wanted this in him, this taste, this chance.

Chance? he thought, *what do I mean by chance?* But before he had time to ponder it, Zach screamed "OHHHH, TREV!" and snarled his fingers in Trevor's hair so hard the strands felt as if they would rip out of his scalp, and his whole thrumming body surged forward and seemed to pour its energy into Trevor. He felt it spilling hot over his tongue and down the back of his throat, crackling from Zach's fingertips into Trevor's temples and straight through his brain, even emanating from Zach's solar plexus in steady waves. His body was like some kind of big nervous battery.

Trevor kept sucking until Zach's penis was soft and slippery in his mouth, until his lips were buried in the crisp, glossy thicket of hair that stood out so black against the juncture of Zach's pale thighs. The taste in Trevor's mouth was much like his own, but had its distinct notes: slightly herbal, slightly peppery. He wondered if his own come would poison Zach's bloodstream with caffeine.

But Zach's body was slowly relaxing into him, twining round him. Trevor slid up on the mattress so that Zach could lie comfortably against him. His fingers traced patterns in the sweat trickling along Zach's spine. He kissed Zach's eyelids and the faint dark smudges beneath his eyes, savoring the tender crepey texture of the skin against his lips, the feathery brush of the lashes, the small secret motions of the eyeball. He kissed the graceful arcs of Zach's eyebrows, the slope of his narrow elegant nose. Then their mouths joined again in a long, lush, sated kiss. It seemed that even with sore lips Zach could not get enough of kissing him. Trevor had never known it was possible to feel this close to someone, had never dreamed he would want to.

"So what do you think?" Zach asked after a while.

"I think it was worth about a million drawings." Trevor felt a guilty pang as he said this. But if the Bird story hadn't been destroyed, this might not have happened. He knew he had more drawings in his hand, in his brain. Zach was right; he didn't need the house to dole them out to him.

Zach shook his head. "If it was enough of an asshole to tear up your story, maybe it'll be sorry. Maybe it'll put the pieces back together."

Trevor snorted. "And Scotch-tape them."

"Yeah, with the *Magic* Tape."

"Yeah, with nine hundred thousand yards of it."

Zach settled into the curve of Trevor's arm. Trevor felt the sweat cooling on their bodies, the damp morning chill that pervaded the room, and pulled the blanket over them. Beneath it, Zach moved yet closer to him. It was like being in a warm pocket of space reserved exclusively for them, like a safe haven, like a womb.

"I'm sorry I hit you," Trevor said. It was way past the time for an apology, but he had to say it anyway.

"I'm not. It got us this far." Zach yawned, pushed his face into Trevor's chest. "I was scared to try anything with you before."

"Why?"

"Well—" Zach shifted position, draped an arm across Trevor's stomach, stroked the small sharp hill of Trevor's hipbone. "I don't usually have sex with people I respect."

"Why not?"

"Because I'm a dumbfuck, I guess. I don't know."

Trevor just looked at him.

Zach began to talk much as Trevor had done yesterday, spilling his sordid history, detailing more damage than he probably even realized: the condoms he masturbated with, the empty French Quarter trysts, the obsessive need to feel other flesh against his own but not to have to think about it.

By the end he was crying again, just a few slow shameful tears.

Trevor cupped Zach's face in both hands and licked the tears away. His tongue darted into the salty corner of Zach's eye, rounded the curve of Zach's cheekbone, slipped back into Zach's mouth. Zach pressed gratefully against him, and Trevor felt himself wanting it all to happen again. He didn't know if it was possible so soon. But Zach seemed to be showing him that anything was possible.

It lasted much longer this time. Zach's hands worked him expertly, stroking, squeezing, fingering and probing, building up a rhythm so exquisite that Trevor thought he would spend his seed between Zach's warm slick palms. That would have been fine, but Zach began to make his way back down, kissing him everywhere, tracing a wet glistening maze of spit along his body, then sucking him deep and slow, excruciatingly, maddeningly slow. It was almost painful, yet Trevor wanted it to go on for hours.

Zach was sprawled between Trevor's legs, his left arm wrapped loosely around Trevor's waist, his right hand doing something ingenious. Trevor felt Zach's penis growing insistently hard against his thigh. He moved his leg against it, reached down and barely managed to graze it with his fingertips. He wanted to do something to make Zach feel good too.

"Can I—how do we both—"

Without breaking rhythm, Zach shifted so that his hips were beside Trevor's head, his boner within easy reach of Trevor's mouth. This position seemed a marvel of physics, but Trevor grasped its advantages immediately; it leaned their weight into each other, pressed the flat planes of their bodies tightly together, and stretched their throats wide open. It seemed as if they *could* go on for hours this way. And so they did, until their exhausted bodies were all but bound together by a moist web of spit and sweat and semen.

Then they slept again, easy sated sleep that lasted into the afternoon. The house was silent around them. Their dreams were set only to the soft patter of rain on the roof, to the slow even rhythm of one another's breathing.

FOURTEEN

A tourist from Atlanta was found murdered Tuesday in a warehouse used to store Mardi Gras parade floats. Elizabeth Linhardt, 36, had reportedly been mutilated and an attempt made to burn her corpse. An anonymous source stated that the victim's head was found in the mouth of a ten-foot bust of Bacchus, partially chewed . . .

Travis Rigaud of St. Tammany Parish accidentally shot himself while cleaning his collection of handguns —five different times with five different guns, twice in the left foot, once in the right calf, and once in each hand, severing two fingers. "I finally sold the handguns," said Rigaud, "but I still have my rifles and this bad luck won't keep me home come hunting season, even if I should miss everything by a mile, no, cherie . . ."

A man was pulled over by state troopers near Chalmette with 148 poisonous snakes in his car . . .

Eddy let the newspaper slip to the floor and draped her forearm across her tired eyes. She wore only a pair of black bikini panties. Her armpits were dusted with the fine dark hair she'd allowed to grow since she quit the Pink Diamond. She still wore small silver rings in her nipples, but she had unclipped the delicate chain that usually connected them. She could smell the sweat on her skin, a faint odor of lemons and musk, and thought soon she might get up and take a shower.

After the cops left, she had gone straight to the bank, then scored the Tuesday morning and afternoon editions of the *Times-Picayune*. Now she was lying on top of seven thousand dollars reading every article and squib and photo caption, looking for more clues from Zach. Her fingers were smudged with cheap black ink. She paid special attention to the weird news, but it was midsummer in New Orleans and there was plenty of genuinely strange shit going on.

But could anyone really shoot himself five times with five different guns? Eddy frowned. It didn't seem possible.

She picked up the paper again and reread the article, and a bell went off in her head. Zach's mother's maiden name had been something Cajun. She was pretty sure it was Rigaud. The other fake story had had a byline of Joseph something-or-other. Joseph was Zach's father's name.

Eddy thought these obscure references to the people who had spent fourteen years abusing him strange, sad, and slightly perverse, but there they were. And this improbable item had his scent all over it, from the gibe at trigger-happy rednecks to the corny patois. "Even if I should miss everything by a mile, no, cherie?" What the fuck was *that* supposed to mean?

No, Cherie . . . N . . . C . . .

She got up and pawed through the books Zach and the Secret Service had left, but of course there was no road atlas. Either Zach had never had one, or he'd taken it himself, or They had snagged it, maybe hoping he'd plotted his escape route in yellow highlighter. She should have gotten a map of North Carolina yesterday, when Zach's first clue appeared in the paper.

Eddy pulled on a pair of denim cutoffs and selected a black T-shirt from the pile Zach had left behind. An artfully torn rag printed with the Bauhaus-like logo of Midnight Sun, a dreadful Gothic sextet that had played around the Quarter clubs last year, then disappeared into whatever void was reserved for truly bad bands. She couldn't imagine why Zach had the shirt, unless he had fucked one of the band members. Probably he had; they'd all been beautiful and stupid.

Those faithful old twin parasites, anger and pain, tried to worm up inside her. Eddy pushed them back down. Never mind who Zach had fucked. She had put up with it and called herself his friend. If she really was his friend, then she had to stay several steps ahead of his enemies, or try anyway.

Outside, the daily cloudburst had come and gone, and the streets were still steaming. Trash piles at the back doors of bars and restaurants gave off a mélange of smells: stale beer, rotting vegetables, fishbones touched with grease and cayenne. She passed a bushel basket of oyster shells still slick with the mollusks' gluey residue, and caught a whiff of the salty seawater odor that always made her wonder for an instant if she needed a bath.

I was going to shower before I came out, Eddy remembered. *I probably smell a little like old oyster shells myself.* But it didn't matter. Nobody was going to get close enough to her to care, and she had more important business to worry about.

A few blocks up Chartres was a used bookstore Eddy and Zach had often frequented together. They could spend hours in there, enveloped in the delicately dusty, dry, alluring scent of books, poring over leather-bound volumes with gilt-edged pages, stacks of ancient magazines, battered paperbacks whose corners were rounded and softened with age. The proprietor, an old Creole lady who smoked a fragrant pipe and read incessantly, never seemed to mind having them natter and browse.

But when Eddy asked for a U.S. atlas, the old lady shook her head. "Maps from the 1920s would be useless to you, no, *chère?* Try the Bookstar by Jax Brewery or one of the chains up on Canal."

"Okay, I guess I will."

Eddy turned to go, but the old lady must have seen some fleeting sadness in her face, for she put a wrinkled hand on Eddy's arm and stopped her. The skin of her palm was cool and faintly silken, and three gaudy rings sparkled on her gnarled fingers. "Where is that handsome young man you come in with?"

"He's, uh . . ." Eddy stared at the old lady's hands, at the stacks of books on the counter. "He had to leave town."

"Love trouble?"

"Law trouble."

"Ahhh." The old lady nodded sadly. "For him, burn a green candle and a yellow one. Are you in trouble too?"

"Maybe."

"For you, take an egg and . . . Have you been questioned by a policeman?"

"Yes."

"How many?"

"Well . . ." Eddy tried to tally broad blue backs and sharp gray suits in her head. "Just one," she said, reasoning that Agent Cover was the only cop who had really questioned her.

"Write his name on an egg," the old lady advised her, "and throw the egg up on your roof. Make sure it breaks. The police will not return."

"Okay," said Eddy, genuinely grateful. She needed any edge she could get. "Thank you. I will."

"Mais non. The poor boy. He is so beautiful, so full of the spirit of life."

"Yes," Eddy agreed. "That he is."

"But always there will be some sort of trouble for him, I think. There is a Creole saying . . . he has *le coeur comme un artichaud.*"

Eddy fumbled for her high school French. "A heart like an artichoke?"

"Oui. He has a leaf for everyone, but makes a meal for no one."

After a hot exhaust-choked walk up Peter Street to the bookstore, Eddy cut back through the shady, humid side streets of the Quarter, stopping at a corner market to buy a green candle, a yellow candle, and a carton of eggs. Back home, she locked the door behind her and spread out her new book of maps on the bed.

She found the state of North Carolina and began scanning

it closely, paying special attention to the small towns just off the main roads, noting odd names. Here were places called Pumpkin Center, Climax . . . Deep Gap, Blowing Rock, Bat Cave . . . Silk Hope, Fuquay-Varina . . . *Missing Mile?*

Eddy looked back at the newspaper article. *Even if I should miss everything by a mile, no, cherie. Missing Mile, N.C.*

That had to be where he was.

But *why*? The first message had implied he was going on to New York. Why had he decided to stay in the South, in a town so small it must be hard to hide there? And why was he so sure of it that he had sent her a message spelling out its name?

Eddy had a sudden flash of paranoia. *He's met someone.* For an instant she was sure of it; she *knew* it was true. *He's met someone and decided to stay with them, three days after telling me good-bye forever.*

But that was silly. There was no way she could know that. And it didn't seem very likely anyway.

Still . . . *Missing Mile, North Carolina?*

She sighed. At least now she knew where he was, or thought she did. Probably tomorrow's paper would have an article telling her he was happily holed up in the East Village. For now, she would do what she could.

Eddy took an egg out of the carton she'd bought and inscribed AGENT COVER on it in large block letters. Then she went down to the street, took careful aim, and sent the egg hurtling toward the roof of her building.

She smiled as she heard a faint wet *splat* far overhead, and imagined the egg frying on the hot rooftop just as Cover's brain must be sizzling with anger that Zach had eluded him.

This is your brain on voodoo, she thought. *Any questions?*

In his cheerless office on Poydras Street, Absalom Cover appeared to be sitting in his shirtsleeves paging through an old *Weekly World News,* but in truth he was concentrating on the Bosch case. Cover knew the kid's file by heart, and now he had the myriad outpourings of Stefan "Phoetus" Duplessis to obsess over as well.

Unfortunately, though Duplessis had proved an extremely tender nut to crack, his concrete knowledge about Bosch didn't go far beyond a grudging admiration for all the terrible things he had done. There was a Hacker Code of Ethics, Duplessis explained, consisting of four sacred laws: *Delete nothing. Move nothing. Change nothing. Learn everything.*

Zach Bosch blew the first three laws to hell every time he turned his computer on. Few others in his electronic circle knew the extent of Bosch's crimes; he was careful, and didn't brag as compulsively as most hackers. He had entrusted Stefan Duplessis with some of this information because Duplessis was a better hardware techie, and could tell him—in purely theoretical terms, of course, probably including diagrams of the theoretical modifications—how to manipulate his system to even greater heights of deviousness. (And also, Cover suspected, because Duplessis wasn't above a little bending of the Hacker Laws himself.) Some of the exploits he credited Bosch with were so extreme that the other agents refused to believe them.

Agent Cover believed. He was beginning to understand the hacker mindset. It required nerves of steel and could generate feats of flamboyant genius, but it was flawed. It was megalomaniacal. Eventually it would slip up on its own sheer daring, and give itself away.

As if to make that very point, Duplessis had also told them about the article Bosch had supposedly planted in the *Times-Picayune.* "Goddess Seen in Bowl of Gumbo." It beat anything in the *Weekly World News,* that was for sure. This headline, for instance: CLAM OF CATASTROPHE, bannering a story about a giant shellfish that ate deep-sea divers, or some such shit. What sort of oxygen-deprived mind came up with these things?

Cover closed the tabloid wearily, leaned back in his chair, and tugged the knot of his tie loose. At least Bosch had some imagination, if he had really planted that story in the *Picayune.*

The other hacker swore he had, though the reasons he gave

for believing so were flimsy at best. He just "knew" Bosch, Duplessis claimed; this was just his "style." And he swore up and down that the girl living in Bosch's apartment, Edwina Sung, had nothing to do with any of it. Agent Cover wondered. Duplessis had obviously known Sung at least long enough to develop a sweaty-palmed, hopeless crush on her.

As of this afternoon, Sung's records revealed a bank balance of just over three thousand dollars, not an unreasonable figure for a young Asian-American who could afford to live in the French Quarter. Most likely her parents were in some lucrative business and supported her. She had no outstanding credit card balances, owed no taxes, had no police record; her employment history was spotty. Probably she was just another scrap of bohemian flotsam, adrift on the warm alcoholic seas of New Orleans subculture.

But Zach Bosch meant something to her. That much had been plain during today's raid. They might be accomplices, lovers, or even blood relations—in an old school ID photo they'd found overlooked in his desk, Bosch appeared extremely young, defiant, and faintly Asian. But whatever they were, Cover thought the girl cared enough about Bosch to keep track of his movements if she could. Maybe she even knew where he was now. She ought to be questioned again.

For that matter, her bank records should be examined more closely. A routine balance check wasn't good enough when a hacker might be involved. They ought to get records of all her transactions for the past month, and see whether she had made any large deposits or withdrawals in the last couple of days.

Frank Norton, the stocky gray-haired agent who had the next cheerless office over, came in and dropped a greasy brown paper bag on his desk. "Here's that sandwich you wanted."

"Tuna?"

"No. Egg salad. It was all the cafeteria had left. Don't you ever go home?"

"Sure. I stopped by a couple days ago. Thanks, Spider." Norton had had the nickname since his days with the DEA, when he'd managed to get bitten by a tarantula during a drug raid on the docks. He claimed someone had thrown it on him. The drug runners swore the huge hairy spiders lived inside bunches of bananas; every fool knew that, and Norton shouldn't have stuck his hand in those bananas even if there *were* five-pound bags of cocaine hidden in them.

Alone again, Cover unwrapped his sandwich. The sulfurous odor of boiled eggs in mayonnaise floated up to him. He hated egg salad. Eating the putrid mush anywhere was bad enough; eating it in New Orleans, where you could get some of the best food in the world, was almost unbearable. But his hands were shaking. He was half-starved.

He took a bite of the sandwich, and a generous glob of egg salad oozed out from between the slices of stale brown bread, hung precariously for a moment, then fell. It left a long curdy streak down Agent Cover's tie and shirtfront. When he tried to scoop it up, half of it plopped onto his pants.

"Shit, shit, shit." He crumpled the paper bag furiously, hurled it in the direction of the trash can, missed. These fancy suits he had to wear were damned expensive, and Cover had no idea whether mayonnaise would stain the pants. His wife would know. Maybe he should go home for a while, get a decent meal. He could deal with little Ms. Sung tomorrow.

Fucking eggs. He hated them anyway.

FIFTEEN

"Let's get some sheets," said Trevor. "That mattress is pretty dirty."

"How about a fan?"

"Yeah, and a coffeepot."

Zach smirked. "Gee, I feel so domestic."

"Well, if you don't want to . . ." Trevor looked sidelong at Zach, then stared at the floor in embarrassment.

"Hey, hey, joking. I've never set up housekeeping with anyone before, is all."

"It makes you nervous?" A small line appeared between Trevor's brows as he frowned. It seemed to cost him an effort to understand moods and motivations that would have been immediately obvious to most. Zach guessed Trevor was probably the most weirdly socialized person he had ever met.

"It makes me hyper."

"Want some Excedrin?"

That was Zach's favorite thing about weirdly socialized people: anything that popped into their heads usually made it out of their mouths. "No thanks, I'm fine," he said, and they caught each other's eye and started laughing.

In the giddy rush that followed waking and more fucking, they had put their clothes on and driven downtown with the idea of getting something to eat. Instead they had wound up in Potter's Store, wandering the dim, dust-scented aisles, browsing through the shelves crammed full of junk and plunder.

Zach watched Trevor's hands plunge into a bin of fifty-cent clothing, sorting out only the black items and quickly discarding them, finally selecting a single plain T-shirt. Zach thought of grasping those hands, of turning them over and kissing the palms.

But Potter's Store was full of old rednecks, mostly the re-formed drunks from the Salvation Army who ran the place. Zach supposed they were used to trendy kids thrift-shopping, but he had no desire to attract extra attention. Hell, these people weren't just Christians, they were probably Republicans. If the right kind of G-man flashed a badge at them, they'd not only tell him anything he wanted to hear, they'd lick his asshole clean while they did it. Goddamn John-Wayne-loving John-Birch-worshiping good country people.

"What are you scowling about?"

"Oh." He looked up into Trevor's face and forgot it all. "Nothing."

Their eyes locked on each other, and for a long moment they might as well have been back in bed, tangled in the sweaty blanket, stewing in one another's juices. Then Trevor glanced over Zach's shoulder. "Hey, there's Kinsey. I bet he'd let us take a shower at his house."

"Feed us too?"

"Maybe."

"Go for it."

Trevor grabbed his coffeepot and Zach his fan, and they slipped through the aisles and homed in on Kinsey's tall form like two hungry cats who know which porch to go to.

Kinsey sat at his kitchen table and listened to the shower blasting away. It had done so for thirty minutes now, and though the bathroom was way at the other end of the hall, the kitchen windows had begun to fog up. If they went on much longer, his zucchini-mushroom lasagna would be ready to come out of the oven and he would have to eat it by himself. The house was getting unbearably hot and muggy.

He went into the hall and switched on the air-conditioning. From behind the bathroom door he could hear water hitting skin, the rattle of the shower curtain, a sound that could have been a laugh or a sob. Were they making love in the steam and spray? Were they crying in there?

He did not even try to guess where the nasty-looking cut on Zach's lip had come from, or why Trevor wasn't carrying his sketchbook.

Kinsey had been surprised when they came up to him in Potter's Store all rumpled and bright-eyed and reeking of sex, as obviously connected as if they were clutching hands. Of all the things Kinsey might have predicted for Trevor's first week in Missing Mile, getting laid was not among them. But he had sent Zach out there, and now here they were. He wondered if he had averted something, or only made the house dangerous for two boys instead of one.

Kinsey hadn't been feeling very good about his own judgment since yesterday, since hearing that Rima had cracked up her car and died on the highway outside of town. It must have happened right after she left the Sacred Yew. If he hadn't been worrying about the stupid dinner special, if he'd taken the time to talk to the girl, to ask the right questions, or better yet, to *listen* . . .

(*"Listen?* Ask the right *questions?"* Terry had raged at him. "You fuckin' hippie! You caught that bitch with her hand in the fuckin' *till!"*

"But maybe if I'd given her the money—"

"THEN SHE WOULD HAVE BOUGHT MORE COKE! Give it up, Kinsey! Give it the fuck UP!")

In his heart Kinsey knew Rima had probably been a lost cause. But her mindless, meaningless death made him wonder how far his good intentions could reach, how much he could ever do for these lost kids he wanted so much to help on their way.

Well, time would tell. This was Kinsey's unofficial philosophy on nearly all matters that did not require his immediate attention.

He opened the oven door and poked at the lasagna with a fork. A sullen little cloud of steam rose from its pale greenish surface. It was still a bit wet, but by the time Trevor and Zach finished whatever they were doing in the bathroom, he thought it might be cooked through. Kinsey sliced a loaf of whole-grain bread, spread it with butter, opened a bottle of sweet red wine, and began to brew a pot of strong coffee.

He might not be able to help them, but at least he could feed them well.

Zach stared at the huge green lump of food on his plate. Trevor was eating automatically, his fork rising and falling, his green lump quickly disappearing, washed down with cup after cup of black coffee. He had grown up in an orphanage; he could probably eat most anything put in front of him.

But Zach just couldn't get started. Though he was usually disposed to like things that began with Z, he thought zucchini might be his least favorite vegetable. It was soggy and nearly tasteless, with only a faint unpleasant flavor like chlorophyll tinged with sweat. If dirty socks grew on a vine, Zach thought, they would taste like zucchini.

The casserole or whatever it was Kinsey had tried to make reminded him of the food in the comic *Calvin and Hobbes* that would jump off the plate and hop across the table or down the kid's shirt making noises like *blurp* and *argh*. But Zach was too polite to pull a Calvin face. Instead he poured himself another glass of wine and wished he were back in the shower with Trevor's hands reaching around to soap his back, with his open mouth sliding across Trevor's wet slippery chest.

"Can I get you something else?" Kinsey asked him.

"No thanks. I guess I'm just not very hungry." In truth, Zach felt slightly nauseated after staring at the green lump for so long, but the wine seemed to be settling his stomach. He caught an odd look from Trevor and remembered that asking Kinsey to feed them had been his own idea. It was a mistake he wouldn't make again.

"You must eat out a lot in New York," said Kinsey, and Trevor shot him another look: *New York*?

"I try to live cheap," he told Kinsey.

"I thought that was impossible in New York."

"Rent control," said Zach helplessly, with no real idea

whether they had such a thing in New York City. Trevor stared hard at him.

I'll explain later, he thought, trying to telegraph it into Trevor's head, and poured himself more wine.

No sooner had they bid Kinsey good night and walked across the overgrown yard to the car than Trevor said, "New York, huh?"

Zach's head was spinning from the wine and the joint they had smoked after dinner. He leaned against the Mustang's fender. "I'll tell you about it when we get home."

"Tell me now. I don't like being lied to."

"I didn't lie to you. I lied to Kinsey."

"I don't like lies *at all*, Zach. If that's really your name."

"What? Did I just hear that from the lips of the famous Trevor *Black*?" Trevor looked away. "Look, I told you I was on the run! I can't just go around telling everyone the *truth*! Now get in the car."

"Can you drive?"

"Of course I can fucking drive." Zach pushed himself off the fender and lost his balance, almost fell headlong into the grass. Trevor caught him and he leaned into Trevor's arms, slipped his arms around Trevor's waist. "Don't be mad," he whispered.

"Are you okay?" Trevor asked.

Zach hadn't eaten anything all day, and he had drunk most of the big bottle of wine. He imagined it sloshing around in his stomach, mingling with all the come he'd swallowed, sweet ruby red swirled with salty pearly white. Zach thought again of the green lump of lasagna and almost lost it, but he couldn't stand for Trevor to see him puke.

"I'm fine," he said. Muffled against the front of Trevor's shirt it came out as one slurry word. "I just got a little drunk. It's nothing." He felt Trevor's body stiffen, remembered that Bobby had been drunk on whiskey when he killed the family. To Trevor, the words *I'm drunk, it's nothing* must sound both stupid and cruel.

Well, they'd find ways to deal with these pitfalls and land mines, even if it meant plowing straight through them. Zach wasn't planning to go on the wagon anytime soon.

And why the hell not? he thought. He liked alcohol—usually —but it wasn't vital to him like pot, wasn't essential to his body chemistry. *You're not in New Orleans where drinking's* de rigueur, *not anymore. Why not just forget about the stuff and make him happy?*

Because I don't WANT to!!! his mind raged in the voice of a cranky three-year-old. *I LIKE to get drunk sometimes, there's nothing wrong with that, it doesn't make me beat people or punch them or kill them! It just makes me . . .*

What?

Well, get laid, for one.

He knew it was true; he had almost always been drunk when he went cruising in the Quarter. It helped him gloss over all sorts of things, like the look on Eddy's face when she saw him chatting up some pretty, empty-headed creature of the night, the fact that he would just as soon spit in Death's eye as wear a rubber, the knowledge that he just didn't give a good goddamn about much of anything beyond hacking and having orgasms and watching slasher movies and thumbing his nose at the world.

Except that now he did. And it seemed as good a time to say so as any.

But just then a vehicle swept around the corner of Kinsey's street and came screeching toward them. A pickup or a four-wheel drive from the sound and size of it, though it was going too fast to tell. Its occupants hung out the windows, all hairy limbs and big bullish heads with John Deere and Red Man caps wedged down firmly over the brow ridge. "FUCKIN' QUAAAAAARES," they heard, and a fusillade of silver beer cans sailed out into the slipstream and came clattering around them in the hot, still night. The truck was already disappearing over the next hill.

The boys had been drinking beer, Zach observed. A fine fascist-owned beer with a bouquet hinting at toxic waste and a crisp, golden, pisslike undertone . . .

He smelled the warm stale beer leaking onto the asphalt, saw a submerged cigarette butt dissolving in one of the little puddles, and lost it. He pushed away from Trevor and sprawled headlong over the curb and vomited in Kinsey's yard. It felt marvelous, like the release of some crushing pressure, like vile crimson poison flooding out of his system. He felt the palms of his hands connecting with the earth, felt energy flowing up into his arms and through his body in huge, slow, steady waves. He was plugged into the biggest damn battery of all.

When he was able to raise his head, Zach saw Trevor staring at him like some interesting but faintly repulsive bug. Zach crawled away from his puddle of vomit and sat shakily on the curb. He took off his spattered glasses, wiped them on the tail of his shirt. Trevor sat down next to him.

"Do you know how many times I saw my dad get sick from drinking?" Trevor asked.

"A bunch, I guess."

"No. Just once. Sometimes I wonder what would have happened, though, if he'd had a few more shots before Momma came home that night. What if he'd made himself sick and passed out? What if Momma could tell somehow that he'd drugged us?"

"It sounds like Bobby was pretty much unstoppable."

"Maybe." Trevor shrugged. "But maybe one more shot would've knocked him out. Maybe Momma would have taken me and Didi away."

"I guess it's possible." More than anything, Zach wanted Trevor to put an arm around his shoulders, wanted to lean into Trevor's solid comforting warmth. But he wasn't sure if Trevor was mad at him. "I used to hope the same thing when my parents would go on a binge," he said. "I'd think, *Just a couple more drinks and they'll pass out. They'll shut up. They won't hit me anymore.* But once they got on a tear, they usually stayed on it for a while."

"And you caught the worst of it."

"Yeah, unless they had something better to do."

"Then how—" Trevor turned to Zach, spread his hands

wide. The expression on his face was half disgust, half genuine bewilderment. "How can you drink now? You saw what it did to them—how can you do it too?"

"Simple. It doesn't do the same things to me that it did to them."

"But—"

"But nothing. Remember what you said last night? *The still doesn't have a choice about making liquor; the choice is up to the person who drinks it?* Drinking didn't make my parents act like that. They *were* like that. I'm not."

"So where does that leave my father?" Trevor's voice was quiet, but deadly.

"Well . . ." This was the all-important question, Zach sensed. If he answered it wrong, he could forget about drinking around Trevor—which meant he could forget about Trevor, because he wasn't going to start letting someone else do his thinking for him. And if he answered it *too* wrong, he wondered if he might see his blood decorating Trevor's knuckles again.

"Maybe Bobby was trying to tamp down his anger," he said. "Maybe he was trying to make himself pass out before your mom came home."

"You think so?"

He wants to believe that. Is it cruel to encourage him? I don't think so; hell, I'd want to believe it if I were him. It might even be true. "I wouldn't be surprised," said Zach. "You know he loved you—"

"No I don't. I know he loved *them*. He took them with him. He left me here."

"Bull*shit*!" Zach didn't care about giving the right answer now; this line of reasoning made him too angry to worry about getting hit. "He wasted everything they ever could have done, could have been. The only life he had a right to take was his own. He *robbed* them."

"But if you love someone—"

"Then you want them to be alive. What's to love about a cold, dead body?" Zach caught himself before he went too far on that track. "Bobby fucked up your life pretty good, but at least he let you keep it. He must have loved you best. If you were dead, twenty years of drawings never could've existed, and I couldn't be loving you, and you couldn't even be wondering about all this—"

"What?"

"I said, you couldn't even be wondering—"

"No. The other part."

"I couldn't be loving you," Zach repeated softly. The words felt so strange in his mouth; they had slipped out before he had even known he was going to say them. But he didn't want to take them back.

"I love you too," said Trevor. He leaned over and kissed Zach full on the mouth. Zach's eyes widened and he tried to pull away, but Trevor held him tight. He felt Trevor's tongue sliding over his lips, worrying at the corners, and finally he gave up and opened his mouth to Trevor. They had already exchanged most of their other bodily fluids; he supposed a little puke wouldn't make much difference.

At last Trevor relented and just held him. Zach felt his shakes beginning to recede, the raw burn of bile fading from his throat.

"So you're really on the run?" Trevor asked after a while. Zach nodded.

"And you told Kinsey and Terry you were from New York?"

"Well, I don't think Kinsey believes me. But that's what I told them, yeah."

"You want to talk about it?"

"Could we get in the car first?"

"Sure." Trevor reached for the keys, and Zach surrendered them without argument. "We ought to get going anyway, before those rednecks decide to come back and kick our asses."

Zach laughed. "Hell, if they did, Kinsey could just come out brandishing his casserole and scare 'em off."

*   *   *

Trevor got a feel for the Mustang quickly. He had once had a brief job driving cars from place to place, reasons unspecified and questions not encouraged by the management. Most of them had been scary old junkers or boring Japanese crackerboxes, but this car was fun to drive. Its engine was loud but smooth, and its wheels chewed up the road like a vicious little wildcat worrying a blacksnake.

There was a sour taste in his mouth like fruit juice gone bad, the ghost of Zach's recycled wine. To Trevor it wasn't much different from having the flavor of Zach's sweat or spit or come on his lips. If you loved someone, he thought, you should know their body inside and out. You should be willing to taste it, breathe it, wallow in it.

He got off Kinsey's road, found his way to the highway, then took a side road that wandered off into the country.

"I like the way you drive," said Zach.

"What do you mean?"

"Fast."

"Just talk to me."

"It has to do with computers," Zach warned.

"I figured as much," Trevor said darkly.

They drove for an hour or more around the outskirts of Missing Mile, past dark fields, deserted churches and railroad crossings, small neat houses lit warm against the night. They passed the occasional bright store or honky-tonk joint, swerved to miss the occasional wet splay of roadkill on the hot blacktop.

Zach told his tale without interruption from Trevor, save for an occasional question. When he finished, Trevor's brain was spinning with unfamiliar terminology, with arcane concepts he had never believed possible, but many of which Zach claimed he had already done.

"You mean you could get information about anybody—*and change it?* Could you get information about me?"

"Sure."

"How?"

"Well, let's see." Zach ticked off possibilities on his fingers. "Do you have any credit cards?"

"No."

"Ever had a phone in your name?"

"No."

"How about a police record?"

"Well . . . yeah." Trevor shuddered at the memory. "I got picked up for vagrancy once in Georgia. Spent the night in jail."

"I could get that easy. Erase it, too. With your Social Security number I could probably get your school and social-services records. And your standing with the IRS, of course."

"I doubt the IRS has ever heard of me."

Zach laughed softly. "Don't bet on it, boyfriend."

They took a roundabout route back to Violin Road. By the time Trevor parked the car behind the house, it felt very late. The clouds had blown over and the sky was a brilliant inverted bowl of stars. Zach saw the Big Dipper, the Little Dipper, and the faint soft skirl of the Milky Way, which pretty much exhausted his store of astronomical knowledge. But he stared up into the universe until he was dizzy with infinity, and he thought he could see the great bowl slowly revolving around them, order born of chaos, meaning born of void.

They pushed their way through the vines and entered the dark living room. The house felt very calm and still. Even the doorway to the hall had gone neutral. It was as if some charge had been switched off, as if some current had been interrupted, though the lights still worked. They brushed their teeth in the kitchen sink, fitted the sheets from Potter's Store onto the mattress in Trevor's room, undressed and lay together in the restful dark, their heads touching on the single pillow, their hands loosely joined.

"So I might bring ghosts into your life," Trevor mused, "and you might bring feds into mine."

"I guess so."

Trevor thought about it. "I believe I'd take my chances with the ghosts if I were you."

"I was hoping you'd say that."

And I guess I'll take my chances with the long arm of the law, Trevor thought as he rolled over and fitted himself into the curve of Zach's body. *Harboring a fugitive is bad enough—they probably have a special punishment if you fall in love with one.* He found that the idea of committing a federal crime didn't faze him much. The thought of being in love still seemed far stranger.

Zach had broken all kinds of laws, he supposed, but Trevor had never had much regard for laws. Few of them made sense to him, and none of them worked worth a shit. He had managed to avoid breaking them very often simply because he didn't have many bad habits, and most of the ones he did have happened to be legal. But if any suit-wearing, mirror-shaded zombie dared touch a hair on Zach's head, or set foot inside the boundaries of Birdland . . .

Trevor didn't know what might happen then. But he thought there would be great damage and pain. After all, this house had tasted blood before, had tasted it again today.

He thought it might be getting a taste for the stuff.

Somewhere in the hazy zone between night and morning, Zach opened his eyes a crack and squinted into the darkness. He had no real sense of the room around him, of where he was at all. He only knew that he was still mostly asleep and about half-drunk, that his head was throbbing and his bladder was painfully full.

He pushed himself off the mattress and stumbled into the hall. At the end of it a soft light glowed like a beacon. All he had to do was make his way to that light and relieve himself; then he could fall back into bed and sleep until the headache was gone.

Zach shuffled down the hall naked and barefooted, trailing a hand along the wall for balance, and entered the bathroom. One of the forty-watt bulbs in the ceiling fixture buzzed fitfully, giving off a dim, flickering light. He stepped up to the toilet bowl and urinated into the small pool of dark muddy-looking water. The sound of his pee hitting the stained porcelain seemed very loud in the silent house, and he hoped he wouldn't wake Trevor.

Trevor . . . asleep in the next room, in Birdland . . .

Zach was suddenly wide awake and very conscious of where he was. His stream of urine dried up. As he let go of his dick he felt a single warm drop slide down his thigh. The ghost of cheap red wine still swirled in his brain, making him dizzy, making him aware of just how easy it would be to panic.

But there was no need. All he had to do was turn, step away from the toilet, and—

—and he knew he hadn't shut the door behind him when he came in.

Though he had been mostly asleep, he remembered groping past it, hearing the knob rattle against the wall. The hinges were caked with rust and could not have closed silently. But though Zach had heard nothing, the door was now shut tight.

He swallowed, felt his throat click dryly.

Well, you live in a haunted house, you're going to have doors shutting themselves once in a while. But that doesn't mean anything in here can hurt you. All you have to do is walk over and turn the knob and you're out of here.

(and don't look at the tub)

That last thought came unbidden. Zach threw himself at the door, clawed at the knob. It slipped through his fingers and he realized that his hands were slick with sweat. He wiped them on his bare chest and made himself try again. The knob would not turn, would not even rattle in its moorings. It was as if the workings of the lock had fused.

Or as if something were holding the door shut from the other side.

He yanked at the door with all his strength. Though he could feel the old wood bowing inward, nothing gave. He wondered what would happen if he managed to tear the knob clean out of the door. If there was something in the hall, would it come rushing in through the hole and engulf him?

Zach let go of the knob and stared around the bathroom. The ancient linoleum had begun to curl at the corners, exposing the rotting wood beneath. The peeling paint was streaked from ceiling to floor with long rusty watermarks. The bare shower curtain rod was cruelly bowed, the bottom of the tub glazed with a thin layer of filth, the black hole of the drain ringed in green mold. He thought of pounding on the wall, trying to wake Trevor to come get him out of here, but the tub was set into the wall that adjoined their room. He would have to lean way over it, or climb right in.

He looked quickly away from the tub, and his gaze fell on the mirror over the sink. It reflected his own pale sweaty face, his own wide scared eyes, but Zach thought he saw something else in there too. Some subtle movement, a rippling in the surface of the glass itself, a strange sparkling in its depths as if the glass were a silver vortex trying to draw him in.

Frowning, he moved closer. The cold lip of the sink pushed against his lower belly. Zach leaned closer until his forehead was nearly touching the glass. It occurred to him that the mirror could simply explode outward, burying razor-shards of glass in his face, his eyes, his brain.

Part of his mind was cowering, gibbering, begging him to get away. But part of him—the larger part—had to *know*.

One of the taps twisted on.

Hot liquid gushed into the sink, splashed up onto his belly, his chest, his hands and arms. Zach jumped back, looked down at himself, and felt his well-trained gag reflex try to trigger for the second time that night.

He was covered with dark streaks and splotches of the blood that was still globbing out of the faucet, pooling in the sink. But this was no fresh vivid crimson like the blood from his lip yesterday. This blood was thick and rank, already half-clotted. Its color was the red-black of a scab, and it stank of decaying meat.

As he watched, the other tap turned slowly on. A second fluid began to mingle with the rotting blood, a thinner fluid, viscous and milky-white. The odor of decay was suddenly laced with the raw fresh smell of semen. As they came out of the faucet, the two streams twisted together like some sort of devil's candy cane, red and white (and Black all over . . . wouldn't Trevor love to put *this* in a story?).

Zach felt hysterical laughter bubbling up in his throat. Tom Waits's drunken piano had nothing on this bathroom. The sink was bleeding and ejaculating: great. Maybe next the toilet would decide to take a shit or the bathtub would begin to drool.

He looked back up at the mirror and felt the laughter turn sour, caustic, like harsh vomit on the back of his tongue.

But for certain familiar landmarks—his green eyes, the dark tangle of his hair—Zach barely knew his own reflection in the glass. It was as if a sculptor had taken a plane to his face and shaved layers of flesh from the already-prominent bones. His forehead and cheekbones and chin were carved in stark relief, the skin stretched over them like parchment, sickly white and dry, as if the lightest touch would start it sifting from the bones. His nostrils and eye sockets seemed too large, too deep. The shadowy smudges beneath his eyes had become enormous dark hollows in which his pupils glittered feverishly. The skin around his mouth looked desiccated, the lips cracked and peeling.

It was not the face of a nineteen-year-old boy in any kind of health. It was the face of the skull hiding beneath his skin, waiting to be revealed. Zach suddenly understood that the skull always grinned because it knew it would emerge triumphant, that it would comprise the sole identity of the face long after vain baubles like lips and skin and eyes were gone.

He stared at his wasted image in fascination. There was a certain consumptive beauty to it, a certain dark flame like that which burns in the eyes of mad poets or starving children.

He put out his hand to touch the mirror, and the lesions began to appear.

Just a few tiny purplish spots at first, one on the stark jut of his cheekbone, one bisecting the dark curve of his eyebrow, one nestled in the small hollow at the corner of his mouth. But they began to spread, deepening like enormous bruises, like a stop-motion film of blighted orchids blooming beneath the surface of his skin. Now nearly half his face was suffused with the purple rot, tinged necrotic blue at the edges and shot through with a scarlet web of burst capillaries, and there was no semblance of beauty to it, no dark flame, nothing but corruption and despair and the promise of death.

Zach felt his stomach churning, his chest constricting. He had never obsessed about his looks, had never needed to. His parents had usually avoided fucking up his face too badly because it might be noticed. He still had faint belt marks on his back and two lumpy finger joints on his left hand from breaks that had healed badly, but no facial scars. He'd never even had zits to speak of. He had grown up with no particular awareness of his own beauty, and once he realized he had it and learned what it was good for, he had taken it for granted.

Now watching it rot away was like feeling the ground disappear from under his feet, like having a limb severed, like watching the knife descend for the final stroke of the lobotomy.

(Or like watching a loved one die, and knowing you had a hand in that death . . . Zach, do you love yourself?)

The faucet was still gushing, the sink clogged nearly to overflowing with the twin fluids. A small black pinhole had appeared in the center of each lesion on his face. As he watched, the dots swelled and erupted. Pain zigzagged across the network of his facial nerves. Beads of greasy glistening whiteness welled from the tiny wounds.

Zach felt a sudden, blinding flash of rage. What the hell was the white stuff supposed to be? Maggots? Pus? More come? What kind of cheap morality play was this, anyway?

"FUCK IT!" he yelled, and seized the edges of the mirror and ripped it off its loose moorings and flung it into the bathtub. It shattered with a sound that could have woken all of St. Louis Cemetery. The faucet slowed to a trickle, then stopped.

Zach took a deep breath and put his hands to his face, rubbed them over his cheeks. His skin was smooth and firm, his bones no sharper than usual. He looked down at his body. No huge blossoming bruises, no cancerous purple lesions. His stomach and hips were hollow but not emaciated. Even the spatters of rotten blood were gone. Nothing felt abnormal but his scrotum, which was trying to crawl up into his body cavity.

His shoulders sagged and his knees turned to water. Zach put a hand on the edge of the sink to support himself. As he did, he saw movement in the tub, something other than his own motion reflected in the fragments of broken mirror, a *swinging* motion that seemed to sweep across the glittering shards, then back, then across again . . .

He stared at it, unable to look away, yet terrified that soon his eyes and his mind would piece together the gestalt of all the infinitesimal reflections. He did not want to know what hung there, swinging in the mirror. But if he looked away, it might be able to get out.

Behind him, the hinges of the door shrieked. Zach spun around, muscles tensed, ready to fight whatever was coming for him. He saw Trevor framed in the doorway, tousled and sleepy-eyed, his face half-bewildered, half-scared. "What are you doing?"

"How—" Zach swallowed hard. His mouth and throat had gone dry, and it was difficult to speak. "How'd you get in?"

"I turned the knob and pushed. Why did you shut yourself in here?"

Speechless, Zach pointed at the sink. Trevor followed the direction of Zach's finger, then shook his head. "What?"

Zach stared at the sink. It was empty, stained with nothing but dust and time. The square of plaster above it where the mirror had hung was paler than the rest of the wall. Trevor noticed it too. "Did you—" He saw the broken mirror in the tub and frowned. Then his eyes fell on the bent shower curtain rod and he looked quickly back at Zach, away from the faintest of shadows slowly twisting on the wall. He wrapped his long fingers around Zach's wrist and pulled hard. "Get out of here."

They stumbled into the hall, and Trevor yanked the bathroom door shut behind them. He stood for a moment with his eyes closed, breathing hard. Then he shoved Zach down the hall toward the kitchen, grabbing his arm and hustling him along when he didn't move fast enough.

"Hey—what—don't—"

"Shut up."

Trevor groped for the kitchen light switch, pushed Zach toward the table, then sat down and buried his face in his hands. Zach saw that Trevor's shoulders were trembling. He reached out to massage the tightly wound muscles, but Trevor went even stiffer, then reached up and slapped Zach's hands away. *"Don't touch me!"*

Zach felt as if his heart had been plunged into ice water. He backed away from the table, toward the kitchen door. "Fine! You don't want me here, your *ghosts* don't want me here! Maybe I'll just get the fuck out!" He glanced around the room, trying to locate the bag containing his laptop and OKI. It was leaning against the fridge, and he would have to walk back past the table to get it. His glasses were still in the bedroom too. So much for grand exits.

But Trevor didn't even look up. "I *do* want you here. I think they do too. Sit down."

"Don't tell me what to—"

"Zach." Now Trevor raised his head. His face was haggard; his eyes had a dazed, shellshocked gleam. "Don't give me any shit. Please. Just sit down and talk to me."

Unmollified but curious, Zach pulled out the other chair. He didn't want to leave, but he hated being pushed away. "What do you want to talk about?"

"What did you see in there?"

"All kinds of shit."

"Tell me."

Zach told him everything. At the end of the telling he found himself angry again, but not at Trevor. He was mad at the house, as mad as he had been when he broke the mirror. *Fuck* its pathetic funhouse scares, *fuck* its cheap moral judgments. He wanted to knock Trevor over the head, drag him out of here forever, then get on Compuserv and score two plane tickets to some remote sun-drenched Caribbean island.

When Zach had finished talking, Trevor didn't say anything for a very long time. His right hand lay flat on the tabletop, fingers splayed wide. Cautiously, Zach put his own hand over it, and Trevor didn't pull away this time.

"What did *you* see?" Zach asked finally.

Trevor stayed silent for so long that Zach thought he wasn't going to answer at all. Then he looked up at Zach. His pupils were enormous, and so very black against the paleness of his eyes.

"My father," he said.

Neither one of them felt like going back to sleep. They stayed in the kitchen talking about other things, anything but the silent house around them.

Trevor was still visibly upset, so Zach tried to distract him, asking about comics he liked and hated, trying to get him to argue about politics. (Zach believed in trying to undermine, subvert, and chivvy away the vast American power structure in as many tiny ways as possible, while Trevor opined that it was best to either go out and blow shit up or simply slip through the cracks and ignore the system altogether.) When Zach mentioned his idea of wiping clean the police records of every drug offender he could find, Trevor interrupted. "Could you . . ."

"What? You want to smoke another joint?"

"No. Could you show me some of that computer stuff?"

Zach smiled evilly, flexed his fingers in front of Trevor's face, and assumed a bogus Charlie Chan accent that had always driven Eddy into paroxysms of annoyance. "Where would honorable boyfriend like to go? Citibank? NASA? The Pentagon?"

"You can break into the Pentagon?"

"Well, that'd take some work," Zach admitted. "Hey, I know what. Let's see if the power's really turned on!"

"You mean break into the electric company?"

"Sure."

"But if it's on, won't they notice and turn it off?"

"We're not gonna *change* anything. That is, unless you want to. We'll just take a look. First we need a number."

Before Trevor could say anything, Zach had his laptop and cellular phone arranged and assembled on the table. He dialed 411, waited, then spoke: "Raleigh . . . the number for Carolina Power & Light, please." He scrawled it on one of his yellow Post-its and showed it to Trevor.

"But isn't that just their office?"

"It isn't *just* anything. It's a seed of information. Now watch what we can grow from it. Turn off that light."

Trevor got up and flipped the overhead switch. Now the kitchen was lit only by the soft silver glow from the computer screen. Zach dialed some more numbers. Then his fingers flew over the keys with a rapid-fire staccato sound. He pointed at the screen. "Check this out."

Trevor leaned over Zach's shoulder and saw:

```
;LOGIN: LA52
PASSWORD:
WC?RA
WC%
```

"What's that?"

"COSMOS," Zach said reverently. "AT&T's central data bank."

"Wow."

"Yeah. So—" Zach typed a few more characters, then entered the phone number he'd gotten from directory assistance. "We get a list of *all* Carolina Power & Light numbers. Including their computer dial-ups. Including accounts." Even as he spoke, this information was scrolling down the screen.

"How did you get into COSMOS in the first place?"

"Stolen username and password."

"Isn't that dangerous?"

"The guy I stole 'em from doesn't even know I exist. All I stole was information. It's still there for him to use." Zach looked up from scribbling another number. "That's the beauty of cyberspace. You can take all the information you want, and nobody loses anything."

"Then how come you're in so much trouble?"

"Well, since They don't even like you ripping off information, just imagine how irate They get when you start siphoning money out of Their bank accounts."

"They?"

"The Conspiracy," said Zach darkly. "Hang on—" He was dialing again, then typing rapidly. "Okay! We're in!"

"Now what?"

"Now I figure out how their system works." Zach scowled at the screen, tapped a few keys, snarled his fingers into his hair and pulled it down over his face. The light from the screen turned his face bluish-white, accentuated the hollows beneath his cheekbones and around his eyes. "You can do a search for either a name or an address. Let's try McGee, Robert . . ."

"I think the bills would've been in Momma's name. Bobby's credit was pretty bad by the time we left Austin."

"Okay . . . McGee, Rosena . . ."

"How do you know my mother's name?"

Zach looked up. His eyes were wild, his mouth slightly open. "Huh?"

"I never told you her name."

"Oh. Well . . . I guess . . . uh . . . I guess I read those autopsy reports in your bag."

Trevor grabbed Zach's shoulder and shook it. He felt Zach cringe a little, and the feeling was more gratifying than he wanted it to be. "Don't you have ANY FUCKING RESPECT FOR PRIVACY?"

"No." Zach spread his hands helplessly. "I'm sorry, Trev, but I don't. I was interested in you, and I wanted to know about you. The information was there, so I looked."

"I would have *shown* you—"

"You would *now*. You wouldn't have *yesterday*. And I wanted to know then."

"Great." Trevor shook his head. "Welcome to the instant-gratification generation."

"Guilty as charged. You wanna look at these electric bills or not?"

"Did you find one?"

"Not yet. Hang on . . . nope, nothing in either of your parents' names, or yours either. But here's the account for the Sacred Yew." Zach gave a long, low whistle of appreciation. "Outstanding balance of $258.50 . . . let's shave off that zero, what do you say?"

"I don't think Kinsey would—"

"Too late. $25.85, that looks better. Let's see . . . Buckett, Terry . . . no, he's all paid up."

"I thought we weren't going to change anything!"

"Oh." Zach looked up at Trevor, grinning like a possum. "I'm just raising a little hell. You wanna see some real *changes*?"

"No! Just find the damn house!"

"Okay, okay. Don't get your panties in a knot . . . Rural Box 17, Violin Road, Missing Mile . . ." Zach typed in the address. "Uh-*huh* . . . Service cut off 6/20/72."

"So that means . . ."

"That means the house is making its own juice."

The kitchen suddenly flooded with stark white light, and they instinctively clapped hands over their eyes. Just as they peeked through their fingers and saw that no one was standing near the switch, the room was plunged back into darkness. Then the light again, for a few searing seconds. Then black.

"LEAVE IT ON!" Trevor yelled. "GODDAMMIT, LEAVE IT ON!"

The kitchen stayed dark. Trevor shoved his chair back so hard that it fell over, crossed the room in three strides, and slapped the light switch on.

"*Leave it*," he said. Zach would not have wanted to argue with that voice.

He logged off the power company system and shut his computer down. They'd raised enough hell for tonight.

"Let's go back to bed," he said. What he really wanted to say was *Let's get the fuck out of here*. But Trevor had been waiting to do this for twenty years, and Zach had only known him for two days. If he wanted to be with Trevor, this was where he would have to be. For now, anyway.

But this place won't get to keep you, he thought as he crawled back into bed with Trevor, settled his chin into the hollow of Trevor's shoulder, draped his arm across Trevor's bony rib cage. *When all this is done, you're coming with me. That much I swear.*

S I X T E E N

All night Trevor felt his father's eyes watching him sleep, trying to infiltrate his dreams and claim them. Bobby's eyes were glazed like pale blue marbles, beginning to cloud over yet still touched with some last spark of awareness, some hellish half-life. Had Bobby been trapped in there, in that body, condemned to the slow secret dissolution of the grave? Or in the bathroom, in the peeling yellow paint and cracked porcelain, imprinted on the hot stale air, woven into the very fabric of time that had stopped there for him?

WHY DID YOU LEAVE ME? he wanted to shriek into that dead face. *WHAT WERE YOU THINKING? DID YOU THINK MY LIFE WOULD TURN OUT GOOD? OR COULD YOU SEE ALL THE PAIN, AND DID YOU WISH IT ON ME ANYWAY?*

He held Zach and tried to lose himself in the warmth of solid living flesh, in the small sleeping sounds and shifts of the other body that already felt familiar next to his. But as he drifted in and out of uneasy sleep, Trevor saw again the form hanging from the shower curtain rod, the rope still turning in tiny aimless circles, stirred by some current or by the tiny movements of Bobby's cooling muscles and nerves.

He had only seen it for a few seconds, and even then it had seemed to shimmer, as if he were viewing it directly with his brain rather than using his eyes. Nonetheless, all the details he had blocked from that long-ago morning had been driven home again. The lividity of the hands and feet, the toes and fingertips ready to burst like purple-black grapes, slow drops of blood oozing out from under the nails. The stark map of veins across the chest and shoulders, clearly visible through the drained skin. The shrunken, defenseless-looking penis nearly hidden in his father's ginger mat of pubic hair.

Suddenly awake, his heart pounding painfully, Trevor clutched Zach tighter. Zach had not seen it. Zach was his talisman, his one thread to any possible life beyond this house. He hadn't questioned Trevor's reasons for being here, hadn't asked to leave even after his experience in the bathroom. He had obviously been terrified when Trevor opened the door. Yet here he was now. Was it because he considered the house some sort of extension of Trevor, and trusted that it would not hurt him?

If that was the case, Trevor reflected, then Zach had more faith in him than anyone else ever had.

Well, anyone since Bobby.

But how do I know it won't hurt you? he thought, pressing his face against the back of Zach's neck in the darkness, tasting salty skin against his lips, feeling velvety hair against his eyelids. *How do I even know I won't hurt you? Your flesh feels so good in my mouth, between my fingers, sometimes I just want to keep pulling and tearing and chewing.*

He fell back asleep remembering the flavor of Zach's blood on the back of his tongue, imagining Zach's skin splitting beneath his fingers, Zach's heart still beating in his gore-slicked hands.

Then suddenly sunlight was streaming through the dirty panes of the window, trickling into the corners of his eyes. His head ached slightly, felt somehow too heavy on his neck. Trevor arched his back and stretched, then rolled his head on the pillow to look over at Zach.

What he saw made him suck his breath in hard and squeeze his eyes shut tight. Zach was lying on his back, arms splayed out above his head, his face battered but serene, very pale. In the center of his chest, just above the arc of the ribs, was a ragged raw-edged crimson hole. Dark blood had bubbled out of it, streaking his stomach and face, drenching the sheet around him.

Trevor could not make himself look again. *Being a true artist means never averting one's eyes,* he remembered Crumb writ-

ing, though he was pretty sure the quote had originated else-
where. But he couldn't open his eyes. Instead, he put out a
shaky hand and felt his fingers bump up against Zach's
shoulder. Slowly he ran his hand over the corrugated rise of
the ribcage. The skin was damp, nearly wet, but whether the
wetness was sweat or blood Trevor could not tell. He moved
his fingers across Zach's chest, exploring it like a blind man,
waiting for his fingers to sink into that raw red hole, into that
soup of muscle and organ and splintered bone.

It didn't happen. Instead he felt Zach's heart beating strong
and steady beneath his hand, Zach stirring and responding to
his touch, Zach whole and alive. The relief that flooded
through him was as hot as the imagined blood had been, but
sweeter.

Zach woke with Trevor's hair drifting across his face,
Trevor's warm wet mouth wrapped around his left nipple,
Trevor's hand sliding along his thigh and over his hip, gently
teasing his already half-erect dick. Thus, he did not immediately recall what had happened in the bathroom. When it did
come to him it felt remote and unthreatening, like a half-
remembered bad dream.

Trevor slid down and started sucking him, and the last of
Zach's low-grade wine hangover dissolved like shreds of a
caul and disappeared. Trevor's tongue made his skin ripple
and his blood quicken. Trevor was no jaded lover like most of
the others he'd had. They knew the same things Zach did:
how to satisfy themselves, how to coax universal physiologi-
cal reactions from whatever body wound up in bed with
them. But Trevor was learning how to pleasure *him*, and Zach
was figuring out what Trevor liked, and every time they woke
up together they learned it all over again. It made so much
difference.

So what changed your mind, Zachary? he heard Eddy's voice
asking him, a little sad, a little reproachful. *What made you
realize you might not turn into a pumpkin if you had sex more than
once with somebody you actually gave a damn about?*

He didn't know. He could only look back with awe on his
life of three days ago, his life that had not contained Trevor

Black, and wonder how he had ever lived it. What had the world been to him without these feelings, without this insane, brilliant, beautiful boy? It was difficult to remember.

Now Trevor's hands were pulling at him, that deft tongue probing him relentlessly. As he grew surer of what he was doing, Trevor was proving to be a near-invasive lover, determined to put his fingers into every fold and hollow of Zach's body, to get every available inch of Zach's flesh into his mouth, to bathe in the juices of sex and perhaps drown in them. It was almost painful—but exquisitely so, like a cerulean wave crashing and foaming on a pure white shore, like the relief of the swollen vein as the junkie slides the needle in.

But suddenly Zach caught himself thinking of his image in the bathroom mirror before he had shattered it. The light of fever burning in the eyes, straight through to the brain. The emaciated face. Those lesions. He thought of all the fluids that had passed between him and Trevor, awash with whatever strange chemicals and subtle poisons lurked in their bodies.

Then he put the thought out of his head, as he always did such thoughts.

But this time it was harder.

In the afternoon they sat at the kitchen table together, Trevor drawing while Zach created a bank account in Raleigh just for the hell of it. Then they ventured downtown for dollar plates of eggs and grits at the diner, which served breakfast all day in keeping with the schedules of its clientele.

Afterward, Trevor was buzzed on brutally strong diner coffee, Zach on the healing energy of a meal he could keep down. They wandered up the street and stopped into Potter's Store to let the air-conditioning soothe their sweaty sex-soaked skin.

Zach stopped to play with an old adding machine, lost himself briefly in the sensual texture of keys beneath his fingertips, then looked up and realized he was alone. He found Trevor in the next aisle looking at something called the Sunbeam Hygenic Cordless Toothbrush. The box was decorated in four-pointed starbursts, the bright colors faded. On its side were the disembodied heads of a WASP family, Mom, Dad, Sis, and Junior, all with gleaming grins—hygienic ones, presumably. Where were those facile fifties faces now, Zach wondered, those vapid, innocent icons of post-war advertising, those manufactured American archetypes?

"Whatever happened to those guys?" he asked aloud.

Trevor looked up from his intense scrutiny of the box art. His eyes were sharp and very clear. "The sixties came along and bashed their little heads in."

Zach was still turning that one over and over in his head as they left the store. Trevor hadn't had to think about it at all before he answered: his life had been a study in exactly what had happened to that kind of mythical family.

They continued down Firehouse Street into the run-down section of town, past papered-over windows, boarded-up doors, abandoned cars sagging on their springs. When they reached the Sacred Yew and heard drums and a bass beat coming from the club so early in the day, they stopped in to see what was up. It turned out to be a Gumbo sound check in full swing.

Terry Buckett was onstage with two other guys, a skinny kid with a bowl haircut and Lennon glasses playing bass and a devilish-looking bleached blond on guitar. The blond, Trevor observed, had a tattoo of Mr. Natural on his left bicep and looked as if he'd been born with a Stratocaster in his hands. He was handsome, too, with a sybaritic face and a lanky, muscular build. Trevor caught himself wondering if Zach had noticed. *How stupid,* he thought, but the thought didn't go away.

The song in progress sounded like a cross between the Cramps and some kind of old surf music. When it ended, Terry got up from behind the drums and crossed the stage to greet them. "I lost my voice!" he said in a hoarse, dramatic whisper.

"Guess we're playing an instrumental set tonight," added the boy with the Lennon specs. "Me and Calvin cain't sing."

"Why don't you cancel the show?" Zach asked.

Terry rolled his eyes ruefully. "Kinsey needs the money real bad. We do too. Trevor, Zach, this here is R.J. He's a nerd, but he's my oldest buddy. And this is Calvin."

R.J. said "Hey" and started tuning his bass. He didn't seem especially bothered at being called a nerd. Calvin looked right at Zach and his face split in a delighted, dazzling grin. He looked as if he would like to eat Zach up right there on the spot. "Howdy," he said. "You new in town?"

Zach started to grin right back, but seemed to catch himself. He gave Calvin an uncomfortable half-smile. "Yeah," he said. "We both are."

"Well, let me know if you need anyone to show you the sights, hear?" Calvin laid a slight emphasis on the *you*, which was obviously meant to be singular.

Trevor wanted to drag him off the stage and smash his head like a melon on the sticky floor. Surely he could see that the two of them were together. Could he also see how clueless Trevor was about sex? Could he read some nameless longing in Zach's eyes?

"Uh, thanks, but I think I've already seen the important ones." Zach turned to Trevor, put an arm around him. "Come on," he urged, "let's see what Kinsey's up to."

They walked toward the back of the club, but in Trevor's mind, Calvin had already suffered all the torments of a particularly cruel hell.

Onstage, Calvin watched them walk away, and Terry watched him watching. Those evil eyes devoured Zach from the top of his tangled hair to the soles of his hightop sneakers. He was just Calvin's type, Terry knew: skinny bones and deathsome pallor, but spiced up with a smartass twist to his lips. "You leave him alone," Terry warned.

"Who's that with him?"

"Bobby McGee's kid."

Calvin's eyes widened. "Is the urge to kill hereditary?"

"You never know. I wouldn't fuck with him. Goddamn, my

throat hurts." Terry grimaced as he picked up his drumsticks. "You wanna run through 'Bad Reaction' again?"

In the bar, Kinsey greeted Trevor and Zach, then went back to his ledger. Zach ducked behind the bar and helped himself to a National Bohemian and a Coke from the cooler. He tossed the Coke to Trevor, popped open the beer, and dropped three dollars on the bar.

Kinsey looked up at the sound of the drinks opening, glanced from the open beer to Zach's face. "How old are you?" he asked.

"Uh, nineteen. Why?"

"You can drink that because we're closed. But during club hours, you don't drink alcohol here. Understand?"

"Huh?" Zach's face registered utter shock. "Why? What did I do?"

"Nothing. You're just too young. I don't know what the drinking age is where *you* come from, but here it's twenty-one. I could get shut down for serving you."

"But—"

"If you want to drink, you can bring in a flask. Don't flash it around, and don't tell anyone I said you could. Those are the rules."

"Rules?"

"Don't they have rules in New York?"

Zach looked helplessly at Trevor. He ought to say something, Trevor guessed. Zach was evidently so poleaxed by the concept of an enforced legal drinking age that his silver tongue had deserted him. But he never should have told that stupid New York story in the first place; he was about as much a native New Yorker as Trevor was a Hindu from Calcutta. And anyway, he had smiled back at that guitarist. Kinsey could keep him squirming.

But Kinsey relented. "You're in the heart of the Bible Belt," he told Zach. "Just be glad you didn't end up in one of the dry counties."

Zach shook his head in silent wonder. Kinsey finished adding a column of numbers, unfolded himself from his bar stool, and headed for the back door. Trevor and Zach were left alone in the bar.

"I bet you won't even buy for me," said Zach.

"You got that right."

"Shit."

The sound check was winding down. Zach went off to the rest room, and Terry and R.J. passed him on their way into the bar. They grabbed frosty bottles from the cooler and sprawled in a booth, looking as if they had done all this millions of times. "Where's Calvin?" Trevor asked, unable to help himself.

Terry pointed down the street, then clutched his throat. "He went to the store to get cigarettes," R.J. translated.

Good, let him die of lung cancer. "Is he coming back?"

Terry looked searchingly at Trevor, then beckoned him over. Trevor slid into the booth beside him, and Terry put a hand on his shoulder and leaned in close to whisper. A few days ago Trevor would have shrunk from the touch out of pure reflex, but now he was able to restrain himself.

"Calvin's all right," Terry said. "He thinks he has to flirt with every good-looking kid he sees, but he's all right. Don't let him bother you."

"He's not bothering me."

"Well, look, if you have to kick his ass, don't break any of his fingers. All the other decent guitarists are out of town."

R.J. snorted into his beer. Terry nodded serenely at Trevor. Kinsey came back in carrying a bushel basket of zucchini labeled FREE and set it on the bar. Trevor wondered whether anyone in this town maintained so much as a passing acquaintance with sanity. But he supposed that was the pot calling the kettle black.

Suddenly, from the restroom, they heard Zach's voice raised in song. Apparently he didn't know how flimsy the walls were, or didn't care. All four heads turned as his clear, strong tenor came soaring through the pipes and particleboard:

"OLD MAN RIVVVERRRR . . . HE DON'T LIKE COTTON . . . TIRED O'LIVINNN', SCARED O'ROTTIN' . . ."

Then they heard the toilet flush, and Zach came back into the bar, saw them all looking at him. "What?"

"I didn't know you could sing," said Trevor.

Zach shrugged, trying and failing to hide his pleasure at being the center of attention. "Cajun blood. You're lucky I don't play the accordion."

Trevor winced, and Zach realized that he had just given away an important piece of his background in front of Terry, R.J., and Kinsey. He couldn't tell if the others had caught it, but Kinsey looked surprised, then vaguely pleased, as if Zach had only confirmed a suspicion he'd harbored all along.

Well, Kinsey hardly seemed likely to call the feds on him. Of course Clifford Stoll was an aging hippie too, and he had busted the Chaos Computer Club, a group of German hackers who weren't doing anything but breaking into mickeymouse American systems and trying rather half-assedly to sell the information to the KGB.

Zach swallowed hard, decided to pretend his slip of the tongue had never happened, and slid into the booth next to R.J. His sneaker found Trevor's under the table and nudged up against it. "I can't really sing," he said airily. "I mean, I've never been in a band or anything."

"Would you like to?" rasped Terry.

"Well—" He looked across the table at Trevor, who was drawing patterns in the moisture left by the beer bottles on the tabletop. "I don't know how long I'm going to be in town," he said, and Trevor looked up.

"How about just for tonight?" R.J. asked. "Think you could learn a few songs that fast?"

"Sure, if you wrote the words out for me and let me look at them for a few minutes."

"Just a few minutes?"

"Well, then I could rehearse with you and really learn the songs. But I can memorize the words real fast."

"Cool." R.J. and Terry nodded at each other. "So you wanna do it?"

"What kind of music is it mostly?"

"It's Gumbo," said R.J. "A little of this, a little of that, and a whole lot of good."

"Uh—" Zach looked again at Trevor, who just shrugged and looked away with a small smile. Probably he thought the whole thing was pretty silly, maybe even stupid. Zach knew that fronting a locally popular rock band, even for a single night in a club way off the beaten track, might not be the smartest course of action for a wanted fugitive. But he couldn't help it: the idea of clutching a microphone, dressed all in black, getting to slink and snarl around the stage for an hour or two in front of his new lover and a big crowd of hipster freaks had already seduced him.

"Yeah," he said. "I want to do it."

The bar phone rang. Kinsey looked up from his account books to answer it, spoke for a moment, then put the receiver down on the bar. "Trevor? It's for you."

Trevor got up from the booth frowning. No one knew he was here. "Who is it?" he asked, but Kinsey just shook his head. Trevor picked up the receiver. "Hello."

"Hi, Trevor? This is Steve Bissette from *Taboo*."

"Uh, hi." *Taboo* was his favorite comics anthology, the one he had meant to submit the Bird story to. Stephen Bissette, a very tasty writer and artist himself, was also its editor/publisher. Trevor had no idea how he could have gotten the Sacred Yew's phone number, or why he would have wanted it.

"Listen, thanks for sending me 'Incident in Birdland.' I think it's a really twisted story and I like your artwork a lot."

"Thank you," Trevor said dazedly. He had never drawn a story called "Incident in Birdland," and to the best of his memory had never yet sent anything to *Taboo*. He'd thought of calling the Bird story "Incident in Jackson," but had discarded that name as too boring, and hadn't titled it at all before it got shredded.

"I really love the ending, where the zombie musicians crucify the sheriffs and burn 'em. I have to admit I didn't see that coming."

"Thanks," Trevor said again. He glanced over at the booth. Calvin had come back and was leaning against the table peeling the cellophane off his Marlboros with elaborate casualness, but Zach was looking at Trevor. He raised his eyebrows questioningly.

"Anyway," said Bissette, "I'd like to buy the story. I just wanted to make sure I should still send your contract and check to this address."

"Could you read it back to me?"

He heard papers rustling. "Rural Box 17, Violin Road . . ."

"No. Send it care of the Sacred Yew." Trevor read the address off a past-due water bill on the bartop.

"Great. And listen, I'd like to see more of your work. But don't send your originals by surface mail next time, okay? It's not reliable. Send me copies or FedEx. Or fax 'em if you want. I can give you the number."

"That's okay. I'll send copies."

They said good-bye, and Trevor hung up feeling as if he'd just smoked two or three of Zach's joints all by himself: dizzy, slightly elated, and disoriented as hell.

He went back to the table and leaned over to speak in Zach's ear. "Can I talk to you for a minute?"

They walked out through the silent gloom of the club, past the softly gleaming graffiti that said WE ARE NOT AFRAID. Trevor wished it were true. The sun was high in the sky overhead, but the sidewalk shimmered with the heat of the day. The sky was the color of bleached denim, heavy with unshed rain.

Trevor recounted the surreal conversation. Zach's eyes grew larger behind his glasses, and he leaned against the building shaking his head. "This just gets more and more fucked up."

"Did you see the pieces of the story after that morning?"

"I thought you picked them up and threw them away."

"I thought *you* did."

They stared at each other, confusion and fear writ large on their faces. At last Zach said, "Are you sure you want to stay there?"

"No. But I have to."

Zach nodded. Trevor watched him for a moment, then asked quietly, "Are you sure *you* want to?"

"No."

"Are you going to leave?"

"No. Not now." Zach took Trevor's hands between his own. "But, Trevor, you know I might *have* to leave. And if I do, I won't get much warning."

"I know. But I've got to stay, at least until I find out . . ."

"What?"

"The reason why I'm alive."

"Trev . . ." Zach slid his hands up to Trevor's shoulders, put his arms around Trevor's neck. "What if there is no reason? What if he was just crazy?"

"Then I have to know that."

They stood on the sidewalk embracing in the hot afternoon. Zach's body felt like a comforting old friend in Trevor's arms by now. His tension ebbed a little. "So are you going to sing with the band?" he asked.

"Yeah. Terry's writing out some lyrics for me. You mind hanging out while I practice with them?"

"I guess not. What do you think of Calvin?"

"I don't know. I haven't said ten words to him. He's okay, I suppose."

"I hate him."

Zach looked up, surprised, and saw that Trevor meant it. "How come?"

"Because of how he looked at you."

Zach laughed, then stopped when he saw Trevor's face. "Don't be stupid," he said. "I'm with you. Understand? I'm crazy about you, Trevor. You have zero competition."

"And because of how you looked at him."

"Goddammit!" Zach grabbed handfuls of Trevor's T-shirt, pushed his face up close to Trevor's. "Your house attacked me last night. It locked me in the bathroom and made me watch myself dying in the mirror. I don't know what else it would have done if you hadn't come in. Now, if you were just a meaningless fuck to me, *do you really think I'd still be here?*"

"I don't know! How should I know what you're going to do?" Trevor seized Zach's wrists, pulled Zach's hands off his shirt. "I've never been in love with anyone before! *Remember?*"

"*Neither have I!*"

Their eyes locked and held. They stood gripping one another's arms, breathing hard, neither giving an inch.

This isn't just about having someone to wake up next to, Trevor realized. *It's about trusting someone else not to hurt you, even if you're sure they will. It's about being trustworthy, and not leaving when it gets weird.* Zach's eyes were very wide, intensely green, his face paler than ever. Even his lips had gone pale, but for the vivid streak of his healing scar. He looked mad as hell. He was so beautiful.

Trevor realized that he was no longer staring Zach down, but studying him, working to commit his face to memory. At the same time Zach's anger seemed to dissolve as quickly as it had come. A wide, goofy grin replaced it. "Hey!"

"What?"

"You sold a story to *Taboo*! That's great!"

"Yeah," said Trevor. "But I wonder what name I sold it under."

SEVENTEEN

Eddy woke up ravenous on Wednesday, went to the Café du Monde for coffee and beignets, read the *Times-Picayune* without finding any new clues, and returned to find that a grimy slip of paper had been tacked to the door of her apartment.

EDDIE: it read, MY PARENTS' HOUSE WAS RAIDED AND MY SYSTEM SEIZED. I AM COOPERATING FULLY WITH THE GOVT. ON THE CASE OF ZACHARY BOSCH, DOB 5-25-73, SS# 283-54-6781. I KNOW HIS CAR. AND I READ THE PAPERS TOO. It was signed SD, along with a local phone number.

She swore and ripped the filthy thing off her door. The paper felt slimy in her hand, eldritch, unspeakably loathsome. Eddy crumpled it in her hand. She wondered how he had gotten past the street gate, then realized that its "security" consisted of an electronic keypad. Presumably such a gadget couldn't thwart a Phoetus of DagØn.

I read the papers too.

Had Stefan the fish-lipped, frog-eyed fanboy seen the same item she'd found yesterday, the one about the Cajun shooting himself with five different guns? Had he wondered about it, and maybe—just as a matter of course—pointed it out to his friendly neighborhood feds? *I don't know if there really is a town called Missing Mile,* she could hear him whining, *but if there is, I think you'd better check it out.*

Well, if he had, at least he'd made a half-assed attempt to warn her about it. Maybe somewhere in his narky little heart he wanted Zach to have a chance.

But, of course, it was up to Eddy to actually *give* him one.

Her brain felt as if it had been dropped into a centrifuge. The cells were whirling dizzily, the synapses separating,

short-circuiting. She sat on the bed and tried to steady herself.
She couldn't help Zach by getting hysterical.

What could she do? First, she needed a way to find Zach
and alert him to the danger. She hoped there was a way to do
that by phone, but if there wasn't, she guessed she would just
have to hie her butt to Missing Mile, North Carolina.

Second, she needed a way to help Zach get away for good.
Probably he would have to leave the country. She might even
go with him. He could hardly refuse her company this time,
not after she had saved his ass.

And before she could do any of this, she needed a safe
phone.

Okay. It wasn't quite a plan, but it was a place to start.

Eddy grabbed a notebook and a pen to write down numbers. Then she set off to catch the streetcar that wound away
from the French Quarter, down St. Charles Avenue and into
the city.

First she called the Pink Diamond. She had missed two
shifts already, so they probably assumed she wasn't coming
back. Still, she hadn't been able to call since the Secret Service
took her phone out, and she wanted to wrap up her loose
ends; that was just the way she'd been raised. She dialed the
office, and the manager's slimy voice answered.

"Hey, Loup, this is Eddy."

"Who?"

"Miss Lee."

"Oh yeah, we figured you ran off back to China." She
heard the wet sinus-damaged snort that passed for Loup's
laugh. "Hey, you got a message here."

"Really?" Her heart quickened a little. "What is it?"

"Well, it's kinda weird. I think it must be from some crazy
customer. Valerye wrote it down"—Valerye was the daytime
bartender—"and she said the guy spelled it out real careful
and swore it was important."

"*What is it?*" she repeated. The phone booth she had found
in the parking lot of a seafood shack near the riverbend was

private, but hot and claustrophobic. Eddy felt the beginnings of a headache.

"Well, it says 'Wax Jism.' "

"What?"

Loup spelled out the two words, and Eddy wrote them down in her notebook. Her head was pounding now. She thanked Loup, told him almost as an afterthought that she wasn't coming back to work, then hung up and stood staring at the ridiculous message. Wax jism. It had to be from Zach. But what in hell did it *mean*?

She looked out at the parking lot. Over the green hump of the levee she could see a sliver of the Mississippi, a tugboat and barge riding on the mighty polluted current. Her eyes slid back to the keypad of the phone, and something clicked in her mind. There were letters on the keys as well as numbers. Eddy looked back at the message. Two words: three letters, then four. The same configuration as a phone number.

Eddy grabbed the unwieldy metal-covered phone book that hung from a coiled cord in the booth. It was battered but miraculously intact. She riffled through the opening pages, found the listing of area codes for all states. Missing Mile had been fairly near Raleigh and Chapel Hill on the map, and the area code was the same for both places. She dropped in a handful of change, punched in the area code, and with shaking fingers picked out the number.

It rang twice. Three times. Then the receiver was lifted, and a slightly hoarse male voice said, "Howdy, this is the Sacred Yew."

"Hi, you don't know me, but I'm looking for—"

"No one's within earshot right now, but we have lots of great shows coming up this week. Wednesday night it's vintage swamp rock with GUMBO!!! Thursday—"

Eddy leaned her forehead against the hot glass, felt hot tears of frustration trickling from the corners of her eyes. It was a recording.

"If you'd like to leave a message for me or anyone who works here," the voice was saying, "start talking at the beep. And remember, please come out and support your local bands at THE SACRED YEW!" The guy sounded nervous and slightly desperate. At last the accursed machine beeped.

"This is a message for a boy named Zach," Eddy said without much hope. She didn't know if he'd be using his real first name, but she was sure he wouldn't be using his last, and she didn't want to give it away. "He's nineteen, about five-eight, skinny, black hair, green eyes, very pale, very striking. If you know him, will you please tell him he's in terrible danger? My name is Eddy. I have to get in touch with him. I'll try to call back." She checked her watch. "I don't know when. Tell him . . ." She realized tears were spilling from her eyes, pouring down her face. "Tell him I'm coming to get him."

Eddy hung up, swiped at her eyes, composed herself. She had one more call to make, to a local number she knew by heart. She dialed it, listened to the phone ring and ring, then closed her eyes in relief as it was picked up. A rhythmic swath of reggae pulsed in the background, and for a moment she thought it was another recording. Then a deep musical voice said "Hello?"

"Dougal," she said. "This is Eddy. Have you heard what happened to Zach?"

"Ya mon. Busted. Terrible t'ing." She imagined him shaking his head, long bright-threaded dreadlocks swaying gently around his face.

Eddy closed her eyes and counted to five. "No," she forced herself to say calmly, "he *wasn't* busted. He got away, but they're still after him, and I think they're closing in. Do you want to help?"

"Oh, ya mon. I would help Zachary any way I can. 'Specially 'gainst de damn government." She wasn't sure, but she thought she heard him spit. She took a deep breath, felt relief spreading through her. At last she wasn't alone in this anymore.

"Could you start by picking me up outside Liberty's Fish Camp? I need to tell you all about it. And I need your help too."

"Sweetheart, don' you worry 'bout a t'ing, hear? You jus' wait right there outside Liberty's. I know de very place."

"Are you sure?"

"Irie," Dougal St. Clair's beautiful voice soothed her. "No problem."

At the Sacred Yew, the rehearsal was still blasting away onstage. Kinsey had gone down the street to get pretzels for the bar. As he came back in, he saw that the message light on the answering machine was blinking. But when he tried to play back the message, the machine just emitted a long series of beeps, then made a sound like a car going up a hill stuck in first gear. Kinsey peered inside and saw that it had eaten the tape. The machine had been on its last legs for weeks, erasing as many messages as it took. Now it was finally dead.

He picked up the phone to call tonight's doorman and realized with much greater consternation that it was dead too, though he knew it had been on earlier because Trevor had gotten that mysterious call.

Kinsey looked at the clock, saw that it was just after five: cutoff time. He'd let the bill go too long. Now there was no way to get the phone turned back on until tomorrow, and Kinsey would have to drive the cash all the way to Raleigh. That was *if* the bar took in enough tonight to pay for it and the other bills too. The phone was important, but water was more so. And in a club, electricity took the highest priority of all; it was what kept the band loud and the beer cold. He had to get that damn power bill paid.

Kinsey had always loved summer in Missing Mile. But just lately it was a cruel season.

Dougal St. Clair lived in a tree in a secluded corner of City Park. His little wooden house was nestled high among the big oak's spreading canopy of branches, accessible by a long, twisty, terrifying rope ladder that was barely visible against the tree trunk. He parked his car at the nearby fairgrounds, made use of public rest rooms and afternoon rainstorms, ate at the city's many fine restaurants with the money he saved on rent, and often relied on the kindness of friends. Dougal had so much slack that it was considered something of a privilege among French Quarter bohos to buy him lunch once in a while.

The outside of his treehouse was painted in a drab brown camouflage pattern. The inside compensated with a riot of color. The walls were red, yellow, green, and purple, covered with snapshots of Dougal's American and Jamaican friends, the former a motley cross-section of New Orleans freak society, the latter invariably dreadlocked and grinning.

The striped ceiling was not quite high enough for Dougal to stand up straight, though Eddy could do so comfortably. The floor was covered with a woven straw mat. There was a nest of blankets in one corner, a crate of books and a boom box with some tapes stacked around it in another. He kept a lot of stuff in his car in case the treehouse was ever discovered, but somehow it never was.

"How do you get phone service up here?" Eddy asked as she settled herself on a gorgeously embroidered cushion. She had told him the whole story on the ride over from the lake.

Dougal held up a sleek black cellular phone. "Present from Zachary."

"I should've known. Can I use that?"

He gave it to her, then pulled a fat straw pouch and a package of rolling papers from his pocket, shook out a generous quantity of fragrant green pot, and started rolling a joint. Eddy dialed the Sacred Yew's number again. It only rang once; then a piercing electronic tone wailed in her ear and a recorded voice said, *"The number you have reached has been temporarily disconnected. No further information is available at this time. The number you have reached—"*

"DAMMIT!" Eddy nearly hurled the phone across the treehouse. Only the fear that it would fly out the window and go crashing to the ground fifty feet below stopped her hand. Her treacherous eyes filled with tears again, though she was sick of crying. "Our only link to Zach has just been severed. Now what do we do?"

"Relax, sweetheart." Dougal handed her the joint, an enormous, tightly rolled bomber. "First we smoke a spleef. Then we t'ink better, an' we plan."

"Speak for yourself. You must have been smoking this stuff since you were born."

"I was smokin' it in my momma's *womb*," Dougal assured her. "But don' worry. This is smart ganja. Relaxes you an' clears your head."

Eddy regarded the huge bomber glumly. Dougal struck a match, offered her the flame cupped between his pink-brown palms. *Oh, what the hell,* she decided, and let him light it for her.

The taste was sticky and sweet, almost cloying. But as it swirled through her lungs and out into her bloodstream, she thought she could feel some of the shadows lifting. By the time she'd had two hits, she actually believed she might see Zach again, might even be able to save him. Another drag and she'd probably be imagining them as an old married couple. She handed the joint back to Dougal. "What is this stuff?"

"Fresh Jamaican." Dougal wrapped his hand around the joint, brought it to his lips, and produced an enormous cloud of smoke. She noticed that he didn't automatically pass the joint back as Americans did, but let it dangle casually between his first two fingers until he was ready to hit it again. When you grew up in Jamaica, Eddy guessed, you always knew where your next joint was coming from.

The afternoon light was very clear, sifting through the canopy of leaves and the cracks in the wood, filling the treehouse with green and gold. Eddy leaned back against the wall, beginning to relax. "Where do you get fresh Jamaican around here?"

"Got a frien' who flies to Jamaica two times a month or so. He lan' at a little strip up in de hills near Negril on de western coast, pick it up an' fly back to his place in de swamp, then somebody else pick it up an' bring it to New Orleans. No problem."

"He has an airstrip in the swamp?"

"Ya mon. Jus' a little shack an' a place to lan' his plane."

Eddy's heart was pounding. "Do you think he might be making a trip soon?"

"I t'ink he could be convinced," said Dougal gravely. "I don' b'lieve he would fly to North Carolina. He don' like to fly over U.S. airspace. But if we get Zachary down to de swamp, I t'ink my frien' would take him."

"I'll drive to Missing Mile. I'll shoot coffee into my veins and drive all night if I have to. I'm not letting them get him."

"You wan' drive my car? You wan' me to go with you?"

"I guess so. We can't bring Zach back through New Orleans. We'll have to go around it and straight down into the swamp. Do you think your friend—"

"My frien' will be there," Dougal soothed. "Don' worry. We call him once we get on the road."

He was smiling at her, his teeth crooked but very white in his dark face, his eyes the color of warm chocolate. She couldn't help smiling back.

"See," said Dougal. "I tol' you we plan better with our heads cleared out. De smart ganja works ever' time."

Agent Cover maneuvered his white Chevy van through the carbon monoxide snarl of downtown New Orleans. A fruitless visit to the French Quarter had left him staring at a lot of dead ends. Edwina Sung's toothbrush was missing from her bathroom, and it turned out she had withdrawn seven thousand dollars from her bank account yesterday afternoon, several hours after the raid. Possibly she was shacked up somewhere, consoling herself over the loss of her favorite wanted criminal. But Cover suspected his exotic little bird had flown the coop.

A short electronic purr came from the region of his armpit. His cellular phone. He wrested it out of his sweaty jacket and thumbed the talk button. "Cover."

"Afternoon, Agent. This is Payne from the DMV."

"Yeah?" Cover perked up a little. A call from the Department of Motor Vehicles could mean good news.

Sure enough, Payne went on, "We got a trace on that name you gave us. Zachary Bosco—"

"Bosch."

"Well, it took us a while to trace 'cause somebody had changed it in the computer. But we got a registration for him. Plate reads LLBTR-5. It's a 1965 Chevy pickup, color red, down in Terrebonne Parish—"

"*Terrebonne?* You mean down by *Houma*?"

"Yep, Houma it is."

"Shit."

"You gotta go down there, Agent? Better be careful. Some a' them Cajuns don't like cops much. Kinda got their own laws an' idears about things an' all. Hot as hell an' swampy as an open grave too. Listen, you need anything else today?"

"No. Thanks, Payne."

Cover terminated the call, tugged the knot of his tie loose, and sat in stalled traffic with the air-conditioning vents aimed straight at his face. He knew Bosch must have gotten into the DMV computer and messed with the plates. *Bosco.* Cute. He probably could have deleted his registration altogether, but that might have set off alarms in the computer, and it was more his style to create as much confusion with as few key-strokes as possible.

A red 1965 Chevy pickup . . . it was all wrong. Stefan "Phoetus" Duplessis knew approximately as much about au-tomobiles as he did about girls, but he swore up and down that he remembered Bosch driving a black Mustang.

Duplessis had been of little help so far. He had found arti-cles in the *Times-Picayune* implying Bosch could be found in, variously, Cancun, Mexico; Bangor, Maine; and Port-au-Prince, Haiti. The newspaper, of course, insisted no hacker could ever violate the sanctity of their system and every word they printed was one hundred percent genuine. And it turned out they *did* have a staff writer named Joseph Boudreaux, the byline on the goddess-in-a-bowl-of-gumbo story. Cover had an agent tracking down the reporter to find out if he'd actu-ally written the story. But there was little doubt that Bosch could have cracked the paper's pathetic security.

Privately, Cover thought the hacker had grabbed his cache of ready money and left the country, in which case they were most likely fucked. Duplessis said Bosch was part Cajun; it was just possible that he had relatives in Houma and was lying low in some fish camp. But Cover thought he was too smart to have stayed in Louisiana. And from other things Duplessis had said about the Bosch family, Cover doubted the kid would *want* to stay with any of his relatives.

He called in an all-points bulletin on the pickup, though he hoped the damn thing was rusting in a junkyard somewhere and wouldn't be found. He knew it couldn't have anything to do with Bosch.

But by the time he made it back to the office, the pickup had already been sighted in Houma, which was only an hour's drive from New Orleans. Cover could think of no excuse that would keep him from checking it out.

"Any word on that hacker?" Frank Norton called as Cover strode past his door.

"Maybe."

"You know, Ab, if you get outsmarted by a nineteen-year-old, you're really gonna have egg on your face."

"Fuck you, Spider."

The old agent let out an annoyingly hearty belly laugh that followed Cover all the way down the hall.

The highway between New Orleans and Houma was precariously close to flooding, as it was much of the year. Cover's tires had thrown off a thin steady spray of water for the last forty miles or so. There were cranes in the breakdown lane, big white birds standing on one leg watching his van slush by, or catching frogs in the reeds and cattails that grew right up onto the blacktop. Huge gnarled trees hung low over the road, draped in Spanish moss. God, he hated the look of Spanish moss.

The local cop in Houma said the truck was parked in somebody's front yard and looked like it hadn't moved in a while. Cover navigated the joyless streets of downtown Houma, got lost several times, finally pulled up in front of the house. The yard was dotted here and there with scraggly chickens. He disliked chickens; his grandmother had kept a henhouse, and even as a little boy the chalky smell of their shit, their scaly feet, and the weird, wobbly red flesh of their combs had filled him with revulsion.

The pickup was a sorry sight, sitting on three flat tires and a cement block, with an ancient paint job that might have once been red beneath the chicken shit. But there was the license plate, clear as anything: LLBTR-5. The cop was leaning against his cruiser taking a steady torrent of abuse from a big black-haired, red-faced man with a flair for dramatic gestures. Relief spread across the cop's ratty little face as Cover pulled up.

"Mister Big Damn G-man!" hollered the Cajun. Cover cringed. He hated being called a G-man. *"Mister G-man, maybe you can tell me for why this stupid cop wants to plague me all damn day, hein? I'm just stirrin' up a pot a' gumbo, me, an' he come knockin' an' ask so many questions I done scorched my roux!"*

"Uh, Agent Cover, this is Mr. Robicheaux," the cop broke in. "He says the truck hasn't been driven for about five years—"

"Damn right it ain't! My wife she made me put on that damn, what-you-call-him, vanity plate. Was a damn voodoo curse, says me. S'posed to stand for *'Laissez Les Bons Temps Rouler,'* an' it ain't rolled since. Now the chickens roost in there."

Agent Cover opened the truck's passenger door. There were three frizzly chickens on the front seat, several more nesting in straw on the floorboards. They cocked their reptilian eyes at him and gobbled frantically.

As if to cap off the sheer perfection of his day, a single egg rolled off the seat and landed square on the tip of his left tassel loafer. Cover stared down at the golden yolk and milky albumen oozing over the carefully polished leather.

Somebody hates me, he thought. He wished he never had to set foot in the sweltering mud of Louisiana again. He wished he never had to interrogate another snotty punk who knew a thousand times more about computers than he ever would or wanted to. He wished he had the coveted White House detail.

But none of that mattered. What was the first thing they had drummed into him at Glynco?

Absalom Cover was a Secret Service agent. And Secret Service agents were granite agents.

EIGHTEEN

Trevor sat in the diner punishing a bottomless cup of coffee, sketching and writing in an old spiral notebook he'd found in the back of Zach's car. His hands shook a little, and the glossy black Formica of the tabletop was scattered with constellations of white sugar. Only by pressing the heel of his right hand against the table and holding the notebook flat was he able to steady his pen.

Eyes, hands, screaming mouths clawed their way across the page and were lost in the drowning pattern. He could never remember drawing this fast, not since early childhood, when he was desperate to get as many things as possible down on paper because he knew that was the only way he would ever get good at it.

His hand began to cramp, and he banged it against the table in frustration. He hated it when his hand cramped; it was like having his mind go blank. Trevor made himself extend and flex the fingers, stretch the muscles of the palm. He flipped through the pages, saw that Zach had noted things here and there in a nearly illegible handwriting full of flourishes and jagged psycho spikes. A trio of phone numbers for Caspar, Alyssa, and "Mutagenic BBS." A bunch of incomprehensible scribblings that looked mostly like this:

    DEC=> A
    YOU=> info ter
    DEC=> all sorts of shit, then A

or "MILNET: WSMR-TAC, NWC-TAC" or "Crap file--> CRYPT Unix<filename." A full page of sixteen-digit numbers

followed by month/year dates, labeled simply AMEXES. The cryptic notation "118 1/2 Mystery—Near Race Track."

Trevor studied these random jottings like hieroglyphics, wondering whether he would know Zach better if he could understand them. But all in all, he concluded, Zach was not driven to record his existence on paper as Trevor was. Only six years younger, Zach belonged to a generation that preferred to leave its mark in other ways: on memory chips, on floppy disks and digitized video, every dream reducible to ones and zeroes, every thought sent racing through fiber-optic filaments a thousandth the thickness of a hair.

He picked up his coffee cup and drained it, heard the china jitter as he set it back down. The saucer was full of cold coffee that had sloshed over the edge of the cup. Trevor signaled the waitress for a refill, turned to a fresh page in the notebook, and began making a list in the small, clear handwriting he had cultivated for lettering comics.

FACTS

It makes things appear. (Hammer, electricity)

It makes us hallucinate. (Bathroom, bed)

THEORIES

It really tore up my story, then put the pieces back together and instantaneously moved them 1000 miles to SB's mailbox.

It made us hallucinate the pieces.

I am completely insane and the mail is a hell of a lot faster than we think.

It can do whatever it wants, and is playing a game with me.

It can only do a few things, and is trying to communicate with me any way it can.

He stared at the list, wondering whether he was wrong to ascribe conscious, willful qualities to an "it" he was afraid to name. What if the house or what was left there had no consciousness, no ability to premeditate its actions? What if the events happening to them were like forces of nature, like a recording he and Zach had somehow gotten trapped in? Trevor thought that might be even worse.

The bell above the door jangled as Zach burst in and crossed the diner in three great bounds, oblivious to the stares he received. He slid in next to Trevor, smelling of sweat and beer and crackling energy. His eyes were bright, his hair wild. "DAMN!" he said. "I fucking LOVE this!"

"What? Being a rock star?"

"YEAH!"

Trevor started to close the notebook so as not to kill Zach's buzz, but Zach saw the list. "Can I read that?"

Trevor pushed it over to him. Zach read it quickly, nodding at each item. "What did you hallucinate in bed?" he asked.

"That I had torn your heart out as we slept." So much for not killing his buzz.

"Oh." Zach turned those shining jade-colored eyes on Trevor, regarded him for a long moment. "When? This morning?"

"Yeah."

"But then you woke me up wanting to fuck."

Trevor shrugged. "Yeah."

Zach thought about it, shook his head, started to say something else but stopped. Trevor didn't press him. Zach picked up the coffee cup and inhaled deeply of its aroma, then actually took the tiniest possible sip. Trevor saw a shiver run up Zach's spine, watched his throat work and his dark-fringed lashes flutter as the homeopathic dose of caffeine took effect. He leafed through the notebook and found Trevor's drawings. "Won't the lines on these pages show up when you reproduce them?"

"I'm not going to reproduce them. These are mine. I don't feel like working on anything else right now."

"But, Trev, they're *all* yours."

"I wonder," said Trevor, staring at his hands. "I really do wonder."

"Well, look, I have to get back. I just wanted to tell you we'll be practicing a couple more hours. You can drive home if you want to—I'll catch a ride with Terry." Zach pressed his key ring into Trevor's hand. Not just the keys to his car, Trevor realized, but to most everything this boy possessed in the world.

"Thanks," he said.

"No problem. But be careful out there, okay?" Before sliding back out of the booth, Zach leaned over and planted a warm, none-too-hasty kiss on Trevor's mouth.

"You're so cool," he said. "See you soon."

Trevor watched him leave, then stared at the key ring as if its worn metal could tell him tales of Zach, then glanced around the diner wondering who had seen them kiss.

In fact, no one had seen it but a neatly dressed, pallid old man sitting in a sunny booth by the door nursing his own cup of coffee. The waitresses called him Mr. Henry. He was a lifelong resident of Missing Mile, and until a few years ago he had lived chastely with his younger sister who taught Bible school. They attended Baptist church services every Wednesday and Sunday. Neither had ever married. Since his sister's massive stroke, which had mercifully killed her on the floor of her own tidy kitchen instead of leaving her to linger in some sterile ward, Mr. Henry had only been waiting to die too and be buried in his own small rectangle of earth beside her.

But that kiss reminded him of a summer's day he had hardly let himself think of in seventy years. A vacation on the Outer Banks . . . a local boy he had met on the beach, his own age, twelve or thirteen. All day they swam in the vast expanse of ocean, dozed on the soft hot dunes, exchanged their deepest dreams and darkest secrets. Far from the ordinary fare of schools and families, they became what they wanted to be; they were unimaginably exotic to each other.

They were only lying in the sand embracing when his father found them. But his father had been a deacon of the

Baptist church, a self-styled Old Testament patriarch who, finding himself trapped in the immoral whirlwind of the early twentieth century, had become a domestic tyrant. His father had beat him so badly he could not walk for five days, could not stand upright for a week. And his father had told him he never deserved to stand upright again, for he was no man.

Mr. Henry had been believing that for seventy years. But seeing the two beautiful boys' lips meet and the tips of their tongues press quickly together reminded him how sweet it had been to kiss the briny mouth of that golden-skinned creature in the dunes, though he knew if his father had caught them kissing he would have killed them both. Now they could do it in public if they wanted to, with the nonchalance of any young couple in love. He wished he had been born in such a time, or had been brave enough to help make that time come.

Trevor saw the old man staring. He flushed to the roots of his hair and returned to his notebook, scowling fiercely. But as he began to draw again, he could still feel those faded eyes on him. He was sick of this place anyway, with its odor of grease and boiled coffee grounds, with its rotating fans that emitted a loud, steady ratcheting sound but did not cool the air.

He got up, left a generous tip on the table to make sure his cup would be kept full again next time, and gave the old man what he imagined was a polite but sardonic nod as he left the diner. To his surprise, the old man smiled and nodded back.

Trevor thought of driving out Burnt Church Road to the graveyard before he went home, but decided against it. The grave of his family had felt too peaceful, too final when he visited it on Sunday morning. It contained no answers for him, only crumbling bones. The answers were in the house, in its dampness and rot, its twenty-year-old bloodstains and shattered mirrors.

And also perhaps in its strange sylvan sensuality, its lushness of green vines twining through broken windows; in the home it was becoming to him and Zach, more than it had ever been his alone; in the succession of shady days and sweaty nights that seemed as if it would go on forever, though they both knew it could not; even in the galaxies of dust that swirled through late afternoon sunlight like golden notes descending on a saxophone, there in Birdland.

Trevor parked the car at the side of the house, went inside, and got a Coke from the refrigerator. He stood in the kitchen drinking it, looking at Zach's stuff on the table. Zach seemed to have chosen this as his room and insinuated himself here. His Post-its were stuck to the edge of the table like some bizarre yellow fringe. On the refrigerator he had plastered a bumper sticker that read FUCK 'EM IF THEY CAN'T TAKE A JOKE. His laptop computer, surely an expensive machine, sat in plain view as if he trusted the house to protect it from thievery or harm. He thought of Zach breaking into the electric company last night, just skating right in as pretty as he pleased, as if anybody could call up and read the whole town's power bills anytime they wanted to. *What a silly kid,* Trevor thought. *What an amazing genius.*

But that reminded him of the kitchen light snapping on, off, on again with no hand near it. And *that* reminded him of his story. *Incident in Birdland.* He finished his Coke and walked slowly down the hall, past the bedrooms, into the studio. The light in here was clear, green, pure in a way that only late afternoons in summer can be. He ran his hand over the scarred surface of the drawing table. He stared at the drawings tacked to the wall.

Then, without quite knowing he was going to do it, Trevor thrust out both hands and tore two of them down and started ripping at them. The paper crumbled between his fingers, dry, brittle, helpless. Destroying artwork was a taboo almost as strong to him as murder. The sensation was heady, intoxicating.

"HOW DO YOU LIKE IT?" he yelled into the empty room. "HOW DO YOU LIKE SEEING YOURSELF TORN APART? DO YOU EVEN CARE ANYMORE?"

The silence was deafening. The last crumbs of paper sifted from his hands. Trevor suddenly felt very tired.

He went into his bedroom and laid down on the mattress. The light in here was dim, more blue than green, the kudzu so thick it was like having the shades drawn. The rumpled blanket and pillow were permeated with a unique blend of his scent and Zach's, a third scent that had never existed in the world before yesterday morning, a scent part musk, part herb, part salt.

He touched his penis. The skin felt stretched, tender, nearly sore. The things he had done with Zach were like nothing he had ever imagined. He loved the raw physical intimacy of it, the utter sense of connection. He thought about having Zach inside him, wondered if it would hurt and realized that he didn't care, he wanted it anyway.

Hugging the pillow to him, imagining his lover's body linked inextricably with his own, he slept.

At the Sacred Yew, Gumbo was running through the last few songs of their set. As promised, Zach had memorized the lyrics Terry had written down for him, then learned to sing them with R.J. singing along softly to cue him. R.J.'s voice wasn't awful, but it was a flat kid's voice that had never been meant to front a band. Zach decided his own voice had been meant for just that purpose. On the songs he hadn't learned, he made up his own words.

Terry gave his cymbals a final crash and brandished his sticks in the air. "Let's knock it off," said R.J. "It's not gonna get any better than that."

Zach had shed his T-shirt at some point during the rehearsal. His chest was streaked with sweat and his own grimy fingerprints where he had clawed at himself with one hand while he clutched at the mike stand or gesticulated wildly with the other. He had snarled his hair around his fingers as he sang, pulled at it until it stood out in a hundred directions.

He saw Calvin looking at him and grinned. "What do you think?"

Calvin's eyes were brazen. "About what?"

"My highly original vocal style, of course."

"Of course." The guitarist let his gaze slide from Zach's face to his chest to his midsection, then back up again just as slowly. "I think it's very attractive."

"How old are you?"

"Twenty-three."

"Will you buy me a beer and pour it in a cup?"

"Why, of course I will." Calvin grinned evilly. "But only if you buy the next round."

"Hell, I'll buy this one." Zach pulled a five out of his pocket and held it out to Calvin. "Leave the change for Kinsey."

Calvin waved the money away. "My treat."

Terry came over to the edge of the stage toweling his hair dry with his bandanna, sucking some kind of throat lozenge. The sharp odor of menthol hung around his head like an invisible cloud. "That was some heavy mind groove, Zach. You're quite a crazed front man."

"Thanks. You guys are pretty crazed yourselves."

"Yeah, we try. You wanna come over for a shower and a toke? I can drop you off afterward."

Calvin came back with two sloshing plastic cups. Their fingers touched damply as he handed Zach one. "Where are y'all going?"

"To my house," Terry told him hoarsely.

"Can I come?"

"No. Go home and take a nap. I know you were up until dawn eating mushrooms last night."

"That's okay. I'm going to eat 'em again tonight."

Terry rolled his eyes. "Great. Can you wait until after the show?"

"Maybe." Calvin's gaze sought out Zach's, fairly sparkling with wickedness. "It depends on what's happening after the show."

For the first time, Zach felt a spark of annoyance toward Calvin. He was cute as hell, he played a mean guitar, and he obviously entertained a healthy lust for Zach. But he also obviously didn't give a damn about Trevor.

Well, maybe Calvin just hadn't picked up on the fact that they were together. Zach didn't mind the attention or the free beer. Calvin probably meant no harm, and if he did, that was too bad.

But Zach saw no reason to piss off his new bandmate if he didn't have to. Calvin might even have extra mushrooms, Zach thought, and be willing to share or sell some.

And he *was* awfully cute.

Trevor woke alone in the dark bedroom. For a moment he could not feel the mattress under him, could not even be sure he lay on a solid surface; he might have been spinning in some directionless black void. Then gradually the dim square of the window became visible, and the larger rectangle of the closet. He became conscious of the empty space on the other side of the mattress. Zach hadn't come back yet.

If it was nearly full dark, the time must be well after seven. Trevor wondered where Zach was, what he was doing right now. Was he still at the club, enjoying the cheerful, rowdy company of the other musicians after having spent so many intense hours with Trevor? Was he wishing he had hooked up instead with exotic Calvin, who played the guitar and wore silver charms in his ears, who would not have needed showing how to make love?

What if he has? What if Calvin offered him a ride home, and their eyes met in some perfect understanding that I could never fathom, and halfway here they pulled off the road and Calvin gave him a blowjob in the car? What if it's happening right now? His hands twined in Calvin's bleachy-fine hair, his back arching just like it did for me, his smooth sweet boner fitting as perfectly in Calvin's mouth as it did in mine. What if he never comes back?

Trevor brought his left hand to his lips, sank his teeth into the fold of skin at the wrist. The pain cleared his mind a little, made the paranoid fantasies stop racing faster than he could talk himself out of them. He knew Zach wasn't with Calvin. But he also knew that, under other circumstances, Zach might have been. Irrational as it was, that hurt too.

Faintly he heard a car pulling up outside, a single door slamming. Then Zach's footsteps were crossing the porch, Zach was feeling his way across the dark living room. Trevor heard him bang into something, curse, and stop. "Trev?" he called uncertainly.

You don't have to answer. You could just leave him standing there, alone in the dark.

STOP IT! he ordered himself. Where in hell had that thought come from? "In here," he called.

Light flooded the hall, sliced across the bedroom. Zach came in, sat on the bed and hugged Trevor through the blanket. Trevor rolled over and hugged back. Zach's hair was damp, and he smelled of soap and shampoo and deliciously clean skin.

"You took a shower?"

"Yeah. At Terry's. He's got a cool bathtub, this big old-fashioned deal up on claw feet."

Obscure relief flooded through Trevor as he remembered Terry's clawfooted tub. *Trust,* he reminded himself. But trust had not been a part of his life for twenty years; it wasn't going to come unconditionally in a couple of days.

Zach's hands strayed beneath the blanket. "I don't have to be back at the club for a couple of hours."

"You never slow down, do you?"

"No," Zach admitted, "not if I have a choice."

"Could you just come under the covers here and hold me?"

"No problem." Zach kicked off his sneakers, slid out of his clothes, and snuggled in next to Trevor. He draped an arm across Trevor's chest, rested his head on Trevor's shoulder. His body was relaxed and very warm.

"Ohhhh," he moaned. "You feel so good. Don't let me fall asleep."

"You can if you want to," Trevor told him. "I just got done sleeping. I'll wake you up in an hour."

"Are you sure?"

"I've never had trouble keeping awake."

"Will you stay here and hold me?"

"Absolutely."

"Mmmm." Zach heaved a deep, contented sigh. "I love you, Trev . . . you're the best thing that's ever happened to me." He drifted quickly into sleep, and Trevor was left staring into the dark, facing down that thought.

He didn't see how he could be the best thing that had ever happened to anyone, let alone someone like Zach. His life had been starred with disaster. He was probably crazy. He couldn't lean on anyone; he couldn't be strong enough for anyone to lean on. Maybe Trevor McGee could have been, but Trevor Black could not.

Still, Zach had said it. And Trevor didn't think Zach had been telling him lies.

He wondered what would happen if Zach had to leave. Would he want Trevor to go with him? And if he did, could Trevor go? Though he had returned to the house thinking he might die here, he found that he no longer wanted to die at all. But he still hadn't found what he had come looking for. Or had he?

You came back looking for your family. Maybe your mistake was assuming that meant Bobby, Rosena, and Didi. Kinsey and Terry took you in, showed you more kindness than any strangers ever have. And who is this you hold in your arms now, if not family?

I don't want him to go. I really don't.

Then Trevor had a thought that made his heart miss a beat, made the spit in his mouth dry up. That thought was: *Maybe Bobby thought Momma was getting ready to leave with me and Didi. And maybe he didn't want us to go, either.*

Then why did he leave me alive? Why did he let me go?

Because he knew you were an artist. That's it, somehow. He knew you would come back. Artists always come back to the places that created them and ruined them.

Take Charlie Parker. He could have lived out his middle years in France, where American jazz musicians were treated like royalty, where racial prejudice was almost nonexistent, where the heroin was strong and clean and there were no hassles from the law. But Bird couldn't. He had to fly back to the tawdry lights of Fifty-second Street, to the clubs where he could no longer play, to the great sprawling hungry land that had made his name a legend, but would kill him at thirty-five. He had to come back. He had to see and hear everything. He was an artist.

Okay, he thought, *I'm here. But I'll draw what I damn well want to draw. And I won't hurt Zach, not ever again.*

As if in response, Zach moaned in his sleep and pushed his face into Trevor's shoulder. Trevor stroked his hair and the smooth curve of his back, wondered what haunted Zach's bad dreams. Was it a heavy grip falling on his shoulder, a set of steel bracelets dragging him away to bloody rape and death in prison? Was it his mother's limpid eyes and cruel tongue, or his father's hands? Or was it something less concrete: an image glimpsed in a mirror, a shadow flickering on a wall?

The night was very quiet. Trevor heard the small secret sounds of the house, the distant thrum of traffic on the highway, the insects shrilling and sawing in the long grass outside. But closer than any of that, as close as his own, he heard Zach's breathing and Zach's heartbeat.

He held Zach tighter and thought about all the things he would not give up.

NINETEEN

The Sacred Yew was already crowded when Trevor and Zach arrived. A warm rain had begun misting down, but kids were still milling about on the sidewalk, basking in the humid summer night. Zach saw lots of black and ragged denim, buzz cuts and long braids and hair dyed all colors. Most of the faces were young, pale, and rapt. Sick with joy, Zach thought, watching their lives unfurl before them, a myriad of roads.

The doorman on duty was a slight, reedy teenage boy with a facial bone structure as sharp and delicate as a bird's. His long dyed-black hair straggled into his face, lightly beaded with rain, and for a moment Zach wanted to swoop the poor starved-looking thing into his arms and give him a jolt of the energy and love crackling through his body. He managed to restrain himself.

The boy stopped them as they entered the club, and Zach spoke the four talismanic words as easily as if he had been saying them all his life.

"I'm with the band."

"What's your name?"

"Dario."

The kid found the name on his list and scratched it off, then nodded at Trevor. "What about him?"

"He's with me."

" 'Kay." The kid picked up a rubber stamp and pressed it into a red inkpad, then against the backs of their left hands. The design was a scary-looking tree with many spreading branches, rather like the mythic Yggdrasil with its roots in hell.

They moved from the warm night into the heat and half-suppressed excitement of the club. "Dario?" Trevor inquired.

"It's my stage name. After Dario Argento."

Then they were in the thick of the crowd and talk became impossible. Zach grabbed Trevor's hand and led him toward the tiny graffiti-covered room at the back of the stage. Terry and R.J. were lounging on a broken-down sofa. A cooler full of the ubiquitous Natty Bohos sat atop a blown-out, gutted amp, and Zach took one.

"So Ghost gets on the phone," Terry was telling R.J., "and says 'What's going on? Did you get a new singer?' "

"No shit!"

"Yeah! And he goes, 'Well, watch out. Somebody's after him.' And then Steve gets back on, and he says, 'Ghost dreamed the FBI or something was looking for your singer.' "

"Huh . . . Hey, Zach. Hey, Trevor."

Terry got up and greeted them with a hug. "Zach, our psychic friend dreamed the FBI was after you. Say it ain't so."

Zach tried to laugh. "Not unless they know about all those cattle mutilations." Trevor squeezed his hand.

"So," Terry said, "you ready to go?"

"Hell, yes!"

"I thought we'd play two sets. Everyone will buy beer during the break and Kinsey will make more money."

"And we can get stoned backstage," said Calvin, coming in. Zach wondered if he had been listening at the door. Calvin was wearing a pair of black cotton leggings and a skimpy rag that might once have been a T-shirt: nearly the same outfit Zach had on, but tighter and rattier. Zach saw that one of his nipples was pierced with a silver ring. Calvin beamed at Zach and offered him a slender black object. An eyeliner pencil.

"Want some?"

Slinking about the stage, his eyes smeared with wanton kohl . . . "May I?"

Calvin pressed the pencil into Zach's hand and turned away, flexing his fingers. He seemed to have toned his act down a little. In fact the whole atmosphere backstage had suddenly become brisk, excited but efficient; these guys were ready to have fun, but they also had a job to do. Terry and R.J. were standing, stretching. Zach felt the first flicker of nervousness like a wing brushing the inside of his stomach. He peered into the tiny lightless mirror Kinsey had thoughtfully provided and began outlining his eyes in black.

Trevor watched him strangely. "What are you doing?"

"Putting on makeup." Zach finished, smudged the corners a bit, then looked up at Trevor. "Do you like it?"

"I think I better go back into the club."

"Okay. Why?"

Trevor leaned in close. "Because if I stay here," he whispered in Zach's ear, "I'm going to fuck you right in front of the band."

Great: now he was going on stage with a boner. "Wait till after the show," he whispered back. "I'll ruin you for life."

"Promise?"

"Mmmmm." Trevor's lips covered his, Trevor's arms slid around him and hugged him tight. Then Trevor looked back at the other musicians. "I hope you have a good show," he said. They all realized they had been staring, smiled a little too widely and offered a ragged chorus of thanks.

The backstage door swung shut and Trevor was gone into the crowd. Terry glanced at the others. "Ready?"

A round of nods. A moment of silence. Then Terry spoke three more of rock and roll's talismanic words:

"Let's do it."

Trevor was standing at the very center of the dance floor when Gumbo hit the stage. He felt the crowd pushing him forward, let himself surge closer to Zach.

Zach was already smiling at the audience as if he wanted to eat it alive. Calvin and R.J. picked up their guitars, slung the brightly colored hippie-weave straps over their shoulders. Terry sat down, leaned forward, and spoke hoarsely into the small mike mounted on his drum set.

"Howdy! We're Gumbo!" A spatter of whistles and applause. "Thanks. You'll notice that tonight we're four instead of three. Say hello to DARIO, our special guest vocalist appearing in a limited engagement of one . . . night . . . only!" A drumstick kissed the edge of a cymbal. "DARIO! A genu-wine Cajun maniac straight from New OrLEEENS!"

Over the forest of waving, fluttering hands thrust up by the crowd, Trevor distinctly saw Zach mouth the word *Shit.* But he recovered fast and ripped the microphone off its stand as Terry gave the three-beat intro to the first song. Calvin unleashed a fast-and-dirty flood of guitar noise, and R.J. backed him with a bass line that made Trevor think of wheels blasting down an open highway. Zach stood with the mike clutched to his chest, arched his back and speared the audience with his glittering eyes.

Trevor thought Zach was looking straight at him as he began to sing.

In fact, Zach had left his glasses in the dressing room and couldn't see much beyond the first four rows of people. But he could feel Trevor in the crowd, could feel a long invisible strand of electricity flowing between them, tapping into the web that connected Zach with Terry, R.J., and Calvin, sending tendrils through the audience and infecting them as well. It was a silver-blue energy, as galvanizing as a slug of moonshine, as effervescent as a champagne chaser.

He opened his mouth and felt the energy come blazing up his spine as he let the words fly. He barely knew what he was singing; his photographic memory gave him back the lyrics and his reptile brain translated them into pure emotion without ever processing their meaning. He twisted the syllables, stretched the long sounds, pushed his voice way down deep to match the bass, then sang with the guitar, high and hoarse and clear.

The crowd pushed right up to the stage. A few kids up front were already dancing. Zach let their movements tug at him, flow over him. Soon he was dancing harder than any of them, remembering to breathe, keeping his voice strong, letting the music control him.

The young upturned faces were sweaty, eyes half-closed, lips parted as if in ecstasy. This was like making love to an enormous roomful of people all at once, like taking control of all their pleasure centers and squeezing hard. It was his best fantasy gone one better. No one was jealous. Everyone was getting off, and getting him off. And somewhere right in the middle of it was his one true love.

"I gotta bad reaaaaction," he moaned, lips brushing the mike, letting his voice crack a little, thinking of Billie Holiday. "Gotta bad reaction to yoooou . . . gotta suck your poison every night, gotta swallow too . . ." He was improvising on the lyrics now as the song ended. Calvin caught his eye and gave him a very dark smile.

The next number on the set list read simply "FUNKY BLUESJAM." Terry had told him to vamp around, make up his own lyrics if he wanted. His shirt was already soaked. He peeled it off as the band eased into a slow, sexy groove. The crowd whistled and hooted. Zach closed his eyes and tilted his head back and just stood swaying at center stage for a long moment, leggings riding low on his hips, lights playing over the sweat on his face and chest and rib cage. He felt them looking at him and he let them look.

Slowly he brought the mike up and started singing again, letting his voice skitter and scat over the music, only gradually beginning to form whole words and lines. "Where the bars never close . . . And the neon screams . . . And the smell of whiskey gets in your dreams . . ."

A boy was dancing front and center, head thrown back in abandon, red-gold hair shaved close on the sides and spiked with sweat, pale skin flushed. His eyes met Zach's and held them, almost defiant. Zach knew that look, had seen it plenty of times in the Quarter. It said, *I am as beautiful as you, and I know it.* The boy wore a thin white T-shirt and loose, low-slung faded jeans. The edge of the shirt pulled up as he danced, revealing a maddening stretch of flat hairless belly, a heartbreaking curve of hipbone.

"Where the gutters run red by the break of dawn . . . And the boys get paler as the night wears on . . ."

Suddenly he saw Trevor in the crowd, not dancing, just standing still in the sea of bodies, letting himself be jostled, gazing up at Zach. His face was intent, but calm; he was taking all this in now to be remembered and maybe drawn later. Zach lost the thread of his lyrics, wailed and sobbed wordlessly for a while. He felt like a torch singer in some smoky little dive in 1929, high on Prohibition liquor and the reefers they were rolling backstage.

He gave Trevor his most smoldering smile, put the mike back on the stand and ran his hands over his face, through his hair. Trevor smiled back a little uneasily, as if afraid people would notice where Zach was looking. But his gaze never wavered. He had to take everything in. The artist as eyeball, thought Zach: lidless, as raw to the touch as an exposed nerve, but seeing and processing all.

The next couple of songs were Gumbo standards with a country-Cajun flavor. Zach whined his way through them thinking of Hank and Patsy and Clifton Chenier, wishing he had a bottle of bourbon, a pair of black steel-toed cowboy boots, and a bushel of tabasco peppers. Terry whaled his skins without mercy, and R.J. moved his feet for the first time that evening. Zach could tell this was the stuff they really loved. They played the blues fine, but they were country boys.

Next came another jam, R.J. and Calvin getting into a riff that was like something out of an old spy movie, sinister and slinky, octopussy; Terry laughing behind the drums, striking up a strip-club beat. Zach hung on the microphone, tilted his face to the lights and closed his eyes. The world was red and gold, sweat and smoke, pain and joy.

The first set was over too soon. Zach stared over at the crowd, unwilling to turn them loose even for twenty minutes. Trevor caught his eye and pointed toward the bar. Zach held up his open hand—*Be there in five*—and reluctantly left the stage.

Entering the backstage room was like walking into a sauna. The other three musicians were as sweaty as Zach, and as buzzed. The little cubicle was saturated with their energy. The smell was like an electrical storm in a locker room.

Terry slung an arm around him. "Good show. Man, you really know how to work a crowd."

"It feels great."

"You're a natural," R.J. told him. "Terry could sing 'Bad Reaction' for the rest of his life and never get 'em riled up like that."

"Aw, fuck you," said Terry. "I'm just a drummer working overtime. Zach's a singer."

Basking in the praise, Zach started to grab a Natty Boho, then realized he had finished his first one onstage and his bladder was full. "Is there anywhere I can take a piss back here or do I have to fight my way to the rest room?"

"Yeah, if you go way back behind the stage, there's a little bitty john in the far corner. Nobody's supposed to know about it because it doesn't have a sink, but you can piss there."

Zach took off in the direction Terry had pointed him. A narrow L-shaped hall hooked away into the bowels of the backstage area, virtually lightless. Zach trailed his hand along the wall to keep his bearings. The cinder blocks felt cool and moist beneath his fingers, as if he were descending into an underground cave. Eventually he came to an open door, felt around until he found a light switch, and beheld the dankest, saddest little water closet he had ever laid eyes on. It was clean, and that almost made it worse: a bathroom this desolate needed roaches and mildew to liven it up. He hated to imagine Kinsey back here scrubbing the toilet.

Zach peeled his leggings down. The stream of pee sounded very loud going into the rusty water, and he realized his ears were ringing. As he readjusted himself, a knock sounded at the door. *I bet I know who that is,* Zach thought.

"Yeah?"

"It's Calvin."

Bing! You win the trip to Acapulco and the set of steak knives too. He opened the door a crack and saw a sparkling eye, a shock of bleached hair, half of a grinning mouth.

"Just wanted to see if you were done. I gotta go too."

Zach let Calvin in and turned to leave. Calvin stepped right up to the toilet, tugged his pants down, and let fly. *Huh*, Zach thought, *so he really did have to piss.*

But as Zach was halfway out the door, Calvin said, "Hey, Dario?"

"Yeah?"

"That was a fuckin' brilliant set. You look great onstage."

"Aw hell, I just like to sing. You guys are the musicians."

"Yeah, right. You're about as humble as me." Calvin flushed the toilet, pulled his leggings up to a point just above the line of his pubic hair, then turned and in one smooth motion grabbed Zach and pinned him against the wall. His chest pressed against Zach's, slick with sweat. His hands slid up Zach's rib cage and his thumbs grazed Zach's bare nipples, then tweaked them gently. Zach found himself instantly, crazily aroused.

Calvin's lips brushed Zach's. "Do you want this as bad as I do?" he whispered.

"Well—yeah, but—"

Calvin's mouth closed over his, hot and lush, full of the golden taste of beer. His tongue slid, searched, teased its way into Zach's mouth. For several seconds they kissed with sloppy abandon. Calvin's unshaven face scoured him, abraded him. It would leave scratches. Zach didn't care.

He felt Calvin's hips nudging against his own, Calvin's dick getting hard against him, pushing into his bare stomach. Almost automatically, Zach moved his hips so that their hard-ons were pressed together, separated only by two thin layers of cotton. The concrete wall was rough and cool against his back. The noise of the club was a dull subliminal roar far away.

He suddenly wondered why in hell he was doing this.

The question was jarring. It made him realize that since the moment he'd said *yeah, but* and Calvin had stopped his mouth with a kiss, he hadn't had a single thought in his head. Not for Trevor, not for himself, not for anything but his own damned mindless pleasure. Zach knew he had often used sex like a drug. But until now, he'd never consciously known that he used it to make himself stop thinking.

The shame of that knowledge washed over him like a caustic wave. But on its crest came a second realization. Being with Trevor didn't make him feel that way, didn't short-circuit his thought processes or cut off his emotions. When they made love Zach's perceptions intensified and his consciousness seemed to expand. Before, fucking had always been like slamming a door on the world. With Trevor it was like opening a thousand doors.

And that meant he wasn't getting anything here that he couldn't get a thousand times better at home.

Zach felt a pang of regret as he broke the kiss and pushed Calvin away. Calvin was what he used to think of as a sweet catch, a beautiful bad boy with a guitar, and in the old days Zach would have loved to take an all-night tour of Calvin's personal heavens and hells.

But whether he liked it or not, those days were gone for him. He couldn't do this to Trevor. Furthermore, he didn't even want to.

"Sorry," he said. "I can't."

"Sure you can." Calvin tried to push back against him. His eyes were wild, his breath coming fast. He was obviously horny to the point of pain, and Zach felt for him. But there were plenty of adorable boys out there, fairly stewing in their own juices. A handsome blond guitarist could take his pick.

"No. I can't. I'm with somebody, and you knew damn well I was."

"Hey—" Calvin twitched one shoulder in the most insouciant of shrugs, but his eyes were hurt. "Saw you lookin', was all. Just tryin' to show the new kid a little hometown hospitality."

"I know I was looking. 'Course I was. You're gorgeous." Calvin's eyes softened a little. "But I'm with Trevor, okay? We're solid. I love him."

Calvin sniffed. "You fall in love pretty fast, don't you?"

"Not really. It took me nineteen years."

"Aren't you scared he'll freak out and murder you in your sleep?"

Zach laughed. "No. If Trevor decides to kill me, he'll make sure I'm awake for it."

Calvin considered this dubiously. "Whatever," he said at last. "You wanna kiss me one more time?"

"Yes," Zach told him honestly. "But I'm not gonna."

He ducked under Calvin's arm and left the guitarist staring after him. As he fumbled his way back along the hall, the noise and the energy of the club grew stronger with every step he took. He felt the invisible thread of his lover pulling him, drawing him.

Zach had done plenty of things he was proud of: survived on his own since he was fourteen, hacked his way into systems that no one else could crack, bailed his friends out of jail and wiped their records clean.

All of that was fine. But he couldn't remember the last time a decision *not* to do something had made him feel so good.

"I sold a story to *Taboo*!" Trevor shouted over the din of the bar.

Kinsey's slightly harassed expression became an enormous grin. "That's great! Have a Coke! Hell, have *two* Cokes!" He slapped them down on the bar in front of Trevor, then held up an apologetic hand and hurried away to serve the customers lining up for beer. Trevor pulled a five-dollar bill out of his pocket and dropped it into the tip jar while Kinsey's back was turned.

Zach had given him a wad of cash this morning. *Just in case you need anything in town*, he'd said, pressing it into Trevor's hand. When Trevor protested the amount—over a hundred dollars—Zach only looked disgusted. *Money is just stuff you trade for things that you want*, he had told Trevor with the air of a person explaining that two plus two equals four. *When you need more, you get it. It may not grow on trees, but accessing a bank account is a hell of a lot easier than climbing a tree.*

Trevor looked around the crowded bar, but saw no sign of Zach. Probably he was still backstage getting stoned with the band. Trevor didn't think Zach would mind if he joined them.

To his own surprise, he was actually beginning to develop a taste for pot. Possibly because it was such a vital component of Zach's body chemistry. But maybe, Trevor thought, he was also ready to start altering his consciousness instead of just exaggerating it.

He grabbed his two Cokes and started making his way back toward the stage. Halfway there, he passed Calvin going the other way. Trevor just nodded, but Calvin reached out and stopped him, put his hands on Trevor's shoulders and leaned in to speak loudly in Trevor's ear. "You've got a *real sweet* boyfriend. He sure does love you. Better hang on to him."

Then he was gone into the crowd. *What was that all about?* Trevor wondered. But Calvin had fucked with his head enough. He didn't care what the guitarist thought of him. Terry and R.J. were better musicians anyway. Calvin's playing had plenty of glitter and flash, but none of their Southern soul.

Trevor let himself into the dressing room and Zach was there, barechested, sleek as a seal, resplendent, taking a long toke on a fat, fragrant joint. The room was already crowded with friends of the band, but Zach saw Trevor right away. He held the smoke in his lungs as he passed the joint, crossed the room, put his lips against Trevor's, and exhaled a long, steady stream of smoke into Trevor's mouth. A shotgun.

Trevor abandoned his Cokes and ran his hands down the curve of Zach's spine. His fingertips came away slick with sweat. He touched them to his mouth, tasted salt.

"Do you want to go somewhere?" Zach whispered in his ear. Trevor nodded. Zach pulled him through the door, along a dark passageway, into a tiny, ill-lit bathroom. They slammed the door and leaned against it, groping and squeezing and clawing at each other, kissing madly. Then Trevor was kneeling on the hard cement floor, licking Zach's stomach, using his teeth to pull down the leggings, gripping Zach's hipbones like handles.

It only took about ninety seconds. "Oh Trev," Zach gasped

as he came, "oh god I needed that, thank you, thank you . . ."

"Sure." Trevor wiped his mouth on the back of his hand. "Can't be a real rock star without a backstage blowjob."

Someone knocked.

Trevor felt Zach's body stiffen. He got to his feet. Zach tugged his leggings up and backed away from the door. "Who is it?"

"Us," said a chorus of sheepish voices.

Zach opened the door. Terry, his girlfriend Victoria, R.J., and Calvin were standing just outside looking embarrassed. "Sorry," said Calvin, "but the break's almost over and we thought you might want some of these." He held out a plastic bag half full of mushrooms. They were pale brown streaked with iridescent blue—the psilocybin—and gave off a crumbling earthy smell.

Trevor saw Zach's hand start to reach forward; then he paused and looked uncertainly back at Trevor. "I like mushrooms a lot. Have you ever done 'em?"

Trevor shook his head.

"Well . . . they'd give you plenty of ideas, that's for sure." Zach stared at Trevor, then back at the bag. "Can I have some for later?" he asked.

Calvin pulled the bag back. "You can *buy* some. I'm not giving them away if you're not gonna do 'em with us."

Zach's eyes met Calvin's. Though these two probably were attracted to each other, Trevor realized, that wasn't exactly what was going on between them. It was rather that they *understood* each other as any creatures of the same species will, especially if it is a dangerous species.

"Okay." Zach pulled out a handful of twenties. "How much?"

"Well . . . oh, fuck it." Terry, R.J., and Victoria had all started staring at Calvin reproachfully as soon as he mentioned money. "I don't care. Just take a handful."

Zach was nearly laughing as he reached into the bag. "Thanks, Calvin. That's real nice of you." Their eyes were shooting silver daggers at each other, but on another level they seemed to be positively enjoying the exchange. Trevor had spent the past two days diving into Zach's character like an unfamiliar river, eager to let it flow over him, to let its current carry him along. Now he was beginning to realize that it had secret tributaries and strange deep pools he might never fathom.

Zach wrapped his mushrooms in a twist of toilet paper and gave them to Trevor to hold. Trevor stowed the little bundle deep in his pocket, then wiped his fingers on his shirt. He wasn't at all sure he wanted to eat those nasty-looking things. Bobby had liked his hallucinogens, Trevor knew, but gave them up soon after he stopped drawing. And Crumb had done all sorts of drugs, though he claimed in a recent *Comics Journal* interview that they had affected his draftsmanship.

But what had Trevor thought earlier? Hyping his consciousness with caffeine had helped him prowl around the edges of his past, but he had not yet penetrated to the heart of it. Maybe it was time to start altering his brain, laying open his very cells. Maybe then he would know enough so that he could leave with Zach, if Zach had to go.

Gumbo kicked off the second set with a thrash-tempo version of the old Cajun song "Paper in My Shoe." Zach shouted what lyrics he knew over a pileup of guitar and drum noise and made up the rest, grinning between the rapid-fire lines. He had never been able to stand Cajun music when he lived in New Orleans. But singing this song here in this club was like going home again.

The crowd was dancing hard. From the stage they looked like nothing but a seething, bobbing mass of heads, waving hands, blissed-out faces. Zach noticed that the beautiful red-haired boy was still at front and center, but he had switched his attention to Calvin. The guitarist kept making eye contact with the boy, playing to him. The boy was dancing so hard that his white shirt had gone transparent with sweat. Zach could see the pink points of his nipples through the drenched cotton.

See, Zach felt like telling Calvin, *you're a knockout, you have drugs, you play guitar in a hot band. You couldn't go home alone tonight if you wanted to.*

They eased into another jam, this one slow, dark, and nasty. The V-neck of the boy's shirt had slipped down, exposing one pale shoulder. Several girls in front were wearing skimpy tank tops, and as they danced their slender arms swayed in the air like branches. Zach found himself thinking about skin. It could be a fabulously erotic substance, smooth under the hands, salty against the tongue. Its color could inspire hatred. It could be flayed and tanned.

He gripped the microphone, leaned forward until his lips were almost touching it. "Dressin' up at night in his suit of skin . . . Cured her ribs in the barn . . . Fried up her heart in a skillet . . . Put her ole hands in a jar . . ."

He caught Trevor laughing in the audience, eyes squeezed shut, mouth wide open: a completely unself-conscious moment. Zach let his lips brush the mike. "Ooooh Ed," he moaned, "what'd you do with her head?"

The kids loved it. Zach hung on the mike stand, threw in a few sultry bars of "Summertime." *Gonna spread your wings, take to the sky . . .*

Too soon they came to the last song. Zach threw himself into it hard, ended up on his knees clutching the mike, howling into it, forcing every bit of air from his lungs, reaching deep into his soul for those blues. Who knew when he would sing for an audience again? He had to make this time good enough to last.

Then it was over. He was backstage, listening to the roar of the crowd through the thin wall. Terry, R.J., and Calvin were slapping his back, congratulating him, assuring him of a gig if he decided to stick around town. After they got high again, the others went out to start packing up their equipment, and Zach found Trevor standing alone at the edge of the crowd.

They lingered in the bar for a while. Soon the other band members drifted in to bask in the post-performance attention. Friends milled around, hoping to be drawn into the circle.

Kids approached them with compliments, smiles, hungry eyes.

Zach saw Calvin talking to the boy who had been dancing in front of the stage. The boy's face was as delicately shaded as a watercolor painting: eyelashes the same red-gold as his hair, pale pink lips, the faintest of lavender hollows above and below his eyes. He made a grand gesture with his hand, lowered his eyelids disdainfully. "I don't know," Zach heard him say. "Last time I did mushrooms they were old and made me sick."

"These are real fresh," Calvin assured him. "I grew 'em myself."

"Well . . ." The boy's eyes tilted up to meet Calvin's. "I guess I will." He smiled.

"Come on backstage with me. We'll do you up real good."

Zach watched them leave the bar together. The thought of those two exquisite creatures having mad hallucinatory sex made him happy for some reason. He looked at Trevor sitting next to him and thought about having some mad hallucinatory sex of his own.

"You want to get out of here soon?" he asked, and couldn't help laughing when Trevor looked absurdly grateful.

Tack at the house, Trevor and
Zach sat at the kitchen table drinking tapwater from freshly
washed glasses. Only a rusty trickle had come out of the faucet at first, but when they left it running for a few minutes it
turned into a clear, steady stream. Zach couldn't help remembering the rotten blood and ropy sperm gushing from the
bathroom tap, but the kitchen water looked and tasted fine.

The mushrooms lay on the table in front of them, next to
the computer, still half-swathed in a twist of Sacred Yew toilet
paper. Both boys kept glancing at them from time to time,
Trevor with intrigued trepidation, Zach with a sort of patient
lust.

As soon as they got home, they had gone through the
house turning on lights in all the safe rooms—the kitchen, the
big bedroom, Trevor's bedroom, the studio. Even the hall
light was burning. Though it was well past midnight, the
house felt almost cozy.

Zach couldn't stop talking about the show. "As soon as I
hit that stage," he told Trevor, "I felt like I was born there. I
haven't felt born to anything since the first time I touched a
computer. What am I gonna do, Trev? Maybe I could disguise
myself and become a famous rock star. Like the guy in that
movie *Angel Heart,* but in reverse, without amnesia. It'd be
the perfect cover!"

"But the guy in *Angel Heart* sold his soul to the Devil."

"I don't have a problem with that." Zach fingered a mush-
room cap, watched a few dark spores sift onto the tabletop.
"You know, I really want to eat some of these."

"Eat 'em, then."

"Are you going to do any?"

"Well . . ." Trevor shifted in his chair. "What exactly happens? Is it like getting stoned?"

"No, it's much more intense. Scarier, your first time. But you'll see all kinds of beautiful hallucinations and feel all kinds of weird physical sensations and have fucked-up thoughts and ideas."

"Sounds kind of like sex."

"We can do that too."

"Do you think it could make me see things that are always here, but that I can't see now?"

"Like what? You mean here in the house?"

Trevor nodded.

Zach took a deep breath. "Trev . . . I don't think we ought to stay in the house too long after we dose. I thought we could go over to Terry's. They ate theirs at the club, so they'll be up all night, and I bet Terry would let us use his spare room. I don't know if I'm into tripping here."

Trevor just looked at him.

"What?" said Zach at last.

"This is a hallucinogen we're talking about, right? A mind-expanding, consciousness-altering drug?"

Zach nodded.

"Okay then. Keeping in mind what I came here for, what I'm living in this house for, *do you really think I'd consider doing it anywhere else?*"

"I guess not," Zach said quietly. "But, Trevor, I think it's a *real bad* idea."

"What do you mean?"

"You know I'm going to have to leave soon. And I know you must have at least thought about going with me."

"So?"

"So maybe it doesn't want you to leave."

"Maybe I don't want to."

The words stung like a slap. "If you stay here," Zach began, then had to stop and take a deep breath. His voice had nearly cracked. "If you stay here, it'll be hard to get back in touch with you. I might not be able to do it."

"You could leave a message for me at the club."

"If They find out I was ever in this town, They could tap the club's phone. They could make trouble for Kinsey. They could tap Terry's phone. They could harass the fuck out of you. A lot of *real scary people* are after me, Trev. I've already left too many traces here. I have to disappear for good now, and you might never be able to find me again. Is that what you want?"

Trevor had been staring stubbornly at the table. Now he looked up at Zach. His eyes shimmered with tears about to spill over. "No."

"Neither do I." *Is it true?* thought Zach. *Am I telling him this in good faith? If I'm going on the run forever, do I really want to take someone with me?*

And the answer was a resounding *yes*. Because he not only wanted to, he had to. If he didn't take Trevor, he might as well leave his brain or his heart behind. It was that simple; that was how deeply people became grafted into you when you loved them like this.

A part of Zach still hated that.

A part of him was grateful that he had at least found the right Siamese twin.

And a part of him rejoiced that this was possible after all.

Their fingers intertwined on the tabletop. They gripped hands tightly for a moment, both fighting back tears. "You could stay here for a while, then go over to Terry's," Trevor said. "I wouldn't mind being alone."

"No way. You don't want to trip alone in this house."

"I don't mind."

"You would." Zach pulled back to look into Trevor's eyes. "Believe me. You would. You may be able to deal with the house, but I know psilocybin. I'm not letting you do that."

"Then stay."

"Okay." Zach let his head fall back onto Trevor's shoulder. *I've just agreed to trip on mushrooms in a haunted house*, he thought. *The Grand Adventures of Zachary Bosch . . . reel three.*

"So," said Trevor, "how do we do it? Do we just eat them?"

"Yes. And I warn you, they taste fucking horrible."

Trevor picked up a blue-streaked stem and nibbled experimentally at it. "They don't seem to taste like much of anything."

"Just you wait."

Zach got up and refilled their water glasses, then began to portion out the mushrooms. There were seven caps and five stems. The caps were the most potent and shittiest-tasting part. He put three caps and three stems in one pile, four caps and two stems in the other.

"Now what?" Trevor asked.

"Getting nervous?"

"No."

"Then let's eat."

Each of them picked up a cap, put it in his mouth, and began to chew. Zach's cap splintered and grew soggy in his mouth. The dry dead flavor trickled between his teeth, over his tongue. He washed it down with a gulp of water.

"I see what you mean," said Trevor after a few seconds.

"You don't have to chew them all the way. Just soften 'em up a little and swallow the chunks."

"Now you tell me." Trevor drained his water glass and got up for more. "God, that's disgusting. It's like chewing on mummified flesh."

"Better lose that thought. You've got five more pieces to eat."

Crunching, grimacing, and swigging water, they choked down the rest of their mushrooms, then brushed their teeth at the sink. "How long does it take?" Trevor asked.

"Twenty, thirty minutes. Shall we smoke a joint and get in bed?"

"Are you sure we ought to be stoned?"

"Yes." Zach nodded vigorously. "Under the circumstances, I'm *very* sure."

Trevor felt the first tickling tendrils of the drug twenty minutes later. Zach was lying half on top of him with his head on Trevor's chest. They had been talking in the darkened bedroom, a meandering conversation with pools of calm clear silence here and there. It was during one of these silences that the sensation seemed to begin in Trevor's stomach and spread, shivering through his guts, swirling slyly through his blood, up his spine, into his brain.

He felt Zach's lips move against his chest. "Do you feel it?"

"Yes."

"Are you hallucinating?"

"I don't think so." Trevor looked at the shadows cast on the ceiling. Veins of pink and purple light were pulsing through them, beginning to creep down the walls. "Well, maybe."

He pulled Zach up to him, cupped Zach's head between his hands, and kissed his closed eyelids. The smudges of shadow beneath Zach's eyes were dark with eyeliner and fatigue. Trevor brushed his lips across them, felt Zach shiver. He kissed Zach's forehead, the narrow bridge of his nose and its elegant pointed tip, his willing mouth.

Kissing soon became a hallucinatory experience in itself. The interplay of their tongues was like a dance. Zach's mouth tasted of mint toothpaste and pot smoke and what Trevor had come to think of as his lover's own flavor, peppery and faintly sweet. Zach's very skin seemed to undulate against him at every point of contact. Trevor imagined it becoming soft as warm caramel and flowing over him, surrounding him. Whether Zach's body was taking him in or being assimilated itself would not matter. Their flesh would mingle, their bones would merge into one complex cradle surrounding the stew of their viscera. What a drawing it would make!

Now Zach was running his tongue along the arc of Trevor's collarbone, leaving a trail of warm wetness that quickly turned cold as it evaporated. He rubbed his face on Trevor's chest, pressed his lips into the hollow just below Trevor's ribs. Trevor felt that bright band of energy connecting them again, as elusive and yet as constant as the particles and waves that made up light, sound, matter.

The room was swarming around him. His drawings waved gently from the walls. The mattress felt insubstantial under his back, as if it were suspended above a great gaping hole that went through the floor and the foundation of the house, as if it could dissolve at any moment and leave him plunging forever, alone in a numb black void, a blank universe. Trevor gasped and clutched Zach tight. It was beginning in earnest.

"It's okay," Zach soothed him. "These are strong 'shrooms, that's all. Keep hanging on to me and you'll be fine."

"Do you . . . can you . . ." Trevor had no idea what he wanted to ask. His teeth began to chatter.

"Trev, just relax and go with it. Look at the lights. Everything feels good. I love you."

"I love you too . . . but it's so strange . . ."

"It's supposed to be strange. That's why we do drugs; they make us feel different. Don't fight it."

Zach stroked Trevor's hair, rubbed his arms and shoulders until the muscles began to unbunch. Trevor's hands had curled into loose fists. Zach coaxed them open, kissed the mirror-image maps of the palms, the pencil-calluses, the intricate whorls of the fingertips. He took a finger into his mouth and sucked softly, heard Trevor's breath catch.

"Your tongue feels like velvet."

"Your hands taste like seawater."

Zach kissed the fold of Trevor's left wrist, then ran his tongue along the forearm and into the soft hollow of the elbow. Trevor sighed and relaxed a little, though his pulse still beat like a frightened bird against Zach's tongue. The veins of the inner elbow: the junkie veins, the veins to sever if you wanted to bleed to death.

Zach slid his mouth down Trevor's arm and kissed the raised white lines of his scars. He had hesitated to do this before, unsure if Trevor would mind. Now the scars' rippled texture was so appealing that he couldn't help himself. Zach imagined the razor going through Trevor's flesh smooth as butter, Trevor's icy eyes screaming out of his impassive face as he watched the blood well up.

Trevor made a soft moaning sound deep in his throat. Zach sucked harder at the tender flesh, and the scar he was kissing opened against his tongue like a torrid kiss. The coppery taste of fresh blood spilled into his mouth.

Trevor felt a silvery stinging sensation in his arm, then another and another, then three at once, a deep bone-shivering pain. He raised himself on his right elbow, saw the old cuts on his left arm opening, parting like little red mouths. Zach stared up at him in confusion, then in horror as he realized Trevor was seeing the blood too. Deep wet crimson ringed his mouth and streaked his face, shocking against the whiteness of his skin.

"Trev? What . . . ?"

Trevor felt weirdly serene. The open wounds hurt no more than they had when he'd made them. It was, rather, a way of draining off pain. He remembered the feeling so well now. "It's nearly here," he said.

"What?"

"Birdland."

Zach's pupils were enormous, glittering. His mouth hung slightly open. Trevor took his hands, pulled him up and held him, smearing Zach's body with blood. He kissed Zach's sticky lips. "Don't be scared."

"But . . . aren't you bleeding?"

"Only for a little while."

"Trevor! Have your stigmata, then, goddammit, but *don't pull this mystical shit on me!*" Zach pounded the mattress. "Don't you dare die—if you die, I swear to God I'll come after you—I'll hunt you down and haunt your damn ghost—"

"I'm not dying. Come here. Hold me." He wrapped his arms tighter around Zach, felt the blood flowing between them, trickling down Zach's spine. *I have to go,* he thought. *You're the only thing that will bring me back.* But that would just frighten Zach worse, so he didn't say it.

He didn't know where he was going, or even how. He knew it would be Birdland, the true Birdland that lay paradoxically far beyond the house and deep within it. But Trevor was realizing that Birdland wasn't just the place of his past, the place in his childhood where he had found his talent, his dreams. It was also the place where his dreams could find him, and some of them were very bad. It was a place of scars, and of wounds that had never healed.

"Just don't leave me here," Zach murmured against his chest.

"I promise."

Trevor remembered lying in bed this afternoon imagining Zach's body inextricably linked with his, remembered his fantasy of Zach's flesh flowing over him, surrounding him. He pressed his body up against Zach's, wrapped his legs around Zach's skinny hips. "I want you to fuck me," he said.

"Huh? Now?"

"Yes. Now."

Emotions were warring in Zach's face: confusion, fear, sorrow, frustration, arousal. Trevor felt Zach's penis growing cautiously hard against the back of his thigh. He reached down and cupped Zach's balls, ran his hand up the silky shaft, streaking it with blood. Zach shuddered, took a deep breath. "Are you sure?"

But apparently he could see the answer in Trevor's face. His eyes never left Trevor's as he wet his hand with saliva and rubbed it up and down his penis, then lifted Trevor's knees and spread his legs and eased in. The sensation was not so much painful as completely alien. Trevor felt his asshole trying to contract, his whole body trying to tense up. He sought Zach's mouth and sucked at his tongue. He would have this boy inside him any and every way he could. It was time.

Then his intestines were loosening and warming, his muscles melting in concentric rings around Zach, drawing him in deep. He linked his hands at the small of Zach's back. Blood ran down his arms, dripped over their bodies, began to soak into the mattress.

"*Ahhh—*" Zach's teeth closed on Trevor's shoulder, a tiny exquisite pain. "You're *so tight*. It almost hurts."

"You can fuck me hard. You can open me up."

"Yeah?" Zach scrambled to his knees, put his hands on Trevor's thighs and pushed them up and back, driving in still deeper. His face was streaked with blood, his expression poised between pain and ecstasy. "Like that? Does that feel good?"

"Yes—but harder—" Trevor groped for Zach's hand,

guided it to his penis. When Zach closed his fingers around the head and began to stroke, Trevor put his hand over Zach's and squeezed brutally.

"Trev, I don't want to hurt you—"

"Harder!" Trevor sobbed. "I have to get there!"

"WHERE, DAMMIT?" Zach grabbed Trevor's chin with his free hand, forced Trevor to look him in the face. Zach's eyes were huge, wild. "WHAT ARE YOU MAKING ME DO TO YOU?"

The pleasure and the drugs overloaded Trevor's synapses with towering sensation. But he felt a vortex beginning to open in his brain. His consciousness swirled around the edges of it, began to be drawn into it. He drove his hips up hard against Zach, impaling himself. The area between his asshole and his balls and the tip of his penis felt like one huge raw nerve. Zach's heartbeat throbbed deep in his guts. Light poured out of the vortex, sparkling, swarming.

Beyond that vortex was Birdland. If he was ever going to be with Zach again, he had to go there now.

Trevor let himself go.

"Trev? *Trevor?! GODDAMMIT, TREVOR!!!*" Zach punched the pillow beside Trevor's head. Trevor didn't move or seem to hear.

Zach had felt Trevor's back arching, Trevor's come welling into his palm and dripping between his fingers, and he had nearly come too. But then Trevor had stopped moaning and his eyes had gone blank and he had fallen back on the mattress.

Zach's heart lurched painfully. He felt for Trevor's heartbeat, listened for his breathing. Both were strong and steady. Trevor's eyes were half-open, blinking slowly. But they were unfocused, and did not flicker when Zach passed his hand before them or peered into them. Zach shivered. Trevor's eyes looked abandoned.

"Trev?" he whispered. "Remember, you promised not to leave me."

No response.

"Trevor? . . . *Please?*" Zach pressed his mouth against Trevor's slack lips, kissed hard. Again no response.

He didn't think Trevor was in there. Or perhaps Trevor had gone so deep that he couldn't hear. A word rang in Zach's mind like the tolling of a deep dissonant bell. *Catatonia.*

The thought scared him so badly that he grabbed Trevor by the shoulders and shook him hard. Trevor's head rolled bonelessly on his neck. A silvery thread of saliva leaked from one corner of his mouth. There was nothing in his eyes, nothing in his face.

Zach clawed at his own face, bit his fingers viciously, sobbed in frustration and dread. Why had he ever thought it was a good idea to feed Trevor mushrooms? Why had he thought either of them could handle such a heavy-duty mindfuck within these cursed, malicious walls?

Suddenly he remembered what Trevor had said right before passing out. *I have to get there.* Had Trevor used the shock of orgasm to detach himself from his body somehow? Was his spirit careening around the house, unable to communicate with Zach, unable to get back in?

Or, worse, was Trevor no longer here at all? What if he went crashing into the spirit world, demanding his explanation for being alive, and Bobby decided to keep him there? What if Bobby just wanted to finish the job he'd left undone before? Embodied or not, Trevor was still tripping his ass off, and that made him more vulnerable than he already was. If Trevor had gone somewhere else, Zach knew he had to follow.

But how in hell was Zach supposed to leave his body? He was used to having orgasms; no matter how intense they were, his spirit did not separate from his flesh, did not extrude on some umbilical thread of ectoplasm, did not detach. He had never thought about how solidly mired in his body he was until now, when he wanted to get out of it.

He concentrated furiously, tried to project himself into Trevor's brain. He'd gotten in once, but it seemed the password had been changed. Zach tried to imagine what the new one might be, tried to feel around the edges of Trevor's blown consciousness. He forced himself to go limp, surrender to the drug, think about anything but projecting. He tore at his hair and his scalp, trying to rip his own ghost out of his skull. None of it worked. Zach collapsed back on the mattress, hugged Trevor and sobbed into his chest. A thin sheen of sweat had come up on Trevor's skin. It rippled with opalescent colors and smelled faintly of coffee.

Coffee . . .

Zach had a dangerous idea.

He tested Trevor's heartbeat again. It remained even and strong. He kissed Trevor's cheek, spoke into his ear. "I love you, Trev. I'm coming to get you. Just try not to go too far in."

He pushed himself up, nearly passed out himself as the blood rushed to his head, tried to let it happen but recovered. He crossed the bedroom and edged into the hall, refused to look toward the bathroom or at the doorway into the living room, would not glance over his shoulder as he entered the kitchen. He had never felt so unsafe in this house.

Zach opened the refrigerator, squinted into the dazzling light, took out the bag of coffee Trevor had bought. He carried it over to the coffee maker from Potter's Store and shook a generous amount into the filter basket, then ran tapwater into the pot and poured it through. A few seconds later the machine began to bubble and a dark, rich scent filled the kitchen. The odor nauseated him: he knew what he was probably going to have to do.

Zach couldn't wait for the pot to fill. As soon as a cupful had collected, he yanked it out and splashed it into a mug. The stream of brewing coffee sizzled against the hotplate. Zach's nerves twitched in sympathy. He thrust the pot back in, flipped the switch off, grabbed the steaming mug, and hurried back to the bedroom.

"Trev? Want some joe? C'mon . . ." He slid a hand behind Trevor's neck and propped his head up, wafted the mug back and forth under Trevor's nose without much hope. As he had feared, Trevor made no response. He was gone, all right.

Zach looked into the mug. The black surface of the coffee

shimmered, as full of subtle sinister colors as an oil slick. To Zach it looked like the surface of death. His heart twinged, and Zach apologized to it in advance for what he was about to do.

He took a deep breath and blew on the demon joe, the drug that bore his father's name. He said a prayer to his various gods, steadied his hand.

Then he raised the mug to his lips and drank the bitter brew straight down.

TWENTY-ONE

Trevor felt himself rising through the syrupy air of the room, through the ceiling and the roof, out into the night. The sky arched above him like a great black bowl pricked with diamonds. He saw the kudzu swarming over the roof, the sturdy little car parked behind the house, the willow tree in the yard where he and Zach had talked that first day, fronds wavering in the terrible razor-edged moonlight. He was rising and rising. He could see the streets of Missing Mile in the distance, dark and still. The house was far below him now, a toy rectangle he could almost forget.

This isn't where I'm supposed to be, he realized. *Got to get back to Birdland . . .*

All at once it was like a film being run in reverse and speeded up; he was falling in a dizzy spiral back toward the roof, through the sucking vines, back through the ceiling and into the rooms and melting down the walls and crackling through the power lines and dripping from the faucets and disappearing down the drains, into the broken fragments of the mirror . . .

He was there.

The thought filled him with a cold excitement that was almost fear. Whatever, wherever Birdland was, he was there now.

The sensations of his body returned. He opened his eyes and found himself standing on a street corner in a city he could not name. It was like a composite of every city he had ever been in, the run-down sections and shady neighbor-hoods: ashen buildings squirming with illegible graffiti, broken and boarded windows, ragged posters stapled to telephone poles, peeling from brick walls. The few splashes of color in the landscape seemed somehow wrong.

The sidewalk and the street were empty. Though the slice of sky above him was an unhealthy purplish color that reflected back the city's light and masked any moon or stars, it seemed very late at night. Trevor saw no signs of life in the buildings around him, heard no traffic, no voices.

But the place did not feel threatening. He thought he recognized it, and he was sure it recognized him. Trevor chose a direction at random and started walking. He thought he heard the wail of a saxophone in the distance, though it kept fading in and out until he couldn't be sure it was there at all.

He passed the dark maw of a parking garage with a length of chicken wire stretched across it, a stretch of vacant lot seeded with broken bottles, a row of pawnshops, laundromats, storefront churches of Holy Light, all closed. Everything had a stark, slick, compressed look, more than two dimensions but not quite three. The buildings were solid enough; he could feel the sidewalk under his feet, the cool night air blowing his hair back from his face, the bones in his fingers moving as he stuck his hands in his pockets—

Pockets? He had been lying naked in bed with Zach. Trevor looked down at himself and saw that he was wearing a black pinstriped suit jacket with wide notched lapels, 1940s-style lapels. Underneath it was a black silk shirt with a loud checkered tie knotted loosely at the collar. His trousers matched the jacket, and on his feet were a pair of scuffed but obviously expensive black loafers. He had never worn clothes like this, but he'd seen hundreds of photos of Charlie Parker in just such a getup.

Trevor kept walking. Once he smelled the aroma of coffee, rich and strong, but he couldn't trace its direction. After a few minutes it was gone.

Soon he came to a row of bars that seemed to be open. The block was lit with old-fashioned wrought-iron gas lamps on each corner. The bars were dark, but neon flickered far in their depths, fitful chartreuse, cool blue, lurid crimson. The narrow alleys between the bars were darker still. A yeasty perfume drifted from them: the smell of a hundred kinds of liquor-dregs mingling, brewing a noxious new poison.

A few cars were parked along the curb, humpy sedans and finned dragsters, all empty. But there was still no one else on the street, and the windows of the bars were opaque, throwing back distorted reflections. The street was full of puddles that rippled with strange light and seductive colors.

All at once Trevor realized what was wrong with the colors here. The place was like a black-and-white photograph tinted by hand, *overlaid* with color rather than permeated with it. It had an appearance at once faded and garish.

Bobby's comic had always been drawn in black and white. He remembered Didi coloring in a page of it with crayons once, just scribbling in a swath of red here, a streak of blue there. That had looked sort of like this place.

Trevor stood uncertainly on the sidewalk, reluctant to enter any of the dark bars, hesitant to leave the signs of life behind him. The street seemed to grow darker in the distance, the buildings larger and more industrial-looking. Already the air was tinged with a faint scorched odor, part chemical, part meat. He didn't want to get lost among the factories and slag heaps of Birdland.

So where *was* he supposed to go? He stepped into the street to get a better view of the bars, scanned their tattered awnings and tawdry lights looking for some clue. He found none. But suddenly someone lurched out of one of the alleys, and Trevor's quick step backward was all that kept the scrawny figure from plowing right into him.

The guy gripped the lapels of Trevor's jacket with spidery fingers, stared imploringly up at Trevor. His face was gaunt, his huge burning eyes set in sockets so deep they looked like they'd been scooped out with a spoon. His flesh had a fibrous texture. His long black coat hung on his shoulders like a pair of broken wings. Its baggy sleeves had slid up over his wrists as he grabbed Trevor. Fresh needle marks ran up both stick-like arms as far as Trevor could see.

"Please gimme some credit," he hissed. "I got a big old shiny rock coming in."

It was Skeletal Sammy. Bobby's quintessential junkie character, all hustle and twitch and promise, animated by his addiction. This was the character Trevor had been trying to sketch at the kitchen table the day he learned he could draw. He remembered Bobby leaning over his shoulder and kissing the top of his head, whispering in his ear. *You draw a mean junkie, kiddo.*

He reached up and encircled Sammy's skinny wrists, gently removed Sammy's skeletal claws from his lapels. He felt an odd tenderness for this character. "Sorry, Sam," he said. "I don't have anything."

"Whaddaya mean? You're the Man, aren'cha? You got *these*, don'cha?" Sammy seized Trevor's hands, held them for a long moment. His flesh was cold as morgue tiles. Trevor felt something gouging his palm. When Sammy let go, Trevor found himself holding a small glittering jewel. It looked like a diamond, but with a faint blue glow at its core. He rolled it over his palm, watched its facets catch the light.

"That's all I got," said Sammy. "I know it ain't much, but I'll make good later."

He reached into the folds of his coat and pulled out a syringe wrapped in a dirty handkerchief. The plunger was depressed, the barrel empty. The needle gleamed dully beneath a thin film of dried blood.

"Just give me a little," begged Sammy.

"I don't have anything. I swear."

Skeletal Sammy peered at Trevor as if one of them must have gone crazy and he wasn't sure which one it was. "I *do* know you, right?"

"Well—" Trevor wasn't sure how to answer.

"You *are* an artist, right?"

"Yes."

"Then c'mon. I'll pay you double tomorrow. I'll suck your dick. Anything. Just be a pal an' roll up your sleeve."

"What for?"

"The red, baby." Sammy clutched at Trevor's sleeve. "That sweet red flowin' in your vein."

"You want my *blood*?"

Skeletal Sammy stared him in the eye and nodded slowly. The naked, wretched need in Sammy's face was like nothing Trevor had seen before. He remembered a phrase from William S. Burroughs. Sammy's face was an equation written in the algebra of need.

Trevor had never been any good at math. But he did know that there were two sides to every equation. If the inhabitants of this universe or dimension or comic or whatever the hell it was could get high on his bodily fluids, maybe he could extract something from them, too.

He put his hand over Sammy's, forced the diamond back into Sammy's palm.

"What if I give you some?" he asked. "Do you know where Bobby McGee is?"

Again that slow nod.

"Will you take me there?"

" 'Course I will," Sammy said. "He's been expecting you." The junkie tried to smile. It was a ghastly sight.

"Okay, then."

Sammy led him into one of the dark bars. The interior was both garish and squalid, with walls of filthy purple velvet and a floor unwashed for so long that Trevor felt the soles of his shoes peeling softly away from it as he walked. A sign advertising a brand of beer he'd never heard of flickered green and gold above the bar. Reflected in a dirty mirror on the opposite wall, it made a dizzy tunnel of light spiraling away into infinity. There was no bartender, no customers. The place was silent.

They sat at one of the rickety little tables. Trevor took off his pinstriped jacket, rolled up the left sleeve of his silk shirt. He saw that his scars were still open, oozing slow tears of blood. The stains didn't show on the black cloth, though the sleeve was wet with it. Sammy's eyes honed in on the blood. He looked as if he would like to lap it right off Trevor's arm.

Instead he reached into his voluminous overcoat, pulled

out a length of rubber tubing, and tied it around his own arm inches above the elbow. "If I tie off ahead of time," he explained, "I can shoot it while it's still good an' hot." He reached over and stroked Trevor's hand. His touch was ambiguous, not quite sexual. "You ready?"

"Clean your needle first. You're not sticking that dirty thing in my arm."

"No, that ain't where you like to stick dirty things, is it?"

Before Trevor could fully process this remark, Sammy got up from the table, slipped behind the bar, and came back with a glass full of neat whiskey. He took out his syringe, immersed the needle in the amber liquor and swished it around several times. Then he pulled out a cheap cigarette lighter, ran its flame along the needle and let it linger on the tip. The alcohol flared up clear blue, burned off fast. Sammy glanced at Trevor. "Satisfied?"

Trevor had no idea if this procedure really sterilized the needle, but at least the scummy-looking crust of dried blood was gone. He nodded, feeling as if somewhere during this transaction he had lost the upper hand.

Sammy bent over Trevor's arm and slid the needle into the open scar closest to the elbow. For a moment he probed, and a scintilla of pain shot through the soft meat. Then the needle found a vein and sank in deep. Sammy pulled the plunger slowly back. A dark flower of blood welled into the syringe. Trevor felt the needle shivering with each beat of his heart.

Sammy kept hold of his hand, idly stroking his wrist and playing with his fingers. But as soon as he had a full hypo, Sammy yanked the needle out of the wound. With absolutely no wasted motion he pulled up his own sleeve, stuck the needle deep into the flesh of his inner elbow, and pushed the plunger. Trevor's blood seemed to rush into his vein as if his own blood were sucking hungrily at it. Trevor saw Sammy's eyelids fluttering, the pinkish rag of his tongue glistening in his mouth. "Ohhh . . . thaasss the sweeeeet red . . ."

Then Sammy's hands spasmed and his eyes rolled back in his head and he collapsed face first on the table. The hypo fell out of his arm and rolled off the edge of the table, the inside of the barrel still coated with a thin film of blood. Sammy's right hand hit the glass of whiskey and sent it spinning to the floor. Its harsh reek filled the bar.

Trevor grabbed a handful of Sammy's hair and lifted his head off the table. It felt as light as a hollow gourd. The junkie's face had gone a sick blue beneath the already-gray cast of his skin. His eyes were closed, his chin slicked with spit.

Then the handful of hair separated from Sammy's scalp like dead grass ripping out of dry dirt, and Sammy's head smacked against the tabletop and split open as easily as an overripe melon.

Shards of his fragile skull went skittering away. Much of it simply sifted to dust. His brain looked like burnt hamburger meat, desiccated and crumbling. Trevor saw a thing like a cloudy marble trailing a length of red string roll to the edge of the table. One of Sammy's eyeballs. It teetered for a long moment, then plopped moistly to the floor. There was very little blood. The tabletop quickly became littered with teeth the color of old ivory, drifts of hair gone ashen gray, dust that smelled like a freshly opened mummy case: faintly spicy, faintly rotten.

Trevor stared dumbly at the wreckage he had made of his father's cartoon character. The running joke about Skeletal Sammy had been that he could shoot *anything*. Morphine, Dilaudid, straight H, you name it. Junk peddlers had tried to poison him with battery acid and strychnine when he got too deep into them for credit, but Sammy just pumped these noxious substances into the old vein and came back for more.

It had taken the son of his creator—his brother, in a way— to give Sammy the kick he couldn't get twice. And if Sammy had ever known where to find Bobby, he wasn't telling now.

Trevor squeezed Sammy's thin wrist. The skin flaked away beneath his fingers until he found himself clutching little more than bone. Once more he was alone in this place that felt as empty as a junkie's promise. Trevor rolled down his sleeve, put his jacket back on, and walked out of the bar.

The street was still deserted. He chose a side street that ran alongside the factories but didn't seem to lead directly into them. He had no tears left for Sammy. He kept walking.

Zach managed to drop the empty coffee mug and curl up next to Trevor before the pain slammed into his chest. For several seconds it rendered him quite unable to breathe, and he thought that was it: he'd killed himself quick and neat with a single dose of a socially acceptable drug used by billions of people without a second thought every day of their lives.

Then his lungs hitched and he was able to suck in a shallow, agonizing little breath, then another. His heart was beating so hard it made his limbs tremble and his vision throb. He rolled closer to Trevor, hooked an arm across Trevor's chest, made sure their heads were close together on the pillow.

Every muscle in Zach's body felt pulled in too many directions, stretched too thin. He imagined the fibers pinging and snapping one by one. The pain was exquisite, electric. It burned and jittered and screamed. The mushrooms in his system only upped the ante.

A red curtain began to draw across his vision. Zach let his eyes unfocus, felt himself slipping. It occurred to him that if he blacked out and had frightening dreams, the stress on his heart might kill him before he could wake up. *I don't care,* he thought. *If I can't find Trevor, I don't have a hell of a lot of reason to come back.*

The pain lessened, then disappeared. He felt as if his weak flesh and his confining brain were dissolving, releasing him. All at once Zach found himself hovering somewhere near the center of the room, staring down at the two bodies on the bed. Their limbs were intertwined, anchoring each other. They looked defenseless, as fragile as the cast-off husks of locusts that would shatter at a touch.

This is real! thought Zach. *I'm having an actual out-of-body experience!* He tried to quash the thought, afraid it might jolt him back into his flesh. Instead he suddenly felt himself skimming along the ceiling, on the verge of being pulled through the wall. Zach dug in his psychic nails and fought to stay in the bedroom. He was afraid to lose sight of their bodies. And on the other side of that wall was the bathroom.

But he was already through, circling madly near the ceiling, so close he could count the cracks in the yellowed paint and the cobwebs that clogged the light fixture. The room whirled faster, faster. Now there was no ceiling, no floor, nothing but a nauseating blur of toilet and tub and sink that looked stained again with rotten blood, though it might have been the shadows. Zach felt dizzy with centrifugal force and terror.

He was in a vortex, being sucked toward the tub. For a moment he thought he would go spinning straight down the black orifice of the drain. But then he saw the glittering shards of mirror and felt himself swirling into them, fragmenting. It was like being forced through a screen, like falling into a kaleidoscope edged with razor blades.

Zach recognized the next place he saw. It was a place he knew well. It was his cradle, his home, his most addictive drug.

It was cyberspace.

The writer Bruce Sterling defined *cyberspace* as the place where a telephone conversation seems to occur. This could be extrapolated to include the place where computer data was stored, and the place a hacker had to travel through to get the data. It had no physical reality, yet Zach had an image of it as vivid and sensibly laid out as the streets of the French Quarter. Cyberspace was part cosmos, part grid, part rollercoaster.

Right after leaving his body in the bedroom, Zach had felt very light and slightly damp, like a breath of water vapor or a spare scrap of ectoplasm. Now he was utterly weightless, without physical properties. He was composed of energy, not matter. He was a creature made of information. He was traveling through cyberspace at a very high speed.

Then suddenly he wasn't, and it knocked the wind out of him.

Zach sat up with a deep burning sensation in his solar plexus, pressed his hand to his chest and touched crisp cloth. He seemed to be wearing some kind of suit. He was reclining in a padded chair, hard sticky floor under his feet, lurid light assaulting his eyeballs. As he became accustomed to it, he was able to make out rows of seats around him, slumped bodies and nodding heads, bloody images flickering across a wide screen. A movie theater.

The film appeared to be a composite of any number of works by Italian splatter film directors, but with an all-male, homosexual cast, set to a screeching saxophone soundtrack. A boy carefully rolled a condom onto another's erect penis, raised a pair of huge gleaming scissors and snipped the whole thing off, then pressed his mouth to the raw hole and drank the fountaining blood. A white man masturbated over a prostrate black man, ejaculated a pearly stream of maggots into the straining, glistening ebony back.

Zach saw that most of the other filmgoers were seated in pairs. Here and there a head bobbed gently in a lap, half-concealed by a dirty overcoat. Zach watched the movie for a few more minutes. Just as he was starting to get interested, someone slid into the aisle seat next to him and put a warm hand on his leg.

He turned with a well-rehearsed *fuck off* on his lips. This was a situation he'd encountered at the movies ever since he could remember, and he wasn't enough of a slut to let some anonymous pervert jack him off, hardly ever.

But instead of letting the words fly, Zach just stared. The person sitting beside him was Calvin.

The guitarist wore a charcoal suit with a black turtleneck sweater underneath. His gaunt grinning face seemed to float on the gloom of the theater. His blond hair was slicked back, giving him a vulpine look. The pressure of his fingers increased. He leaned over to whisper, and his lips brushed Zach's ear. "Do you want this as bad as I do?"

No, I just want Trevor, thought Zach. He opened his mouth to say so, and what came out was "Hell, yes." Then Calvin's mouth was attacking Zach's, Calvin's hand was sliding up to his crotch, tugging at his zipper, freeing his eager, treacherous dick. Calvin's fingers squeezed and stroked him expertly.

Zach wrapped his arms around Calvin's neck and kissed back hard. Their tongues exchanged molten secrets.

This was all we ever wanted from each other anyway, Zach thought, *a down-and-dirty, no-strings-attached fuck. What was so wrong with that?* He couldn't remember why they had stopped the first time.

The skin of his balls was tightening, his dick aching and throbbing. Zach broke the kiss and gasped for breath. Over Calvin's shoulder he caught a glimpse of the movie screen. A hand was sliding up and down the shaft of a penis he recognized as his own. The camera panned back until he could see a tangle of naked limbs, including an arm whose bicep was tattooed with a little cartoon character Zach could just make out as Krazy Kat. He guessed Mr. Natural hadn't been invented yet in this universe. *Well,* he thought incoherently, *Krazy Kat was a fag.*

The camera zoomed back in on the hand. Its quickening rhythm matched Calvin's. Zach felt himself getting ready to let go hard. The screen filled with glistening purple flesh, huge slippery fingers. Then come was pulsing from the enormous lips of the movie penis, and from his own aching dick as well.

But Zach saw only what was happening onscreen. The come made a deadly rainbow arc in the air, landed on the hand, and began to dissolve the skin. Tiny holes appeared where it hit, sizzling and spreading, reducing the layers of flesh and muscle to blackened lace. The matter dripped off the framework of the bones, oozed down the shaft of the penis. Still the huge skeletal fingers stroked. And still Calvin's hand moved in his lap.

Calvin leaned in for another kiss and Zach saw his face, no longer just gaunt but emaciated. Zach shrank back against the seat as Calvin's skin blossomed with purple lesions like the ones he had seen on his own face in the bathroom mirror. Calvin's tongue was a dead dry sponge thrusting between his lips, questing toward Zach's mouth, seeking moisture.

Then it wasn't Calvin at all; it was the clerk from the convenience store in Mississippi. Leaf. Those elegant cheekbones were hideously exaggerated now; those honey-colored eyes were like chips of topaz set in a ruined mosaic. His lips twitched as he leaned toward Zach. He stroked Zach's thigh with a disintegrating hand.

"Oh," he whispered, "*just come over here and let's fuck . . .*"

Then he was the person before that. And then he was the person before that. And then *she* was the person before *that.* And they just kept changing, and they just got worse . . .

Zach shoved himself out of his seat and stumbled backward down the row. He tripped over a tangle of feet and turned to apologize, but the pair of faces that tilted up to him were blotched with purple, horribly withered. He saw his lover pushing itself up, supporting itself on the seat backs, making its way slowly toward him. Above the blaring soundtrack Zach heard labored breathing, dry, painful coughing. All over the theater other figures were beginning to stir, to rise.

Zach turned and ran. He vaulted over the tangled legs, sprinted up the aisle, and burst out into the lobby. A set of glass doors led out onto the street. At the last second before he grasped the handle, Zach *knew* they would be locked. He would be trapped here in the lobby with the zombies coming for him, and when they got him they would smear him across the glass like a crushed strawberry. He had seen enough movies to know what happened when the zombies got you.

But the doors weren't locked, and Zach slammed through them at high speed. On the far side of the street, pausing to push his glasses up and catch his breath, he glanced across at the theater. Its facade was lavishly decorated in art deco tiles and marble, deep crimson, jade green, jet black. The marquee was wrought of fluted, gleaming chrome like a 1930s dream of the future. On its sign was spelled out—in red block letters a foot high—THE GARDEN OF EARTHLY DELIGHTS.

"Cute," he snarled, and started walking fast, looking behind him every half block or so. The street remained empty. He guessed the zombies were quarantined in the theater.

Zach held his hands up in front of his face and stared at the palms. The lines in them were dark pink, healthy-looking enough though slightly damp with sweat. He had always heard that if you were really sick, the lines in your palms turned gray.

But he felt fine. Was the place trying to scare him with its rotting mirror images and its wank-house zombies? Or was it trying to warn him of something?

If he ever got out of here, Zach decided, he was going straight to the nearest health clinic and getting a blood test. He didn't want one, but he thought maybe it was time to start considering things other than what he wanted.

Soon he was far from the theater. The deserted streets felt half-familiar. This place wasn't New Orleans, but Zach thought New Orleans had been used to flavor it like a spice. He could see it in the gas lamps on the corners, the high curbs, even a cast-iron balcony or a gate leading into a shadowy courtyard here and there. The night air was cool on his face, though it smelled nothing like the alcoholic haze of the French Quarter. The odor here was more like Toxic Alley, the poisonous stretch of the Mississippi River between New Orleans and Baton Rouge, a faint ghost of chemicals and burning oil.

He saw a fountain bubbling fitfully in a tiny concrete park and stopped to rest. The fountain struck him as odd, and after a moment Zach realized why: there were no coins on the bottom, not even pennies. He had never seen a public fountain without pennies on the bottom. Instead there seemed to be a few small faceted jewels, so translucent in the clear water that Zach could hardly be sure they were there at all.

Well, you're in a hallucination now, he thought. *And it isn't even your own. Better get used to seeing some weird shit.*

He stared at his feet and suddenly registered that they were clad in shoes he'd never seen before, two-toned wingtip loafers polished within an inch of their lives. For the first time he thought to check out the rest of his outfit.

Some kind of suit, he'd thought in the theater. But what a suit! It was woven from nubbly-textured cloth of the palest shell pink, cut loose and baggy, with vast lapels. Underneath he had on a cream-colored shirt and an extravagant red silk tie with a tiny paisley figure. Zach felt something on his head, reached up to investigate. A beret. Wouldn't you just know it. Even the lenses of his glasses seemed to have taken on a smoky hipster tint.

Birdland might try to fuck with you at every turn, Zach thought, but at least you got to dress cool.

He heard a ripple of music nearby. The clear voice of a saxophone, leisurely rising, then descending. The sound was getting closer. By this time Zach would not have been surprised to see Charlie Parker (or his zombie) come swaying round the corner, eyes shut tight and forehead wrinkled, blowing the horn as he walked. Bird used to come onstage like that, Trevor had told him, after the rest of the band had already been playing for an hour or so. He would start somewhere way off in the bowels of the club, and the other musicians would gradually fall in with him as they heard his approach, until by the time he walked onstage Bird was leading the band.

But what rounded the corner instead was, in the most literal sense of the term, a solo instrument. Walking on four multijointed, chitinous-looking legs, depressing its own keys with two equally insectile three-fingered hands, brass gleaming through a web of scuffs and scratches, came an unaccompanied alto saxophone.

"Oh now," Zach muttered, "this is just silly."

The music stopped, and a low fluting voice spoke out of the instrument's bell. "Hey, cat—you in a cartoon, dig? Cartoons is s'posed to be silly. Here, have a stick of tea and you be gettin' silly too."

Zach could see no speaking apparatus anywhere on the thing, nothing that vaguely resembled lips or vocal cords, yet the voice did not sound synthesized. The alto reached one of those spiny claws deep into the curve of its bell and pulled out a fat twisted cigarette. This it tossed to Zach, who caught it eagerly.

"Pick up on that tea," the sax advised him. "Don't be lettin' zombies bring you down. They ain't cool or viperish neither. Not like us."

"Hey, thanks."

"*De nada*," said the instrument suavely. "Any descendant of Hieronymus is a friend o' mine." It began to noodle off down the street, playing a few bars of "Ornithology."

"Wait!" Zach stuck the joint in his pocket and hurried after it. "Do you know where any of the McGees are? Trevor? Bobby?"

The alto switched to "Lullaby of Birdland" but did not otherwise reply. It had a half-block start on Zach, and it always seemed to stay just a little too far ahead of him, dropping to all fours and scuttling like a roach on those barbed legs, still playing itself with its spiky little hands, the gay tune spiraling behind. Zach's fancy new shoes pinched his feet when he tried to hurry. He could not catch up. Eventually the thing disappeared down an alley and lost him altogether.

Now Zach was in a narrow street lined on both sides with dark buildings that seemed to lean forward over the sidewalk, swaying slightly. Many of the buildings had old-fashioned stoops and stairs leading up to recessed entryways that might have once been elegant, but all were in a state of advanced decay. He saw fanlights with the stained glass broken out, only a few shards remaining like jagged multicolored teeth in the frames. Overhead he could barely make out a purple slice of sky. The place was deserted. Zach reached into his jacket, knowing somehow that there would be a streamlined silver lighter tucked in a pocket. There was.

He leaned against a stoop, stuck the joint in his mouth, and lit up. An acrid, bitter taste filled his mouth, nothing remotely like marijuana. He burst out coughing. "A stick of tea," the alto had said, and Zach assumed it was talking beatnik slang. Now he remembered a panel from *Birdland* of cat-headed smugglers at a river dock, unloading bales of Darjeeling and Earl Grey under cover of darkest night. It really *was* tea.

Well, fuck it. Caffeine had started him on this journey; maybe it would preserve him. Zach took another hit off the stick of tea and found himself getting a delicious dizzy high, as good as that from the sticky green bud Dougal used to sell in the French Market. He felt a sudden wave of homesickness, wondered if he would ever see New Orleans again.

But if he didn't get his ass moving and find Trevor, he might never even see Missing Mile again. Zach took a couple more tokes, bent over to snuff the joint on the sidewalk. And then all at once a premonition hit him, stronger than any he'd ever had before: *Get the fuck out of here. Now.*

Zach began to straighten up, heard a door slam and heavy footsteps pounding down the stairs behind him. He dropped the joint, but before he could turn, a hard shove sent him sprawling across the sidewalk. He managed to get his hands under him and his chin up fast enough not to break any teeth, but he felt the healing cut on his lip burst open, saw fresh blood spatter the cement. His palms screamed agony. He felt sidewalk grit working its way into raw subcutaneous layers of flesh.

"You stupid fuckin' kid! Leave you alone for five minutes and I find you smokin' dope on the street corner!" A boot ground into the small of his back. The voice was familiar, deep and faintly gravelly. *Shit, no, please, no,* thought Zach. *Make me fuck a zombie. Let me watch my own face rotting in the mirror. Please, anything but my dad.*

Zach twisted away from the boot. A large hand wrapped around his wrist and hauled him up. He found himself staring up into the pale exasperated face of Joe Bosch, and remembered one of the scariest things about his father: even when he was beating the crap out of someone, usually his wife or son, his face never lost that wide-eyed, slightly harassed expression. It was as if he sincerely believed he was inflicting this damage for the good of all concerned, and was only pissed that they couldn't see it that way.

When Zach left home, his father had been a foot taller than he, skinny but muscular. Since then Zach had grown six inches and gained thirty pounds. Joe must have kept growing too, for he still seemed just as big. Zach had always looked very much like his mother. He had her pallid coloring, her slender bones, her narrow nose and sulky underlip and thick blue-black hair. The almond shape of his eyes was hers too.

Joe didn't look so different; he was fair-skinned and dark-haired with sharp intense features, and could have been Evangeline's brother. But Evangeline's eyes were Cajun black. Joe's were the color of jade.

His father's relentless stare bored into him, dissected him, mirrored him. Zach could not even try to pull away. He remembered the consequences of evasive action all too well. The trick of being beaten up was to take what you couldn't avoid and show just enough pain to appease their anger, but not enough to make them want more. If you awakened their lust for pain, they would make you bleed, break, burn.

But there was one thing Zach had never been able to control, one thing that had gotten him hurt more times than he could remember, and that was his smart mouth.

He looked straight into Joe's eyes, wondering if there was anything of his real father in there or if this was a phantom like Calvin in the movie theater, a distillation of Birdland and mushrooms and his own fear.

"I know you can kick my ass," he said, "but can you talk to me?"

"Talk?" Joe sneered. Zach saw a gold tooth, remembered a night when he was four or five, his father staggering in with blood pouring from his mouth. It looked as if he had been vomiting the stuff. He'd been in a bar fight over some woman, and Evangeline had screamed at him all night.

"Sure, *Zach-a-reee*." His mother had named him after her own grandfather. Joe hated the name, always spoke it that way, with a taunting twist to his lips. "We can talk. What do you wanna talk about?"

"I've got all kinds of shit I want to talk about." Zach had never dared say these things to his father. If he didn't say them now, he never would. "Tell me why you hate me so much. Tell me why I have belt scars on my back that haven't faded in five years. Tell me how come I could leave home and support myself at fourteen but *you couldn't even deal with your fucking life at thirty-three!*"

He tensed, expecting to get slapped. But Joe only smiled. It turned his eyes brilliant and dangerous. "You wanna know all that? Then take a look at *this*."

Joe stuck his free hand into his shirt pocket and pulled out a used condom. Holding it by the rim with thumb and forefinger as if his own seed were distasteful to him, he thrust it in Zach's face. The reservoir tip was split open, and a long thin string of come dangled from it, glistening in the purple light. The Bosch family heirloom.

"This is why I hate you," said Joe. "I didn't want a kid any more than you want one right now. I could've done anything with my life. Your momma didn't want you because she was scared of being pregnant and too lazy to take care of you once you got there. But *I had a future, and you killed it*."

"BULLSHIT!" Zach felt his face flushing, his eyes burning with anger. "That's the stupidest thing I've ever heard! I'm just your excuse for being a failure. Nobody made you—"

Joe jammed the rubber between Zach's lips and deep into his mouth. The thing slithered over his tongue, squeaked nastily against his teeth. Zach was so startled that he almost sucked it right down his throat. For a moment his father's fingers scrabbled over his tongue, hard and dirty; then they withdrew, and there was only the slimy feel of the rubber, its latex-and-dead-fish flavor.

Zach felt bile rising in his throat. He twisted his face away from Joe's hand and spat the thing out on the sidewalk where it lay like a severed skin in a pool of spit. The taste of Joe's come still filled his mouth, like sulfur and salt and murdered dreams.

"Swallow it," Joe told him. "It could have been you."

Zach felt his mind beginning to drift away on a thin tether. "This isn't happening," he said. "You aren't real."

"Oh yeah?" said Joe. "Then I guess this won't hurt." He cocked his right arm. Zach saw the flash of a big gold ring an instant before the fist smashed into his face.

The pain was like a sunburst exploding through his head. Zach inhaled a freshet of blood. Behind his eyelids he saw a sudden flare of electric blue. He'd read that when you saw that color, it meant your brain had just banged against the inside of your skull.

Joe hit him again and his lips smeared wetly across his teeth, soft skin splitting and shredding. This made the time Trevor had punched him look like a love tap. Joe let go of his arm and Zach crumpled to the sidewalk. He couldn't open his eyes, though hot tears were searing them. He curled into a fetal position and wrapped his arms around his head. His father was screaming at him, half sobbing.

"You goddamn smartass BRAT. Always thought you were smarter than me. You and that CUNT, with your pretty faces. How pretty are you gonna be NOW? How smart are you gonna be with your fuckin' BRAINS STOMPED INTO THE SIDEWALK?"

Joe's boot connected with the base of Zach's spine, sent a hot wave of pain up his body. *He's going to kill me,* Zach thought. *He's going to kick me to death right here in the street. Will my body back at the house die too? Will Trevor wake up next to me with my head bashed in and think he did it?*

The idea was unbearable. Zach rolled over, saw the boot drawing back to kick him again, grabbed his father's ankle and yanked hard. If Joe went down, Zach knew in that instant, he wasn't getting up again. Zach would kill him if possible—with a bottle or a chunk of brick if he could grab one, with his bare hands if he couldn't. Fuck not fighting back; all bets were off.

But Joe didn't go down. Zach managed to throw him off balance and he stumbled, then recovered with a great roar of rage and drove the toe of his boot into Zach's shoulder. The muscles instantly contracted into a shrieking knot of agony. *Well, that's it,* Zach thought through the pain. *That was my chance and I blew it and now he's just gonna kill me worse.* He could already taste the dirty boot heel plowing into his mouth, his teeth splintering, blood spraying over his tongue.

But instead of stomping his face, Joe reached down, grabbed Zach's arm, and pulled him back up. It was obvious that Joe would be perfectly willing to yank his shoulder out of its socket if Zach resisted. "You're smart enough to get into places but not smart enough to know when you're not wanted," he hissed into Zach's face. His breath was scented with peppermint and rotgut gin. "You're meddlin' here and I'm gonna stop you. Don't fight me or I'll put out one of your eyes. I swear it."

Zach believed him. He remembered a time just before he had left home for good that Joe had thrown him against the wall and held a lighted cigarette less than an inch from his right eye, threatening to burn it if he blinked. Evangeline had snatched the cigarette, taken a slap across the face that knocked her down, then cussed Zach to ribbons for having provoked his father with some smartass remark. Later he had noticed that his eyelashes were singed.

Joe pulled out the poor man's weapon he had always carried on the streets of New Orleans, a knotted sock half full of pennies. The black wool was stiff with dried blood. He slapped it against his palm thoughtfully, then grinned and swung it around his head, winding up for the blow.

Trevor, Zach promised silently, *if I see you again—no, WHEN I see you, I'm taking you away to the cleanest, whitest, bluest, warmest beach you ever saw, and I'll buy you all the paper and ink you want, and we'll keep each other as sane as we want to be and love each other as long as we're alive. We'll let go of our pasts and start making our future.*

Then his father's slap plowed into his skull. Joe hit him so hard that the sock split right open. In the instant before his mind went out, Zach saw its contents raining down around his head, shimmering, sparkling.

Not pennies. Tiny diamonds.

Trevor kept following the street he had chosen. It led him deeper into the factories where he wasn't sure he wanted to go, but there were no cross streets anymore, and he would not return the way he had come. There was nothing in those bars for him, nothing but the bottles frosted with dust and filled with poison, nothing but Skeletal Sammy's crumbling bones.

He passed a shining, bubbling pool of black liquid enclosed

by a chain-link fence, a vast decrepit building with white steam billowing from hundreds of broken windows, a rail-yard where rusty boxcars lay scattered like children's blocks. There was a weird toxic beauty to the landscape. Like alien terrain, Trevor thought at first; but this desolation was peculiarly human.

His fingers itched for pencil and paper. He could actually feel the satisfying sensation of the graphite tip gliding over the page, the slight textured catch of the paper's grain, the minute sympathetic vibration in the bones of his hand. He thrust both hands into his pockets and walked on.

The street began to curve away in a strange perspective, as if the horizon line didn't quite mesh with the sky. He saw the corner of another empty lot up ahead, then realized it wasn't empty after all as the edge of a building became visible, set back farther from the street than the others. Something else was odd about the building, and after a moment Trevor realized what. It was made of wood. The structure he saw was a wooden porch, here in this industrial wasteland of steel and concrete.

It cast a flat black shadow on the ground, the shadow of a peaked roof and spindly railings, like any of a million porches on a million rambling old farmhouses. You saw them plenty driving around rural areas of the South. You didn't see them much, though, in the industrial sections of vast gray deserted cities.

A few more steps and his conscious mind saw what his back brain had known all along. It was the house from Violin Road, set down stark and solid in the middle of this necrophiliac dreamscape, the same as it had ever been, hardly looking a part of the world it now inhabited.

If not the seed of Birdland, the house was surely its rotten core; if not an actual part of this dead world, the house was surely its source. Trevor knew he was going back in there now. If he died this time, it would be as if he had never lived these twenty years. If he didn't, then the rest of his life belonged to him.

And to Zach, if he still wanted any part of it. *It's the house where you lost your virginity after a quarter century, too,* Trevor reminded himself. But that was another source of its power over him, as visceral as the deaths.

Remember, he thought dreamily, *you still have plenty of time to get down to Birdland . . .*

But now there was no more time. Now he was all the way down.

Without its yardful of weeds and green veil of kudzu the house looked stark, broken-backed, sculpted of splinter and shadow. The windows rippled with opaque colors, reflecting some light Trevor could not see. As he crossed the featureless lot they flared violet, then faded to bruise.

He mounted the steps, pushed the listing door open, and went in. The living room was just as he remembered it: ugly chair and sofa sagging but not completely gone to mold and mildew; the turntable surrounded by crates of records. His heart missed a beat as he saw another figure in the dim room.

Crouching near the hall doorway was a slender woman in a loose white camisole and a red skirt with matching elbow-length gloves. Long black hair spilled over her shoulders and down her back, rippling with unearthly blue highlights.

Her head swiveled and her face tilted up to him: pale, sharp-featured, startlingly lovely. Her enormous dark eyes were slightly tilted, smudged with shadows. Trevor realized three things at once: the woman looked just like Zach; she was holding something in her cupped hands; and she was wearing only a white one-piece shift, no gloves. The skirt was so stained with blood that he had thought it a separate piece of clothing. Her arms were swathed to the elbows in gore.

She raised her hands and showed him what she held. Trevor saw a gelatinous glob of blood shot through with dark veins, the black dot of an eye, five tiny curled fingers.

"I didn't have the money for a doctor," she said, "so I hit myself in the stomach until it bled. I just wanted the damn thing out of me. Do you hear? Out!"

Trevor advanced on her, stared her down. A quick hot vein of anger pulsed in his head. Zach had suffered unforgivably at the hands of this woman. "You did not," he said. "You didn't want him but you had him anyway, and you two tortured him as long as you could get away with it. That was nineteen years ago and your baby's doing fine. Where are *you* now, you fucking evil *bitch*?''

The woman crumpled back against the door frame. The bloody mess slid out of her hands. Trevor had to resist the urge to scoop the lonely detritus into his own hands and sob over it. That mangled thing wasn't Zach, couldn't be. It was only a neverborn phantom.

He remembered that Zach's mother was named Evangeline, like the poem. ''Go away, Evangeline,'' he said. ''Get out of my house. I hate you.''

Her huge stricken eyes settled on Trevor. He couldn't tell if she was hearing him; she hadn't responded directly to anything he said. ''You're a ghost,'' he told her, ''and you're not even the right one.''

Her head fell back. Her hands curled into claws. A shudder went through her, and for a moment the outlines of her body blurred, as if she were passing through some unseen membrane. Then all at once her hair was turning to cornsilk shot through with streaks of darker gold, matted with blood. Her features grew softer, rounder, her breasts heavier. Her arms hung by her sides, a mass of blood and bruise. Trevor found himself looking at his own mother, Rosena McGee, as he had discovered her that morning.

He remembered the first day he had come back to the house, when he switched on the light in the studio and saw Bobby's drawing of this scene, identical to the one Trevor had done on the bus. At the time Trevor thought maybe Bobby had drawn it before her death, as a sort of dry run. But it was too exact; with Rosena struggling, he never could have landed the blows as precisely on her flesh as he had done on paper.

No. He had killed her, and then he had sat down here with his sketchbook and drawn her. Then he had tacked the drawing to the studio wall before he went in and killed Didi. Trevor had no proof of this sequence of events, but he could see it all too clearly. Bobby hunched on the floor before her broken body, hand flying over the paper, eyes flickering with manic intensity from Rosena's dead face to the page and back again. But why?

His mother's eyes were open, the whites filmed with blood. There were deep gouges in her forehead, her left temple, the center of her chest. All had bled heavily. From the head wounds had also trickled some clear substance—cerebral fluid, he supposed—that cut pale tracks through the blood. Trevor noticed that unlike himself and Skeletal Sammy, Rosena was not in forties-noir costume; she wore the same embroidered jeans and cotton dashiki top she'd had on the night she died.

What the hell did that mean? What the hell did *any* of it mean? He suddenly wanted Zach here with him as badly as he had ever wanted anything. Zach could unravel intricate patterns of logic, perhaps explain them. And if there was no logic in Birdland, then Zach could hold him, give him somewhere to hide his face so he would not have to keep looking into his mother's bloody eyes.

No. This was what he had come for. He had to see everything.

Rosena's body blocked half the doorway. Trevor edged by, careful not to let his leg brush her. He could picture the stiff sprawl of her limbs if he were to knock her over, could hear the hollow sound her head would make hitting the floor. When he was nearly past, he could also imagine how it would feel if she reached out and wrapped a hand around his ankle. But Rosena remained motionless. He could not believe that she would ever harm him.

He pushed open the door of Didi's room and looked through the crack but did not enter the room. There was a tiny body sprawled on the mattress. Even in the dim light Trevor could make out the dark stain surrounding the head.

Had Bobby drawn Didi after killing him too? Maybe, but Trevor didn't think so. It would have been getting very late by then, and Bobby didn't want to see another dawn. But where had he gone next? Straight into the bathroom with his rope, or somewhere else?

So many questions. Trevor was suddenly disgusted with himself for asking them when there seemed to be no answers. What the fuck did it *matter* what Bobby had done? What difference could it make to him now? He should never have eaten those mushrooms, should never have catapulted himself over into Birdland. He had left Zach behind, and he didn't know how to find his way back, and everything here seemed like a senseless dead end.

Maybe he was hallucinating it all. This world *seemed* as tangible as the other: he had felt the sting of Sammy's needle going into his arm, smelled the fresh blood and raw sewage stink of the bodies. But he was on an unfamiliar drug. Who knew what could happen? Maybe he would enter his bedroom and see his own body asleep on the mattress, curled around Zach. Maybe he could get back through.

You came for answers, he reminded himself. *Did you think they would be written on the walls in blood? Are you really ready to go back to the real house, to the empty house? Are you ready to stop trying to fit yourself like an odd piece into the puzzle of your family's deaths, to fly away with Zach, to start your own life?*

He didn't know. There seemed to be an invisible barrier between him and all he saw, as if the house were letting him look but not touch, telling him *You were never a part of this* as if he needed to hear it again. The dead were linked in a terrible intimacy, and Trevor was the living, the outsider. *You never had anything to do with it. Bobby left you out completely. They all left you. Go back to the one person who cared enough to stay.*

Trevor found himself standing before the closed door of his own room. He felt as if he were walking a thin line between his past and his future. If he fell, he would have neither. Balance was everything.

As if in a dream, Trevor saw his hand reaching out, his fingers closing on the knob. Very slowly, he opened the door.

The man sitting on the edge of the bed looked up. His eyes locked with Trevor's, ice-blue irises rimmed in black, pupils hugely dilated. His gaunt face and his bare chest were smeared with blood. His ginger hair was matted with it. In his right hand he held a rusty hammer, its head glistening thick sticky red, its claw a nightmare of tangled blond hair, shredded skin, pulverized brain and bone. Slow rivulets of blood ran down the handle, coursed in dark veinlike patterns over his arm.

Trevor was dimly aware of someone else in the room, a small still form on the mattress, breathing deeply, shrouded in covers. But he could not focus on it; the membrane seemed to shimmer and grow opaque at that point, like a wrinkle in the fabric of this world.

For a long, long moment he and Bobby simply stared at each other. Their faces were more alike than Trevor had remembered. Then Bobby's trance seemed to break a little, and his lips moved. What came out was a broken whisper, hoarse with whiskey and sorrow. "Who are you?"

"I'm your son."

"Didi and Rosena—"

"You killed them. You know me, Bobby." Trevor advanced a few steps into the room. "You *better* know me. I haven't stopped thinking about you for twenty years."

"Oh, Trev . . ." The hammer fell out of Bobby's hand, landed with a heavy thunk on the floorboards less than an inch from his bare toes, but Bobby didn't flinch. Trevor saw tears coursing down his face, washing away some of the blood. "Is it really you?"

"Go look in the mirror if you don't believe me."

"No . . . no . . . I know who you are." Bobby's shoulders slumped. He looked ancient, desolate. "How old are you? Nineteen? Twenty?"

"Twenty-five."

"Do you still draw?"

"Goddammit!" Trevor remembered the drift of shredded paper on the mattress, the pillow, their bodies. "You ought to know!"

Very slowly, Bobby shook his head. "No, Trev. I don't know anything anymore." He looked up again, and Trevor saw by the naked pain in Bobby's face that it was true. A terrible suspicion drifted like a cold mist into his mind.

"Why didn't you kill me?" Trevor asked. He had been

waiting so long to say those words. Now they sounded flat and lifeless.

Bobby shrugged helplessly. Trevor recognized the gesture; it was one of his own. "I just kept sitting here," Bobby went on, "looking at your drawings on the wall, wondering how in hell I could hit you with that thing, wondering how I could bury that chunk of metal in your sweet, smart brain, thinking how *easy* they'd been compared to you. They were like anatomy lessons. The body is a puzzle of flesh and blood and bone . . . you understand?"

Trevor nodded. He thought of the times he had wanted to keep biting Zach, to keep pulling and tearing at Zach's flesh just to see what was under there. Then he thought of fighting at the Boys' Home, of slamming the older kid's head against the tiles of the shower stall. Of tendrils of blood swirling through warm water.

"And when you kill the people you love, you watch what your hands are doing, you feel the blood hitting your face, but all the time you're thinking *Why am I doing this?* And then you get it. It's *because* you love them, because you want *all* their secrets, not just the ones they decide to show you. And after you take them apart, you know everything."

"Then why . . ." Trevor could hardly speak. It was true what he had suspected all along: Bobby hadn't loved him enough to kill him.

"Why did I leave you out? Because I had to. Because I sat here watching you sleep, thinking all that. And then you came in, just now.

"And I can't do it, Trev. If I have any talent, any gift left at all, it's in you now. I can kill them, I can kill myself, but I can't kill that."

He picked up the hammer again, stood, and walked toward Trevor.

"Wait!" Trevor put out his hands, tried to touch Bobby. Bobby stopped just out of reach, and his hands closed on air. "Are you seeing . . . Is this . . ." He didn't know how to articulate what he wanted to ask. "What about Birdland? What happened to it for you?"

"Birdland is a machine oiled with the blood of artists," Bobby said dreamily. His tone was as detached as if he were giving a lecture. He came closer, held out the dripping hammer. "Birdland is a mirror that reflects our deaths. Birdland never existed."

"But it's right outside that window!" Trevor yelled. "It's where I just came from!"

"Yes," said Bobby, "but I stay in here."

He pressed the hammer into Trevor's hand. Then he spread his arms wide and wrapped Trevor in an embrace that felt like warm damp fog. His outlines were blurring. His flesh was softening, melting into Trevor's.

"NO! DON'T GO! TELL ME WHY YOU DID IT! TELL ME!!!"

"You don't really want to know why," he heard Bobby's voice say. *"You just want to know what it felt like."*

Trevor felt the viscous fog seeping into his bones, curling up in his skull, blotting out his vision. He felt blood running down the hammer handle, coursing warm and sticky over his fingers, mingling with the blood from his own scars. From the corner of his eye he saw his drawings fluttering on the wall like trapped wings.

"Tell me," he whispered.

You're an artist, the voice whispered back. It was deep inside his head now. *Go find out for yourself.*

Then the world blinked out like a blown bulb.

TWENTY-TWO

Zach was plummeting through cyberspace. *Imagine,* he thought dazedly, *I never needed a computer at all; you can get here just by drinking a cup of coffee and having someone hit you in the head hard enough to knock your eyeballs out.*

He was going faster and faster, at the speed of light, of information, of thought. Beyond that there was no consciousness, no identity. There were no federal spooks, no United States, no New Orleans or Missing Mile, no one named Zachary Bosch. There was no such thing as a crime, no such thing as death. He felt himself dissolving into the vast web of synapses, numbers, bits. It was complex but unemotional, easy to understand. It was comforting.

It was *so cold . . .*

Zach struggled against the web in sudden panic. *No!* He didn't want to stay here and be assimilated into cyberspace, or Birdland, or the void—whatever it was, he did not want to become a small part of a greater good or evil, a streamlined fragment of information that meant nothing on its own. He wanted his troublesome individuality, with all its attendant difficulties and dangers. He wanted his body back. He wanted Trevor.

With every particle of will left in him, Zach strained toward the waking world.

He felt a cold electric flash, became aware of his body's weight and the mattress under him, felt his heart hammering in his chest. He was uncomfortably sure that it had just started back up. Blood was draining from his nasal cavities into his throat, nearly choking him. His head buzzed and throbbed. His hands felt as if someone had gone at them with coarse sandpaper.

Either everything he remembered had really just happened, or this was one intense motherfucker of a trip.

Zach forced his eyes open and saw Trevor sitting on the edge of the bed staring vacantly at the opposite wall. His tangled, sweat-soaked hair streamed over his naked shoulders and down his back. His arms and hands were still bloody, but the scars seemed to have closed.

Clutched in his right fist was the hammer, glistening with blood and other matter. Zach knew Trevor hadn't hit him: if all that gunk was his, he wouldn't be breathing now. But what *had* Trevor done? And what did he *think* he had done?

He propped himself up on one elbow, felt his head spinning, his vision going blurry. He realized he had lost his glasses somewhere. "Trev?" he whispered. "Are you okay?"

No response.

"Trevor?" Zach's hand felt rooted to the mattress. He managed to lift it a few inches, extend it for what seemed like miles. His fingers just brushed Trevor's thigh. The flesh felt cold and smooth as marble. Zach's fingertips left four parallel smudges of blood on the pale skin.

He had scraped the hell out of his hands. There was nowhere in the house he could have done that. *Of course not*, he thought, *it happened falling on the sidewalk in Birdland, trying not to bust your teeth out on the curb. Joe pushed you, remember?*

And if he had met Joe, what had Trevor seen?

He pushed himself closer to Trevor, tried to sit up. "Trev, listen, you didn't hurt me. I'm fine." A wave of dizziness washed over him, threatened to become nausea without further notice. "Are you okay? What's going on?"

Trevor turned. His eyes were like holes drilled in a glacier, black gouges going down deep into the ice. His face looked hollow, haggard, used up. His skull seemed to be trying to wear right through the skin.

"He saw me," said Trevor. "He saw me in here."

"Who? When?"

"My father." There was recognition in Trevor's eyes, but no

warmth. Looking into them was like falling through the void again. "He saw me come in here that night. He talked to me."

Oh man, thought Zach, *bad trip. Bad, bad trip.* "Where were you?" he asked cautiously.

"Birdland."

Of course. Where else? "No, I mean . . ." What the hell *did* he mean? "I mean, where were you on the space-time continuum? *When* were you?"

"This house. That night. I saw my mother dead. I saw my brother dead. Then I came in here and Bobby was alive, was sitting on the bed deciding whether to kill me. He saw me, *spoke* to me, and decided he couldn't do it. It was my own fault."

"I don't understand. You mean you woke up and talked him out of it?"

"NO! He saw me the way I am NOW! He talked to ME NOW, and then he went and HUNG HIMSELF! LOOK AT THIS! DON'T YOU SEE?" Trevor gestured wildly with the hammer. A tiny gobbet of gore hit Zach's already-bloody lip. He shrank back against the wall and surreptitiously wiped it away.

"He talked to you at age twenty-five?"

"Yes."

"He was haunted by your ghost."

"Yes."

"Shit." Zach's head was beginning to clear a little; it almost made sense. He thought of loops, which were computer programs designed to repeat a set of instructions until a certain condition was satisfied. Zach had previously suspected that hauntings, if they existed, might operate on much the same principle. This was borne out by most of New Orleans' famous ghost stories, in which the ghost usually appeared in the same place and repeated the same actions again and again, such as pointing at the spot where its bones were buried or rolling its decapitated head down the stairs.

The idea still seemed to make sense somehow. This was one hell of a complicated program, but maybe Trevor had managed to break into the loop.

A drop of blood landed on Zach's chest, trickled in a wavy line down his ribs. Then Trevor reached out and laid the head of the hammer ever so gently against Zach's face. He traced the curve of Zach's jawline with it, stroked the underside of Zach's chin with the claw. The metal felt cold, slightly rough, horribly sticky. Trevor's face was exalted, nearly ecstatic.

"Trev?" Zach asked softly. "What are you doing?"

"I'm getting ready."

"For what?"

"The puzzle of flesh."

Whatever that means. "Okay. I'll help you with that if you want. But could you put the hammer down?"

Trevor just looked at him with those drilled-ice eyes.

"Please?" Zach's voice was little more than a hoarse whisper now.

Very slowly, Trevor shook his head. "I can't," he said, and raised the hammer high. His eyes never left Zach's. They were full of lust, pleading, naked terror. Zach saw clearly that Trevor didn't want to be doing this, hated doing this; he saw just as clearly that this was the only thing in the world Trevor wanted to be doing.

He also saw the trajectory of the hammer: next stop, Zach's own beloved pineal gland, the spot where his third eye would be. Zach slid off the other side of the mattress, scrambled around the bed, and tried to get to the door, but Trevor followed and blocked him. The hammer crashed into the wall, tore through a drawing. Brittle fragments of paper sifted to the floor.

"WHAT ARE YOU DOING?" Zach yelled.

"I'm finding out what it feels like."

"WHY?!"

"Because I'm an artist," Trevor said through gritted teeth. "I need to know." He caught Zach's right arm and forced him back against the wall. Trevor was only slightly bigger and stronger, but he seemed to have the mother of all adrenaline rushes pumping through his veins. He raised the hammer again.

"Trevor—please, I love you—"

"I love you too, Zach." He heard genuine truth in Trevor's voice, saw the hammer descending and flung himself sideways. The blow glanced off his shoulder, and the muscle sang with pain.

Trevor pulled the hammer back. Zach got his left arm up, grabbed Trevor's wrist, locked his elbow and held Trevor's arm away with all his strength. It was slippery with sweat and blood, hard to hang on to. He stared deep into Trevor's eyes.

"Listen to me, Trev." His heart felt like a ripe tomato in a blender. He gasped for breath. Trevor strained against him. "Why do you need to *know* how it feels to kill somebody? You have an imagination, don't you?"

Trevor blinked, but did not stop shoving his body against Zach's.

"Your imagination is better than Bobby's. He might've had to do it to find out how it felt. *You don't.*"

Trevor hesitated. His grip on Zach's arm eased the slightest bit, and Zach saw his chance. *Fight back for once!* his mind screamed. *Don't think about what he'll do to you if you fuck up! You'll be dead for sure if you don't try, and so will he. Just DO IT!*

Zach let out a long wordless howl and drove his knee straight up into Trevor's crotch. At the same time he shoved Trevor's arm backward as hard as he could. The angle of the knee thrust was bad, but it caught Trevor by surprise and threw him off balance. Zach twisted Trevor's wrist brutally, and Trevor lost his grip on the hammer. It sailed across the room, hit the opposite wall with a loud crack, thudded to the floor.

If Trevor went after it, Zach decided, he would make a break for the door and try to get out of the house. Maybe Trevor would follow him. Maybe things would be saner outside.

Trevor's eyes were very wide, very pale. He stared at Zach with something like admiration, something like love. His gaze was hypnotic; Zach could not make himself move.

"Fine then," Trevor said softly. "I always imagined doing it with nothing but my hands."

He lunged.

Zach dodged aside and managed to get to the door, then through it. Trevor was right behind him, blocking the way out, driving him down the hall. He tried for the studio, thinking he could go out a window. Trevor caught a handful of his hair and yanked him off his feet. Zach's neck snapped back. He stumbled heavily against Trevor, and Trevor pinned his arms.

"I just want to know how you're made," Trevor breathed in his ear. "I love you so much, Zach. I want to climb inside you. I want to tàste your brain. I want to feel your heart beating in my hands."

"It can only beat in your hands for a few seconds, Trev. Then I'll be dead and you won't have me anymore."

"Yes I will. You'll be right here. This place preserves its dead." *Like hitting a SAVE key*, Zach thought, and that reminded him of loops again. Had some kind of homicidal loop been set in motion in Trevor's head?

And if it had, how could he interrupt it?

He felt Trevor's sharp hipbones pressing into his buttocks, Trevor's arms wrapped tightly around his chest. For a moment the contact was nearly erotic. He thought Trevor felt it too; his penis was stirring against the back of Zach's leg, growing half-hard.

Then Trevor lowered his head and sank his teeth deep into the ridge of muscle between Zach's neck and shoulder.

The pain was immediate, huge, hot. Zach felt fresh blood trickling over his collarbone and down his chest, felt muscle fibers twist and rip, heard himself screaming, then sobbing. He tried to drive his elbow back into Trevor's chest, but Trevor had his arms clamped tightly to his sides. He tried to kick, and Trevor lifted him off his feet and dragged him into the bathroom.

He's taking me to his hell, Zach thought, *and he's going to eat me there, he's going to rip me apart looking for the magic inside me, and he won't find it. Then he'll fulfill the condition of the loop, he'll kill himself. What a stupid program.*

Trevor kicked the door shut. The tiny room was dark but

for the fragments of mirror in the tub, which seemed to suck in light, infect it with noisome colors and send it swirling back over the leprous walls and ceiling. The sink was stained black with blood. Zach wondered if the come was there too, dried to a translucent scale.

The pain in his shoulder ebbed a little. Zach stopped struggling. He felt dizzy, remote. Trevor's hold on him was shoving his ribs up and crushing them inward, making it difficult to breathe. He was going to die right now. These sensations of pain and disconnection were the last he would ever feel, these fleeting, panicky thoughts the last he would ever have.

Stupid fucking program . . .

Then Trevor slammed him into the wall face first, and Zach grayed out completely.

Yielding flesh in his hands, hot with fear, sticky with sweat and blood and already smelling of heaven. Helpless bones his to crack, helpless skin his to rip open, sweet red river his to drink from. He had to do it. He had to know. With his eyes and his hands, with all his body, he had to *see*.

Trevor shoved Zach into the space between the toilet and the sink, *his* space. He clawed at Zach's chest with his fingernails, ripped furrows in that smooth white skin. Blood sparkled on his hands, sprayed across his face. He pushed his mouth into the spray, lapped at it, then tore at the skin with his teeth. It was easy. It was right. It was *beautiful*.

Zach's hands came up and tried to push Trevor's head away, but there was no strength left in them. Trevor slid him farther back into the corner, into the cobwebs, felt tiny multilegged things skittering away. He ran his tongue over the long shallow wounds his fingernails had made on Zach's chest. They tasted of salt and copper, of life and knowledge.

He stroked the concavity of Zach's stomach. All the body's bountiful secrets, cradled between the pelvis and the spine. He would sink his hands in to the wrists, to the elbows. He would reach up under the rib cage and make the heart beat with his fingers. He would find the source of life and swallow it whole.

"Trev?" said Zach. His voice was weak, paper-thin, barely there. "Trevor? I can't fight you. But if you're gonna kill me, please tell me why."

Trevor closed his teeth on Zach's earlobe and pulled at it, wondered how the soft little mass of flesh would feel going down his throat. "Why what?"

"Why pain is better than love. Why you'd rather kill me for the thrill of it than try to have a life with me. I thought you were brave, but this is some pretty cowardly shit."

Tears were trickling down the side of Zach's face, into the fine hair at his temples. Trevor traced their salty path to the corner of Zach's eye, flicked his tongue over the lid, then sucked softly at the eyeball. It would burst in his mouth like a bonbon. He wondered if that amazing green would taste of mint.

"To see everything," Zach whispered, "you have to be alive. If you do this to me, you're gonna die too. Tell me you're not."

Maybe he was. Of course he was. But hadn't he always known this would be the last panel, the crucifixion and con-flagration, the way his life was supposed to end? And wouldn't it be worth it?

But suddenly Trevor remembered something Bobby had said to him in the other room, in the other house. *Birdland is a machine oiled with the blood of artists.*

He looked down at Zach. Blood had run down over Zach's face in thick black rivulets from a wound in his scalp. Blood leaked from his nostrils and his torn mouth. He had a lurid purple knot on one shoulder, an encrusted bite mark on the other. His chest was crisscrossed with furious red scratches. Where it wasn't cut or bruised, his skin was absolutely white. His eyes held Trevor's. His expression hovered somewhere between terrified and serene.

"Whatever you want," said Zach. "It's up to you."

The words jarred Trevor completely from his dream of rending flesh, of crawling inside the body to find its secrets.

Because it *wasn't* just a body, he realized. It wasn't a puzzle or an anatomy lesson or a source of mystical knowledge, it was *Zach*. The beautiful boy he had watched strutting and moaning onstage tonight, smartass and criminal anarchist and generous soul, his best friend, his first lover. Not a box of toys to tear apart, not a rare delicacy to rip open and devour still steaming.

And Zach was right. Whatever Trevor did next would be his own choice, and he would have to live with it until he died, even if that was only a matter of minutes. And if he died, would he go to Birdland? He thought of Bobby, alone with those two broken bodies forever. What if Trevor ended up in his own house, trapped with his own dead?

Yet Bobby had put the hammer in his hand and told him to go find out what it felt like.

Trevor imagined a crisp new autopsy report: *Zachary Bosch, transient, 19 yrs . . . Cause of death: blunt trauma, exsanguination, evisceration . . . Manner of death: Murder . . .*

Was that what his father considered art these days? Or was Birdland thirsty for blood to grease its cogs?

He shoved himself off Zach, out of the cramped space between sink and toilet. He stared at his hands, and for a moment he thought they were slicked with Zach's blood, that he had sunk them deep into Zach's insides, that he had really done it, and woken up too late. *If I have any talent, any gift left at all*, he heard his father saying, *it's in you now.*

Fuck that, he thought. *I'm not doing your dirty work.*

He turned away from Zach and stepped into the bathtub. Broken glass gritted and scraped beneath his bare feet. Trevor stared down into the fragments of mirror, into the swarming light. "I won't do it," he said. "I don't need to know what it feels like. I don't need to draw it. *I can live it.*"

He made his right hand into a fist and drove it straight through the wall.

The damp old plaster splintered, sifted away, disintegrated beneath his knuckles. It hadn't hurt at all. He *wanted* it to hurt; he wanted the pain he had been so ready to inflict on Zach.

He fell to his knees and began slamming his fist again and again into the hard porcelain, into the broken glass.

Zach thought he heard a bone crack in Trevor's hand. He tried to push himself up. His head felt numb and leaden, his vision blurry. He could not get off the floor to go to Trevor.

So, with the last of his strength, he crawled.

The tub seemed very far away, though Zach knew it was only a couple of feet. He had to grab its edge and drag himself the last of the distance. The porcelain felt loathsome, slick as teeth and cold as death, shaking with Trevor's blows. Trevor's fist hitting the tub sounded like raw meat slamming into a stone floor now. Zach clung to the edge with one hand, reached out and touched Trevor's back with the other.

Trevor whirled on him. His face was contorted, his eyes crazed with grief and pain. *This is it*, Zach thought. *He's gonna kill me now, and then beat himself to death like a moth against a windowpane right here where Bobby can watch. How stupid. How utterly useless.* He felt no more fear, only a great hollow disappointment.

But Trevor didn't grab him again. Instead he just stared at Zach, his face almost expectant. *Something I said made him stop hurting me*, Zach realized. *What can I say to make him stop hurting himself?*

"Listen," he said. "Bobby killed the others because he couldn't take care of them anymore and he couldn't let them go. Then he killed himself because he couldn't live without them. Right?"

Trevor made no response, but he didn't look away. Suddenly Zach had a flash of intuition, the way he sometimes did when hacking a troublesome system. He thought he knew what was on that loop in Trevor's brain. "Is it about love?" he asked. "Trev, do you think you have to make all this keep happening to prove you love me?"

At first he thought Trevor wasn't going to answer. But then, ever so slowly, Trevor nodded.

We're so fucked up, Zach thought. *We could be the Dysfunc-*

tional Families poster kids if either of us lives long enough. Thanks, Joe and Evangeline. Thanks, Bobby.

"But I *know* you love me, Trevor. I believe you. I want to stay alive and show you. I don't need you to take care of me; I can take care of myself. And if you come away with me I won't leave you ever."

"How . . ." Trevor's voice sounded husked out, used up. "How can I know that?"

"You have to trust me," said Zach. "All I can tell you is the truth. You have to decide the rest for yourself."

Trevor looked up from the hypnotic swirling pattern in the mirror shards, looked into Zach's battered face. The pain in his right hand was enormous, hot as a skillet on the burner, then cold all the way to the bone. His knuckles were torn to bleeding ribbons. He thought he had broken at least one finger. The feeling of it made him heartsick. But the terrible anger was gone.

He had been ready to go plunging down, down, down. And he had nearly taken Zach with him.

Zach was kneeling before him, naked and bloody as if he had just been born. Pain needled through Trevor's legs as he stood. His feet were sliced up pretty badly too, he realized; he had been grinding them into the broken glass, trying to obliterate some image he could not piece together. The mirror fragments were opaque with his blood now, reflecting nothing.

Trevor climbed out of the tub and helped Zach up with his good hand, grabbed him with the other arm and buried his face in Zach's stiff hair.

"What can I do?" he asked. The question seemed terribly inadequate, but he could think of no other.

"Leave with me. Now."

Trevor expected to feel the house clenching like a muscle around him, trying to hold him in. But he felt nothing coming up through the floorboards to mingle with the blood from his feet, nothing in the walls around him. He looked over Zach's shoulder at the buckled shower curtain rod and felt only an echo of the old sorrow tinged with dread. That was where Bobby had ended up, where he had chosen to end up. Trevor could choose to go anywhere he wanted to.

The realization was like seeing infinity suddenly unfold before his eyes. A million mirrors, and none of them broken. A million possibilities, and more branching out from each of those. He could leave this house and never see it again, and he would still be alive. And it was by his own hand: he had chosen to be with Zach, had chosen to eat mushrooms and go to Birdland, had sought out the house and turned the knob and walked in on Bobby's eternity. They were all choices he had made. It was up to *him.*

Zach opened the bathroom door and pulled him into the hall. The house was full of a clear, still blue light. The night was over.

Trevor looked down into Zach's ill-used, blood-smeared, weary face. *I choose you,* he thought, *but I can't believe you still want me.*

They stumbled into the bedroom and sat on the edge of the bed. Zach found his glasses unharmed on the floor and put them back on. Trevor saw the gouge in the opposite wall where he had tried to hit Zach, saw the bloodied hammer in the corner. He stroked Zach's hair with his good hand, kissed his eyelids, his forehead. He hoped an electrical current would have run up his arm and shocked him to death if he had violated this wondrous brain.

Zach leaned against him. His head lay heavy on Trevor's shoulder. "I need to get out of here," he whispered.

"Okay. Where will we go?"

"I don't know." Gingerly, Zach touched Trevor's right hand, which he was cradling in his lap trying to keep still. "This looks bad. You need to get it set. And I think I might have a concussion."

"Oh . . . Zach . . ."

"You didn't do it. My dad did."

"Your dad?"

"Yeah. Look, we have to talk, but I can't right now. I feel like I'm gonna pass out. We need a hospital."

"The closest one's twenty miles away. Can you call Kinsey on your cellular phone?"

"His home phone's cut off. I heard him say so last night . . ." Zach trailed off. His eyes were half-closed now, his breathing quick and shallow. His skin felt cool, slightly damp.

"Can you drive?"

Zach shook his head.

"But your car has a stick shift."

"I know. I'll shift for you if I can stay awake. If I can't, it's gonna hurt you like hell, and I'm sorry. But I can't even see straight. I'd run us right off the road."

"All right, then." Trevor tried to flex his hand. Great bolts of pain shot up his arm. The two middle fingers were stiff, swollen shiny, suffused with blood. The skin felt as tight and uncomfortable as an ill-fitting glove. His knuckles were so badly abraded that he thought he could see a pale glimmer of bone beneath all the red, though he didn't look too closely.

I can't hold a pencil with that, he thought. But he was too worried about Zach to care much.

Zach helped Trevor dress, tugged his sneakers on and tied them for him. Trevor felt the linings tugging at the cuts on his feet, blood soaking into the soles. Then Zach dressed himself and helped gather their belongings. Trevor took nothing but his Walkman, his tapes, and his clothes. If his hand healed, he would get new pens and sketchbooks later. He couldn't imagine using the old ones again.

After some consideration, he held a match to the envelope containing his family's autopsy reports and burned them in the kitchen sink. It felt a little like smashing his hand had felt. But he thought they belonged here.

He helped Zach out through the living room, half holding him up as Zach carried both bags. The air was thick as syrup, sucking at Trevor's legs, pulling at his feet. *You could stay,* it whispered. *There is a place for you forever, here in Birdland.*

But Trevor would not listen. It was only one of a million possible places, and it wasn't the one he wanted anymore.

Zach clung to him until they were out of the house and off the porch. The sky was a deep watery blue streaked with rose. A few stars were still visible; they seemed too huge and bright, their glitter too intense. The whole world was silent.

Wet grass brushed their knees as they made their way to the back of the house where the car was parked. Trevor helped Zach into the passenger seat, then slid in behind the wheel. Zach fumbled with his seat belt. Trevor wanted to wear his too, but he didn't think he could fasten it himself, and he was afraid to ask Zach to lean across the seat and help him. Zach looked sick and sweaty, on the verge of blacking out.

Trevor fitted the key into the ignition with his left hand and turned it awkwardly. The engine roared into life. Pain flared in his foot as he stepped on the clutch. The Mustang began to roll through the yard and down the overgrown driveway.

"Zach?"

". . . yeah . . ."

"Put it in second."

Zach groped for the shift stick and pulled it down into second gear. The car picked up speed. They were at the end of the long driveway now, turning onto Violin Road. Trevor steered with his left hand, braced his right forearm against the wheel. He glanced into the rearview mirror. The house was barely visible through the shroud of weeds and vines. It looked like an empty place. Trevor wondered if it ever would be.

He let the car coast down the rutted gravel road. "Okay," he said. "Put it in third."

No response. Trevor looked over at Zach. He was slumped back against the seat, eyes shut, glasses sliding down his nose, bruises blooming like dark flowers on his pallid face.

"Zach!" he said. "ZACH!"

". . . mmm . . ."

Trevor slowed the car to a crawl, made sure Zach was breathing, speeded back up to twenty or so. If he rolled through stop signs, he could drive all the way to Kinsey's house in second gear. It would be hell on the clutch, but he didn't care. If anything happened to Zach now, Trevor might as well go right back into that house and nail the door shut behind him.

"Stay awake," he told Zach. "I don't want you slipping."

". . . mmmmmm . . ."

"Zach! Sing with me!" Trevor tried to think of a song whose words he knew. The only thing that came to mind was one he had been made to learn at the Boys' Home. It would have to do. "YIPPIE KI YI YO-O," he sang loudly. "GIT ALONG, LITTLE DOGIES! Come on, Zach. Please . . . IT'S YOURRRR MISFORTUNE, AND NONE OF MY OWWWWN . . ."

"Yippie . . . ki yi yo," sang Zach in a ghostly voice, barely a whisper.

"GIT ALONG, LITTLE DOGIES . . . c'mon, louder . . ."

"YOU KNOW THAT WY-OMING WILL BE YOUR NEW HOOOOOME," they finished in unison.

Trevor glanced over at Zach. His eyes were open, and there was a tired smile on his face. "Trevor?" he said.

"What?"

"You're a lousy singer."

"Thanks."

"And, Trev?"

"What?"

"That song really sucks."

"So?"

"So . . . you want this thing in third gear?"

"Take it up to fourth," said Trevor, and pushed the pedals to the floor.

TWENTY-THREE

rank Norton chewed on a stale glazed doughnut and regarded the improbable figure that had just appeared in the doorway of his office. The kid looked seventeen or eighteen, his skinny body awkwardly put together and slightly hunched. Dirty brown ringlets of hair hung in his face. The lenses of his glasses were as thick as Coke bottles. His beady little eyes peered suspiciously through them.

"Is Agent Cover here?" he demanded.

Should've known he was looking for Ab, thought Norton. *Who else has teenage nerds in his office at seven in the morning?* "Nope. He had a rough time chasin' down a Chevy pickup yesterday and he's not in yet." The kid stared blankly at him. "Can I help you?" he added.

"My name is Stefan Duplessis. I'm assisting him with the Bosch case."

Ah. The stoolie. "Sure, Stefan. What can I do for you?"

"I've found a very important clue." Duplessis held up a sweat-stained piece of newsprint. "I think Zach Bosch planted this article in the *Times-Picayune*. Furthermore, I think he's in North Carolina. The first article said so, and this one does too. I've even figured out the name of the town!"

Furthermore. Jesus. "Is that so?" Norton asked politely. Ab was really grasping at straws on this case. That hacker was probably living it up in Australia by now. "Well, Stefan, I'm afraid that's not my case. You'll have to leave it on Agent Cover's desk."

"But I need to talk to him *now*!" The last word was pronounced *naaaaow*, like the noise his sister-in-law's Siamese made when Norton pulled its tail.

"Sorry, kid. You can't."

"Then I'll wait till he gets here. This is too important to leave on his desk."

"Suit yourself. There's a bench in the hall."

Duplessis made his exit with an air of wounded dignity. *Ab Cover isn't a Secret Service agent,* Norton thought. *He's a goddamn babysitter.*

A few minutes later he got up to get a cup of coffee and saw the hacker sitting forlornly on the hard wooden bench, still clutching his section of the *Times-Picayune*. Norton's curiosity got the better of him. "Hey, kid, can I take a look at that?"

Duplessis handed him the paper. It was smudged with the gray whorls of his fingerprints, and he had circled the article in green felt-tip.

> Travis Rigaud of St. Tammany Parish accidentally shot himself while cleaning his collection of handguns —five different times with five different guns, twice in the left foot, once in the right calf, and once in each hand, severing two fingers . . .

Norton handed it back. "That's real nice, Stefan. He'll be happy to see it."

Ab Cover isn't even a babysitter, Norton decided with vast amusement as he poured himself a cup of coffee and settled back down with his doughnut. *He's a fucking lunatic.*

Kinsey Hummingbird was having a nightmare. It was a dream he often had, in which irate rednecks kept dropping off decrepit, barely running cars and pickups at the Sacred Yew, telling him to have them ready by six o'clock this evening. Kinsey would look up at the club's sign and see that it had been repainted to read s. YEW GARAGE & AUTO PARTS.

Someone was leaning rudely on a car horn now, demand-

ing service. *WHOOOOOONK!!! WHOOOOOOOOOONK!!!*
The sound blared loud and long through his bedroom. Kinsey
opened his eyes. It was just getting light outside, and he
thought he could still hear the horn. The sound had never
carried on after he was awake before. Perhaps he was going
slowly insane from overwork.

No. Well, maybe; but someone *was* blowing a horn outside.
It sounded again, sharp and clear in the hush of dawn. Kinsey
sat up and twitched the curtain aside, peered out the window
above his bed. He saw Zach's black Mustang in the yard,
wheels cutting deep swaths through the unmowed grass.

Kinsey slipped his bathrobe on over his pajamas and hurried through the blue-lit house. He realized too late that he
had forgotten his slippers, let himself out the front door, and
crossed the soggy yard to the car. Trevor was behind the
wheel, his face drawn with exhaustion and pain. He finally
looked his age, Kinsey thought, perhaps even older. Beside
him, Zach was alternately pulling at his own hair and beating
his hands on his knees. His face was a bruised, bloody mess.
Kinsey saw crisscrossing stripes of blood beginning to soak
through the cloth of his shirt, adding random touches of gore
to the exploding Kennedy head already printed on it.

"I'm keeping myself awake," Zach said when he saw Kinsey looking in at him. "I have a head injury. We kinda could
use some help."

"What happened?"

"Could we tell you on the way to a hospital?" said Trevor.
He held up his right hand, which had been hidden in his lap.
Kinsey stared at it, aghast. The hand was purple, swollen to
three times its normal size. The two middle fingers were
twisted at dreadful angles. It looked like Wile E. Coyote's
hand after he'd managed to smash it with the giant wooden
mallet intended for the Roadrunner.

Kinsey opened the car door for him, and Trevor climbed
out carefully, as if his whole body was sore. Zach got out the
other side by himself and promptly fell over. Trevor and Kinsey hurried around the car, but he had fallen on the soft rain-
soaked grass and was only lying there cussing helplessly

through his tears. "I can't *think* straight," he said as they helped him up and led him to Kinsey's car. "It's the worst feeling in the world. It's like opening a bad oyster . . . it's like . . . um . . . shit . . . um . . ."

"Keep talking," said Trevor. He helped Zach into the back seat and climbed in after him. "It's like a bad oyster? Why?"

" 'Cause my thoughts feel all slimy and rotten but I've already swallowed them and I can't . . . um . . ."

"Regurgitate them?"

"Yeah!"

Kinsey listened to conversation in this vein for more than twenty miles. Occasionally he interjected a comment or question to help Trevor out, but he did not press them for details of what had happened, though he was madly curious and more than a little concerned. They would tell him when they could.

The emergency room in Raleigh was nearly deserted at this early hour. Kinsey sat in an orange plastic chair designed to conform to no human ass in existence, paged through an assortment of magazines that no one would ever want to read. He listened to Trevor check himself in, then help Zach check in under the name "Fredric Black," telling the nurse only that they had been in an accident.

"How would you like to pay for this?"

Zach fumbled in his pocket. "I have some credit card numbers . . ."

"Cash," said Trevor hurriedly. He had Zach's entire bankroll on him, and it was considerable.

"Marital status?" the nurse inquired. Zach stared wildly up at Trevor. "Single," Trevor told the nurse. "He's with me."

The nurse looked at them for a long moment. "Brothers?"

"Uh, yeah." Trevor nodded at Kinsey. "That's our uncle over there."

"All right. You can go back together." The nurse handed them their forms and waved them down the antiseptic green corridor.

Another nurse washed the blood and plaster off Trevor's hand, then picked seventeen slivers of mirror glass out of his knuckles with a pair of tweezers. He was given an ice pack to hold while the doctor looked Zach over, probed the wound in his scalp, shone a light into his eyes, and finally pronounced his concussion genuine but not serious. "Make him rest," he advised Trevor. "Don't let him move around a lot."

"I have to," protested Zach. "I'm a professional rock star."

"I won't," Trevor promised. He helped Zach down from the examining table with his good arm. The doctor glanced at the gash in Zach's head again. "Jesus, kid, maybe we ought to stitch that up."

"No! No stitches!"

"Well, it's your head . . . What hit you, anyway?"

"Diamonds."

"Couldn't have been diamonds. You'd be dead. That's one of the hardest substances known to man."

"It was diamonds," Zach insisted.

The doctor glanced at Trevor. "He may not be, uh, real lucid for a day or so."

"I understand." Trevor squeezed Zach's arm. *I believe you,* he thought. *It was diamonds, just like the one Skeletal Sammy pressed into my hand.* He had no idea what the significance of diamonds might be. But it meant Zach had been in Birdland too.

The only bad part for Trevor was when the doctor pulled his fingers straight to splint them. He gripped Zach's hand and made himself ride the waves of pain instead of sinking beneath them. He had done this to himself. He would endure whatever he must to fix it. And when it was healed, he would draw whatever he wanted to for the rest of his life.

On the way back to Missing Mile they huddled together in the back seat, Zach lying with his head in Trevor's lap. Trevor tried to give Kinsey a comprehensible version of the night's events. Kinsey didn't say much, but seemed to believe everything.

"I don't know what we're going to do," he told Kinsey. "Could we hole up for a couple of days with you?"

"Sure. As long as you want."

"I don't think it'll be very long." *I like everything else about*

Missing Mile, Trevor thought, *but I don't even want to be in the same town with that house anymore. I know what I need to know now. And Zach has to fly soon.*

He glanced down to make sure Zach wasn't falling asleep. The doctor had said not to let him do so for another hour.

But Zach's eyes were open, watching Trevor steadily, the color of jade shining in the clear morning light. He looked wide awake, and very glad to be alive.

The morning red-eye express took off from New Orleans International at eight-twenty. Agent Cover had just enough time to scrape together the bare bones of his original raid team and notify the Special Agent in Charge at the Raleigh office that they were coming. The SAIC was supposed to meet them on the other end with cars.

A stewardess pushed a gleaming cart of drinks along the aisle and stopped beside their row with a saccharine smile. "Can I get you somethin'?"

"Coffee," said Loving, Schulman, and DeFillipo.

"Coffee," said Cover.

"Cream and sugar?"

"Black," they said as one.

Cover flipped open the Bosch file and stared at the newspaper article. His heart had sunk this morning when he arrived at the office and saw the pasty, sniffling boy waiting in the hall. Duplessis pored over the papers until they were soft and sweat-stained, unpleasant to handle. And all his "discoveries" so far hadn't amounted to shit.

But when Cover read this one, he got excited right away. The other article had mentioned North Carolina outright; this one seemed to hint slyly at it, which could mean Bosch was there and had decided to stay for a while. And there was a town called Missing Mile. And no one could really shoot himself five times with five different guns.

The clincher came when Schulman delivered the news that Joseph Boudreaux, *Times-Picayune* reporter, had never even heard of the goddess Kali.

Agent Cover thought Bosch had finally fucked up.

He stared out the window at the bright blue morning sky, at the sunlight washing over the creamy tops of the clouds. He always felt safe at twenty thousand feet. He took his mirrorshades out of his breast pocket and put them on, then glanced back down at the file. The little photo of Bosch stared up at him, lips twisted in a punk sneer, eyes accusing.

I'm coming for you, he thought. *I hope you had a ball in North Carolina, because you aren't going anywhere else for a long, long time.*

He was a little surprised to find himself elated. He was supposed to be a granite agent. Instead he felt like a kid on an Easter egg hunt, closing in on the big chocolate bunny.

Terry drove his Rambler into town around two, sent his afternoon worker home, cranked up R.E.M.'s first album, and sat behind the counter at the Whirling Disc staring contentedly at the shifting patterns of sunlight on the opposite wall. He always felt wonderful the day after doing mushrooms. The visuals took about twenty-four hours to fade completely from his brain, and they gave the next day a distinct psychedelic edge. Even his throat felt better.

R.J., who still preferred to live like an eleven-year-old kid most of the time, had just said no and gone home to bed. Terry tripped with Victoria, Calvin, and David, the redheaded boy Calvin had met at the show. David turned out to be a brilliant twenty-year-old exchange student from London who entertained them all with witty banter until Calvin dragged him off into one of the bedrooms. Terry and Victoria took the other one. There was nothing quite like sex on hallucinogens to strengthen a relationship.

Around four-thirty A.M. they'd all met back up in the kitchen, bedraggled and happy, and managed to make a batch of popcorn. Then they put *Willy Wonka and the Chocolate Factory* on Terry's VCR, snuggled up on the couch, and thrilled to the sinister tale until dawn, rewinding it again and again at the part where Gene Wilder said "*WE* are the music makers, and *WE* are the dreamers of dreams." After that Terry and Victoria crashed while Calvin and David went zooming off to breakfast, still full of crazed fungal energy.

Terry suspected that psychedelic drugs affected the body chemistry of gay men differently than straights. He could never eat greasy diner food on 'shrooms, and though he'd enjoyed Ecstasy the couple of times he'd done it, he hadn't felt remotely like dancing to disco music all night. Or techno, or rave, or whatever was the current noise of choice. Calvin and David had kept wanting to drive to Raleigh where they imagined they could find some glamorous after-hours club and do just that.

That made him think of Trevor and Zach. Terry had hoped they would show up again, but they never did. He wondered if they had spent the night tripping in that house. The thought made his nuts crawl. Terry remembered scaring his younger friends with the story of the murders as a teenager, wondering aloud if the McGees' ghosts still lived in the house, daring them to go inside with him.

Eventually, of course, they had. At first it had just looked like any old abandoned house, all sagging wood and ancient dust and shadow. But as they approached the bloodstained doorway to the hall, the shadows had seemed to *shift* around them, to *change*, and for a moment they were no longer in the house at all.

He didn't know if it had been a group hallucination or what. He doubted so, because it didn't seem to have anything to do with the murders. Terry had seen a city street around him, a boarded-up slum, wavering like a mirage but definitely there. R.J. had seen a dark deserted bar with shattered glass on the floor and cracked mirrors on the walls so dusty that he could not see his face in them. And Steve would never say what he had seen, except that it had legs like a bug.

They had all felt that the place was *sucking* at them, that they could get lost in here and never come back. What Terry hadn't admitted to the others—but suspected they'd felt as well—was that for a moment the idea of getting lost had tempted him. Here were sweet poisons and twisted dreams.

Here were things he could never touch with hands of mere flesh and bone . . .

They had run out yelling, slapping high-fives but not fooling each other for a second. They had tumbled off the porch and across the weed-choked yard, toward the small stubborn figure of Ghost far away on the other side of the road. None of them had ever gone back. But Terry had dreamed of it, that strange seductive slum. And he would be willing to bet Steve and R.J. had had dreams of their own.

Terry realized he had been woolgathering. Two kids were standing by the imports section eyeing him speculatively. One was a lean black guy wearing a Yellowman shirt and voluminous multipocketed fatigue pants, long color-threaded dreadlocks pulled back in a thick ponytail from his amiable, slightly horsey face. The other was an absolute knockout, a stunning Asian girl with short hair that accented her large tilted eyes and exquisite bones. She wore a lot of earrings, but no makeup. Terry hadn't seen either of them around town before.

"Help you with something?" he inquired. Probably they were looking for Steve and Ghost. Kids from the fringe had started drifting into town over the past year, since Lost Souls? had managed to get their tape distributed to record stores up and down the East Coast. Most just wanted to see a show; a few wanted to camp out in the band's yard, or thought Ghost was their true soulmate due to secret personal messages they heard in his lyrics. It was a little unnerving, but it had brought in tons of business when Steve worked at the store. Even now that Lost Souls? was touring, when Terry pointed out that he had played drums on their tape, these kids would always buy a Whirling Disc T-shirt.

The girl stepped forward and, to Terry's surprise, pushed a photograph of Zach across the counter. The photo had been taken at night, and Terry recognized the locale as New Orleans, probably during Mardi Gras. Zach was hanging on to a lamppost with one hand, clutching a Dixie beer with the other, wearing a purple jacket and a shirt made of black fishnet and a huge shit-eating grin, obviously drunk within an inch of his life.

"We're looking for this boy," she said. "His name is Zachary. He's a good friend of ours, and he's in a lot of trouble."

"He looks like he might be." Terry picked up the photograph, pretended to consider it. "Nice young kid, though. I'd hate to see the cops get hold of him."

"We're not cops! We're trying to *warn* him about—" The girl shut her mouth as if she thought she'd already said too much. Her companion approached the counter.

"We come in peace," he said, holding out a large slender hand. "We are his brudda an' sista. My name is Dougal. The lady is Edwina. Eddy."

Terry took the hand and shook it. Dougal spoke with a thick Jamaican accent, and his eyes were sharp, kind, stoned. The girl's burned like embers. Terry believed they were Zach's friends, though probably not his actual brudda an' sista. They smelled faintly sweaty, as if they had been driving all night. And the photo was worn, rubbed around the edges. Someone had spent a lot of time looking at it, and Terry was willing to bet that someone was Edwina. Eddy.

Still, it was one thing to trust people based on a gut reaction; it was quite another when the feds might be involved. He was glad they hadn't happened upon Kinsey first. "How come you to ask in here?"

"Because Zach's a freak," Eddy said simply, "and freaks tend to frequent record stores."

Terry couldn't argue with that. "Well—look—you understand I want to be sure you're cool. Give me something I can trust."

"How 'bout we all relax a little firs'," said Dougal, and pulled out a straw pouch and a package of rolling papers. As soon as he opened the pouch, the sweet sticky reek of absolute primo weed filled the store. Terry saw a double handful of tightly packed bright green bud bristling with tiny red hairs. Dougal pinched off a generous amount and started rolling a huge spliff right there on the counter.

"Okay! Okay!" Terry jumped up. "Hang on! Let's go in the

back room and talk this over." He locked the door, flipped the sign to the side that read BACK IN 5 . . . OR 15 . . . OR WHENEVER.

In the back room, among piles of records, tapes, and CDs, stray equipment stored here by various bands, and posters rolled into unwieldy, unstackable paper tubes, Dougal fired up the joint and Eddy gave Terry a quick rundown of their situation. She didn't offer many details; only that Zach had managed to get himself into an awful lot of trouble with his computer and they wanted to help him get out of the country. Terry had read about computer hackers and been intrigued by them, but he didn't know they ever ripped shit off on the scale Eddy implied Zach had.

He hit the joint, which tasted even better than it smelled, and held the smoke in for a long time. He didn't think so much of theft, but it was hard to feel sorry for vast bloated corporate entities like Citibank and Southern Bell. They loved to talk about how the cost of such theft was passed on to the consumer, Terry reflected, but when was *any* cost of big business *not* passed on to the little guy at the bottom of the ladder?

Whatever Zach's morals (or lack thereof), Terry genuinely liked him. If there was even a slim chance that feds were heading for Missing Mile to nab him, Terry knew he had to help Zach get away.

"Okay," he said. "Truth. Zach's in town."

Eddy's face lit up with a beautiful, delighted smile. She was obviously crazy for Zach—along with half the world, it was beginning to seem. Terry refused to be responsible for breaking the news of Trevor to her. It wasn't his damn business anyway. But he had a hunch that the plane out of the country was going to be carrying an extra passenger, and not the one Eddy probably hoped it would be, either.

"He's staying with a friend," Terry said. "In an abandoned, haunted house. Now I'm not going out there, and I don't guess you better go by yourselves either. But I'll take you over to my friend Kinsey's. He doesn't mind ghosts. He'll go tell Zach you're here."

Someone pounded on the front door. All three heads jerked up; all three faces snapped toward the sound.

"Wait here," said Terry. "Don't come out unless I call you. If you hear any other voices, go out the back door over there." He picked up a can of Glade air freshener and tossed it to Eddy. "Here, spray some of this crap around."

Terry ducked under the curtain and went to the front of the store. Two broad-shouldered guys in suits and mirrorshades were at the door, already pounding again. "Hold your fuckin' water," Terry muttered. He unlocked the door and opened it a crack. "C'n I help you?"

"Absalom Cover, U.S. Secret Service." The taller dude flashed a badge at Terry. He was lean and hard-jawed, with dark hair slicked back from his narrow face. Terry thought he could make out the bulge of a pistol beneath that well-cut jacket. "This is my partner, Stan Schulman. May we step in and ask you a few questions?"

"Uh . . . actually, no." Terry slipped out through the door, pushed it shut behind him. The sidewalk was bright and dazzling, and he realized he was about as stoned as he could be. But he knew his rights. If they didn't have a warrant, he didn't have to let them in the store.

"I'm doing inventory," he explained, "and there's stuff piled up everywhere. I can't have a bunch of people walking around knocking my stacks over. You wanna ask me something out here?"

"Your name?"

"Terry Buckett. I own this place."

The other agent, Schulman, reached into his jacket. He looked dumpy and unkempt next to the sleek Cover. Terry could see oily beads of sweat standing out on the man's scalp, clearly visible through the thinning hair. There were even a few in his mustache. Terry tried to imagine what it would be like to have a job that made you wear a jacket and tie in the heat of a Carolina summer.

Schulman pulled out a small photograph. "Have you ever seen this person before?"

Terry studied the photo, managed not to laugh at Zach's fuck-you scowl. "No . . . I don't think so."

"You must see a lot of kids in your line of work," Schulman urged. "Try to be sure. His name is Zachary Bosch. He's nineteen years old."

"And he's a dangerous criminal and a menace to society, right? Nope, sorry, I haven't seen him." Terry folded his arms across his chest and stared at the agents. He saw himself reflected in their sunglasses, four little images of his ratty hair and faded blue bandanna cheering him on. *Bosch*. It figured.

"We know he's in town," said Schulman. "They gave us a positive ID up the street at the diner. We've got this whole place blanketed. If you know where he is and don't tell us, all sorts of bad things could happen to you."

" 'Scuse me?" Terry tapped the side of his head with the heel of his hand. "I must be hearing wrong. I thought I woke up in America this morning."

"You did, Mr. Buckett." Cover leaned in menacingly. "And possession of marijuana is illegal in America. Aren't you a little *stoned* right now?"

Shit. "I don't know what you're talking about, but I gotta get back to work. If you want to waste your time getting a warrant and searching my store, go ahead. You won't find anything. I thought you guys were supposed to guard the President, not harass innocent citizens." He saw both agents' jaws go stiff when he said *President*.

"We do our jobs, Mr. Buckett." That was Cover, cold and deadly. "We expect *innocent* citizens to help us out when they can."

"And the rest of us are guilty, huh?"

"Of something, Mr. Buckett." Even with mirrorshades on, Cover managed to look smug. "Everybody's guilty of *something*. And we can find out what. Good afternoon."

"And a terrific afternoon to *you*," said Terry as he went back into the store and locked the door behind him. He stood there for a minute watching them walk away, cold shivers running up his spine. He couldn't help but wonder what in hell he was getting into here.

But he knew which side he was on, and that was about all he needed to know. Terry looked at the phone, thought of calling Kinsey. But what if the agents were hiding around the corner, waiting to see if he would jump on the phone as soon as they left?

He stuck his head through the curtain. The back room reeked of pine air freshener. "Bad news. The spooks are here looking for him."

Eddy's eyes went very wide. "Did they follow us? Did we lead them here?"

"I don't think so. They didn't seem to know you were around. I got the impression they were acting on some kind of tip."

"The newspaper. Shit! Goddamn that fucking Phoetus!" Eddy pounded her small fists against her knees. Angry, with her jeweled ears and spiky haircut and elegant Asian face, she looked like some sort of feral-eyed Tibetan goddess. A couple of extra arms and a lolling tongue would have capped off the image perfectly.

"Look," said Terry, "I'm gonna sneak out and make a call."

Dougal reached into a pocket of his baggy fatigues and pulled out a cellular phone. "You wan' use this?"

"Well—sure." Terry examined the sleek little gadget. "Where do you turn it on?" Dougal showed him. He dialed Kinsey's home number, heard a truncated ring, then a piercing electronic voice.

"The—number—you—have—reached—has—been—temporarily—disconnected . . ."

"Goddamn, I wish that guy would keep his bills paid. I guess we better get over there."

Eddy tapped his arm. "Was one of those spooks named Cover?"

"Yeah, the spookier one."

"I can't go out there. He'll recognize me."

"I think they're gone—"

"Our car is parked all the way down by the hardware store. I can't take the chance."

She was right, Terry realized. "Okay, wait here by the back door. We'll pull up in the alley and get you."

Terry and Dougal left the Whirling Disc together and walked with elaborate nonchalance along a series of back streets, gradually winding toward the other end of town. Terry imagined agents lurking behind every telephone pole, peering through every tinted window. "Doesn't your car have Louisiana plates?" he asked Dougal. "Won't it be dangerous to drive through downtown?"

"No mon. We stop on de way here at a—what you call de toilets by de road?"

"Rest stop?"

"Ya mon. We fin' a car broken down but still have de license plate, an' I take de liberty of borrowin' de plate."

Terry nodded, marveling. He had met plenty of freaks in his time, complete fuckups and brilliant artists and everything in between. But for sheer resourcefulness, he thought, these kids outdid them all.

Still, they didn't have the U.S. Government on their side, weighing the scale down with money and power. Street smarts wouldn't be much use against a loaded Uzi.

Terry didn't stop sweating until they had Eddy safely in the car, crouching in the back seat with a towel over her head, and they were well on their way to Kinsey's. Even then, he couldn't quit looking in the rearview mirror.

TWENTY FOUR

Kinsey moved Zach's car into the driveway and parked his own behind it. The Mustang wasn't exactly camouflaged, but it was less noticeable than it had been sitting in the middle of the front yard. He settled Trevor and Zach in his bedroom, then folded himself onto the couch. He had only been in bed for two hours when the Mustang pulled up in his yard, and he had to open the club later. Soon he was asleep again, his dreams blessedly free from blaring, whining horns and the smell of engine grease.

In the bedroom, Trevor lay flat on his back staring at the ceiling. His splinted hand felt heavy and remote. Zach was nestled into the crook of his left arm, legs thrown over Trevor's, fingers idly playing with Trevor's hair. They had each taken one of the painkillers the doctor had prescribed for them, and they were numb but contented. Enough so, eventually, to talk about the night before.

"What were you wearing there?" Zach asked.

"A suit with wide lapels. A tie. And fancy shoes."

"Me too. But I had a beret."

"You were Dizzy."

"Huh?"

"Dizzy Gillespie. Bobby used to look at pictures of him and Charlie Parker to draw his characters' clothes. They always wore these real sharp suits."

"We were in the same place, weren't we?"

"We were in Birdland."

"What does that mean?"

"It means we were inside my father's brain. Or we were in

hell. Or we were hallucinating. How the fuck should I know? You were there. You saw it.''

There was a silence. Trevor wondered if he had spoken too sharply, but he did not want to pick apart what had happened in the house, not yet. He wasn't sure he ever would.

Finally Zach asked, ''Where should we go next?'' His voice was beginning to fade out. He pressed his face into the side of Trevor's chest and closed his eyes.

''Have a dream,'' Trevor told him, ''and make it be about a beach. It has pure white sand and clear turquoise water, and the sun feels like warm honey on your skin. Stop someone on the beach and ask them where you are. Then remember it, and we'll go there.''

''Ohhh, yes . . .'' He felt Zach's body relax completely. ''. . . love you, Trev . . .''

''I love you too,'' he whispered into the cool silence of the room. It was true, it was all true, and they could both be alive to believe it. Trevor was still amazed by this knowledge.

You could kill someone because you loved them too much, he realized now, but that was nothing to do with art. The art was in learning to spend your life with someone, in having the courage to be creative with someone, to melt each other's souls to molten temperatures and let them flow together into an alloy that could withstand the world. He and Zach had used each other's addictions to hurl themselves into Birdland. But addictions could fuel talents, and talents surely fueled love. And what else had brought them back but love?

Zach's breathing was slow, even: a wholly peaceful sound. Trevor wondered if he might be able to sleep too. He let his body settle into Zach's, synchronized his breathing and his heartbeat with Zach's.

Minutes later he was as deeply asleep as he had ever been, and his sleep was dreamless.

Dougal's ancient station wagon pulled up in front of Kinsey's house. Eddy saw the black Mustang in the driveway, and her heart leapt. ''That's Zach's car!''

Terry and Dougal followed her up the walk. Terry knocked, waited, knocked louder. Eddy could not make herself stand still. After a few agonizing minutes, the door opened a crack and a bright blue eye peered out. Then it swung all the way open, and a very tall, very thin man in rumpled pajamas smiled blearily at them. "Mornin', Terry." He nodded at Eddy and Dougal, then stood there rubbing his long skinny jaw and looking politely puzzled.

"Mornin'," said Terry without a trace of irony, though it was just past three P.M. "Kinsey, it seems we got some trouble. These are Zach's friends from New Orleans, and his enemies aren't far behind."

"Well, come on in, sit down. Zach's asleep. Trevor too." Kinsey ushered them through the door.

Terry made introductions, then told Kinsey about his run-in with the agents. Eddy stared around the cozy living room. Her thoughts were speeding out of control: *Zach's in this house, I'm going to see him, I'm going to save him . . .*

"What did you do after the show last night, anyway?" Kinsey asked.

"We ate mushrooms and watched a movie. Trevor and Zach went home, but Calvin gave them some 'shrooms too." Terry frowned. "Why?"

"Well, they met up with some kind of accident."

"The car looks okay."

"Something happened in the house."

"I knew it!" Terry slapped his forehead. "That damn place is haunted! I went in there once, me and Steve and R.J., and you wouldn't even believe what we saw—"

"What?" said a quiet new voice. "What did you see?"

Everyone turned. A young man with long ginger-blond hair stood in the hall doorway. His right hand was splinted and swathed in bandages. He was shirtless, and his cotton pants rode low on his hips as if he had just tugged them on one-handed. His pale intense eyes rested briefly on Eddy and Dougal, then moved back to Terry.

"Hey, Trevor." Terry looked embarrassed. "I, uh, I'd rather

not tell you what I saw, if you don't mind. I shouldn't have been talking about it.''

''That's okay,'' said Trevor. He glanced at the newcomers again. ''Who're these?''

''Well . . .''

''We're from New Orleans,'' Eddy interrupted. ''We're friends of Zach's. If you're his friend too, we need your help.''

Trevor's eyes narrowed. He looked at Kinsey, who shrugged. ''What do you want?''

Eddy could tell by the way he said it that he had slept with Zach. What a surprise.

''How much do you know?'' she asked him.

''Everything.''

''Prove it.''

''I remember now. You're Eddy. He left you ten thousand dollars as a going-away present.'' He looked at Dougal. ''And you're the guy from the French Market. I don't remember your name.''

At least he mentioned me, Eddy thought bleakly. But something was odd here; this Trevor didn't seem like one of Zach's one-night stands. He looked intelligent and talked as if he had a brain. And Zach evidently trusted him a lot.

''Is he all right?'' she asked.

''He will be.'' Trevor stared at her. ''Tell me what you want.''

''Trev? What's going on?'' A pair of skinny arms appeared out of the dark hallway and encircled Trevor from behind. A moment later, Zach peered over Trevor's shoulder. His face was sleep-webbed, naked without his glasses. From what Eddy could see, he wore nothing but a pair of skimpy black underwear. He squinted at the roomful of people. When he made out Eddy and Dougal, his eyes went almost comically wide. ''Fuck! I think I'm hallucinating again!''

''No, you're not. They're really here.'' Trevor guided Zach to the couch, sat him down beside Kinsey, then sat on his other side and put a protective arm around his shoulders. ''They haven't said why, though.''

''We want you to leave with us,'' said Eddy. She looked at

no one but Zach, though she couldn't tell if he was really seeing her or not. He seemed unfocused, not quite *there*. "The cops raided your apartment. They also arrested your friend Stefan, who ratted on you just as fast as he could. Now they're in Missing Mile. We can help you get away."

"Hey, Ed. Hey, Dougal. It's great to see you. Uh . . . where would you take us?"

"*Us?*"

Zach stared at the floor, then back up at Eddy. A fog seemed to clear from his green eyes, and she saw the old evil spark. He was in there after all. "Yeah, Ed. *Us*. Me and Trevor. If there's a problem with that, I guess we'll have to get away on our own."

He laid his hand on Trevor's leg, high up on the inside of his thigh, and looked evenly at her. There was no trace of guilt in his expression. She supposed guilt simply wasn't part of his genetic makeup.

"Just tell me how you could do it," she said.

"Do what?"

"Fall in love so fast after refusing to do it for nineteen years, you *ass!*"

Zach shook his head. Eddy could see that this question honestly bewildered him, and that hurt most of all, because she knew exactly how he felt. "I don't know," Zach said. "I just found the right person."

She looked at Trevor, who met her gaze steadily. His eyes were so clear that Eddy thought she could look straight through them to his brain. Was that what made Zach love him? She imagined those lips kissing Zach, those graceful long-fingered hands touching him, Zach's head resting on that smooth bony chest. There was chemistry between them, and passion; it was obvious just watching them sit together.

"Okay," she said. "Fine. I hope it makes you happy. I'm going outside for a few minutes. You guys decide what you want to do, and let me know." Eddy stood up and groped her way out of the room with tears blinding her eyes, found herself in the hall, then in a bedroom. She was sobbing now, unable to see anything, barely able to breathe. She stumbled back into the hall, nearly tripped over her own feet, then felt a large, gentle hand on her shoulder, a tall form looming behind her. Kinsey.

"Back door's this way," he said, and guided her into the kitchen.

"Th-thank you . . . I'm sorry to freak out in your house . . ."

"No apology needed. I understand." He opened the door for her. "The yard's very private. Stay as long as you like."

"I don't think we have long."

"I'll try to get them moving," he promised.

Eddy sat on the back steps for several minutes, staring into the jungle of the yard, letting the tears course freely down her face. She believed Zach really was in love; that was the hell of it. She could see it in his face and Trevor's, in the way their bodies touched. And she didn't think Zach would lie to her about such a thing. It was easy enough to understand. She hadn't been what Zach wanted. Trevor was.

But she still didn't want to see him go to prison. She still had to help him.

Eventually her tears dried up, and she sat with her chin propped on her fist, watching a bee circle Kinsey's overgrown, zucchini-laden garden, savoring the country quiet. She loved the French Quarter, but sometimes it was difficult to think there, what with all the street musicians and exploding bottles and screaming queens and blaring traffic. And if there was anything Eddy needed just now, it was time to think.

Left to their own devices, the ragged crew in the house would sit around talking until Agent Cover showed up with his minions. But by the time she stood up and went back inside, Eddy had a plan.

"So where would we go?" Zach asked Dougal.

Dougal favored him with a crooked white grin. "I fly you home wit' me, mon. You always say you wan' go get lost in Jamaica someday."

"Jamaica?" Zach turned to Trevor. "That's where I dreamed about. Like you told me to. I was walking down a clean white beach with bright green palm trees and a guy said 'Ganja, *smart* ganja' so I stopped—"

"That's Jamaica," Dougal assured him. "Always got de smart ganja. I got some now if you wan' it." Zach and Terry nodded. Dougal rolled another bomber and passed it around. Soon the room was filled with sweet herbal smoke.

"Goddammit, are you all just going to sit around and get STONED?"

Eddy stood in the doorway, arms akimbo, face tear-stained and royally pissed and lovely. He had missed her since he left, Zach realized, and he would miss her wherever he was going. She was so tough.

"The Secret Service is ALL OVER TOWN! The agent in charge of your case showed up at Terry's record store!" She crossed the room to Zach, grabbed him by the shoulder and shook him. "Don't you think you better GET GOING?!"

Trevor knocked her hand away. "He has a concussion! Leave him alone!"

"Well, if you don't move your asses, he'll have plenty of time to recover in a *jail cell*! Is that what you want?"

"You guys shut up. Please." Zach scowled and rubbed his temples, trying to clear his head. "She's right, Trev. If they're already here, we have to go."

Zach stared miserably up at Eddy. "I'm sorry about all this, Ed. I wish I could do something to make it up to you."

"Give me your car."

"Huh?"

"You heard me. Give me your car. I've always liked it, and you won't be needing it anymore. Dougal can take you back to Louisiana to catch your plane. Do you think you could get into Louisiana DMV again and register the car to me?"

"Well . . . sure. What are you gonna do?"

"Drive through downtown and try to lure them after me. I'll go east on 42 while you guys sneak out of town the other way. They won't be looking for Dougal's car."

All five men stared at her with wide awed eyes. Finally

Terry said timidly, "Won't they chase you down and arrest you?"

"I'll lead them as far as I can. Maybe they'll arrest me, but maybe they won't have a damn thing to charge me with if they can't prove Zach was ever here. I'll say the Mustang was mine all along, and the computer will back me up. Right?"

"Right," Zach said.

"After that, who knows? I may drive to California. I may meet William S. Burroughs in Kansas. I may wind up stranded in Idaho. I don't really care. I just want some time alone."

She pulled her key ring out of her pocket and tossed it to Dougal. "You know where my apartment is. You and the rest of the French Market gang can have everything in it. Zach, do you want anything out of your car?"

"Umm . . . no, I've got my bag."

"Then could some of you guys come help me unload it? I don't want to get busted with a hot computer and a bunch of boys' clothes."

"I'll take everything to Potter's Store," Kinsey offered.

"Keep the computer," Zach told him. "It's got all kinds of good stuff on the hard drive. You'll never have to pay a bill again."

"Thanks, but I'll pass."

"I'll take it," said Terry.

The others carried five loads in from the Mustang while Zach dialed up the Louisiana DMV computer and made the necessary changes, plus a couple of embellishments. Eddy selected several items from the piles of Zach's stuff: a bulky army jacket, a pair of sunglasses, the broad-brimmed black hat Dougal had sold Zach in the French Market less than a week ago. When she put these things on, it was obvious that from a distance she could easily pass for Zach.

Eddy walked over to the sofa. "Excuse me," she said to Trevor, and leaned down and kissed Zach square on the lips. Then she turned and went to the front door and smiled back at them. It was a rather rueful smile, but not a bitter one.

"It's been nice knowing all of you," she said. "Really it has.

Good luck to you. I think you'll all need it. Give me about ten minutes' head start."

The door closed noiselessly behind her. A few moments later they heard the smooth purr of the Mustang pulling out of the driveway.

Everyone gazed uncertainly at each other. Then Trevor asked Zach, "Did you really dream about Jamaica?"

Zach started to nod, winced, and said, "Yes."

"Then let's go."

They looked up to see Kinsey, Terry, and even Dougal grinning like proud parents at a wedding.

"Maybe we got time for jus' one more little smoke," said Dougal. "I t'ink we got somet'ing to celebrate."

Eddy drove along Kinsey's road, stopped the car for a long moment at the intersection, then turned right at Farmers Hardware onto Firehouse Street. She didn't know where the agents were or what their cars would look like, but she figured she could make them see her.

She tugged the black hat down over her face, pushed the sunglasses up on her nose, and gathered every particle of her nerve. She was going to have to do some fancy driving. But the car could take it; Zach had once driven her down Highway 10 at a hundred twenty miles per hour. And she could take it too.

She was sick of hot, humid weather that sapped the strength but teased the libido. For that matter, she was sick of the libido. She was sick of beautiful boys, geeks, and the assorted mutants that fell somewhere in between. She was going to have adventures she damn well felt like having, ones that didn't depend on some man. One way or another, this would be the first.

She saw the Whirling Disc up ahead on her left. Halfway through downtown now. They'd had plenty of time to notice the car, plenty of time to read the license plate if Stefan had been able to give them that.

Eddy revved the engine, stomped the gas, and went blasting through Missing Mile. The needle jittered up to sixty, seventy-five, eighty. She glanced in her rearview mirror, saw three white Chevy vans pulling away from the curb behind her, and let out a howl of pure triumph.

They hit the open road going ninety. Eddy kept pushing the Mustang, watched the vans fall behind. She tried to keep the needle steady at a hundred. She didn't want to lose them too fast, not until Dougal's creaky old station wagon had had plenty of time to slip out the other way.

Eddy turned on the tape player, cranked up the volume. "YORE CHEATIN' HAWRRRRRT," whined Hank Williams. She hit the EJECT button, risked a glance at the other tapes on the dashboard, tossed Hank in the back seat, and slapped on Patsy Cline.

Crazy. Crazy for lovin' you . . .

Not anymore, kiddo.

Maybe they would catch her. But they couldn't keep her; her money and her car were no longer traceable to Zach. She trusted him on that one. And after that, she would go where she wanted.

Eddy saw a wide, bright highway heading west, with the marvelous clean flatlands beginning to unfurl before her wheels. Prairie, mesa, desert stark and dry as a bone, stretching all the way to the Pacific Ocean.

It was hers to have, and she wanted it.

Thursday night and Friday morning were a long confusing blur. Zach remembered getting dressed, Kinsey and Terry hugging him, then climbing into the back seat of Dougal's station wagon and promptly falling asleep in Trevor's lap.

Somewhere near Atlanta, he thought, Dougal stopped the car in a pretty little suburb and ushered them into a houseful of Jamaicans. A Hefty garbage bag full of fragrant marijuana sat in the middle of the living-room floor and massive joints were constantly being rolled. They were given bowls of spicy goat stew and glasses of fresh ginger beer. From the boom box in the corner, Bob Marley sang that every little thing was gonna be all right. Zach was beginning to believe him.

They all grabbed a couple of hours' sleep. Then Dougal drove straight through to South Louisiana. "Lay low, Zachary," he thought he remembered hearing Dougal whisper once. "We pretty close to New Orleans now. But we be at Colin's soon." Then nothing but green swamp light for miles and miles, and Trevor holding him all the way.

They arrived at Colin's place at dusk. It was a small shack deep in the swamp, surrounded by still water, bright green vines and other vegetation, great moss-encrusted stands of cypress and oak. Out back in a large cleared area was the runway. It was built atop the mud, Zach thought, on the same basic principle as a cracker balanced on toothpicks sunk into a dish of thick pudding. On the runway sat Colin's plane, so small and spindly it looked like a toy. They would be taking off in the morning. They stared at the ramshackle contraption, then at each other. "Adventure," Zach murmured, and Trevor nodded.

Colin was a wiry, jet-black Rastafarian with dreadlocks hanging halfway to his waist. The inside of his shack was a single large room with sleeping bags on the floor. Trevor and Zach crawled into a single bag and fell asleep. Dougal and Colin sat up most of the night, talking and smoking.

They climbed the steps into the cargo hold at dawn. Zach's stomach dropped as he felt the wheels leave the ground. But once they were in the air the motion was soothing, lulling him back to sleep with the weight of America lifting off his back.

He woke up once on the flight to the sound of someone gagging, realized it was himself. Trevor was awkwardly holding his head up while Dougal offered him a neat little plastic-lined bag to puke in. "Colin keep these in de plane," Dougal explained. "It's jus' de Bermuda Triangle make some people sick a little. Soon pass."

Zach felt horrible. His food-deprived body must have sucked up the goat stew already; he only had the dry heaves. Soon the nausea subsided a little. Dougal handed him a smoldering joint and he dragged on it gratefully. "We're over the Bermuda Triangle?"

"Jus' a little on de edge."

Zach handed the joint back to Dougal, who crawled up to the cockpit to pass it to Colin. He closed his eyes and leaned back against Trevor. "What do you think, Trev?" he whispered. "Am I a fun date or what?"

He was pretty sure he knew the answer. But he fell back asleep before he could hear it.

Sometime later Trevor shook him awake and gripped his hand. The plane was full of light. Dougal motioned them toward the cockpit. Peering over the pilot's mass of dreadlocks, Zach could see a calm clear expanse of water the color of turquoise, a stretch of beach like a wide white ribbon unfurling out of sight, a lush green country in the distance.

The place he had seen in his dreams. A place for him and his lover to get lost together.

"Welcome home," said the Rasta man.

ONE MONTH
LATER

The asphalt of Firehouse Street had begun to soften in the July heat by the time Kinsey let himself into the Sacred Yew. The summer had gotten hotter and wetter until all the days seemed to run together in a long soggy blur. It would continue like this straight on through September. Kinsey could not bring himself to concoct any dinner specials; one did not want to cook in this weather, did not even want to eat.

The Secret Service agents had come back at the end of June to ask more questions. It seemed they had been mistaken about the car Zach drove, and were now looking for a tan Malibu registered in his name. Of course, no one in Missing Mile knew anything. None of the kids had ever seen that pallid raven-haired boy whose picture the agent kept flashing around. No one remembered the night Gumbo had had a guest singer, especially not the ones who had been in the crowd at that show, galvanized by a wild voice now tragic, now raucous, now joyous.

Kinsey grabbed a Natty Boho from the cooler and stood at the bar sorting through the day's mail. Electric bill, surprisingly low . . . gas bill . . . collection agency notice . . . and two postcards. One was postmarked Flagstaff, Arizona, and read KINSEY, YOU FORGOT TO PAY THE PHONE BILL. LOVE, STEVE. Below that was scrawled *Krazy Kat lived here* and an amorphous swirl that might have been a *G*.

The other card was creased, smudged, ragged at the edges.

But Kinsey thought it still bore a faint breath of sun and salt. The picture side was a closeup photograph of some *ackee*, the peculiar Jamaican fruit that was deadly poison before it burst open, but could be scrambled like eggs afterward. Creamy yellow curds of flesh bulged from dusky pink three-lobed skins. Embedded in each fruit were three glistening black seeds as large and round as eyeballs. Kinsey had read about *ackee* in his cookbooks, but never actually tasted any. He imagined it would be rather like brains.

The other side of the card was bordered with tiny faces and hands: graceful, gnarled; screaming, grinning, serene; all sorts of hands and faces exquisitely drawn in ink of black ballpoint. The postmark was too smudged to read, but the message said *K: I drew for 3 hours today. It hurts like hell—but who cares? And Dario is growing dreads. Play some Bird for me. Your Friend, T.*

Kinsey put on his favorite Charlie Parker tape, propped open the doors, and let Bird go soaring out over Missing Mile for the rest of the afternoon.

Trevor opened his eyes late one night and found himself staring at a vivid green lizard on the wall inches from his face. The shack was so bright that its scales seemed to shimmer.

Trevor blinked, and the creature was gone in an iridescent skirl.

He turned his head and looked at Zach, asleep on the narrow mattress beside him, naked atop sweat-dampened sheets in the steamy tropical night. The moonlight turned Zach's skin pale blue, his knotty hair and the shadows of his face a deeper indigo. The nights here were as blue as the days; the sky deepened in color but never truly darkened.

They were living in the countryside near Negril, which was something of a hippie mecca on the western coast of the island, deep in the heart of ganja country. They had no electricity, no plumbing, and they didn't care. When they missed these comforts, they hitchhiked into Negril and spent a night or two in a luxurious hotel room for about twenty dollars American.

Sometimes they visited Colin's friend's farm way up in the hills and spent a couple of days getting ridiculously stoned. Zach would amaze everyone by eating fresh scotch bonnet peppers right off the bush. The Jamaicans thought he was showing off, but Trevor knew Zach loved the pretty little globes of fire. Trevor himself had already put away gallons of Blue Mountain coffee. But not as much as he used to drink. He didn't have to keep himself awake anymore.

More often they lounged on the small cove of white sand beach a few hundred yards from their shack. Zach lathered himself with the strongest sunscreen he could buy, then lay for hours in the brilliant blue water, his head cushioned in the soft sand. He stayed as pale as ever, but his cheeks took on a faint tinge of color, and some of the dark smudges around his eyes began to fade. He wanted to learn to sing reggae.

The sun had bleached Trevor's hair pale blond. He had to tuck it up under a hat when they went into town; else Jamaican women would descend on him stroking it, praising its beauty, wanting to braid it. The first time this happened, Trevor had endured the reaching, grasping fingers for about ten seconds, then flailed out from under them with an enraged snarl that sent the ladies scattering and left Zach sprawled on the ground, helpless with laughter.

His right hand ached all the time, but it was a healing ache, the feel of bones knitting back together and muscles remembering how to move. He drew every day for as long as he could stand it. Then Zach massaged the stiffness from his hand, gently tugging the knots out of his fingers, rubbing the cramps out of his palm. The muscle at the base of his thumb sometimes throbbed until Trevor wanted to drive his fist through the wall again. But he was through hitting things forever.

He sent a postcard to Steve Bissette asking him to donate payment for "Incident in Birdland" to the production of *Taboo* or other comics.

They talked intimately and obsessively, fucked as often as

their bodies could stand it, sometimes combined the two. It was difficult to remember how short a time they had known each other. But at the same time, they were starting to realize how much they had yet to learn. They began to unlock each other like puzzles of astonishing intricacy, to open each other like marvelous gifts discovered under the Christmas tree.

Sometimes Trevor thought about the house. Sometimes he dreamed about it, but remembered only frozen images from these dreams: the shape suspended from the shower curtain rod, slowly turning; the terrible dawning recognition in Bobby's eyes as he looked up from the bed of the sleeping son he had meant to kill after all, but could not.

Had Bobby meant to die already, or had the sight of his elder son grown, in Birdland, driven him to his death? Trevor would never know. He no longer worried much about it.

Sometimes sensations came back to him as well: the impact shuddering up his arm as the hammer crashed into the wall inches from Zach's head; the thousand tiny pains of the mirror fragments sliding into his flesh. He never wanted to forget those.

He remembered what Birdland had meant to him when he was small. It had been the place where he had discovered his talent, the place where he could work magic, where no one else could touch him. Trevor believed in magic more than ever. But he had learned that living in a place where no one could touch him was sometimes dangerous, and always lonely.

Birdland was a mirror. You could shatter it and cut yourself to ribbons on it, you could obscure it with blood. Or you could be brave enough to look into it with eyes wide open and see whatever there was to see.

He realized Zach was awake, had been watching him for some time. The moonlight turned his green eyes a strange underwater color. He did not speak, but smiled sleepily at Trevor and reached for his hand. The night was silent but for the distant shush of the sea on the sand and the sound of their breathing. The air smelled of flowers and salt, of their bodies' unique chemistry.

Yes, Trevor thought, he could have ripped himself apart on the jagged edges of Birdland just to learn how Bobby had felt doing it. He probably could have dragged Zach down with him. And he could have deluded himself into believing he did this without choice, that it was his destiny.

But it was all choice. And there were so many other choices to make. There were so many other things to learn. He wouldn't mind living for a thousand years, just for the chance to see a fraction of everything in the world.

Trevor could not be grateful to Bobby for leaving him alive. But he could be glad he had not died in that house, with all those possibilities untapped, sights unseen, ideas unexplored. He could make that choice. He had made that choice. It was all up to him. The boy whose hand he held was living proof. Zach had shown him that anything was possible. Zach was the one who deserved his gratitude.

Trevor found ways to show it straight on through till morning.